ACCLAIM FOR MATTHEW QUIRK'S
COLD BARREL ZERO

"Matthew Quirk's *Cold Barrel Zero* is an unputdownable blast. The writing is spare and masterful, you care about the characters, and the action is hair-raising, authentic...even mesmerizing. One of the must-read thrillers of the year!"

—Ben Coes, bestselling author of *Coup d'État* and *Independence Day*

"*Cold Barrel Zero* is gripping and utterly convincing. It's the tale real agents and operators would tell if they had Quirk's storytelling genius." —Steven Pressfield, bestselling author of *The Afghan Campaign* and *The Legend of Bagger Vance*

"Thriller Award winner Quirk goes flat-out explosive in this superior military adventure novel....There's plenty of cool cutting-edge technology, but in the end it comes down to action, and the riveting battle scenes are among the best in the business. Readers will look forward to seeing more of the skilled and deadly John Hayes." —*Publishers Weekly*

"The action dazzles....The threats seem all too real....Quirk delves deep into the world of international terror and covert operations and writes with such authority you half expect his prose to be riddled with redactions."

—Chris Holm, *Los Angeles Review of Books*

"Matthew Quirk has elevated to must-read thriller status faster than seems possible. *Cold Barrel Zero* is a brilliantly researched and written tour de force from an author who understands both high-stakes action and fine writing."

—Michael Koryta, author of *Rise the Dark*

"A relentlessly paced military thriller.... Sophisticated storytelling and whiplash pacing.... *Cold Barrel Zero* delivers some clever twists and startling surprises." —Art Taylor, *Washington Post*

"Fast-paced.... A dangerous adventure. Highly recommended for fans of rapid action with down-to-the-wire conclusions."

—Susan Moritz, *Library Journal*

"Quirk takes a major step forward.... A lethal game of cat and mouse fuels Quirk's third and best novel.... The story is expertly stripped down, the action relentless, and the characters multi-layered." —*Kirkus Reviews*

"A deadly high-stakes, high-tech chase on land and sea. Quirk, whose two previous novels centered on corruption in the corporate world, spins an adrenaline-fueled, military-based action adventure just as skillfully. Characters, most known only by their last names, are well drawn and motivated, and their exploits are hair-raising. Another hard-to-put-down adventure from Quirk, this is even more chilling for its air of plausibility. A fine thriller."

—Michele Leber, *Booklist*

COLD BARREL ZERO

ALSO BY MATTHEW QUIRK

The 500
The Directive
Dead Man Switch

COLD BARREL ZERO

MATTHEW QUIRK

MULHOLLAND BOOKS

Little, Brown and Company

New York Boston Toronto

Copyright © 2016 by Rough Draft Inc.
Excerpt from *Dead Man Switch* © 2017 by Rough Draft Inc.

Hachette Book Group supports the right to free expression and the value of copyright. The purpose of copyright is to encourage writers and artists to produce the creative works that enrich our culture.

The scanning, uploading, and distribution of this book without permission is a theft of the author's intellectual property. If you would like permission to use material from the book (other than for review purposes), please contact permissions@hbgusa.com. Thank you for your support of the author's rights.

Mulholland Books/Little, Brown and Company
Hachette Book Group
1290 Avenue of the Americas, New York, NY 10104
mulhollandbooks.com

Originally published in hardcover by Mulholland Books, March 2016
First Mulholland Books trade paperback edition, January 2017

Mulholland Books is an imprint of Little, Brown and Company, a division of Hachette Book Group, Inc. The Mulholland Books name and logo are trademarks of Hachette Book Group, Inc.

The publisher is not responsible for websites (or their content) that are not owned by the publisher.

The Hachette Speakers Bureau provides a wide range of authors for speaking events. To find out more, go to hachettespeakersbureau.com or call (866) 376-6591.

Library of Congress Cataloging-in-Publication Data
Quirk, Matthew.
  Cold barrel zero / Matthew Quirk. — First edition.
    pages ; cm
  ISBN 978-0-316-25921-7 (hc) / 978-0-316-25919-4 (pb)
  I. Title.
  PS3617.U5926C65 2016
  813'.6—dc23   2015024562

10 9 8 7 6 5 4 3 2 1

LSC-C

Printed in the United States of America

For my father,
Commander R. Gregory Quirk, USN (Ret.)
Reveille! Reveille! Reveille!

COLD BARREL ZERO

THEY WOULD COME for him at night, so Hayes was awake. He finished with his codes and laid his Bible on a makeshift table: a plank set across two splintering crates. He never really slept anymore, just rested for a few hours during the day, lying dressed on the floor on top of a thin blanket.

He brushed a mosquito from his arm where a patch of rough scar showed under the sleeve of his T-shirt. Once it had been a tattoo—a combat diver and jump wings, the seal of the First Force Reconnaissance Marines—but two years ago he'd had to take it off.

A sparrow perched on the branch of a tree outside. As Hayes watched it, his thoughts drifted back to the dead.

It flew off. Another bird followed, then a dozen more. The rustle of wings surrounded the hut as hundreds of them rose, filled the sky, and blotted out the stars.

Hayes stood, slung his rifle over his shoulder, grabbed his bag, and sprinted through the door of his compound, leaving the light on behind him. He stopped after seventy-five meters—danger-close range for the Hellfires—and ducked behind the trunk of a Meru oak. He could have gone farther, but he needed cover between him and the sky.

Drones are silent, despite all the myths locals like to believe about death buzzing over their heads. If the machines allow themselves to be heard, it's a show of intimidation. When they come to kill, they stay high and make no noise. Hellfires move faster than sound, so the target dies unaware that he has been hit.

He knew it was futile, but he scanned the sky anyway. The odds of catching a reflection from the sensor ball were almost nil.

A hare bolted across the savanna. Above him, a sparrow returned, looked at him hiding behind the tree, and cocked its head.

"I know," Hayes said, and took a deep breath. Too long running. Too long alone. The paranoia was getting to him. He'd been speaking a mix of Egyptian Arabic and French with a Belgian accent for the last month, passing himself off as a mineral engineer. He needed to get across the border.

The rest of the flock settled. He relieved himself against the tree, then started back toward the house. Three seconds later, a sonic boom punched him in the stomach and ears. It felt like a small, close explosion.

The shock wave from the blast knocked him back on his heels. Flames licked red through the rising cloud of black smoke. As the debris showered down, he threw himself behind a tree and waited a moment for the disorientation to pass.

He stayed there until the smoke expanded enough to cover him from above, then ducked low and stepped through the wreckage toward his truck, an ancient Land Rover Defender.

Strong winds blew from the east. The smoke would lift in a few seconds and the drone would see him with its infrared cameras.

He'd run the drill himself dozens of times, calling in strikes with an infrared laser. The drone would circle back and then clean up the squirters with its second missile.

A smoldering piece of plywood lay on the ground beside him, a foot from the waist-high grass that surrounded the compound. He needed cover. The fire might work, or it might kill him. There was no time to think twice. He kicked the wood into the brush. White smoke twined up and joined the last black fumes from the demolished house.

He stepped into the truck. The natural instinct was to speed from the blast, from the eyes above, but he waited, calm.

The wind caught the embers, and the grass became a wall of fire rushing toward him. He started the engine but didn't move. Only when the flames reached the rear bumper did he touch the throttle and begin to roll along slowly, keeping a few feet ahead of the blaze roaring behind him. The heat wavered the air in his mirrors. The curtain of smoke and heat would conceal everything the Predator had, visual and IR. He would be safe as long as he stayed cradled in the fire. It grew, faster now, and he just outpaced it, bucking at twenty, thirty, forty miles an hour over the rutted tracks through the grasslands, moving with the flames toward the wooded foothills and highlands beyond.

The fire jumped ahead. He checked the speedometer. Any faster and he would break an axle.

The rear window blew out from the heat.

The forest was close. It would give him cover. There were too many ways in and out to find him. The fire leaped ahead and swallowed the truck.

He pressed the pedal to the floor. He had to get through to warn the others.

The hunt had begun.

CHAPTER 1

MORET YAWNED AS she walked past the only grocery store in town, a Chinese-run market. Dust caked her skin. She had been on the highlands for three days and nights. She spent most of her time hunting, both to feed herself and to cover her expenses with guide work, trophies, and bounties. A pool of brown, foul water filled half the square. She circled around it.

She left her dog, a boxer mutt, in the passenger seat of the truck with the window cracked and headed for a storefront off the main path. She came every week. *Fax* and *ADSL* were hand-painted on the window below Arabic script. She pulled her headscarf forward, looked away from the security camera, and took a terminal in the far back. She opened up the browser and went to Hotmail.

She double-checked the date—the twelfth of October. From her shoulder bag, she pulled out a small volume with a cloth cover over the original leather. It was a Bible, the most common book in the world, the King James Version.

They were using a book cipher based on the date. The twelfth;

she counted off twelve books, which brought her to the Second Book of Kings. October, the tenth month; she went down ten chapters. And, finally, she used the last two digits of the current year to count down verses. Her finger rested on the page:

And he said, Take them alive. And they took them alive, and slew them at the pit of the shearing house, even two and forty men; neither left he any of them.

She took the first letters of the first ten words and typed them in as her username: *ahsttaattt@hotmail.com.* Then she proceeded to the next verse and used the number and the first ten letters as her password: *15AwhwdthloJ.*

She had done this every Sunday for the past two years, and every Sunday she had found nothing. She was starting to hate this ritual. It felt like rolling over in the morning and reaching for a spouse long dead.

Each account was used only once. She clicked on the spam folder and skimmed the page. There wasn't much because of the randomness of the username. Then she saw it—the fourth message down. She thought at first it must be a mistake, but no; it was what she had been waiting for. It read like any other prescription-pill come-on, but for two years she had been waiting to see this sender's name: John Okoye27.

She clicked on the e-mail. *Best and Cheapest Premier Pharmacy!* the text read. What interested her was the embedded JPEG file at the bottom of the screen. It showed a blue diamond-shaped pill. The colors looked normal to the naked eye, but the pixel data had been manipulated, with extra bits written over the least significant color codes.

Photos modified with this embedding technique, called steganography, appeared as normal file attachments. An encrypted message wouldn't be able to withstand the NSA's deciphering tools, and encryption would only draw attention to it. That was why Moret's instructions masqueraded as spam, hiding in plain sight, just one more drop in the sea of garbage coursing through the web.

She downloaded an open-source program from the Internet and extracted the message embedded in the photo. It was a sequence of fourteen letters and numbers, which she broke into grid-zone designator, 100,000-meter square ID, and position north and east, down to the meter. They were MGRS coordinates, the military's version of latitude and longitude.

She memorized them, then took a disc from her bag and inserted it in the computer. It spun and began wiping the machine's hard drive.

She returned to her truck, a rusting Toyota Hilux. She kept everything she owned in it. A battered Pelican case behind the seats contained an Mk 11 Mod 0 sniper rifle, a nightscope, and a suppressor. She'd removed the passenger airbag to make room for a hidden compartment, known as a trap. The only way to open it was to press down both window buttons and the hazard lights for three seconds. Inside there was $90,000 in U.S. currency, five passports, and a 1911 pistol with no serial number.

The boxer cocked his head at her. She opened the door and led him out of the car. She ran her hand over his head a few times, then climbed back in and drove off. In the rearview, she watched the dog fall back, sprinting after her through the mud, disappearing slowly in the distance.

Seventy-five hundred miles away, a screwdriver rested on the open pages of Speed's Bible. Electronics and machinery spilled their insides over every horizontal surface of his one-bedroom house. It hadn't taken long for word to spread through the peninsula about his ability to fix anything. The pocket watch in his hands had been a labor of love; he'd carefully tweezed apart the workings, even milled a new balance staff. He had been planning to drop it off at the apartment above the billiards hall on his way out of town when someone knocked on his door. He wiped the sweat from his face, drew back the mosquito netting, and answered, as always, with a pistol drawn.

It was Emiliano. The people in the village loved to watch Speed work, piecing together gears and screws a few millimeters wide, his long fingers moving like spiders. But today he just handed the boy the watch through the partly open door, refused the crumpled pesos, and sent him away. He packed his tools and a few leather cases marked *Falle* in his backpack, walked the half a mile to the coast road, and waited an hour to catch the fifty-year-old yellow school bus that now served as the intercity line.

Speed found a seat. His bag held two kilos of HDX high explosive. He set it down between his feet next to an old woman's purse and a sack of red potatoes.

At the same moment that Sunday, in a time zone eight hours ahead, Green locked the front door to his Communist-era apartment building. He took the key off his ring and dropped it through the grate of a sewer. He had been planning to move on anyway. He had helped out his neighbor's daughter first, resetting a badly broken radius and ulna. Soon more came, because they couldn't afford a doctor, or because they couldn't afford to draw attention to their injuries. Too many people were looking for him, and more and more were showing up with professionally laid-on bruises and welts, which meant internal security, which meant trouble.

He rounded the corner and saw the girl climbing in the apartment complex's playground. The arm had healed nicely. She waved to him from the top of the slide. He waved back as he passed through the gate, then he tucked his chin down against the freezing wind and headed for the footbridge over the highway.

One by one they opened their Bibles and made their way to the stashes: cash, explosives, small arms, frequency-hopping radios, false papers, instructions on the target, and specifics of how to slip across the U.S. border.

They knew the stakes if they were caught. Aiding the enemy was punishable by death. But that didn't matter. They were coming home, all of them. He was calling. It was time.

CHAPTER 2

A MAN SOME called Hayes put his spotting scope down on the passenger seat. The skin on his forearm was mostly healed from when he'd burned it in the brushfire.

Hayes had been waiting for the moment for a long time. They were on the kill list. He knew the routine all too well: find, fix, finish. They would be tracked down one by one. That's why he had sent the messages, why he had gathered them together. He was already inside the United States. So was Green. The time for running was past. He had to make a stand, to take them down from the inside. And soon he would have the means.

But first, he had to see her, even though he knew it was a mistake. He crossed Orchard Road, then skirted the split-rail fence. Daytime, suburbs, male; he'd picked clothes to blend in. He wore Dickies and a short-sleeved button-down, just another contractor, pest control if stopped. The movements came automatically as he closed the distance: fast when the wind blew and the rustling leaves covered the noise of his steps, tall and relaxed through the dead space behind a knoll, slow when out of cover. He stayed downwind, moving closer and closer, everything he'd learned in the stalk, everything he'd taught to so many. He missed the weight of his rifle.

At the edge of the trees, he paused and looked over the house, a ranch on two acres. A basket of black-eyed Susan vines hung in the kitchen window. Lauren's clothes swayed gently on the drying line in the back. It was as if nothing had changed. She had parked the F-150 so the two passenger-side wheels rested on the curb. He saw her walk away from it, balancing the oil pan with both hands. Her hair was up in a ponytail, and she was wearing one of his old flannel work shirts.

He saw movement fifty feet away; at the edge of the backyard, a two-year-old girl in a puffy vest climbed up a pile of mulch.

Hayes thrived on stress, enjoyed the stimulation. It's why he was chosen, how he survived, through selection and a dozen deployments. He could regulate his breathing, lower his heartbeat, manage his cortisol levels. But suddenly he didn't trust his body, doubted his control.

The girl jumped off the top, landed hard, fell, and came up with dirt all along her right side. She examined her arm for a moment, then looked his way and began walking straight toward him. He was a little disappointed that after everyone he had killed, unseen, with one shot from a cold barrel, he'd just been made by a toddler. It was impossible, unless he'd wanted to be seen.

Hayes felt his heart rate rise, easily past a hundred and ten now. This was a mistake. He was putting himself in danger, which didn't matter, but he was putting them in danger too.

She moved closer, picked up a long stick, and dragged it behind her. She stood fifteen feet away. Hayes watched her. He didn't move, couldn't move. She had his mother's eyes. He prayed for strength.

She turned her head to the side. "Who?" she said.

"Hey, kiddo." He'd never seen her before and now she was in front of him, speaking. His pulse raced, past counting. He swallowed and it caught in his throat.

The girl looked back to her mother, then to Hayes.

"Mom!" she shouted. "Stranger!"

Good girl, Hayes thought. He watched her mother as she came around the corner of the house. Lauren looked older, with more gray in her hair than anyone deserved to have earned in two years, but still as beautiful, even more so.

How had she survived the shame he had brought her? He wanted to tell her how sorry he was, how the regret burned in him like a disease. He wanted more than anything to hold her, to feel their breath rise and fall together. But he had already gone too far. They didn't deserve any more pain. And she was most likely armed and liable to call in the FBI.

No. He stepped back into the shadows. He couldn't live like this, but the answer wasn't here. He would use any means necessary to get back to them. He would do what he had been trained for, ingrained after so many years. Develop the situation. Increase the tempo. Audacity above all.

He slid through the woods, silent as sunlight, until he reached his box truck. He opened up the back door and pushed a camera with a telephoto lens to the side, then picked his radio up off a coil of detonation cord. Everything was ready. He'd be home soon, in this life or the next. The time had come to find out which.

CHAPTER 3

HELEN MCREARY WAS always the first to arrive at the Applications Personnel Support Office. The pain in her hands tended to wake her before dawn and by then her terrier was whining at the side of the bed. She looked forward to the quiet of the empty office, sitting at her desk with a travel mug of strong black coffee from home.

She opened the door, entered the bland front foyer, and brought her right eye a few inches from a plastic and steel box on the wall. The bolt retracted with a clunk. She stepped inside a short hallway and took a sip of coffee. As soon as the door behind her closed, the door ahead unlocked.

The gray slush outside had soaked her sneakers. She took them off, slid them under her desk, and pulled a pair of flats from her shoulder bag. She dialed the combination into her filing cabinet, opened the drawer, and flipped the sign stuck in the handle from the red side marked Closed to the green marked Open.

She took her hard drive from the drawer and inserted it into the dock on her computer. As it powered up, she put her smart card into the reader and logged in with her PIN. Once her terminal was ready, she checked her messages and navigated a secure database, noting on an index card the paper files she would need to pull that morning. She shut and locked the drawer, flipped the sign back, took her keys from her bag, picked up her mug, and crossed the office.

A fine metal mesh was embedded in the walls, floor, and ceiling, and copper contacts were built into the doorjambs. These transformed the entire suite into a Faraday cage, from which no electronic or radio signals could emerge. The outlets were filtered for the same reason, and there were no connections to the public Internet.

At the far end of the room, she turned her key in a lock, opened a steel door, and entered a corridor. Along one side were vault doors. She walked to the fourth and dialed in the combination. Five revolutions right, four left, three right, two left, and then a final spin until it stopped, which meant the bolt had drawn. The door opened slowly due to its weight. She flicked on the fluorescent lights, consulted her card, searched out the appropriate file drawer, and pulled it open.

The coffee mug slipped from her hand as she let out an uncharacteristically foul obscenity. As she grabbed for the falling mug, a gush of hot liquid ran over her hand. She ignored the burn, picked the cup off the floor, and stared into the drawer.

The cabinet was three feet wide and one foot deep. The thousand folders that normally filled it had been filed left to right. Now it was empty. She tried the one above it: empty. The next one over: gone.

She went to the vault door. The lock was intact, perfect. There hadn't been a single thing out of place. It was as if the documents had simply vanished.

She entered the corridor and opened the next vault. The racks were empty; they had taken the hard drives too. She needed to make the call. At her desk, she pulled a directory from her drawer and picked up the phone. She looked under Joint Special Operations and dialed the Special Security office.

"I need rapid response at APSO. The records are gone."

"Which records?"

"All of them."

"I don't understand. Is this urgent?"

McReary dropped the index card into the burn bag. "This is your career on the line. Put me through now."

The command in her voice was unmistakable.

"Hold, please."

She waited a moment as she was transferred and then explained what had happened.

"So this was a break-in?"

"There must have been a breach, but I don't understand," she said as she scanned the room. "There's no trace. The biometrics are fine, the locks, the vault doors too. It's like it all just disappeared."

Six hours later, Cox knelt at the vault and examined the dial of the Sargent and Greenleaf combination lock. It was perfect, with no sign of any manipulation or forced entry, none of the marrings characteristic of a robot dialer. Cox's formal title was special assistant to the secretary of defense. His job was to make problems go away. He was a brigadier general but traveled in civilian clothes.

The officer with direct oversight of APSO, Lieutenant Colonel Barnard, had come from Bragg and stood over him, arms held loosely behind his back. Cox had flown from DC on a C-20, the navy's version of a Gulfstream jet, normally used only by general officers. That set Barnard on edge. Cox made no mention of his own rank. He found it easier to read people when they weren't kissing his ass.

"If there's no damage, we must have an inside job," Barnard said. He put his hands on his hips, a tic to project authority. "Do we have the audit logs? We'll simply find who entered and then case closed."

Cox removed the last screw and pulled the back off the safe lock. "We already did." Without standing up, Cox held a printout over his shoulder.

Barnard took it, scanned the entries for the previous night, and saw only his own name. "Me?" He made a noise that was a cross between laughing and clearing his throat. "I wasn't here. This is impossible."

"Not quite impossible. A high-res shot of your iris, superimposed over a live pupil; either a contact lens or a good printout could do it." He unscrewed the wheel pack from the threaded rod. "What worries me is the Abloy Protec up front and the Sargent and Greenleaf here. There is no sign of picking or bypass."

He held up a long threaded rod with the safe dial on the end, shone a light on it, and lifted his glasses to examine it up close. "I almost missed it. It's too perfect. Zero wear. This is a new spindle and a new dial."

"Well, let's get the camera footage and see who it is."

"That won't help. I checked. They did the whole thing in the dark."

"You're telling me that anyone can just waltz in here and defeat four layers of the hardest security the U.S. government and Joint Special Operations Command can manage?"

"Not anyone. No." Cox stood and wiped off his hands. "Only one of our guys could do it. The night-vision, the Abloy decoder, the tools for the safe bypass; we have them. No locksmiths. Only USG, a few teams at JSOC, the NSA, the CIA, and the FBI."

This office had two names, one official and one known only to a few. That is why a C-20 had been sent to the front of the line on the tarmac at Joint Base Andrews with Cox on board. Applications Personnel Support Office was a cover, something for the org charts and paychecks. It was a name that could be handed out when an employee needed to list a reference for a bank or a landlord.

In reality, this office housed the security roster of the Defense Cover Program, which provided false identities to members of classified units within the Joint Special Operations Command. Their records were pulled from the normal military personnel system and stored here under lock and key with any connection between present and past erased. The members of these special mission units lived as civilians, under cover. That allowed the president to disavow any tier-one assets who were caught working behind enemy lines. It also firewalled the day-to-day identities of the soldiers in order to protect them and their families from enemy reprisals during and after their service.

"Good, then," Barnard said. "That gives us a short list to work from. We'll just narrow it down."

"They stole everything we'd need to make that list. That's probably the point."

"You know we have assets unaccounted for. We lost track of Hayes and his team after the air strikes," Barnard said. "But that would be insane, to enter the lion's den."

"If it is them, it's brilliant."

"We need to find these people."

"Every cover identity available to them, every passport, every safe house, every cache of arms and currency is now lost to us. We barely know their real names."

"But this entire program is designed for deniability, to protect us against them."

"Now it's working the other way. And the measures to guard their families against the bad guys are going to hide them from us. They stole the records of everything we'd use to find them in the United States: next of kin, associates, means of support."

"For Christ's sake. Someone has to know who these people are," Barnard said. "We have the material from the investigations."

"The annexes were kept here." It had been Barnard's order, a way to control the political damage to JSOC by limiting access to the details of Hayes's crimes.

"You're telling me that we have war criminals loose in the United States and they are goddamn ghosts! You know what these men are capable of."

"I do," Cox said. This was what these soldiers had been trained to do: assume a name, a face, a life. Hide out for years if necessary. "We can work backward. Everyone leaves a trace, even if the paper's gone. We know he came from Marine Special Operations. We can go back to his old unit. He stole his personal file, but we can pull the unit rosters by hand, talk to those who served alongside him, commanded him, reconstruct what we can about where he is likely to go and who is likely to help him stateside. He'll need support.

"Some of it may be on magnetic tape in a bunker, though that'll take weeks to drag up. It's going to be a lot of legwork."

"Well, we should get started."

Cox already had. "I will."

"Jesus," Barnard said, surveying the empty file drawers. "They took the files for every cover identity in the field. They could sell those to our enemies. It would be a slaughter. Worse than Hanssen, worse than Ames."

"There's that," Cox said.

"You don't think that's his game?"

"If he hadn't taken all of them, we would know where to start. He had no choice."

"So he's covering his tracks. He's on the run. This could be his last step, a disappearing act."

Cox shook his head. "No. He can disappear anywhere. This is overkill. He'd take a risk this great only to avoid a greater one later."

"Say what you mean."

"He's back in the U.S. It's suicidal, but that's his psychology, why we selected him: he'll always choose duty over self-preservation. He's coming for us. He's going to finish this. And now"—he waved his hand at the empty racks—"we won't be able to see him coming."

"You're on top of this?"

"Yes. And it would be wise to let Colonel Riggs know, so he can take precautions."

"I'd like to keep this close to the vest," Barnard said. Behind his back, he held the printout with the record of his biometric entry into the office.

"Hayes nearly killed Riggs. He is likely to finish the job."

Barnard nodded. "You're right. You find them, under whatever names, whatever lies they are living, and then we go after them with everything we have."

"I will," Cox said, and he was already in motion, striding away with the safe dial in one hand and his phone in the other.

As soon as his cell got a signal, he punched in a number, put the phone to his ear, and said, "Give me MARSOC."

CHAPTER 4

IN THE BACK of a box truck, Hayes laid two packets down on a steel shelf. The magnets inside clunked onto the metal. He picked up a simple Nokia cell phone, dialed a number, and placed it beside the devices.

Each packet was about the size of a hardcover book and had a Nokia bound to the top with electrical tape. The phones' plastic cases had been pried open, and a small piece of breadboard circuitry covered each keypad. As both phones rang, Hayes held the probes of a multimeter across the open wires and checked the current. It was plenty. He reattached the wires to the detonators and went through the continuity on the circuits one last time. Then he handed the packets back to Speed.

"Strong work," he said.

Speed gave them a last once-over, kept one for himself, and handed the second to Moret. They stowed their packages in messenger bags and hopped out of the back of the truck. Two motorcycles were parked beside it. They climbed on. Green waited behind the wheel of a Nissan pickup, and Foley drove the Ford Taurus.

The bikes pulled out, nearly silent. The two other vehicles followed behind as they left through the gated entrance to the lot. The convoy disappeared around the corner, past a truck-repair depot that was closed for the night.

The box truck would stay behind for a few minutes. Cook stood guard outside. Ward was in the cargo area, leaning over a laptop on top of the communications rack. She handled comms and the tracking of the GPS in the packets. Hayes crouched beside her. He ran his finger over the gold cross embossed in leather on the cover of his Bible, then opened it and laid it on his knees.

His headlamp glowed red on the book of Matthew, the betrayal of Jesus. He read the passage where a disciple cuts off the ear of a servant of the high priest: *Then said Jesus unto him, Put up again thy sword into his place: for all they that take the sword shall perish by the sword.*

Hayes turned to the Gospel according to Mark, then Luke, then John. Only Matthew mentioned that line.

He thumbed back to the Last Supper and Jesus's instructions: *And he that hath no sword, let him sell his garment, and buy one.*

The last verse he found with no trouble. The spine was creased and the pages seemed to open to it on their own. It was from Matthew: *Think not that I am come to send peace on earth: I came not to send peace, but a sword.*

Hayes ran the back of his hand along his chin and read it again.

"More codes?" Ward asked.

He watched her for a moment before he spoke. "In a way. Reading, mainly."

"Don't spoil the ending for me. We found the target. They're at the airport."

"On the move?"

"Yeah."

Hayes closed the book. He had waited years for this. It was vulnerable in transit. He had one chance.

"Execute."

The armored truck rumbled along Sepulveda Boulevard, approaching the tunnel where the road passed under the runways of Los Angeles International Airport. The man at the passenger window reached his hand into the bag from In-N-Out Burger. He shoved three fries in his mouth as he gazed at the multicolored towers rising one hundred feet into the night sky around LAX.

"The loose ones are the best, man," he said as they inched through traffic into the tunnel. He was the messenger. In a normal armored truck, he would make the pickups. The man in the middle was the guard; he would stand outside the truck with his gun drawn and provide cover. The driver would stay with the truck, the most lethal weapon any of them had. This, however, wasn't a normal truck. The selectors on their firearms went from single-shot to full auto. Only a handful of security companies in the United States were authorized to use those guns. Most of the ones who did dealt with nuclear facilities.

"Whoa," said the driver as he stood on the brake. "Look lively."

Horns blared. Brake lights lit the tunnel red. The Nissan truck in front of them slammed to a stop. It had brushed fenders with a Ford Taurus that was trying to change lanes. The drivers argued through their open windows, blocking the path ahead. Traffic stalled, hemmed in the armored truck on all sides. A plane landed on the airstrip overhead, and the screech of tires filled the tunnel.

"We're sitting in a kill zone," the guard said. "Get around them."

The messenger dropped the paper bag to the floor and lifted his MP7 across his chest. The driver twisted the wheel to force his way into traffic, but two motorcycles were coming up fast on either side, between traffic, splitting the lanes.

"Where the hell did they come from?" With all its armor, the truck had huge blind spots. But he hadn't heard a thing as they approached. The bikes' headlights glared in the side-views, blinding the three men in the truck.

"Just my luck, getting killed for an empty truck." The messenger slid a metal tab to his right and rested the muzzle of his submachine gun in the gun port.

The pickup's reverse lights lit up, and it backed toward them. "He's going to hit us!" the guard shouted.

The Nissan's bumper stopped a foot from the front of the armored truck just as the motorcycles passed on either side. The one on the left swerved around the pickup as it shifted into drive and pulled ahead. The driver of the Taurus shouted a few more curses at the Nissan as it drove off, then he continued on as well.

The traffic eased, and the armored truck went with it, out of the tunnel. The messenger kept his gun up, his eyes darting around.

"Relax, dude," the driver said. "Shut the port. We've got runflats and armor good up to fifty-cal."

The messenger let his gun fall to the end of its sling, then lifted the manifest that detailed what they were supposed to be picking up.

"A coffer?" He turned to the guard. "What is that?"

"I think it's like a dresser or a trunk."

The driver pulled through the airport gates and drove along the tarmac. He glanced at the manifest, the photocopied bill of lading written in a language he couldn't understand.

"I thought it was a safe."

A squad of armed guards waited around the plane. The messenger laughed as he saw them and the weapons they were carrying.

"This better be some dresser."

He reached down for the paper bag between his feet, but by now the fries were cold.

The cost of security on an armored truck is dead space. The narrow, high windows blind those in the cab to anything that comes close alongside. The convex mirrors bolted onto the sideviews help, but in the tunnel they had been blinded by the bikes' headlights. As an added measure, Green in the Nissan pickup had distracted the guards by nearly reversing into their front bumper. There was no way that anyone inside the truck could have seen the motorcyclists attach the devices to the rear wheel wells.

CHAPTER 5

THE BOX TRUCK parked outside the cargo terminals. A blue vinyl sign on its side read *A&S Fire Protection Systems*. Hayes jumped out, pulled a ramp down from the rear, and waited. The cargo offices were closed. He looked through an open gate to the runway. The perimeter security was a joke.

Two headlights appeared at the end of the access road. Speed and Moret cruised toward the truck on their motorcycles and drove straight up the ramp into the back. Moret pulled her helmet off and let her hair down. It flowed past her shoulders.

"Both wheels?" Hayes asked.

"Yes," she said.

"They never stopped, never checked," Speed said. "We're good."

Foley drove up in the Taurus, the Nissan pickup right behind him, as Hayes lifted his spotting scope and watched the armored truck enter the cargo area through a gate a quarter of a mile away. It cleared security and parked beside an Emirates SkyCargo plane, a triple-seven freighter. The ground crew parked a scissor lift beside the hold and began to unload it.

Hayes examined the guards. He noted the MP7s on slings, pistols on chest rigs, stances at once relaxed and commanding. They looked like operators, not ten-dollar-an-hour security. His scope passed over the guard who stood outside the armored truck, then he brought his attention back and fine-tuned the focus.

"Hmm. Little Bill," Hayes said.

"Is that ironic?" Moret asked. None of the guards looked like they weighed less than two hundred pounds.

"No. His dad's also Bill. I oversaw his SERE course at Swick. He's former Special Forces. Good guy; twenty-four with four kids when I met him."

Hayes would have preferred more easily rolled opponents. He did have the advantage of having designed a lot of their training. He could account for them, and, most important, they would recognize a detonator when they saw one.

Thirty minutes later, the ground crew rolled a crate onto the lift, lowered it, then loaded it into the back of the armored truck.

Disguising the shipment was good tactics, but when you do the low-value, hide-in-plain-sight trick, you have to go all the way. When Hayes worked with the Secret Service on presidential security overseas, he had a chance to watch the Brits do it right. Americans would never settle for less than a sixteen-car package for the president, while the Royal Protection Branch liked to shuttle the queen around London in an unmarked Vauxhall sedan. These men didn't have the nerve to go that far with tonight's shipment. It had gone regular cargo out of the Emirates, but the extra security on the ground stateside gave it away.

Getting to the wheel wells had been the decisive point of the operation. Hayes had timed it for when their guard was down, when the truck was empty.

He stepped into the back of the box truck. "Any crypto?" he asked Ward.

"No," she said. "It's all single-channel. Easy to listen in. They're bringing it back to the compound. No word on the route. You want to wait?"

He considered doing it here. Urban terrain favors the guerrilla. It's ideal for ambushes, for melting away. The truck exited the cargo area, riding noticeably lower on its springs. Hayes had spent enough time in LA to know that one of the favorite local sports, up there with Lakers basketball, was car chases. It seemed like there was one on the news every night, and a half a dozen helos could be found overhead at any moment.

Hayes checked the maps of the mountains to the east. He knew that Riggs's primary compound was in rural Riverside County. There were two main routes the truck could take to reach it. Both ran through foothills, miles of sparsely populated terrain. He traced the roads, the switchback approaches to the passes. There were plenty of spots.

"Yes. Fall in behind them. Stay out of sight. We'll hit them in the country."

The three vehicles—box truck, pickup, and sedan—let the armored truck go ahead and then picked up the pursuit. They were two minutes behind it on the 105. They had GPS on the truck now, and Ward could track the radio signals as well.

The truck continued inland and eventually began winding its way through the hills. It was clear which route it would take.

Hayes pored over the maps, tracing topographic lines in the Santa Ana Mountains. The highway ahead narrowed to two lanes. Hayes checked the contours. The 5 percent grade would slow the truck. Two switchbacks would give cover, and the steep pitch on either side of the road would block the escape routes. He knew the men in the armored truck were seasoned. They must have known, or figured out by now, that they were carrying a high-value shipment. The usual tricks—fake cop, stranded woman—would send them straight into evasive action. Hayes and his team had to take them head-on, one shot.

"Green, go ahead," Hayes said into the radio. The pickup accelerated. In a minute, Green caught sight of the armored truck. He passed it easily as it labored up the hill and then raced off ahead.

Hayes took one more look at the map, then his GPS.

"Two minutes," he said, and he glanced into a corner of the truck. "Wake him up."

Speed had folded himself up between the wall and the motorcycle and was snoring. Ward kicked the wall a foot from his head. He stirred, wiped the corner of his mouth, and made a noise like he'd just had a really good meal.

There was little double-checking or fussing. They'd test-fired their weapons before they headed out. This was routine infantry against armor ambush: blind, halt, destroy. They had drilled it, done it, and taught it for so long it was about as exciting as parallel parking.

Speed rubbed his eyes, pulled a silver and orange can from his pack, drank it down, and shivered.

Hayes waited at the rear door beside Cook. "Any fishing while you were out in the wilderness?"

"Yeah," Cook said. "Pretty much lived off dogfish."

They didn't talk much about where they had been, never shared specifics. It was better to keep things in compartments.

"One minute," Hayes announced. The team lined up behind him. "I thought those were trash fish."

"Ugly, sure, but I love them. Did you get out on the water?"

They pulled onto the shoulder of the highway, a quarter mile behind the armored truck.

"Free diving. Lobster, mainly. Did some spear too."

Hayes reached down and threw open the door.

"Remember, we need them alive," he said and jumped onto the gravel as the truck came to a stop. They hauled out the ramps. Cook climbed on one of the bikes inside the truck. Hayes rode behind him in order to keep his hands free.

"Did you hear about the dog that does magic?" Cook asked Hayes.

"Things are bad enough without your jokes."

"It's a Labracadabrador." He smiled and flipped down the night-vision goggles on his helmet.

"I can't believe I actually missed you, man."

Moret straddled the other bike. Speed looked like he was going to complain about sitting behind a woman, but after one glare from Moret, he let it go and climbed on.

They were dual-sports, essentially street-legal dirt bikes with high clearance and long-travel suspensions. Cook started the engine. It never failed to impress Hayes. The bikes were electric, with baffled motors, nearly silent. He'd first used them in Kunar. Cook and Moret flicked switches for the headlights. Nothing happened. The lights were infrared, visible only through the NVGs. To anyone else, the bikes were blacked out, invisible.

"Block the road," Hayes said into his radio.

Behind them, Foley pulled the Taurus across both lanes. He'd fastened an Oversize Load sign to its bumper and clapped a flashing amber dome light onto the roof. The road switchbacked up the mountains. The armored truck had gone around a steep curve and was on the far side of the ridge above them, proceeding slowly up the grade. Two miles ahead, Green pulled his pickup across the road and put his flashers on. The armored truck was cut off.

The two bikes took off straight up the ridge. They would come over it through a gully to avoid being silhouetted against the sky as they approached the truck. The landscape glowed green through their goggles.

All Hayes could hear was the rush of the tires and the wind past his ears. They ran through a slot between two peaks and closed in on the armored truck from its blind spot at five o'clock. The country was more open than Hayes had expected. He was glad to be silent and unseen.

The safe standoff distance for the IEDs was two hundred and fifty meters, but Hayes's crew needed to get closer before they blew. They would be vulnerable to gunfire until they were in the dead space around the truck, almost touching it, which would make the firing angles from the gun ports impossible.

Hayes pulled out a cell phone as they bounced along the chaparral. He'd been in trucks hit with these kinds of explosives before. They were a twenty-first-century update to the sticky bomb. One had blown the legs and genitals off a radioman beside him. There was no time to think of the men inside the truck. Blow the IEDs, race to the dead space. That was all.

He lifted the phone and pressed the green Call button. The screen read: *Call 1 ... dialing.*

Flames flared twelve feet out from the rear tires of the armored truck. Hayes watched the pressure wave spread across the ground, driving a wall of dust and flattening the scrub until it smacked him in the chest as hard as a phone book.

Both motorcycle drivers accelerated, half blind from the flying sand. The bikes rocked back as the electric motors gave instant torque. They had six seconds to get inside the dead space.

A truck tire rolled toward them. Fire trailed from the rubber as it wobbled and then jumped end over end. Cook swerved around it, banked the bike hard. The armored truck plowed the asphalt as it dragged its back end and came to a stop at the edge of the highway.

They curved in through the smoke onto the road. Before the men inside the truck could react, all four members of Hayes's squad were standing in the dead space, feeling the heat from the blast.

Muzzles flared through the gun ports in three-round bursts of automatic fire. The bullets came within feet of the team outside but couldn't reach them. The rear-wheel-drive truck had been reduced to a stalled prison. The men inside were at Hayes's mercy.

Speed walked to the back of the truck in a crouch, then stepped on the bumper and started laying explosives along the four hinges of the rear doors. They were linear-shaped charges, thick strips of C-4 explosive fixed to a long V-shaped piece of copper about an inch wide. The open end of the V pressed against the plate steel.

Only one shooter inside the truck continued to waste rounds firing at them. He was probably too worked up to know better. Speed paid no mind as he finished his task. The explosives would deform the copper and send it shooting out at twenty-two thousand miles per hour, essentially squeezing it into a liquid razor that would slice through the metal before the explosion had a chance to melt the copper. He plugged two detonators into each charge, then stepped down and tossed the wires to Hayes, crouched alongside the truck.

Hayes plugged the wires into his detonator, then crawled under the passenger-side gun port and stepped out a dozen feet in front of the truck, fully lit by its headlights. He normally used a smaller trigger, but tonight he'd picked a multiline unit with a key and a red button. Theatrics mattered for this one.

The driver hit the gas again. What was left of the rear axle and differential ground uselessly against the road. The damaged metal tore against itself and shrieked. Next to the truck, Cook and Speed helped boost Moret onto the roof. The noise and shuddering from the drivetrain succeeded in covering the sound of her movements as Moret dragged herself along the top of the vehicle until she was over the cab.

Hayes lifted the detonator into view, pointed to the doors, and mimed an explosion with his hand. He turned the key and raised his right hand, fingers outstretched to start the countdown.

First five, then four.

The men in the cab watched him. He could see them talking, still composed despite the explosion. The man in the middle reached down—for a heavier weapon, Hayes guessed. The other two lifted their MP7s. He wished they hadn't. They were readying for an assault. He wanted them alive. He'd spent a lot of time with Speed working through the charge calculations and precisely splitting sticks of M112 to avoid juicing the guards. Killing them would have been much easier, but it would muddy Hayes's message, and the message was all that mattered in unconventional warfare.

Little Bill's mouth dropped open as he locked eyes with Hayes, his old instructor.

Hayes held up three fingers.

Hands on doors inside the cab. He could tell by their eyes, the way the muscles in their faces tightened: they were coming out fighting.

He tapped the radio mounted on his shoulder.

"Moret, get the bang ready. Doors are opening."

He raised two fingers, holding it for a long count to buy time as Moret took a grenade off her vest, pulled the pin, and held the spoon.

The doors opened. Moret let the spoon fly, tossed the grenade in the cab, and rolled back across the roof of the truck just as all three men inside jumped out, guns ready.

White light filled the cab as the explosion deafened them. The concussion grenade hit with enough force to disorient them for ten seconds. The driver, blind, kept moving, then tripped and fell hard. Little Bill leaned back against the truck and crumpled, hands over his ears, while the messenger staggered in a half circle, groping for the shotgun he had dropped.

Cook, Speed, and Moret rushed them and had all three guards facedown on the ground with flex cuffs biting into their wrists before their senses returned. Hayes's crew knelt on the men's backs and dug pistols into the bases of their skulls.

"I tossed the keys, assholes," the driver said. "You'll never—"

Hayes hit the detonator. The hills flashed bright as midday. As the crack echoed, quieter with each distant canyon, the rear door fell off the truck and shook the ground.

"That won't be a problem," Hayes said. He radioed to Ward to bring the box truck.

The guard was talking nonstop between panicked breaths. "Is this? Are these the goddamn guys? We're dead. We're—"

"They'd have killed us already if they wanted to," the driver said. "You'll wish they had."

Little Bill said nothing. He watched Hayes with hate in his eyes.

"Just calm down," Hayes told them. "Hey, Bill, you all right?"

He didn't respond.

"You know who I am?" Hayes asked.

"Yes."

"Good. That'll save time. You notice you're all still alive."

"Am I supposed to thank you for not killing me?"

Hayes knelt next to him. "No. Just tell your boss: We have what we need. The past is coming for him."

Less than three minutes had elapsed since the first explosion. Ward arrived in the box truck and backed it up to the armored vehicle, out of sight of the captives. The team ran the ramps straight across and rolled the crate out of the wrecked truck.

Hayes radioed Foley and Green to pull back the traffic-control points. Foley had detoured one car without incident.

The ramps flexed under the thirteen-hundred-pound weight of the shipment. Once it was in the truck, Ward and Hayes pulled a copper mesh over the crate to block any GPS or RFID signals. Hayes pulled the vinyl wrap signage from the side of the box truck, leaving it white, and swapped its stolen plates for a new set. With the crate inside, there was barely room to stand.

Green pulled up in the Nissan truck. After they loaded the bikes into the bed, the team split up among the three vehicles and drove deeper into the mountains. They left the three men trussed by the side of the armored truck. The explosions were bound to draw attention. It wouldn't be long until someone came by.

There was no backslapping among Hayes's squad. As they drove off, it was like the raid had never happened. They took separate routes, then reconnected in a valley forty miles away, at the end of a long service road between groves of almond trees.

The team gathered at the back of the box truck. Desert air blew dry and cool. Moret rubbed her shoulder. It had been banging against the crate the whole drive.

"I give," she said, shining a light over the customs form stapled to the raw pine. "So, what is it, some kind of artifact?"

Hayes had kept the details to a minimum as they organized the op. Cells were the safest way to operate, here at home, behind enemy lines. They all trusted him absolutely. They deserved a look. And to be honest, Hayes wanted to see it too. He pulled back the mesh, then wedged his knife in under the top of the crate, pried back a corner, and worked his way up the lid. Ward helped him pull the top off with a squeal of nails against wood. He lifted some of the packing.

"Is that ivory?"

"Bone."

Speed was resting, slumped against the bulkhead. The others crowded in.

Hayes reached down and lifted the inner lid. They stared at it for a moment.

Green turned to Hayes. "Holy shit."

"Sell your cloak and buy a sword," Hayes replied, and he ran his hand over the shipment. "Now the real work starts."

CHAPTER 6

Cox scanned the images of the burned-out armored truck once more, cursed under his breath, then shut his laptop. He had set up in an office on the second floor to run the search for Hayes and his team. While he worked the phone, assistants ferried in faxes and scans and couriered CDs full of data: old pay records, state rolls, unit rosters, vouchers from the adjutant general's office. By that evening, stacks of files were piled high and rising on his desk.

He put his coffee down on top of a sheaf of papers. He picked up the phone and started calling night-action desks in and around Washington. He began with the National Counterterrorism Center, the FBI, and the DHS and added what names he could find to the watch lists.

Barnard appeared in the doorway. Cox waved him in and finished his call.

"I need to get to California," Cox said, "but I found some more names for the local police and FBI to check out. They're former teammates and friends of Hayes, and one's an old mentor. He may go to them for support. Many are former Special Operations, so we're telling law enforcement to use caution."

"You think they would help him after everything he did?"

"They might. Hayes has a way of bringing people under his spell."

Barnard looked down the list while Cox lifted his cup and sipped the cold brew.

"This guy's a doctor now," Barnard said. "He hasn't worked with Hayes in more than a decade."

Cox pointed farther down the page. "Look at the commendations. He killed nine enemy in ten minutes with a back full of shrapnel and saved Hayes's life. A few years ago he left the navy and for all intents and purposes disappeared. Let's be careful with him. He's not just some white coat, and he's staying a couple hours away from the site of the truck bombing."

Barnard looked at the name, stained by a ring of coffee: Thomas Byrne.

CHAPTER 7

I was guilty of many things and had been waiting to fall for a long time. But I never expected it to be like this.

I eased the door handle down and entered the room without a sound. The lights were off. She was still asleep. I was exhausted and covered in sweat but felt the best I had in years. I crossed the carpet, opened the bathroom door, and stepped onto the cold tile when I heard her voice calling from behind me.

"Where did you go, Tom?"

I turned. My eyes adjusted to the dark, the morning sun barely filtering through the shades.

"For a run. I couldn't sleep."

Kelly mumbled, "Mmm-hmm," then rolled over and pressed her face into the pillow. I thought she'd nodded off until she spoke again.

"You never sleep." She turned over, opened one eye, and ran her hand through her hair. "Bad dreams?"

She pulled the sheets up to her chin, then fell back asleep. I looked around the room and there was the other woman. She had green eyes, like Kelly's, and like Kelly she was young and strong and beautiful. Her eyes were open, as peaceful as if she had just woken from a long sleep, but her body was a shambles.

They had troubled me at first, these shades that followed me around. Now what bothered me was that I had almost grown used to them, that I could go on finishing my coffee or climb back into bed beside Kelly even with the dead girl in the room.

"Tom?"

I approached the bed. My eyes followed the curls of Kelly's hair and the curve of her neck. I smiled. "I never remember my dreams."

She propped herself up on her elbow. The sheets fell away. She reached for my wrist and pulled me into bed. I wrapped her up in my arms, looked at her for what seemed a long time, then rolled her on top of me. She kissed me, buried her face in my neck.

"I'm all sweaty," I warned her.

"I don't care." She closed her teeth on the muscle at the side of my neck and made hungry noises. I caught her hands, pushed her back. She came down on her side on the bed. I moved closer, lying behind her. She backed into me. I grabbed her hips, felt her press harder, arch her head back as my lips found her ear, her cheek, her mouth.

We moved together, lost in each other's bodies.

Afterward, she fell asleep, on her side, tucked under my arm, with her head on my shoulder. I wanted to join her, to give in to the drowsiness, but I couldn't. I hadn't slept—really slept—beside a woman in two years, only passed the night half awake, remembering the last time I'd given in to sleep beside someone. When I woke up, she was torn apart, and the blood was on my hands.

Kelly didn't really know anything about me, though we'd been together for almost a year, long distance. At the beginning it had been mainly physical, but it had become something more, even if we didn't acknowledge it. I'd never fallen into such an easy rhythm with someone.

She didn't ask about why I had left the navy. Maybe she sensed it wasn't something she wanted to know.

We were in San Diego for only a few days. I'd come to town on business, a medical conference, and she joined me afterward. She lived in Boston, and I had been moving around a lot.

With these weekends together, these sudden intimacies, the absences between, it was getting more serious than it would have if we'd lived near each other. I couldn't let the past repeat itself, couldn't let that happen again, not to her. I had been alone for a while now, and I hadn't felt this way in a long time, but I couldn't give in to it. It would be my weakness, and she would suffer.

Boom-boom-boom. A fist pounded on the door.

Kelly sat up in bed. "What's that?"

"I got it."

She held the sheets up to her chin. I pulled my shorts and a sweatshirt on and checked the peephole. It was a man in his forties with deep-set eyes. His lower lip was tucked behind his front teeth, making him look anxious and angry. Short-sleeved black uniform, SDPD badge: a local cop.

"Who is it?"

"Police."

"About a case?" Kelly asked as she stepped out of bed and pulled the hotel robe on. I'm a doctor, and I sometimes talk to cops around the emergency department. "I don't know," I said, and I opened the door. Beside the local police officer, there was a man in a dark blue suit.

"Are you Thomas Byrne?" he asked.

"Yes."

"I'm Special Agent Cruz with the Federal Bureau of Investigation. You'll have to come with us." He lifted a warrant: *You are commanded to arrest and bring before this court Thomas Byrne*. It was a material-witness charge.

"Let's go."

"Is this about a patient?" I asked, and I started thinking back over the recent victims of violent crime who had been on my operating table. "I'm on vacation. Can we do it some other time?"

"Don't make this any harder than it needs to be."

Kelly stepped beside me. "Is everything okay?"

"Yeah," I said.

As I reached down, the agent and the local cop pulled their guns. "Stop right there!"

I lifted my hands.

"My wallet."

Cruz turned, saw it, picked it up, and handed it to me.

"Where are you taking him?" Kelly asked.

"Local precinct."

"I'm coming with you."

"That's not possible."

"Stay here," I told her, picking up my cell phone and keeping my voice calm and even. "I'll get this sorted out."

I kissed her, then stepped outside onto the terraced walkway that ran around the exterior of the hotel. The agent cuffed my hands behind my back as Kelly stood in the door, a shocked look on her face.

"You're done," Cruz whispered in my ear as he jacked my arm up. I crossed toward the stairwell and could only imagine what Kelly was thinking.

They had come with the tactical teams: four vans, a loose perimeter with security at every exit, and deputies carrying rifles.

After all those years of guilt, I had expected some reckoning, pictured a thousand variations. But this didn't make any sense.

They marched me downstairs to the parking lot and stuffed me into the back of a Chevy Tahoe. Two officers stood in front of Kelly. They had stopped her on the walkway near the top of the stairs. There was fear and confusion in her face, and a question: *What did you do?* She had been too smart to ask it.

I watched her through the window as the Tahoe pulled away. A material-witness charge, Feds, and long guns; they'd come for me with everything they had.

CHAPTER 8

"Boston, Seattle, Homer, Flagstaff, Silver Spring." Cruz shut the file. "You've lived in five cities in the last year."

"That's right."

I rested my elbows on the metal table. We were at the police station, in an interview room with cinder-block walls painted white. A mirror, which I assumed was one-way glass for observation, was set into the blocks over Cruz's head.

"What are you running from?"

I shook my head. "Nothing. I move around for my job."

"You're a doctor. Emergency medicine, right?"

"A trauma surgeon. I work in emergency departments or trauma units. Locum tenens."

"What does that mean?"

"Placeholder. It's a doctor who goes where he's needed."

"And you chose to be this kind of doctor?"

"For now. It's good money. A chance to travel."

"Like I said, what are you running from?"

It was a good question, and I took my time answering it. I'm wary of people who are smarter than they look. They're the dangerous ones.

I thought back to my last hospital, to the chief of the department's office. I'd just finished cleaning myself up after a surgery. The medical center was in Prince George's County, outside DC. We had a lot of gunshot wounds, a lot of PCP and bath-salt cases. The place was a knife-and-gun club, which kept me busy, which I liked. The chief offered me a permanent position, which was a great compliment, but I had to pass. I couldn't stay.

"How many died?" I'd asked him. I had to know.

"Sorry?"

"From my table, how many died post-op?"

"Two," he said.

I looked down, took a long breath in and let it out through my nose. "I'm sorry."

"It's the best record we've had in this hospital by far. I don't even know that they could have been prevented."

I said nothing.

"People die. You can't save them all, and you can't take it personally. Are you sure you won't reconsider?" he asked.

"I appreciate it, really. But I'm going to be moving on."

What are you running from? Where do you go, Tom? I had a few ideas, but I wasn't about to share them with Cruz.

"You're just a doctor, huh?" he said; he ran his tongue over his teeth and lifted a file. "I don't think so."

He took out a sheet of paper and whistled. "You're in a world of hurt here, Byrne. Let's start from the beginning. When did you fly into Southern California?"

Question by question, I went through every minute of the last four days, and then Cruz started again from the beginning.

"I just told you."

"Tell me again."

He was looking for inconsistencies, for cracks. I ran through it all three times. They worked on me in turns—Cruz, a man from DHS, and another who didn't bother identifying himself—asking me questions that made no sense: Had I been to North Carolina? When was the last time I'd left the United States?

"You can't bullshit me, Byrne," Cruz said. "I want the names of everyone you spoke with since you arrived here, from the top."

I had dealt with guys like him before, in the navy, during the long investigations that came down right before I left. The secret to holding out against them is counterpoise: the angrier they get, the calmer you become; the more terrifying the stakes, the more you relax. Pushing back only lands you in trouble. They want emotion, a fight, anything to get you talking. They can't stand trying to rattle the Buddha.

"I would like to talk to a lawyer," I repeated, again. He was exhausted, I could tell. I was too. They hadn't let me go to the bathroom for the past three hours. My head hurt; as they were escorting me into booking, they had banged my forehead on a door frame, causing a small laceration.

Cruz ignored me and started reading from the paper in front of him. "Use of a weapon of mass destruction. That's life right there. Game over. And just for kicks, we add conspiracy to use a weapon of mass destruction and conspiracy to commit an act of terrorism transcending national boundaries. Not even your ghost will see parole."

"What the hell are you talking about? Will you just tell me—"

"Conspiracy to destroy property by fire and explosive, twenty years. Use of a firearm during and in relation to a crime of violence, life. Carjacking."

He was dumpy; his head was shaved, and the back of the neck looked like a pack of hot dogs. With my past and my job, I'm pretty good under pressure, even enjoy it after a fashion. But what little I knew about material-witness warrants made my mouth go dry with fear. I'd read stories in the paper about trumped-up national security charges, stupid mistakes, Feds run riot. People would be arrested and disappear—no lawyers, no press, no details to the family; they'd just be locked in windowless boxes for months or years.

Why hadn't they read me my rights? Or let me call anyone or talk to a lawyer?

"Listen," I said. "I have a lot of respect for the work you guys are doing. But there must be some sort of mistake. Like I told you, I'm just a doctor getting some R and R after an acute-care symposium. If you would explain why you've brought me in and let me call my girlfriend or a lawyer, we can sort this out without—"

"The only mistake is yours, cocksucker." Cruz stood, shoved his chair back, and put his face in mine, his mouth shut tight, eyes slit in anger like he was about to deck me. I balled my fists until my fingernails bit deep into the flesh of my palms. I could feel the fury surge through me.

He put his hands on his hips and stuck out his chest, enjoying the fact that he was getting to me.

No. It's what he wanted. If they couldn't get me for a crime, they would just twist me until I gave them some reason to lock me up. This was a test, and the best way to get back at this man would be to deprive him of the pleasure of provoking me.

He was in his glory, with a genuine bad guy on his hands, puffed up like a boy playing soldier. But behind it there was fear. He kept his eyes fixed on me at all times, never turned his back. If anyone really thought that this case matched up to the charges he had listed, they would all be absolutely terrified of screwing it up, and of me.

"You're not going to hit me, so drop the act and let me go to the bathroom."

He shook his head and gave me a disgusted look.

"I am requesting counsel," I said.

"Public-safety exception," Cruz sneered. I could see my calm demeanor was setting him on edge more than any tough-guy act would. "I know you were in on that hit on the truck last night. So tell us. Where is the shipment?"

Last night. That was the first real detail anyone had let slip.

"I know you and all the other guys in your unit went to school for this. Survival, Evasion, Resistance, Escape. We know the tricks."

My unit? What was he talking about? I didn't go to SERE.

"What am I supposed to have taken?"

He moved in close again, kissing close, then brought his mouth to my ear. "Pandora's box. And we're going to nail you for it."

"Last night?" I asked. "Last night, between six and eleven p.m., I was at the home of Allison Archambault in Laguna Niguel. Have you tried talking to her yet?"

"So you know nothing except when the crime occurred."

"You said last night!"

"And what, you have some accessory lined up with a ready-made alibi?"

"It was a fund-raiser for pediatric cardiology at UCLA. I was there the whole time. I spent forty-five minutes talking to the host. I can give you her number. She's the former mayor."

I watched his Adam's apple bob up and down twice. The agent glanced up at the camera. I looked at it too.

"Please. This is a mistake. Just call."

He turned the list of charges around and left it on the table in front of me. It was six lifetimes of prison. I could guess what they were doing. No one could be more brutal to me than I could, so they'd left me alone to stew.

As the door closed, I saw him again. Every time they moved me, every time a new face appeared, the people holding me eye-checked a man who was wearing a light gray suit that cost a thousand dollars more than everyone else's.

And no matter how wrong they were, with stakes like these, the time was working on me. One wrong word could mean my life was over. I didn't know who the agent was talking to. Those crimes could easily be rounded into a capital case.

An hour passed. And another. And being locked up alone was bad enough, but soon the dead came, one by one, slumped in a corner of the room or leaning over my shoulder and whispering in my ear: *We finally got you.*

A beautiful woman from my past sat in the chair across from me, her body torn apart, and she asked me why she was dead and I was still alive.

I watched the red hand sweep on the interview-room clock. Six hours I'd been here. I hoped for Kelly's sake that she had packed up and left, but I knew she'd be waiting for me. She had no idea what I did to people.

She was a civil engineer and served part-time in the Massachusetts National Guard. I had been a doctor with the navy, a surgeon.

She came into the ER a year ago, a workplace accident on a bridge construction. A cable had snapped and opened up her shoulder. I sewed her up. She was funny, reminded me of another girl I once knew with green eyes and a no-bullshit affect. Doctors have to be careful about patients falling for them, careful about taking advantage of the trust and power that comes with the ability to heal. I didn't like the doctors who crossed that line. But with Kelly, I didn't really have a say. She was getting discharged just as I wrapped up my shift. I was leaving town in two days. She told me she had a beat-up 1980s Honda motorcycle waiting for her back at the site.

"You shouldn't be riding," I said.

She looked at my keys and then at me. It was a look I knew pretty well.

"I don't date patients."

She lifted her papers. "I'm not your patient, and I don't really have time for dates."

"You don't want anything to do with me. Let me call you a cab."

"I don't need to be told what I want."

In the end, I didn't stand a chance.

She asked me only once about what I'd done in the service. Before I became a doctor, I was a corpsman, the navy equivalent of a medic. I had been attached to a Marine expeditionary unit. The Marines are technically part of the navy, and the navy takes care of everything that has to do with medicine. I went through the training for the Fleet Marine Force, wore the Marine uniform with U.S. Navy insignia, followed Marine discipline, and deployed with a squad. It was called going greenside. The photo and statue of Marines raising the flag on Iwo Jima is actually four Marines and one navy corpsman.

It's not uncommon for Marines and navy guys to beat the shit out of each other in bars, but when I went out with the infantry guys, we all did fine. Once your Marines start trusting you as a corpsman, they call you Doc as a sign of respect.

After Kelly and I got together that first time, she asked me why I'd left the navy. I started to say something, then stopped. It was dangerous territory. She never asked again.

I had told her early on, straight out, that if she knew what was good for her, she'd find someone else.

She just laughed. "I like what I see so far."

There had been women since, but none like her. It was the first time I'd thought, I'd hoped, I could change, for her sake, and for mine.

But she couldn't say I hadn't warned her.

The door opened. It was Cruz. I was innocent; innocent of everything he had thrown at me, at least. But that didn't matter. The waiting, the seconds were wearing me down.

Cruz conferred with the man in the gray suit just before he entered.

"You're free to go," he said.

My mouth dropped open. I had questions, sure. I almost started to ask one, but my first priority was getting the hell out of there. I stood and walked straight through the door. They gave me back my wallet and pink-slipped my cell phone. It was in Evidence. The clerk hadn't even finished the report.

I'd been in that room so long, the sun's light blinded me as I exited the building. I jogged across the street, looking for anyplace that wasn't a police station where I could use the bathroom.

I walked out of the McDonald's with a cup of coffee and a handful of change.

Nothing about it made sense. They had had me in for everything short of treason, and then they'd let me walk without a word. I scanned the street for a pay phone.

I found one, dropped the quarters into the slot, dialed Kelly's number, and held the sticky receiver an inch from my ear. My eyes remained fixed on the station house down the street. It was probably because I was still rattled, but I felt certain this wasn't over. I had to find her and get out of town, fast.

CHAPTER 9

SUNLIGHT AND SUNBURNED tourists filled the airport. Kelly had picked me up and we checked out of our hotel. We returned our rental car and made it to our terminal with fifteen minutes to spare. We were on the same flight out of town.

"Boarding group two," the gate agent announced.

We merged into the crush of travelers. I looked down the Jetway, glad to put some distance between us and whatever those cops were up to, though it had cost us the last day we had together on this trip.

I relaxed some as I handed our boarding passes to the gate agent. The machine returned a red light. He examined the screen.

"We're good with an exit row," I said.

"That's not it. Could I see your IDs?"

"Sorry?"

"Your IDs. I have to double-check your date of birth. Sometimes we get false positives."

"We showed it at Security."

"Please, sir. We don't want a scene."

"It's all right, Tom," Kelly said, trying to calm me down. I swallowed, then leaned over and pulled my wallet from my bag.

She handed her license over first. The agent held it, then took mine. He checked the computer and conferred with the other person working at the gate. Her eyes went wide. A few travelers behind us grumbled about the holdup.

The gate agent fidgeted with his tie. "Could you step to the side for a moment," he asked.

"What's wrong?"

"Please move to the side."

We stepped out of line.

"Away from the gate, sir," the man said. He held his arms tight against his body, his hands balled into fists.

A manager walked over and picked up the phone. She saw me looking, and she covered her mouth and whispered into the handset. I watched the boarding groups disappear, one by one, down the Jetway. A few stragglers jogged toward us.

"We can't miss this flight," I said. When I turned, I saw a police officer doing his best to keep up with a young TSA agent heading toward us.

"I'm afraid you won't be able to fly today," the woman said. She had waited until she had backup.

"What's the problem?"

"Perhaps you should talk to these men."

"What's going on?"

The TSA agent held her palms up toward me. "It's a security precaution, sir. We're going to have to ask you to leave the sterile area."

"You're kidding," Kelly said.

They moved closer, flanking us. "We would be happy to explain the procedures, but I'm afraid we need to relocate you outside security."

Maybe I wouldn't make it through today without snapping after all. "We paid for our tickets. We're boarding that plane," I said, and I picked up my bag.

The cop's mouth tightened to an asterisk. His nostrils flared. Then his hand went for the Taser hanging off his belt.

Kelly put her hand on my chest. I laughed wearily, and we started walking back to the security checkpoint.

I spent the next two hours in a cubicle in a hot back office filled with the sound of jet engines, talking in circles with the TSA agent. There is no such thing as a no-fly list, I was told. Dozens of different agency and law-enforcement watch lists get dumped together by the Terrorist Screening Center. The DHS enforces it, but they say they have nothing to do with it. No, you can't know if you're actually on it. That's classified. And no, you can't find out which agency has blackballed you.

The woman gave me half a dozen forms and said something about the interagency compliance-redress memorandum of understanding. She told me my name probably just matched that of someone on the list, in which case there was no point in appealing the decision, since I wasn't on the list at all.

"So I can fly?"

The agent looked at me like I was thick. "Of course not."

Kelly had been sitting quietly, but I could see her shoulders tense up. She stood and approached the woman. She was about to tear into her. I laid my hand on her arm. "Our problem isn't with the TSA," I said. She looked from me to the agent and then back to me, and relented.

We brought our luggage to the taxi line.

"It's the police from before, isn't it?" Kelly asked.

I had told her about the questioning and how they had let me go once they verified where I'd been last night. And we looked up the news about the armored-truck robbery. No wonder they had been so on edge.

"They must have flagged my name. The stuff Cruz rattled off at me—terrorism—it was crazy. I'll get it sorted out."

She looked at me for a moment. She had every right to bolt. She probably should have. I could see the suspicion in her eyes, that evaluating gaze.

She leaned over and kissed my forehead, then took a close look at the bandage they'd placed over the cut there. She shook her head and bit her lower lip lightly, looking ready to kick someone's ass. There was something deeply attractive about that.

"You want to go back to the Coronado?" I asked.

"It was a little Mayberry. Maybe someplace new."

"La Jolla?"

"What's that place near the cove? La Valencia?"

"I don't remember."

"Let's give that a shot. Tom? Does that sound good?"

My attention was fixed on the short-term parking lot. "Do you recognize that car?" I asked.

"I don't think so."

"I think he was ahead of us the whole way to the airport."

"He was following us from ahead?" She put her hand on my arm. "Babe, I think this is getting to you."

Our cab rolled up. "Maybe," I said, and gave the driver the address.

I called on the way, using Kelly's phone, and made a reservation. When we got there, I was still so out of it I nearly crashed into a man at the main entrance. The hotel was a 1920s throwback set on Prospect Street, painted pink. The dining room was framed in palms with French doors opening onto a terrace and panoramic views of the ocean.

I took my wallet out and was about to get in line for the front desk when I saw a waiter thread through the tables carrying a loaded tray. The ache in my stomach reminded me I hadn't eaten anything all day. "You want to grab some food first?" I asked Kelly.

"Sure," she said. "I'm starving. Then we can figure out the flights."

We parked our bags at the side of the room. The tables were all full, so the hostess seated us at the bar. I handed Kelly the wine list. "Go nuts," I said. We might as well enjoy ourselves.

She picked out a bottle and we ordered appetizers.

"You are staying at the hotel?" the bartender asked. I told him we were as he opened the bottle and poured us two glasses. I raised one to Kelly. "There's no one I'd rather be stuck with."

She clinked mine and smiled. "So you're stuck with me, hmm?"

I laughed and we drank. Kelly put her hand over mine.

"What was the room number?" the bartender asked.

"We haven't checked in yet," I said.

"Okay. Can I have a card for the tab, then?"

I lifted my wallet. The bartender swiped it at his terminal, then pressed his lips together. "Hmm...didn't go through," he said. I took out my bank card. No luck.

Kelly took her wallet out of her purse. "Try this one." I protested, but she handed the card over.

The bartender swiped again.

"No. I'm afraid not."

We went around and around, four or five cards between us. Nothing worked.

"Do you have any cash?" Kelly asked. I opened my wallet. As

we'd left the last place, the Hotel del Coronado, half a dozen captains, bellhops, and stewards materialized. "No. I tipped it all out."

"I spent my last forty on the cab."

"There must be some kind of travel freeze on our cards."

"Let me check with the manager," the bartender said.

A man with dark hair slicked back came over and listened as we explained the situation. He eyed us up for a moment. I wondered if I looked like a guy who had been in jail half the day.

"Do you have some ID?" the manager asked. The politeness was still there, but behind it was a new wariness. "We can send you a bill," he said.

My license was loose in my pocket. As I fished it out, the pink slip from the police station fell to the floor. The manager picked it up and glanced at it as he handed it to me.

The goodwill disappeared. He eyed our open bottle of wine, our glasses three-quarters full. Then he looked up, shook his head, and mouthed *No.* I turned to see a confused waiter standing ten feet behind us holding our food. Kelly watched the appetizers with longing as the waiter turned around and headed back to the kitchen. The bartender took the bottle of wine off the bar.

"I can send a bill for the bottle of wine to your home address."

"And we have a reservation for tonight," I said.

"How many nights were you hoping to stay?"

"It depends."

"I am sorry, sir, but without a valid form of payment, that won't be possible."

I looked around the room, an odd mix of bridge ladies and Arab and Mexican moneymen. My issue wasn't with this guy. I was looking for a fight only because I was hungry and pissed off. It was Cruz I wanted to throttle.

I signed a bill he printed up. We picked up our bags and started walking. I heard the bartender say something about us not looking the type.

Prospect Street was lousy with tourists. We turned downhill, toward the water and the setting sun and, I realized a few minutes later, the smell of grilled onions coming from a food truck. There was a music event in the park overlooking the cliffs and the cove. We were starving, broke, and stuck without a place to stay. This was a great opportunity for a blowup, but Kelly just rolled with it. We watched the sun go down, which lifted the mood for a moment.

"Should we call that agent? Cruz?" she asked. "This is obviously a mistake."

I scanned the street for someone following us but saw nothing strange among the palms and luxury cars.

"No. It's not."

"Then what the hell's going on?"

"They put a scare into us, set us loose, cut us off from all support, and trapped us here to see what we would do, who we would contact, where we would go."

"What are you looking for?"

"They're probably watching us right now."

"That's crazy."

"I know. But they think we're part of something. We're bait."

"Tom, what aren't you telling me? I need to know—" Kelly put a hand to her stomach. "You know what? Save it," she said. "I'm getting a little shaky. I've got to eat something and then we can talk."

"We look decent," I said, surveying the streets above us. "There are happy hours. Corporate events. We could crash."

She appraised me for a moment. Kelly was big on eye contact, on fixing you with those beautiful greens while she thought about what you had said and prepared to speak her mind. I had done nothing wrong, but this was still somehow my fault. And everything she had seen suggested I was some kind of criminal suspect. I squirmed, felt like a bug pinned through the middle in a glass case. Maybe it was too much. We were both hungry. My stomach felt full of acid from sitting empty for so long. If she wanted to lose it on me, that was understandable.

"I saw a Samsung thing at the Grande Colonial. Just follow my lead."

"Perfect."

She followed my gaze to a takeout container perched on the edge of a trash can—the remains of a club sandwich.

"Don't even."

"I wasn't." Though the thought had crossed my mind. A seagull swooped down on the Styrofoam.

"You're a good guy, Tom Byrne," she said, and kissed me. "We'll figure this out."

We started walking up a steep hill toward Prospect Street. The path followed the bluffs. Below us, seals played in the caves, and pelicans flew by in a low chevron.

A car passed.

"Did you see that?"

"What?"

"That Taurus. It's following us."

I scanned the sidewalks behind us. The wind shifted. The reek of guano from the cliffs became overpowering. We continued up the hill. The smell only strengthened. It was like a cloud of chemicals.

"Tom. I've got to get out of here."

We marched fifty feet toward Prospect, and I suddenly doubled back.

Kelly turned. "Where—" I pulled her into the stairwell of a parking garage.

"He's coming," I whispered.

"Who..." she started to say, then lowered her voice. "What are you going to do?"

I was going to grab whoever was after me and shake the living shit out of him. It probably wouldn't help matters, but I didn't care. I wanted answers.

A faint shadow stretched toward us, cast by a man standing in front of a yellow streetlight. Then I noticed ours; we were lit by a flood at the top of the stairwell. The man must have seen our shadow too. He turned around, fled back up the hill. I stepped out, sprinted after him, and saw him go down Prospect.

Kelly ran behind me. I pursued him as far as the Valencia, but he had disappeared. I scanned the streets—no sign of him—and then ducked back into the hotel's lobby. I remembered the man who had bumped into me when I came through those doors the first time. He was all muscle; it had been like walking into a wall of granite. It was no accident.

I looked around the lobby: same bartender; same old ladies through the French doors, but I didn't see my man. As Kelly entered behind me, the manager spotted us. He arranged his shirt cuffs with two sharp tugs and marched our way.

"Do you have Cruz's business card?" I asked Kelly. "Enough is enough."

I took her cell phone and called Cruz's number. An operator answered.

"Tell him Thomas Byrne is calling. He'll want to take it."

He put me on hold. The manager approached Kelly. "Did your credit card start working?" he asked.

"No. We...we thought we left something behind."

He looked me over nervously. I was breathing fast through my nose like a bull. I'm sure I looked like a maniac, but I'd had it. Anger overpowered me as soon as Cruz picked up the phone.

"Listen. Don't think you can coerce me with this Gestapo bullshit. I told you everything I know. You flag me at the airports. You freeze my accounts. Enjoy it while you can. Because I'm going to destroy you. Wrongful arrest and imprisonment; I'm going to have your badge and make a belt buckle out of it. And tell these assholes following me that I don't—"

"Who's following you?"

"Don't play dumb."

There was some muffled cross talk as he checked with someone. "Give me the phone," I heard a voice say.

"Thomas. My name is George Hall. I'm an army major and I have been helping with this investigation."

"Gray suit?"

"What? Yes...that was me. You are in danger. Where are you? Can you see the men? Are they armed?"

"I chased one and he ran. Tell me what's going on."

"Get him as far away from innocent targets as possible," said a voice behind Hall's.

I could see the manager talking to Kelly, pointing to the door, telling her to get out.

"I'll explain, Byrne," Hall said. "But first, where are you?"

"La Jolla. La Valencia hotel."

"Stay there. We're going to send some people."

"I've been through that already. No, thanks."

"We're not bringing you in. It's for your protection. Trust me. Whatever you do, do not approach or confront these guys. They are no joke, all right?"

In the background, someone asked Hall about the bomb squad.

"Stay by this phone." He hung up.

The manager had overheard my tirade, and it hadn't helped matters. I spent a minute or two trying to calm him down. He disappeared and came back ten minutes later with two security guards.

"I'm calling the police," he said.

Sirens filled the street.

"They're already here," I said, and Kelly and I walked outside.

A black Chevy Tahoe parked in front of the hotel and a black Suburban pulled up behind it. Patrol cars cut across the two nearest intersections, lights flashing, and blocked them off. Traffic came to a halt.

Cruz stepped out of the Tahoe and started giving commands to the cops. They spread out, scanning the roofs of buildings and the streets.

The man in the gray suit, Hall, walked up to me. "You all right?" he asked.

"Never better," I said. "Though it sounds like I have a decent risk of being detonated."

"It could be worse, much worse. I'm sorry about the confusion and the incident back at the station. The local cops can get a little worked up when we come by. They like to show off. What did the man who was following you look like?"

"I'm not helping you. I have no idea what you idiots landed me in the middle of." I had blood on my hands, but that was from years ago. It had nothing to do with whatever these cops were so afraid of right now.

"Tall?" Hall asked. "Well-built but lean, like a backpacker? Bearded, or maybe recently shaved, pale around here?" He indicated his chin.

That was the man who had crashed into me. "Is someone going to tell me what's going on?"

"During the truck ambush last night, a shipment related to national security was stolen. Based on military records, we thought you might possibly have links to the men who took it. And you were in the area. Those men may now be following you."

"They're soldiers?"

"They were."

"What do they want with me?"

He let out a breath. "That's what we're trying to find out."

"What did they steal?"

"I can't talk about it here," he said. "If you come with me, I can explain. There's someone you should meet. He can make things clear. And then we can get this travel mess sorted out."

I looked to Kelly.

"You're not safe here," Hall said.

"We were perfectly safe until you hauled us in," Kelly said, and she turned to me. "You're really going to go with this man?"

I needed to get out of crisis mode, and I wanted answers above all.

"If I come, you unfreeze our accounts and let us go home."

"I can help with that," Hall said.

I walked toward his truck, then leaned in close to him. "She stays out of it. I'll need some money for her, for food and a place to stay so she can get squared away. You tell me what's going on. Then I'm out of here. Deal?"

"Deal," he said. It was nice of him to act like we were on equal footing. The fact was, he and the police could have hauled me in at any moment with that warrant. I was already in checkmate, with no money and nowhere to go. What did I have that he wanted so badly?

He took some cash out of his wallet, then scrounged some more from the driver. I took the bills and folded them. "I'll pay you back as soon as you unlock my accounts."

I walked over to Kelly and put the money in her hand. She spread it out. "And what do I say when people find out I traded my boyfriend for a hundred and thirty dollars?"

"Tell them you got a great deal. Get a hotel and something to eat."

"I'll call the bank and start reaching out to people who might know what's going on."

"Good. Leave me a voice mail. I can check it without my cell. Tell me where you are. I'll be back in a couple hours."

"You know what you're doing?"

"No clue."

I kissed her and then joined Hall by the Tahoe. The guard opened the back door, and I climbed inside.

"Don't worry," Hall said as we pulled away. "You'll be safe with us."

CHAPTER 10

HAYES SAT IN the driver's seat of a Chevy S-10 pickup parked in a pay lot down the street from La Valencia. He watched Byrne talking with the police outside the hotel. His squad had swapped out the vehicles from the armored-truck ambush.

On the bench seat beside him, Ward and Cook kept up the good-natured argument they'd been having for the past four years over who would win in a fight between Jean-Claude Van Damme and Steven Seagal. Cook was the youngest of the group by six years and still eager to prove himself to the more experienced operators.

As Byrne climbed into the black Tahoe, Ward worked the keys of a computer on her lap. A wire ran from it out the window to a small probe about the size of a pencil that had been fixed with a magnet to the windshield pillar of the truck.

There was a graph on the computer screen with a red line bright against the edges.

"The calibration must be off."

"Do you have it? They're on the move," Hayes said. The Tahoe inched ahead in the traffic going toward the 5.

She adjusted the settings. "Wait. Where is Speed?"

"Under the cap." Hayes tilted his head toward the bed of the truck.

"I'm overloaded. He's glowing with the stuff." She opened the small window that looked onto the truck bed.

"Did you wear a glove when you painted Byrne?" she asked.

"It would have looked pretty weird to be wearing a surgical glove, wouldn't it?"

"Wash your hand off with this." She gave him a small plastic bottle. "Then get back to the other car before you completely drown out the scent."

Speed crawled out and walked to the Toyota 4Runner parked on the street, the squad's second vehicle. Ward watched the colors change as the chemicals dissipated. When Speed had bumped into Byrne at the entrance to the hotel, he'd tagged him with a per-fluorocarbon tracer, a near-perfect tracking chemical. PFTs don't exist in nature, and they are detectable down to one part tracer to one quadrillion parts air—one followed by fifteen zeros. They penetrate closed buildings, locked doors, and sealed luggage. They last for weeks. The existence of a real-time portable sensor to track PFTs was still classified top secret in a special-access program.

"Working now?" Hayes asked as the Tahoe disappeared over the hill.

"Yes," Ward said.

Hayes put the truck in gear. Ward watched the colors shift on her screen and glanced up at the road and the coming intersections.

"Straight ahead."

It was a long, difficult process. They would lose the trail and double back to pick it up again where the target had turned. The PFTs lingered in the air behind Byrne and Hall. Hayes closed in on them but never approached, never moved within sight of his quarry or the police. The trail snaked through the dark, visible only to Ward's spectrometer.

It led the two trucks on a route parallel to the coast, then departed the main highways and wound along a rough access road. The land narrowed, and ahead they could see an isolated point banked in fog. The tracers drew them on. The terrain fell sharply away on both sides, desert plants on the south, lush green on the shaded north.

They tracked the scent to a small collection of buildings set at the very end of the point, almost surrounded by the ocean. There was a utility building that bristled with microwave and radar antennas, a decommissioned lighthouse, and a white stucco house with a red-tile roof. Hayes drew the Chevy as close to the fences as he could get without being spotted and got out. He looked over the target building. It would be easy to cut off by land.

Speed stepped out of the Toyota and surveyed the perimeter barriers. Two parallel chain-link fences, set thirty feet apart, cut across the peninsula to protect the base.

"What do you think?" Hayes asked.

"Stacked microwave along the face of the fence. Good construction. Climbing's out. Bridging will be tough." The hill they stood on ran down toward the fences. "The topography will help out."

"Power?"

Speed traced the electric lines. "The transformers are over there. Should be easy to black out."

"And once we're past the fences?"

"Hard to say. My guess would be infrared."

"Ugh," Hayes muttered. "Bring the silicone spray and the shields."

They took a few minutes to unload the gear out of the trucks, then started hiking. They stayed low, crouching along the back of a knoll, until they were about twenty feet from the fence.

"Pizza cutters," Speed said. The easiest way to bypass a perimeter is to simply place a long board up against it and bridge over. Outside corners often form dead spots in the sensors, but these had circular blades set at the top of each one.

Speed took out a twenty-meter rope and tied a hook at the end.

"You sure there's no vibration?" Hayes asked.

He surveyed the fence one more time, looking for the telltale black boxes.

"Yes. Ready?"

"Wait," Hayes said. He watched the sky. A minute passed, then two. The moon was setting. He watched as a thick layer of fog rolled in, blocking the pinpoint white glow of Jupiter.

"Go."

Speed spun the hook and flung it over the top of the fence. He dragged it to the left until it set securely against a post, then looped his end around the base of a short tree, gnarled and pruned by salt water on its ocean-facing side. He and Moret pulled it tight and tied it off in a wireman's knot.

"Is there enough room to land?" Hayes asked.

Speed looked again. Every fifty feet or so, a small black rod stood out from the gravel between the two fences: reference markers. That was a mistake. It indicated that there were two microwave sensor paths running down the middle of the no-man's-land, but there was room to move just inside either fence.

"If we drop straight down," he said.

One by one, each lay on the rope and hooked a foot around it. They crawled over on their bellies on top of the line, picked their way over the barbed wire, then dropped to the gravel.

"You see the markers?"

"Yeah," Hayes said. He dropped to his hands and knees on the stones.

"Closer," Speed said. Hayes crawled toward the beam.

"There."

The others lined up twenty feet down the fence. One at a time, they sprinted at Hayes, planted a boot on his ass, and vaulted high over the microwave beams that ran between the fences. Cook, all two hundred and forty pounds of him, went last, and Hayes could barely stifle a groan. Hayes stood, leaned over to stretch the sore area on his behind, then sprinted, cut, and dive-rolled over the path of the sensors.

He stood with the squad beside the inner fence.

"Huh," Speed said, looking back.

"What?" Hayes asked.

"Deer."

"So?"

"Well, with wildlife, they usually have a speed cutoff on the microwaves. To avoid false positives. So we probably could have just sprinted across."

Hayes rubbed his lower back. He tilted his head and gave Speed a dead look.

"Probably not, though."

Hayes climbed up the inner fence and dropped to the other side. The others followed. They were inside the base, but motion detectors peered down at them from the corners of the buildings.

"Passive system?" Hayes asked.

"No," Speed said. He took an IR laser pointer from his chest pocket and adjusted his night-vision goggles. The detector's field would refract the light. "Follow me," Speed said. "Stay close."

They moved in a tight file. The beam of Speed's laser wavered at the edge of the detectors' range. He led them in a staggered pattern like a lightning bolt. They took cover beside a storage shed with a view of the main house.

Hayes surveyed the buildings. He switched his goggles over from infrared to thermal. The night went from a world of green contours to a full rainbow of heat signatures. "Transformer at two o'clock. One hundred meters," he said, then turned his attention to the main building.

The blinds were down, but he caught three ghosts as they passed in front of an open window on the first floor of the house. He counted off the sentries posted at the main doors, on the roof, at each corner. He saw six. Best to assume a dozen, and six to eight more in the building based on the number of vehicles outside.

As Moret readied a charge, Hayes scanned again. He saw a faint red patch in his goggles, next to what looked like a diesel tank, a hundred and fifty or two hundred meters to their left. It was either the largest hot-water heater ever made or a generator. Backup power. "We have to get the genny too." He lit it with his IR laser.

Speed navigated the detectors and led Moret to the transformer. She planted a small charge against the bushings around the main wires to the compound. The detonator was on an RF switch. Speed's light glowed through their goggles as he traced the invisible maze to the generator, and Moret planted a second explosive.

They returned to the squad.

"Are we going to wait for the guards to go off?" Moret asked.

"No," Hayes said. "We can't risk any more time here. We'll just have to hit hard. Ready to black them out?" Moret armed the detonator remote and handed it to him.

They all crouched, prepared to sprint.

"What's your boy's name again?" Speed asked.

"Tom Byrne," Hayes said.

"Will he give us any trouble?"

Hayes remembered Byrne stabbing him in the chest, picking up an M249 machine gun, and vaulting over a wall toward enemy fire.

"Maybe," Hayes said, and he put his thumb on the detonator. "He was never very good about taking orders."

CHAPTER 11

HALL AND I rode in the back of the Tahoe while his driver navigated to the end of the peninsula then pulled up to a security checkpoint. The guard spoke with the driver, then waved us onto the base. There was a second chain-link fence after thirty feet. As we passed through the inner gate, I could see the red-tile roof of the main house through a break in the fog. We rolled down the driveway.

A lighthouse stood in the distance to our left, and beside us was a storage yard full of rusting model ships, a whole fleet of carriers, destroyers, and frigates, dozens of them, four to twelve feet long.

We parked in front of a Spanish-style mansion at land's end. Hall led me to the front door as two members of his security team followed behind me. I paused on the stoop and took a look around but could see only the stucco facade and faint lights glowing through the fog in the distance. The guards behind me stiffened.

"What is this place?" I asked Hall.

"A safe house," said a voice behind me. A man stood, silhouetted in the door frame, then stepped into the glow of the porch light. "The E Ring decided we need to be babysat until we can round up the soldiers who came after you today."

"Thomas, this is Colonel Riggs," Hall said.

He was solidly built, a bear, though it seemed middle age had softened him a little around the jaw. He had deep creases beside his eyes and a look so direct it made me want to take a step back.

"Tom Byrne." I reached my hand out toward his right.

"Doesn't work," he said and offered his left. I took it and felt the embarrassment showing in my face.

"Sorry."

"Don't be. I'm used to it. Come in." He entered the house, limping slightly on his right leg, before I could say another word. I turned and watched the fog pull back along the twin fences high on the hill above us. I thought I saw movement.

"What's up?" Hall asked.

I looked again. "Nothing." I followed them inside.

"You want water or coffee or anything?" Hall asked.

"Coffee." It would cover up my hunger for a while.

The interior looked like an officers' club from the early twentieth century: wood paneling, a model ship on the mantel. Most of the furniture was covered in drop cloths. The three of us walked past an open window toward a dining room. The drawn blinds moved in the breeze.

"We have instant. Still getting settled." Riggs stepped into the kitchen and leaned against a sideboard. "They have us going to the mattresses here. It seems like overkill, but I've underestimated the people who are after you before."

He pointed to his disabled hand. A scar that looked like the result of a gunshot wound covered the back of it. "This was their work."

Hall started a kettle and poured a foil packet of coffee crystals into a Fort Campbell mug.

"Colonel," I said. "I don't have anything to do with any armored truck or any of these men you're after. My bank accounts are frozen. I can't fly. Could you tell me what's going on?"

"Standard procedure when we find someone with a nexus to terrorism."

Hall poured the water and set the mug on a wooden table beside me. "Sit down."

I took a chair. "Terrorism? Come on. This is obviously a mistake. If you keep coming after me with this stuff, you're only going to hurt your own career—"

"My career is already over, Dr. Byrne. So you can save the threats. They're pretty weak anyway. I'm retired, though DOD calls me in to consult fairly often. Most of my time is spent on a project I have that provides employment opportunities to warriors after their service. I wish I were done with the Pentagon, but they can't seem to let me go."

"I had nothing to do with this."

He lifted a stack of papers on the side table and let them fall. "You seem to check out."

"What is that?"

"Your past."

"Good. I'm cleared. So I can go home."

"That's out of my hands. And besides, these papers could be the dog that didn't bark."

"Whose hands is it in? Because I'd like to talk to them instead of wasting my time here."

Riggs stepped next to me, put his face close to mine. "No more bullshit. Did you help him attack that truck?"

"I told you, no. I don't even know who you're talking about."

"Come off it. You know who he is. You're helping him. You're in over your head. Come clean now and save yourself the pain."

I took a deep breath. "Baiting me isn't going to work. I don't know anything."

He let the aggression drop, deflated slightly. I gathered it had been his last stab at me, and he seemed to accept the truth of what I was saying. "So you really were just in the wrong place at the wrong time. You poor bastard." He shook his head. "Well, whether you make it home depends entirely on the soldiers hunting you."

"Who are they?"

"You saw one today, tailing you at the hotel. Their leader sometimes goes by the name John Hayes."

I looked down and put my hand to my forehead, trying to make sense of it. I hadn't heard that name in more than a decade. Hayes had been my sergeant when I was attached to a Marine squad. I could see Riggs trying to read something into my look of recognition.

"I served under him when I was a corpsman. But I haven't seen him or talked to him in years. Why would Hayes ambush a truck inside the U.S.?"

"Revenge," Riggs said. "That's the least worrisome motive." He pulled a chair out and sat next to me.

"Let me tell you what we're up against here. Captain Hayes was the leader of a task force under my command. We were deployed overseas; doesn't matter where. He and his team came from Joint Special Operations Command's special missions units. Those are all classified, black.

"We train them to go behind enemy lines, to disappear, to survive indefinitely with no support, to fight, to hunt, and to kill. We take them to the edge. Sometimes they go over.

"While coming out of a denied area, Hayes and his team committed grave crimes against innocent civilians. Rather than face punishment for their actions, they fled. Now they're in the U.S., and they're on the warpath. We don't know their ultimate target or their motives. It could be revenge or an attempt to eliminate the people who can testify against them."

He opened a folder and slid a photo to me: a bombed-out armored truck surrounded by burned scrub and torn metal. It looked like news footage from Afghanistan.

"The truck attack. They did that in less than three minutes."

I looked at the scorched metal where the doors had been sheared off. It was a surgical hit.

"What did they steal?"

"Something very dangerous. This is the latest in an escalating pattern of strikes. And now they seem to be after you."

"But why?"

"You tell me."

"No clue. I don't know why you or the police would think I have anything to do with Hayes."

"We've been over your file. You two nearly died together at K Thirty-Eight. You're going to tell me you're not close?"

"I haven't seen him since then."

"Hayes's first target inside the U.S. was an office building in North Carolina," Riggs said. "It's an annex of the Defense Cover Program that handles classified-unit personnel records. It is as secure a building as we know how to make, and they went through it like a breeze.

"He and his team destroyed their personnel files, the information we would need to find them and their aliases, associates, and family members. Pentagon investigators are attempting to reconstruct those records."

"You didn't know him well?"

"Few did. He was in the field for most of the time I commanded the task force. Your name surfaced when we canvassed past teammates and associates of Hayes. That's why the FBI picked you up when they found out how close you were to the assault on the truck."

"Jesus." I lifted the photo and shook my head. "You thought I would help him do that? I'm a doctor now."

"He can assume identities with ease. Some people thought you *were* Hayes. We know better, now that he's following you. He may try to contact you or coerce you into helping him. It's one of his strengths. Don't let him lure you in. He's done it to many people, and it's a fatal mistake."

"I'm nothing to him."

"That can't be true. You saved his life."

"I was just doing the job." I took a sip of coffee, then leaned back in the chair. "How about this: Is it possible Hayes is watching you, hunting you?"

Riggs looked around the safe house. "Certainly."

"He probably saw the police and Hall drag me in. And now he and his team are checking me out. It's pretty simple."

"Help us find him, and we'll protect you and sort out your travel and financial issues."

I clamped both hands around the mug and took a long breath. I was innocent, but they were going to keep treating me like a terrorist unless I made myself a target for the real bad guys. I would suffer for an obvious mistake made high above me that no one could be bothered to correct. Boy, I missed the military.

"I don't want anything to do with this."

"I imagine Hayes's crew are already none too happy with you. Why else would they be following you? And now that they've seen you talk to the police and us, I don't think they'll consider your jawing over coffee with me any worse than what you've already done. They can't kill you twice."

I muttered a curse. This was insane. "Even if I wanted to, I couldn't help you because I don't know anything. Unless you want to use me as chum to draw them out."

Riggs gave me a disingenuous look: *Heaven forbid.*

"This is extortion," I said.

"You can do some good here."

"No."

Riggs stood suddenly. His chair skittered back. He tripped with his weak leg, stumbled, and then caught himself. Hall went to help him, and Riggs shoved him away.

"Hayes," Riggs growled. "Blood on his hands, and still you people line up to help him. He's the goddamn pied piper." He turned to Hall. "Give it to me."

Hall handed him a folder.

"Do you have a clearance?" Riggs asked me.

"No."

"I could go to prison for showing you this," he said, then shrugged. "To hell with it."

He laid a photo in front of me. It looked like doll parts at first, then I made out a shipping container in the background and got a sense of scale. It took me a second to understand what I was seeing. It was a pile of bodies, many dozens, heaped like trash in a landfill—men, women, children, some two or three years old, all of them torn apart by gunfire, massacred. I knew I would never be able to unsee it. Those bodies would mingle with my own ghosts, making themselves at home.

I pushed it to the side.

"That's more of their handiwork," Riggs said. "Hayes and his

team are in the late stages of an operation. You are a target, in-
dividually and as an innocent citizen. Everyone you know and
love is at risk. I am here to stop them. I am here to save you. So
have some basic human decency and help me. Because that"—
he tapped the photo—"is a warm-up. Will you help us stop
him?"

I looked back at the eight-by-ten, at the bodies. I had enough
blood on my hands and I wasn't going to get Kelly involved in
this. I finally had someone to lose. "I can't. I'm sorry."

Riggs straightened up. "Get Nazar," he snapped to Hall.

"What's going on?"

"There's someone you need to meet."

Hall stepped away and opened a sliding door. I looked around
the room. There were guards at both exits. I didn't like the setup.
I peered through the door after him, expecting some enforcer to
emerge. But in the slanting light, all I could see was an older
woman leaning over a table in a sunroom. He beckoned me in,
and I stepped through the door.

Windows filled most of the two far walls, looking out over a
courtyard. The patchy fog pressed against them, condensed on the
glass, and streaked down. I could hear waves crashing.

Hall said something to her, and she looked up from her work.
She had been writing in a slanting script, filling a page of letter
paper. I looked at the book on the table in front of her.

"*The Odyssey?*" I asked. I didn't recognize the language she was
writing in, but it was clearly verse. She was translating it.

She pushed back her chair and stood. She wore a flowing
printed dress and had gray hair up in a loose bun. As she turned, I
could see scars beside her eye.

"Tom Byrne," Riggs said. "This is Nazar. Nazar, Tom Byrne."

We shook hands. She gave me a kind smile, though there was

something sad about it. She was tall and thin and carried herself in a manner that struck me as old-fashioned, European.

"Nazar is your last name?" I asked. It felt impolite to call her by her first.

She began to speak, but Riggs interrupted. "Let's just stick with Nazar for now."

He stepped closer, between us. He wanted to protect her.

"Nazar was one of our interpreters—no, much more than that, a fixer, my trusted local guide. She worked with Hayes occasionally."

"Just a translator, really," she said, laughing quietly. "The colonel makes me sound like Gunga Din. I'd rather be hiding out among these books."

I pointed to the open volume. "I remember a part where he goes down into the underworld, and he meets all these people he knew who died."

"The shades. The shadows of the dead. The Greek is *skia*, the Latin *umbra*. Dante used similar language."

Her English had a faint British accent. Something else too— a trace of a hard burr I couldn't place. I took another look at the scars, then caught myself.

"It's okay, Tom," Riggs said. "We're the bang-and-dent section. And we're the lucky ones. I understand your reluctance. You'd be an idiot if you didn't try to avoid these men. So don't ask any questions. Just listen."

"You were at the massacre," I said to her, and I turned to him. "Hayes did this?"

Riggs nodded. "We survived."

"What happened?"

Through the windows, I could make out guards on the widow's walks and upper-floor arcades looking down at us.

"I'm afraid I can't say where exactly we were fighting. It's a borderland. A bad neighborhood, geopolitically. Hayes's team was preparing the battlefield."

I'd heard that phrase—*preparing the battlefield*—before. It's a bit of Pentagon jargon. The Department of Defense uses it to broaden its activities around the world. As long as it claims it is preparing the battlefield, the DOD can conduct clandestine operations. The CIA functions under a different set of laws, rules that govern covert actions. The terms may sound similar, but there is a world of difference between them.

The Pentagon, unlike the CIA, can conduct clandestine missions without presidential authorization and without telling Congress, operating with zero civilian oversight. That's why more and more intelligence work has been pouring into the military side.

"Two years ago, the men and women under Hayes's command conducted a low-visibility clandestine operation," Riggs said. "It was dangerous and complex. A long incursion into enemy territory that was crucial to U.S. national security."

"Men and women?"

"There's an all-female division in the Intelligence Support Activity and other women in the special mission units. We borrowed the tactic from the Mossad. Sending eight jacked young men into a hostile area raises suspicion. Couples have far less trouble. If the enemy thinks we have no women operators, we damn well better have some.

"Hayes was given an exceptional amount of autonomy for a captain, though he was no ordinary captain. Several members of his team were killed on the mission. Perhaps we had them working for too long out in Indian Country, under too ambiguous a moral compass. But they came back to the safe house, the forward base they had been operating out of, and..."

He trailed off. He still had the photo from the massacre in his hand, but he brought it down beside his leg. I could see he felt embarrassed, as if it were indecent to let Nazar see it.

"It's fine," she said, and she stepped toward Riggs. She laid a hand on his arm to reassure him, took the photo, and held it in the light. "I can't go for more than a few minutes without seeing it up here, anyway." She gestured to her temple, then looked at the faces of the dead.

"My niece and nephew, here. And this is my sister." Her finger moved across the glossy surface of the eight-by-ten. "She was always the pretty one. We used to tease her."

She smiled, then shut her eyes hard, waited for the emotion to subside. She cleared her throat.

"Yes, well," she started, in control again. "Captain Hayes came back to the base and began to gather the interpreters. We were all essentially refugees," she said, and she glanced down at the book she had been translating. "From…"

She looked at Riggs.

"No details, please," he said.

"From a country hostile to the United States. We had been persecuted, some of us killed, for what we believed and what we looked like. The colonel gave us shelter, protection. He was good to us. And Hayes, he was good to us too. We all loved him."

She pressed her lips together and shut her eyes again, let the anger flow through her. "He had a way of making people love him, making them trust him. That is why we followed him on the day of the massacre."

"You have to understand," Riggs said. "Hayes was much more than a door kicker. He trained with the CIA at Camp Peary and Harvey Point. He was born to be a spy, spent his whole life blending in, winning confidences, making everyone his accomplice. That's why he was so lethal. You have to be careful with him, Byrne. He could turn you without your even knowing it. He draws people in, uses them as tools to kill others, then discards them. And we've never seen anyone better."

"He played on our hopes," Nazar said. "All we wanted was a home, a safe place for our families. Hayes told us we had been granted asylum in the U.S. and Europe. We gathered our relatives, what possessions we could carry—none of us really had much more than that anyway—and went to meet him. I've never seen such joy among my people. For generations we had wandered, lost and hunted, and soon it would be over.

"Hayes and his team gathered us in the village square. My sister was crying, she was so happy. They lined us up in front of a mud wall and told us a helicopter was coming."

She wiped a tear from the corner of her eye and kept on, calm. "Then Hayes shouldered his rifle, and they began to fire."

She looked at the photo, examined the bodies.

"Hayes executed them," Riggs said. "Everyone who had interpreted for Hayes, their families, and all who witnessed his crimes on that day. He killed them all."

"I was hit twice," Nazar continued. "But I was fortunate. I lay among the bodies, beside my niece and sister, as still as I could manage while the bullets cracked. And Hayes—I couldn't believe it was the same man I had worked with. It was like a devil took him."

She looked my way, and I could see she was still trying to make sense of it. I knew Hayes as a good man, but I had seen him in battle, seen him kill face-to-face with a cold efficiency. It was as if, when we flicked our weapons' safeties to fire, something switched inside him too.

"I'm sorry," I told her. The words sounded weak and uncaring, almost cruel. We stood in silence. Nazar commanded the center of the room. I wanted to avoid her gaze, the simple moral insistence that burned in her, but I didn't look away.

Riggs cast his eyes to the ground. "I failed to protect them."

"He did everything he could," Nazar said. "He came and tried to stop Hayes. They shot him in the chest, and he still fought."

"It wasn't enough. Only Nazar survived, lying among the dead. To this day, her work, reading and writing, pains her." I had seen how Nazar bent close to the page, almost touching it.

"I was an air force colonel," Riggs said. "I came up as a fighter pilot. And now I'm useless for anything but holding down a chair."

"What were they hiding?" I asked.

"What do you mean?"

"They targeted their interpreters. Were they covering their tracks?"

"I can't talk about that. One of the team members was raised in the U.S. but has family connections in Turkey, an area known as a transshipment point for the al-Nusra Front. It's a very worrisome scenario."

"What was in that truck?"

Riggs nodded. "These are the right questions, Tom, but I can't discuss the answers. After the massacre, Hayes and his team took arms and equipment that would allow them to work independently of the command. Based on their movements and the impunity with which they have been operating inside the United States, we believe that they are at full strength at the squad level, possibly higher.

"I killed one of them on the day of the massacre, and Nazar and I are the chief witnesses in proceedings against them. Our safety is the least of our concerns. These soldiers have gone over. Hayes is not the man you knew. He has done things from which there is no redemption. We sent them into the dark, and the dark came back with them. They are in this country. And last night they stole something very dangerous to all of us.

"The United States spent decades and hundreds of millions of dollars training them for exactly this: to enter a nation and destroy it through violence from the inside. The problem is that their target is now the United States. And after last night, they have the means. So, Tom Byrne, how about a little help, if that won't inconvenience you too much?"

I didn't answer. I didn't care what happened to me, but Kelly was still out there, alone.

Hall looked at me with disdain. "You were on a good track. Fleet Marine Force. Accepted into Special Amphibious Recon. Why didn't you go on with Marine Special Operations?"

"I wanted to be a doctor."

"But you and your guys got shot up pretty bad at K Thirty-Eight?"

"Yes."

"And *then* you started working on getting your commission. Got your bachelor's during active duty, applied to the USUHS." That's the military's medical school.

"Correct."

"Intern. General Medical Obligation. Resident. Fellow." He read down the sheet, ticking off the steps. "That's a lot of time hiding out in libraries and hospitals. And then you were at Camp Dagger?"

"On the forward surgical team."

Hall put the papers down. "This tells me a story, Tom. You were on track to be a good soldier. Then K Thirty-Eight happened. You saw some real bloodshed and you quit, ran away, tried to find someplace safe. But even as a doctor, you couldn't escape it.

After the Dagger attack, you left the navy the first chance you got. Milked us for everything, then bailed."

He stood over me like a prosecutor wrapping up a closing statement.

"You nailed it," I said.

Riggs leafed through the papers. "I don't think so. You're hiding something. You volunteered for a frontline trauma spot. Commendation with valor for K Thirty-Eight. And you earned the Navy and Marine Corps Medal at Dagger. They don't give those out to just anyone."

"After they mop up the blood, they go looking for heroes. Sometimes they just need a chest to pin a medal on."

Riggs frowned.

"You can do some good here." He lifted the folder. "Make things right. Save lives."

I remembered that day at Camp Dagger, remembered a woman, young and strong and beautiful, remembered how peaceful her face looked. The shadows. I couldn't live with any more of them.

"Dr. Byrne," Nazar said. "Will you help us?"

I thought back to the chief of surgery at the last hospital. Even one death was too many. *You can't save them all,* he had said. But I had a feeling the patients on my table wouldn't mind if I tried.

"All right," I said. "What can I do?"

Riggs turned to Hall. "Bring me everything you have," he said. Hall left. Nazar, Riggs, and I remained in the sunroom.

Hall returned with a file and offered it to me. "To start, we want you to look at some photos. Tell me if you recognize the men who followed you today."

I reached for the folder. As my fingers closed around it, the lights went out.

CHAPTER 12

"Did you hear something?" Hall asked.

"Will someone check the goddamn fuse box" came Riggs's voice. "This place is ancient. Don't worry. We have a backup—"

A muffled crack cut him off. It sounded like lightning behind the fog.

"Who has a radio?" Riggs asked. There was movement in the dark, then a crash from inside the house.

I heard the crack and static of an open radio channel: "We lost power. You see anything out there?" Riggs asked.

"Nothing," a guard replied.

"Keep your eyes open."

My vision slowly adjusted to the dark, but I could still barely make out the contours of the figures standing three feet away, like shadows in the fog.

A man lifted a radio beside me. "We're on the porch. Get down here with some lights." It was Riggs.

"Rog. We'll—" The guard's voice cut off, and then three cracks boomed from the radio speaker.

"Say again. Say again," Riggs ordered. But there was only silence from the other end. I could feel my heart pumping in my chest. "Say again," Riggs demanded.

Finally, a new voice broke in on the radio.

"Someone's inside."

"Where?" Riggs asked.

A moment passed. No one answered.

"Get to the courtyard," a guard said. The words came over the radio between fast breathing, like a man running, and squelches of static. "Lock yourself in."

I followed the voices. We stepped through a door onto weathered tiles.

"Byrne, you here?"

"Yes."

"Hall?"

"Yes."

"Nazar."

"Yes."

I moved closer until I could see the others.

"Good. We'll be safe here," Riggs said. "There are sentries above us. Everything's locked. The only easy way in is through that door."

He pulled out his sidearm, thumbed down the safety, and stared at the door that led back into the house. We formed a loose circle, fanned out with our backs to a stucco wall.

"We're in the courtyard," Riggs said into the radio.

"We haven't found anyone. They blew the generator. Sit tight."

My vision narrowed. Every sound seemed to grow louder. Time slowed. I moved on autopilot. There was fear and a flood of adrenaline. I felt strong and wanted the fight. *Come on. Come for me.* Jesus, how I had missed this rush.

"I need a weapon," I said.

"None to spare."

His mistake. We waited. The other men were nearly hyperventilating. I felt like they were right beside me. The fog muffled the sounds, warped the sense of distance.

This was bad. We shouldn't be bunched up together. It was a basic rule when expecting contact. I took a few steps to the side.

"Don't move," Riggs said.

Far up, to my right, I saw blue flashes, and then I heard a *rat-tat-tat*. It seemed too quiet for a gun.

"Are those shots?" I asked. "Suppressed?"

"No," Riggs said. He lifted the radio. "This is Riggs. Come back. Come back."

There was nothing.

"Come back."

I heard a cry and a thump from inside, straight ahead of us. The colonel raised the pistol and aimed it at the door. A moment passed with no noise, no movement, just our breath in the fog.

"Come on, assholes," I heard Riggs whisper.

"Let's get out of here."

"No. They want us to panic."

We waited. Time stretched my nerves to the breaking point. I turned toward the colonel and saw a shadow moving silently down the wall from the second story: a man, slipping in like a wraith.

"Riggs, behind you!"

The figure let go of the rope and dropped to the floor. I lunged toward him. Metal clinked against brick. White light blanked out the world. The explosion hit me like a crashing wave, thumping my chest and deafening me. I fell back. My head hit the ground.

I staggered up on my hands and knees. I could hear only a high-pitched whine in my ears, some aftereffect of the blast, could see only blue, like I'd stared into the flash of a camera. I took one step and fell forward, caught a wall with my hand, steadied myself as my eyes adjusted. The blue softened to red, and finally the black murk took over again.

"Byrne." I felt a gloved hand on my shoulder. "This way. We'll get you out."

I followed, arm extended, touching the guard's back as we moved through the house. I don't know how he managed to navigate. There was no light. The reek of explosives bit at the back of my throat, sent me into a fit of coughing. We crossed the foyer and made it outside. I could feel the damp as we started moving down the hill, toward the sound of crashing surf.

The fog eased as we moved lower. I picked my way down the eroded hillside, the tufts of scrub and washed-out gullies above the cliffs. I heard the churn of an engine coming from the water below. Floodlights glared down at us from the house, filtered through the brush. The man I was with wore canvas utility pants and a gray long-sleeved shirt. He had no insignia. He blended into the shadows with black streaks of face paint.

I stopped. Gunshots cracked behind us. I saw red flash through the fog to our left, coming from the house.

The man with me wasn't one of the colonel's guards. It was one of the fugitive soldiers Riggs had described. He knew my name. I tried to think.

"Thank you," I said. He stood downhill from me. I moved closer to him. The waves boomed below us.

"Don't mention it. We've got to move. There's a boat waiting."

"Is that it?" I pointed. He looked. I planted my foot on his shoulder, shoved him to the ground, and started toward the house, using my hands and feet in the crumbling dirt on the steepest part of the hill.

I could hear rifle rounds tearing past us, coming close. "Don't shoot!" I shouted. "It's Byrne! Friendly!"

He came from my left side, hit me hard, tackled me. A puff of dust exploded, and a sandstone bank let go where I had been crawling. The bullet would have torn through me. We tumbled down the hill, and suddenly, my stomach went light. We dropped in a free fall.

The cold seized my body like an electric shock. I gasped as my head went under the blackness. I came up and cleared the salt water from my mouth and nose. The waves slammed into the rock face, threw spray twenty feet in the air. The water surged again. A swell carried me up, ready to throw me against a stone wall half covered in jagged shells.

I felt the water suck me back, try to hurl me with the lip of the wave. I dived, expecting the blow any second. It pulled me down, but I made it out the back of the wave. I swam through the white water. I was in the middle of a set. I dived down again and came up to see another wall of black water feathering and crashing toward my head. I went under once more, no time for a breath. A third wave, a fourth, a fifth. I had no air left, could barely see them coming as I pulled myself down into the freezing water and fought the foam. I tried to breathe, sucked in air and frothing water.

I heard an engine cut close. A black object materialized out of the fog. A rigid inflatable boat maneuvered twelve feet away, the pilot pivoting the engine perfectly to keep it steady as it slammed over the surf. My legs cramped from the cold and effort. I started to sink. With the last of my strength, I sidestroked through the lip of a wave and hauled myself to the gunwale. I grabbed the rope and pulled my body up, coughed out water against the rubber. I waited like that for a moment, breathing slowly, fighting the urge to hyperventilate. I wrapped my hand around a thwart and pulled myself up. A man stood over me. He reached down, grabbed the seat of my pants, and heaved me up and onto the floor as the engines revved. There were three men aboard.

The boat took off planing, launching off the back of the swells, dropping six feet to flat water. I slammed against the deck with each crash. The others took them like it was nothing, some standing, not holding on to anything for support, absorbing all the momentum with their knees.

The cliffs whipped by. I grabbed the column of the pilothouse as we picked up speed, accelerating to thirty-five, maybe forty knots. After each jump, we bottomed out; it felt like a car crash.

Black waves flew past. The wind was up. The swells capped. We were maybe a mile out. I couldn't see land or horizon, only fog. I knew I probably wouldn't survive if I dived off.

"What do you want with me?" My teeth clattered around the words.

A man stepped over. I asked it again, as loud as I could over the roar of the twin diesels. It was the guy I had tangled with on the hill.

"Relax, Junebug," he said, and reached into a lockbox. He pulled out a damp wool blanket and handed it to me.

I hadn't heard that in years. My sergeant had given me the nickname at Field Medical Training Battalion, where they put the corpsmen through infantry training so we could hack it with the Marines. We had been drilling on the yard, and as I ran with my class, I inhaled a bug. I doubled over and caused a three-corpsman pileup in front of the command master chief. I'd never lived it down.

The man who'd given me the blanket brought his face in front of mine and ran his hand through his wet hair.

"Hayes?" I said.

"Good to see you, Byrne." He pounded me on the back. "I'll bring you up to speed in a minute. For now, just hang on."

CHAPTER 13

CARO STOOD OUTSIDE the school, with its gleaming glass facades and angular architecture. He was in Al Bateen, an affluent neighborhood of villas in Abu Dhabi that was popular with diplomats and the Western expats. He had chosen to live here in the Emirates' capital. It was more self-assured, in contrast to the flash, the transience, the arrogance of Dubai.

His Mercedes idled beside him, the driver at the wheel. Caro crouched beside his daughter, took a linen handkerchief from his pocket, and wiped the corner of her mouth.

"What's that smell, Father?"

"I don't smell anything."

"It's like chemicals."

"They probably changed a filter in the car," he said. "You're going to be late." He ran his hand over her hair, gave her her backpack, and watched as she walked up the steps to the school.

He got back in the car, took off his Ray-Bans, and hung them from the pocket of his bespoke suit.

"Ready, sir?" the driver said, and he put the S550 in gear.

"No."

He looked at the stragglers entering the school. His blue eyes scanned the windows as he watched the children climb the stairs and gather in the classrooms.

It was a beautiful winter morning. He sniffed his jacket. Yes. It was unmistakable: burned plastic. It had been a long day. He had flown back to the Emirates from Central Asia this morning and hadn't had a chance to shower after visiting the cells.

The whole trip had been a waste of time. He'd sat in as two men, trained by his deputy, entered the latter stages of interrogation in a detention facility they had set up in an abandoned refinery. They were in a basket-case former Soviet republic that offered complete freedom of operation for a price.

The subject had been tied to the table, mottled with blood and filth. The two questioners took turns. One gripped what was left of his hair and shouted questions while the other held a torch to an empty water bottle and let the molten plastic drip onto the skin. It would fall, burning, and fuse with the flesh.

"Where were you going?" one barked.

He said nothing. The scalding was the easy part.

The second man waited, let the plastic harden, then grabbed its edge.

"Who were you going to meet?"

He jerked it back, bringing the flesh with it. It was a favorite trick of Saddam's Mukhabarat. Now everyone used it.

The man began to sputter.

"What? What? Speak up!"

He broke. They asked the questions in a rapid-fire sequence. Names, dates, addresses; it all came in a torrent.

The two interrogators turned to Caro, the senior commander,

though he held no official role. That would have circumscribed his freedom of movement, made him far too interesting to other intelligence agencies.

It was a common problem; the young men would try to impress him, go too far to prove their viciousness. It was amusing, in a way, because if they'd known whom he was working for, they would have executed him on the spot. They thought in black and white. They couldn't understand the nuances of the great game.

"You brought me here for this?" Caro asked.

One man stepped closer, the concern clear on his face.

"Just stop," Caro said.

The man on the table mumbled what thanks he could.

"But he just told us."

"He would have told you anything," Caro said.

"Didn't you hear?"

Caro's temper broke through. He took the torch and held the flame to the bottle, then laid a line of burning plastic from the man's temple across his cheek to his neck, just below the jawline.

He ignored the screams, simply looked at the two interrogators, a patient teacher.

"Was Kyenge there?" Caro barked at the captive.

"Kyenge?" the man asked, desperate.

Caro tore the strip away in one clean stroke. Even the interrogators blanched at the damage.

The first screamed words were unintelligible, but then they became loud and clear: "Yes! Yes! Kyenge. He was there. I know him. I can show you where."

Caro looked to the two juniors, who avoided his gaze with shame.

Kyenge had been dead for eight years. The man was lying.

Caro stood close to him, nearly whispering in his ear. "It's all right. It's all right. It's over now."

"Please," the man said. "Please—"

"It's okay," Caro said. He took the man's jaw firmly in his left hand, then reached his right into the man's armpit and slid him up the table until his head just hung off the edge. He shoved the man's face straight down toward the floor. The head fell back and dangled at a strange angle.

The body shuddered and then relaxed completely, voiding on the table. The table's edge had dislocated his cervical vertebrae and severed his spinal cord. The dead man's member rose, taut, toward the ceiling; angel lust, a phenomenon that, even the hundredth time, never failed to unsettle Caro, though he gave no sign.

He was grateful to the man for supplying the lesson so many of the younger fighters forgot. Terror wasn't an end in itself, some pure expression of power or some innate evil, as the blacks and whites of the American outlook had it. It was a tactic, pure and simple. These boys had done too much killing and not enough reading—Qutb, Clausewitz, Robespierre. Terror was necessary, of course, but it had to be applied with care. Against a stronger man, it might have been appropriate, but this man was weak, and in the face of such pain, he crumbled. Fear was a means, a tool like any other. The ends were what mattered.

Caro thought of that lesson again as he looked at his daughter's school through the tinted windows of his Mercedes. Several buses rolled into the lot; today was a class trip. The children's faces lined the windows.

He watched them, their eyes wide open, inches from the glass.

He turned away, paused, then looked back.

The eyes. The glass.

He would have to double-check the details of the operation. There would be a show first, a distraction before the main event, to draw them to the windows, and the charge would be much smaller, because terror was a tactic, and it's far too easy to forget the dead. There are things worse than death. Knowing those things intimately was his specialty and his curse.

One more day.

"Sir, there is some traffic on the way to the airport."

Caro looked away from the school. He had been in Abu Dhabi, the closest thing he had to a home, only long enough to see his daughter, swap out his suitcase, and pick up a different passport. He didn't like being home, with the strange smells and sounds of a hospital coming from the rear of the apartment.

"Let's go," he said. He had to make his flight to Los Angeles. His associates now had the shipment inside the United States. He would have his hands on it soon, and in twenty-four hours he would pull the trigger.

CHAPTER 14

THE BAG OVER my head hung close, damp with my own breath. I smelled fried food and chlorine. I had been stripped naked and searched. They took my clothes and my wallet and cut them apart stitch by stitch with a fixed-blade knife.

My whole body was electric with fear, my skin goose-pimpled and my hair on end, but there was no panic. When things got bad, whether it was back in the navy or in surgery, it was always the same: I would slow down, grow quiet, focus.

They pulled the hood off. I'd been wearing it for the last ten minutes. I sat naked on a wooden dining chair.

My eyes focused on the stainless-steel shelves to my right and left. I was in a walk-in commercial freezer that wasn't running. The space was warm, the air stale. Craning my head, I could see through the open door into the restaurant's dining room. It looked long abandoned, and a sign that read *Mariscos* hung over some smiling Day of the Dead skulls.

In the part of the kitchen I could see, all the windows were blacked out with plywood, and four rucksacks leaned against the wall. One man rested on the concrete floor.

"No cell phone?" Hayes asked me.

"The police kept it."

He handed me a pair of work pants and a long-sleeved gray shirt. I pulled them on.

"Hayes," a woman called from somewhere out of sight.

He walked out of the freezer.

The man who had been sleeping approached the door, yawned, and then gave me a hard stare. He held his rifle ready, his finger just outside the trigger guard. No hoods or masks for him. That was a bad sign. I could identify him, if I lived.

"We've got to keep this batch on track. What's the temperature of the water bath?" I heard Hayes ask.

"Twenty-eight degrees."

A chlorine smell wafted in and burned my nostrils slightly as I sniffed. I kept my head up but didn't lock eyes with the guard. In captivity, you need to strike a balance between keeping your pride (any cowering can invite a sadist) and being overly confrontational (which can also set one off). Hayes returned and took the man at the door aside. They spoke too quietly for me to hear the words, but I could tell that the man with the rifle was agitated. Hayes seemed to be reassuring him, talking him down, keeping him from violence. It could have been an act to gain my trust, a strategy to make Hayes more sympathetic, the good cop.

He walked into the freezer, and the movements of the air crinkled the plastic sheeting hanging from the wall behind me.

It was strange to see that much gray hair on a man so fit. It made him look much older than his years.

"How have you been, Hayes?" I asked. I was trying to build rapport, to get him to see me as a person, not an object. It's harder to kill someone you know, though from everything I had heard, that wouldn't present Hayes with any problems.

"I've been better, Byrne. You?"

"Likewise. Are we in Mexico?"

"More or less."

The guard watched me through the door, still cradling his rifle. Hayes gave him a nod, then leaned toward me, raising his callused hand to my neck.

I pulled away, seized his wrist. He seemed more amused than annoyed. The guard shouldered his rifle, finger on the trigger, and stepped inside, the muscles in his jaw drawn tight. "Your neck," Hayes said. "I'll have that cut stitched up for you if you want."

I touched the skin. I'd thought it was just a scratch. Only then did I feel the crust of blood.

"I'm good."

"Suit yourself, shipmate."

I saw a woman walk past the door with a bottle marked *Concrete Etch*. Acid. Eats through organic material. I checked out the plastic sheeting again and shifted in my chair as the fear balled up my lower belly. "It's been a long time, Hayes. What's going on?"

He leaned against the shelf. "We are here to help you, Byrne. We have been watching Riggs and his men. We saw him take you in. We thought he might be setting you up. Or about to threaten or coerce you."

"I'm only trying to get home," I said. "I don't want anything to do with this."

"We all want to go home. You spent a while with Riggs."

"Let me walk away. I won't talk."

"You're free to go. This isn't a kidnapping."

I looked around. "You had me fooled."

He smiled. "I can see how you might interpret it that way. We had to take a few precautions in case he was tracking you. Word to the wise: Don't play ball with Riggs. Once you're no longer useful, he'll throw you out. He was gunning for you, Byrne."

I remembered the shot that nearly killed me as I ran toward the cliffs on the peninsula.

"What did he tell you about me?" Hayes asked. "Did it square with what you remember?"

It didn't. But there was another Hayes I'd only glimpsed. I remembered the first time we took contact close up. I had finished bandaging up one of our guys and saw Hayes walking away from an enemy KIA, wiping off his Ka-Bar. He'd driven it through the man's eye. I had to clean up a bite wound on Hayes's forearm.

"Let me guess. He took the false-humility route, brought out Nazar, and played the martyr. Did he talk about helping soldiers find jobs?"

"Something like that."

"He runs a security-contracting company like a personal army, poaches the most experienced operators from their units after the U.S. spent millions training them, runs off-book logistics—ships, trucks, matériel—for the Pentagon, and charges three times the going rate to keep his mouth shut." In the banquet room behind him, a man opened a trunk and start piling ammunition inside it.

On the way back from the peninsula, they had landed and swapped out the boat for late-model SUVs. They had all the gear you would need for amphibious direct action or an on-the-water interdiction. I didn't know who was helping them, but they had serious support.

"I know the scenery doesn't help. You've got no reason to believe me. That's fine. I was just trying to give you a heads-up. Check out what Riggs told you, though. Some of it's true. The truck ambush. That was us. The records office too. No one was injured beyond a few scrapes and bruises. At the point, we went in nonlethal. Riggs and his guys shot back. Think about it. Stay away from him, for your own sake."

"That's a threat?"

"It's good advice."

"I can walk out of here?"

"We'll need to make some arrangements. Give ourselves a head start. But, essentially, yes. I can't say what Riggs will do. If you walk out there, you're on your own."

I had a feeling this was a ploy to test my loyalty, see whether I could be turned. If I left, I might get about twenty feet before they shot me in the back of the skull.

"If Riggs is lying, tell me the truth."

"He's full of shit," Hayes said. "But I can't read you in on the rest. The colonel's good at all that politician stem-winder business. We keep our mouths shut. Live by it. Trust has to be earned. I wish I could tell you more. I owe it to you to change your mind, but I can't. I swore. I'll just say this: We can protect you, keep you safe until this blows over. Or you can walk away. That's fine. You bailed before. I'll understand if you do it now."

"I haven't seen you in over a decade. And after everything I've heard, you think I'll join you? That's..."

Hayes ran his hand back through his hair. "Insane. I agree. But that's the way it is. I can see the bind you're in, not knowing who to trust, Riggs or me." The corner of his mouth ticked up. "I guess you could see which one of us kills you first, then go with the other guy."

One of the women outside called for Hayes. He stood in the door. I took a step closer to hear.

"We've got company coming," she said.

"What is it?"

"Riggs. Five, maybe ten minutes out."

"Pack it up. Get those trucks out of here. I'll burn everything exploitable left behind."

I stepped into the doorway and looked over at the rest of the kitchen. The guard had joined the others in loading out.

On the counter, a glass retort sat over a low flame. Red vapor rose through the sphere, gathered in the neck, and dripped down the long glass tube into a beaker. A soldier stacked thick sections of milled pipe in a trunk and then closed the lid.

I was in a bomb factory. Used filter paper coated in white crystals lay at the very end of the counter. I looked away, tried not to betray what I had seen and understood.

A hand gripped my shoulder. It was the guard. I had seen all their faces. I could identify them.

"What are you looking at?" he asked. "And how the hell did Riggs find us so fast?"

"You got the tag from his wallet, right?" Hayes said.

"Yeah."

Hayes stood on the other side of me. "Anything you want to tell us, Byrne?"

The man at my shoulder pulled his sidearm. It was suppressed, good for an execution.

Hayes stepped a foot away from me and looked me over. Then he reached for the bandage on my head, grabbed the corner, and tore it off.

I winced from the sting as the laceration opened up again.

"Riggs is three minutes out!"

"This guy is fucking doubled," the man Hayes had called Speed said. He pulled me closer and put the gun to the back of my head.

Hayes took his knife out and stood in front of me. He folded the bandage over the blade and cut through it. Silver filaments glinted in the light.

"Pretty good," he said.

"They put that on me at the police station," I said. "What is it?"

"Radar-responsive tag. We've been fielding them only over the last couple years. Flash radar at it and it bounces back a unique ID pattern from miles away."

He passed it to Speed. "Flush that." The man headed down a corridor. The rest of the crew was in motion, hauling gear toward the main doors.

Hayes faced me. "We've got to run. You're coming with us, Byrne. No time to sort this out now."

"I get it." I moved toward the open doors in the rear of the kitchen. There were too many of them for me to escape out the back. I needed a distraction. "Can I help load?"

"Sure." He went along, tossing gear into duffels. I walked to the far wall, near the door, and rested my hand on the counter as I leaned over to lift a Pelican case. I pinched one of the pieces of filter paper as gently as I could and hid it in my palm. It smelled like bleach, which probably meant it was primary explosive. That could easily blow from friction, shock, heat, or nothing at all, and it would take my hand off. As I reached down for a second case, I slipped the packet into the jamb of the door leading from the kitchen to a storage room. Then I knocked the doorstop out. The door slowly started to swing closed.

A man and a woman rolled a heavy crate toward the banquet room, and as they forced it across a threshold, the moving blanket over it fell forward.

Arabic writing covered the side, and I couldn't help but think that whatever weapon had been stolen from that armored truck was sitting fifteen feet from me. I watched as the door closed the last few inches to the jamb and steeled myself for a sprint. The filter paper blew, barely a gram of explosive. Without a second's hesitation, Hayes's crew shouldered their weapons and ran toward the blast. I sprinted the other way, shoved the rear exit open, and ran into an alley behind the restaurant.

Cool, dry air enveloped me. The night was pitch-black, and after the explosion and the lights inside, I couldn't see anything. I stumbled over something, heard what sounded like a plastic bucket skitter off to my right. My eyes adjusted and I saw ten feet of concrete-block wall looming at the end of the alley ahead of me.

It was a dead end. I sped up, jumped, planted my foot, and got the tips of my fingers onto the top of the wall. The rough edge of the concrete cut into my skin. My shoes skidded as I tried to push myself up, but I managed only to push out and tear myself off the wall.

Footsteps came from behind me.

Silhouetted in the door of the restaurant, a gunman raised his rifle toward me. There was no cover, nowhere to run.

A crack broke through the quiet, echoed off the walls. With what they were firing, that meant the bullet was already here. My body tensed. But there was no pain. I looked back to see the truck pull away at the far end of the alley. It must have been the lift gate slamming down.

A second figure appeared in the doorway and leaned toward the gunman, who lowered his weapon.

"Good seeing you, Byrne." It was Hayes's voice. "Be careful out there."

I dragged a pallet over, propped it against the wall, and climbed the wooden slats like a ladder. I jumped off the top as it fell back and then hauled myself over the wall.

Hayes had called off the shot. I appreciated it, but it would take more than not killing me for him to earn my trust. Maybe he just couldn't afford to make that kind of noise and give away his position. Or maybe I was supposed to draw fire. I had to get to the colonel before he decided I was one of Hayes's men and before Hayes's crew had a chance to pick me up again.

The next alley was like a UN of garbage, with dumpsters for a Chinese restaurant, a taco shop, and a Thai place. Most signs were in English. I must have been just north of the Mexican border. What I thought was a shadow was a crowd of rats that flowed away like a parting sea as I passed through.

I ran for a few minutes until I found a pay-phone kiosk. As I came around, I saw it was empty except for a few burger wrappers. The phone had been ripped out. I was on a commercial drag of one-story buildings, all vacant or closed for the night. A car rolled by at the far end of the street. I stepped back into the alley and walked along the rear of the stores.

I looked through a high window and saw a phone in an office. The caulk around the glass was dried out, the frame rotting wood, the window single-glazed, about eighteen inches high and three feet wide.

The putty gave way easily as I dug it out with my thumb. After a minute, the glass started to lean out from the frame with a creak. I wriggled it out, then hauled my chest up to the ledge, pulled myself through, and tumbled forward onto the beige carpet. I picked up the phone on the desk.

"Directory Assistance."

"I need the police, nonemergency."

It took a few minutes to raise the local cop from the interrogation. They dropped the call on the transfer, and I had to start from scratch. Finally, a desk sergeant who'd been around that afternoon put me through to the officer's cell. He gave me Hall's number.

Hall sounded out of breath and surprised that I had called.

"Byrne? Where are you? Are you okay?"

"I'm fine."

There was a loud noise as someone took the phone away.

"This is Riggs. Where are you?"

I looked out the front window and gave him the address.

"Are you with the operators?"

"I got away."

"Do you know where they are?"

"They're close by, but I'm alone." I heard something in the alley, ducked behind the desk, and lowered my voice. "Can you get me out of here?"

"We're almost there," he said. "Sit tight. Do not move. You'll be okay."

"I'll be here."

See which one of us kills you first. Hayes had been joking, but maybe it wasn't such a bad idea.

CHAPTER 15

Colonel Riggs stood beside the open door of a van. Inside it, a tech sat hunched over a laptop.

"What happened to the signal?" Riggs asked.

"We lost the pattern. They may have removed the tag. It's going to take another minute or two to triangulate the last position. We're within a mile."

He turned and barked to the men. "Get ready!"

A black Mercedes pulled up. From the back stepped Caro. He had arrived at LAX two hours earlier, connecting through Frankfurt on his way from the Emirates.

Caro stepped out of the car, buttoned his suit jacket, and marched to meet Riggs. They greeted each other, and Riggs took him aside.

"The shipment is gone," Riggs said. "Hayes took it. We tracked him here."

"Does he have it with him?"

"We don't know."

"How far is he?"

"Within a mile."

"We knew this was going to be difficult. The right thing always is. We'll get it back."

Caro's arrival had brought Riggs calm for the first time since the cargo was stolen. Caro came from a hard part of the world. He and Riggs had been through a lot of ugliness together. And Caro understood, in a way few Americans did, about means and ends, the necessities of small savagery here and there to achieve a larger peace.

A voice came from Riggs's radio. It was Hall. "Byrne called. We have his exact location. He wants us to get him out."

"And the rest?"

"Rough location. Within five hundred meters."

"Good."

Riggs briefly outlined the situation to Caro.

"Do you have someone you trust to take care of Byrne?" Caro asked. "Who knows the whole story?"

"Hall."

"Put him in the lead."

"You came straight from the plane?"

Caro nodded. Riggs gave him a SIG Sauer. Caro checked the brass in the chamber and switched it to his left hand.

"May I borrow that?" he asked and pointed to Riggs's pocket.

"Sure," Riggs said. He pulled out a knife, a black Benchmade folder. He flicked open the five-inch blade. It would be more useful to Caro, who liked to work quietly and up close.

Caro gave the edge a quick inspection. "Thank you," he said. "Why don't we go after the single man first and see what he has to say about the others before we take them out. What did you say his name was?"

"Byrne. Tom Byrne. It should be easy. He thinks we're coming to save him."

"Good." Caro closed the knife. "Let's try to take him alive."

CHAPTER 16

As I CROUCHED in the dark, waiting for the colonel to arrive, I thought about the last time I'd seen John Hayes, or at least the last time I could remember him distinctly. I'd stabbed him in the chest with a needle, with five needles, really. When someone loses a lot of blood, the vessels constrict. It's impossible to find a vein and start an IV, so there is a tool called a FAST1 that looks like an EpiPen. You slam it into the breastbone just below the throat. The five needles go into the marrow of the sternum, allowing you to deliver fluids without having to go through a vein.

Hayes and I survived that day. Our team had been sent to scout a roadside cluster of buildings to see if anyone was making IEDs there. We called the highway through the area Shakedown Street, because of all the contact we took when we drove through. Our objective was at kilometer marker 38, so we called it K-38.

It turned out to be a major complex for the enemy militias. One moment we were walking through a silent village. The next, gun-fire poured in from three sides.

The RPG that cut up most of my guys left me with a grade-three concussion, so I'm hazy on the details. The official write-up says I killed nine.

Corpsmen and medics are combatants first. The tactical-combat casualty-care guidelines lay it all out: Your first duty is to return fire, take cover, and put down smoke. Only after you eliminate the enemy fire do you look after your Marines. There's no point in stopping a hemorrhage if more bullets are coming. You or the casualty or both are just going to get hit again.

The explosion knocked me out for a moment. When I came to I was still deaf from the blast, and when my hearing started to come back I heard men crying through the ringing in my ears.

"Corpsman! Corpsman up! Doc!" I saw them, bleeding out on the fine dust.

My reaction was mostly automatic, muscle memory from all the training. I yelled for them to put the tourniquets on, find cover, and return fire. Hayes and I were the last ones standing, separated by about ten meters, flanked on both sides. I had taken some shrapnel in my back. Blood soaked his uniform blouse and trousers. A squad of bad guys with T-shirts tied around their mouths were coming down my sector. God knows where the air support was.

I picked up the squad automatic that Farrell had dropped. Hayes and I engaged the enemy until Hayes was shot several times. I found cover farther forward and then went over it to kill the last man.

Gunny Mullins managed to get his tourniquet on, but he must have bled too much to keep it tight. I crawled over. None of the others had a pulse. Standard procedure for care under fire is to leave the men you can't save and start with the guys who have signs of life. Hayes was the only responsive one.

His pulse was weak. I sheared his pants up to the thigh and saw a gaping wound, frothing blood, bright red: arterial. I held pressure hard. He groaned, a good sign. I filled the cut with QuikClot.

He'd lost a lot of blood. I wanted to start an IV, but I couldn't find a vein, so I prepped his chest, slammed the FAST1 into his breastbone, and started pumping him full of Hextend.

Gunny Mullins, Rubino, and Farrell died. They'd been moving after we were first hit. I don't know if I could have saved them, but I might have been able to give them a shot at least, held them together until they made it to shock-trauma.

But my orders were to kill first. And that's what I did. Nine enemy KIA.

I found out two things that day: I was good at killing. And, worse, I loved it, in a way, that primal release of pure hate for the men who had hit us and the pleasure of tearing them apart with precise spurts of 5.56 from a smoking barrel.

"Administer life-saving hemorrhage control *as the tactical situation permits.*" That's from the field manual. Such dry language, but it's haunted me for a long time, along with the images of my three Marines laid out as their blood clumped the dust.

Did I go too far? Lose myself in the killing when I should have been saving lives?

Our objective became a rallying point for the enemy. The battle lasted for a week and came to be known as K-38. Something strange happens to you after most of your squad gets killed and you come out alive with nothing more than a concussion and some metal in your back.

I was in a sort of daze for a while after the ambush. And maybe it was more in my head, but I caught guys looking at me, and I was sure they were asking themselves the same thing I was: *Why are you still here? What makes you think you deserve it?*

During the speech on the day they pinned that medal on me, they said I'd killed nine, but I counted twelve. They forgot to include Mullins, Farrell, and Rubino.

While I recovered from the injuries, I got rolled from SARC, the training to be a doc with Force Recon and Special Operations. I was only a few credits shy of my undergrad degree. I started doing the premed prereqs while on active duty, studying biochemistry by headlamp. Most people thought I was crazy. Corpsmen sometimes go on to be nurses or PAs, but the whole enlisted-to-officer-and-full-MD route was rare.

Hall and the colonel had asked me what I was hiding, why I had dropped recon to be a doctor.

I'd wanted to learn how to do more than plug a guy up, scrape him together, and put him and the pieces on a helicopter. I wanted to learn how to fix him, heart and lungs, everything. I never wanted to watch friends die, to have to make that choice again. I wanted to put men back together, not take them apart.

And above all, I was scared, scared at how easily I took to killing.

I must have seen Hayes at the funerals, but I don't remember it all that well. He was the kind of hard-ass but fair sergeant who everyone loved like a father. We were all trying to earn his respect. Despite the cool distance Hayes kept from his subordinates, everyone I talked to on the squad thought that he was the sergeant's favorite. He inspired a kind of fanatic loyalty among his boys.

Even after all the other guys started calling me Doc, Hayes stuck with Junebug, or just June. I didn't let on that I gave a shit.

But after I saved his life, I thought he might quit and start calling me Doc too. And I remember Hayes turning to me—it's one of the few things I remember clearly from the hospital—and he said thanks, and then he called me Byrne.

It was a start. I could never read him then, and I sure as hell couldn't read him now.

Engines gunned in the street. The colonel was here.

CHAPTER 17

RIGGS DIRECTED THE lead truck to stop around the corner from the address Byrne had given. Men climbed out in full assault gear, wearing black balaclavas, carbines across their chests. He led them down the block and pointed out the address, a store that sold cowboy boots and western clothes.

"Go around the back," Riggs said. "He'll be expecting us from the front. Put two men out of sight on the south side in case he runs."

"You want to call the local cops for a perimeter?" Hall asked.

"No. He's by himself. This should be easy enough. And they'll restrict our rules of engagement."

Hall looked confused. "Sir?"

"You heard me."

He understood what Riggs meant. Byrne might know everything by now. If Hayes had told him the truth and he got away, it would be the end for Riggs, and for all of them.

"Try to get him back here alive," Riggs said. "But make sure you get him."

"Yes, sir."

They surrounded the building. At the rear door, one man pulled a sledgehammer from his pack and stood on the hinge side. Against the wall behind him, Hall crouched, his carbine ready, while the man beside him held a flash-bang and took out the pin.

"Breach," Hall said. The man in the lead brought the sledge back, swung it forward with both arms, pivoting from his legs as he brought the head hard against the bolt of the lock. The door flew open. The second man threw the grenade. It was like a flash of lightning inside the building. "Man in, left!" Hall barked as he rushed the door and sprinted for his corner. His team followed, their gun-mounted lights slicing through the space.

As the smoke thinned, Hall smelled cowhide. Boots lined the shelves.

"Go!"

One covered while the two others moved down the hallway, one high, one low. They kicked in the flimsy interior door to the office, then the doors to the dressing rooms, and finally fanned out through the front of the store.

It was hard to see through the smoke. A man stood in the corner of the room, a black silhouette.

"Hands! Raise your fucking hands!"

No answer.

"Hands or I will kill you!"

"Hands!"

A shot cracked. Fire licked through the dark. The bullet tore through the figure, and something fell to the ground with a crunch.

This was all wrong.

Hall hit the overhead lights as the smoke cleared. He walked over to the fiberglass mannequin and looked through the hole in its chest to the street outside. The figure was wearing a cowboy shirt in black with silver thread. Its head lay on the ground.

Hall lifted a white Stetson off the floor and tossed it to his teammate, whose mouth tightened into a thin line from embarrassment.

"You should only kill the black hats."

Their flashlights shot through the display windows onto the street, where the other members of their team were crouched. Hall opened the front door.

Riggs stepped forward. He turned to Caro, then shouted to Hall, "Where the hell did he go?"

"It's a trick," Hall said, his eyes scanning the rooftops across the street. "Byrne was never here."

I watched the gunshots flashing behind the store window from a building down the street. The whole scene felt surreal, like a film or a nightmare, but I knew this was the reality I had to face.

They were certain I was alone. And still they came for me with grenades and shot to kill. The tin taste of fear dripped down the back of my throat, but there was no time to pay any heed or let my mind run in circles trying to grasp the full extent of the mess I was in. I ran out the back door of the building where I had been hiding, and I was five blocks away when I first heard the sirens. Either the police had heard the commotion themselves or Riggs had called in the local cops to hunt me down.

The streets led me toward a steep hill going down to a freeway, blocked off by a fence. The wash of cars on the road below was like distant surf. The lights flowed red and white at the bottom of the canyon. It was a dead end. I needed to find a way out. I skirted the fence above the highway as it curved, but it was steering me back toward the police. As I made my way through the parking lots, away from the larger roads, the sirens seemed to be everywhere.

I came out between a uniform shop and a pay-as-you-go-cell-phone store and looked across a four-lane street with light traffic. As I stepped onto the roadway, a patrol car appeared at the end of the block. I turned and started walking away, head down, fighting the overwhelming urge to run.

The cruiser passed on the opposite side of the street. I forced myself to take a couple deep breaths.

Whoop.

The cop U-turned through the red light at the end of the block. I cut back through a used-car lot and sprinted away, turned at random on one street and then another, and finally threw myself over a low wall. The sirens grew louder, and floodlights closed on my position.

I recognized the street ahead. It was where I had first escaped, the restaurant Hayes and his team were using as a safe house. As I started toward it, I heard the squawk of a police radio. A beam of light hit the corner where I had been standing.

"There!" I heard someone yell. I took off running, but they were almost right behind me. There was nowhere to hide. As soon as they rounded that corner, I was done.

"Byrne!" The voice was nearby. It couldn't be the police. No one was that fast. I looked over my shoulder and saw an open door beside a loading dock. "Get in here!"

It was Hayes. There was nowhere else to go. I wheeled around, sprinted, and threw myself through as the police came around the corner and fanned out down the street toward me.

We were in a loading area, closed off by a steel rolling door. A man lay on the dock, eyes shut, bandages around his hand and throat. The door shut, plunging us into darkness. Light leaked under the rolling door, passing back and forth: the police. Someone pounded on the door I had just entered. The knob rattled. Another pound. Then the light moved away.

A minute passed in silence. I waited until I was sure they had left. "What happened to your guy?" I asked.

"Gunshot wound, neck. And he smashed his hand."

"Is he still bleeding?"

"I don't think so. Here." He felt for my arm in the dark and placed something in my hands. "Put that on."

They were night-vision goggles. I slipped them over my head and saw the loading area in different shades of green and black. The injured man still had his eyes clamped shut. On the bandaged hand, two fingers pointed off at the wrong angle; serious trauma, but not life-threatening.

"The gash on the neck was probably a graze," Hayes said.

I checked the bandages. The bleeding was under control.

"Good work," I said, and I ran my hand under the man's body to feel for any other injuries.

Open neck wounds are tricky. Most of your blood is under higher than atmospheric pressure; that's why you bleed *out*. But above the lungs, it can be lower, and a wound can pull air in. With small amounts of air, that's not usually a big deal (the idea that you can murder someone by injecting him with a little air bubble in a syringe is a myth), but a larger air embolism can block the flow of blood to the lungs and kill a person pretty easily.

The trauma kit was open on the floor. I pulled out an occlusive dressing, basically Saran Wrap, and taped it down on four sides over the gauze. That would keep the air out until I had time to stitch him up.

I checked his airway and pulse. He was in and out of consciousness.

"We can move him. Is that door the only way out?"

"No. Follow me," Hayes said.

The door to the showroom was locked by a keypad. Hayes shone a pen light on it.

"Some of the keys are worn," I said; the 1, 6, 8, and 9 were dull from use.

"Birthdays," Hayes said. "It's 1968 or 1986."

He entered 1968. The red light flashed. Then he tried 1986: green.

We went back, lifted the casualty, and crossed through into a room. We were in a manager's office. Through the CCTV displays I could see it was a massive, warehouse-style used-furniture store.

"Things didn't go too hot with the colonel?" Hayes asked me.

I remembered crouching in the shadows and flinching at the sound of gunfire. "No. Same with you?"

He looked over at his injured teammate. "We stayed behind to cover the trucks. They shot Green. He was my medic."

Hayes looked straight at me. He needed a doc.

"At least it's his left hand," I said.

He shook his head. *Left-handed.*

"That's rough," I said. "Would Riggs go after family? Loved ones?" Kelly was still out there, and if she got hurt because of me, I wouldn't be able to go on, not again.

"That's why we came out of the woodwork, why we destroyed our Defense Cover records. He would come for our people to get to us."

I rubbed my hands together. Everyone said I was crazy to think that I was some kind of jinx. And then days like today happened. I pointed to the screens. "The front?"

He tapped the monitor. There was a cop on the corner I had completely missed.

"How about this side exit?"

"Better than nothing," he said. I looked at the cars on the external camera, moved closer, squinted at it.

"Think you can steal that one?" I said and pointed to a FedEx truck.

"It should be easy—no engine immobilizer—but it's probably the slowest car on the block. Why would we take that?"

I told him what I had seen just before his men hooded me on the drive out.

"Can you take us back to that spot?" I asked.

"It's not too far. And the sun will be up soon." He considered it for a minute and seemed to like the plan. "It's good to have you back, Byrne."

I took Green's radio and earpiece, and we carried him to the side door. Hayes opened it a crack, then ran to the truck in a crouch and set to work on the padlock that secured the rear gate.

I keyed the radio: "Car coming."

A patrol car pulled to the mouth of the narrow street and lit it like day with the light mounted on the side of the cruiser. Hayes dropped, crawled under the truck, and just missed being caught.

"Hold," I said. "Hold. He's just looking. I've got you."

The light moved forward. The cop pulled away.

"You're good."

A minute later Hayes said, "I'm in."

He ran back and we carried Green and loaded him onto the truck. The medic moaned, muttered a few words I couldn't make out, and then asked for seconds of mashed potatoes as we closed the rear door; he was totally disoriented. There were faster cars on the street—I had passed an older BMW 540i—but the FedEx truck had one advantage that I hoped we wouldn't have to use. I expected Hayes to mess with the wires, but he just jammed a screwdriver deep into the ignition, gripped it hard, and twisted it until something cracked. The engine chugged twice, then started running.

He drove the speed limit, trying not to attract attention. We saw two police cars pulled over ahead of us near an intersection with a four-lane boulevard. I ducked down. He pulled past them, stopped at a light twenty feet away from the cops. We waited. I lay on the floor, looked up, and watched dawn stain the sky blue-gray.

We rode away and were about thirty seconds past the intersection when I heard the sirens cry. Hayes punched the gas. I slammed into the passenger jump seat folded up against the wall. I crouched, looked in the mirrors, and saw two cop cars in pursuit.

We rounded a corner at speed and the van began to tilt. Hayes worked the wheel and fought the van's oversteer. "I'm starting to think this is the worst plan I've ever heard."

"Keep going!"

The cruisers closed in. I could see that the colonel's trucks had joined the convoy. I looked through the window and pointed past the next intersection. "There!"

Hall pressed the throttle down. The six-liter V-8 roared. They were closing in on Hayes. There was no way he could get away.

"Faster," Riggs said. "I'll hold the police back. We should get to them first."

Caro watched calmly from the center of the rear seats. He had guided Riggs as they closed the noose around Byrne. He didn't like surprises, as a rule, but did enjoy a good fight. Byrne was proving to be interesting prey. Caro braced himself against the door. He looked forward to getting his hands on this doctor.

The cruisers ahead slowed and whooped their sirens to stop

traffic coming through the next intersection. A tractor-trailer slammed its brakes, blocking the route ahead.

"Don't slow down!" Riggs yelled.

"What?"

"Go around!"

Hall swerved to the left to get by the eighteen-wheeler and hit the median curb as he curved back into his lane. The Suburban bucked and tossed the men in their seats. Riggs looked in the rearview at the semi. It was a FedEx distribution truck.

There were three FedEx box trucks ahead of them.

"Which one is it?"

More trucks, identical, pulled out from the side streets. Some came from the other direction.

"Which should I follow?"

"What the fuck is going on?" Riggs asked.

Caro saw it first, a warehouse to their right that filled the whole block. Over the entrance was a sign: *FedEx Distribution Center.* Everywhere they looked, more white vans trundled off, dozens of them, spreading out through the city on their morning rounds. He understood instantly. Byrne and Hayes had outplayed them.

"Where are they!" Riggs screamed, punched the dash, then shut his eyes against the pain and lifted his hand to his lips.

They tracked one, then another.

"Did you get the tags?"

"No."

"Tell the police to stop them all."

He lifted his radio and shouted orders.

Caro sat back, and watched the dawn light streak across the sky. "It's too late. There are too many." It was a nice bit of camouflage, but there were other ways to get Hayes and Byrne. They were only delaying the inevitable.

Riggs fumed as the trucks disappeared. He gripped the door handle so hard his knuckles went white.

"The girl with Byrne. Where is she?" Caro asked.

"The Island Colony Motel."

Caro watched a pair of women in tank tops waiting at a bus stop, their bodies displayed for anyone to see. The weakness of the women in this country was their immodesty, their vanity. He weighed the knife in his hand. All Caro needed to do was draw a few lines across Byrne's girlfriend's face with a blade, and he would cooperate.

"Let's get her," he said.

CHAPTER 18

WE MET THE rest of the team at a rally point about eight miles away. It was a 1980s motor home parked on an access road in an area of corrugated-aluminum shipping depots and factories. Half of the buildings looked abandoned.

Hayes's team had a decent trauma setup in the RV. I took care of Green's neck and splinted the broken fingers. He would live, but it would take months of physical therapy if he ever wanted to hold a fork with his left hand again, and he might never have the dexterity to insert an IV. His hands were his livelihood, his reason for being. The physical piece would be the easiest part to recover.

As I worked, I fell seamlessly into the rhythm of the team, but I couldn't get my mind off that box, the crate Hayes had stolen containing God knew what. I wasn't going all in yet. But I would do what I needed to get me and Kelly to safety.

I finished on Green, and before I could say anything, Hayes spoke. "Your wife, or girlfriend. Where is she?"

I borrowed a phone and checked my messages. When I gave

it back, he removed the battery, then pulled the SIM card and cracked it into four pieces.

"Island Colony Motel." I gave him the address. "Where are we?"

"Close to the border, maybe twenty minutes if we move now."

We took a 1998 Honda Civic. Hayes didn't hotwire it. He took out a set of keys he called jigglers and rattled them around in the ignition until it started. I leaned forward in the passenger seat, willing the throttle down, but Hayes kept it at three miles per hour over the limit in the right-hand lane. We blended in with the flow of traffic.

"Thanks for taking care of Green."

"Don't mention it."

"You should have come with me to MARSOC." That's the Marine Corps Forces Special Operations Command, which had been carved out of Force Recon.

"That wasn't for me."

"You ended up in shock-trauma?"

"Yes. The forward surgical teams. I wanted to be close to the battlefield, save who I could. Did you say Green was your *medic?*"

He nodded and picked up on my line of thinking. Medics were army.

"In MARSOC, after I got commissioned I ended up working with a lot of the Seventh Special Forces guys. We were all part of a joint task force. I got into backpacking with them, and I liked the SF crowd, the culture piece, the languages. It's more than just kicking in doors. So when they told me I should try for selection to the unit, I figured what the hell, it's just a long hike."

A lot of people use the term Special Forces to mean any American commandos, but the proper name for that is Special Operations Forces. Special Forces refers to a particular U.S. Army unit with a specific mission: to go into foreign countries and train the locals to fight. Popularly known as Green Berets, they spend as much time cramming languages and geography as they do shooting and grappling. People say that they're anthropologists with guns.

They are one of the main sources for the army's elite counterterrorist unit, once known as Special Forces Operational Detachment–Delta, or Delta Force, then Army Compartmented Elements, then Combat Applications Group. They'd changed it again, but I hadn't heard the new name.

The guys in it never called it anything. They didn't talk about it, just spoke elliptically about "the unit." I'd heard about Delta selection. Just a long hike, my ass. They take the hardest Special Forces and Rangers—elite units to begin with—and usually only a dozen or so from each two-hundred-and-forty-man class of candidates make it through. The weeding-out culminates in a forty-mile trek with a heavy load, back and forth over a mountain of sheer cliffs, bushwhacking for twenty-four hours straight with the instructors doing everything they can to torture you. It was open to all branches of the military, but going from the Marines to Delta was rare and insanely difficult.

"Army," I said, and shook my head.

"I know, I know."

I found myself trusting him, which scared me. I thought back to what the colonel had said: *He could turn you without your even knowing it.*

Hayes could blend in anywhere, win confidences, exploit them. He had the perfect look, mixed ethnicity, with features that would let him pass as a local all over the world.

I remember him talking about that with me and one of the corporals. I'd finally gotten up the nerve to ask him about his background. Even Hayes didn't know. He'd been given up for adoption as an infant but never found a permanent placement. He bounced around with foster parents, a new town, a new family, every few years. That must have been part of what drew him to Special Forces, his ability to slip from one culture to another. No wonder the guy was a chameleon. He'd never had a home. Never knew where he belonged. An outsider, he always had guys coming after him for fights, and it taught him how to hold his own.

We passed a speed trap. A police cruiser pulled out behind us and turned on its flashers and sirens.

Kelly sat down on the bed of room 220 at the Island Colony Motel. Her face was red from exertion. After being cooped up in the room all night, she needed fresh air. She didn't want to go too far, so she'd opted for hill repeats on the steep grade just down the street: a quarter mile at a 12 percent grade, over and over, a dozen times until her chest was heaving and every muscle on her body stood out in clear definition.

She checked her phone. She had been calling everyone she could think of who might be able to help, getting nowhere, trying to find out why they couldn't fly and where the hell Tom had gone.

No one had called. Where was he?

She went into the bathroom, showered, then wrapped herself in a towel. As she crossed into the bedroom, there was a knock on the door. The clock radio said six fifteen in the morning. Too early for housekeeping. She hoped there wasn't some problem with the deposit. She needed a base.

"Kelly Britten?" the voice said through the door. "I'm a detective with the San Diego Police. I'm sorry to bother you. It's about Thomas Byrne."

She looked through the peephole. A man stood on the other side of the door, hands held loosely in front of him, eyes away. Kelly figured him for a detective. "What is it?" she asked.

"He's been hurt."

"What?"

"Can I come in?"

"Jesus. Okay. But can you hold on a minute while I get dressed? And do you have credentials? Things have been a little crazy."

He patted his pockets, then reached inside his jacket, where a pistol hung in a shoulder holster.

Hayes and I watched the cop speed toward us, then change lanes and pass us on the left. I sat back and tried to relax. We drove another three-quarters of a mile and exited the 5 onto a four-lane highway.

"So why is Riggs trying to kill me?" I asked.

"Don't take it personally. He's trying to kill all of us. He told you about those dead interpreters?"

I nodded. "Said you killed them."

"How?"

"Gathered them up and executed them."

Hayes said nothing.

"What did happen?" I asked.

He palmed the wheel through a right on red, took a turn through a shopping center, then checked the rearview.

"We were part of a joint task force. It was a mixed unit, and I handled an element of the advance force operations, the black Special Ops. Someone at Central Command decided that his protégé Riggs would look better to the promotion boards if he had a combat joint duty, so they rotated him in as a CO.

"Riggs had been a decent pilot but spent most of his career riding a chair. He'd never worked Special Operations before. That's fine. Normally, they all make the same mistake: overly complicated battle plans. They want to do everything with drones and Hellfires and helicopters, never get their hands dirty. Instead of listening to the men on the ground, they spend all their time glued to a video teleconference, micromanaging and getting micromanaged by the CENTCOM boys in Tampa."

His eyes went to the mirrors again.

"But this guy was different. I don't know what kind of political cover he had—he was young for an oh-six—but he had decided he was Lawrence of Arabia. The CIA handled the black money. They'd bring in a C-130 with pallets full of cash. No accounting. Bundles went missing. Riggs was skimming, and we knew he was up to something with a few of the local clans and militias.

"He was taking meetings with the men who ran the borderlands. It was a tribe the colonial powers had cut up when they drew the boundaries, divided it among three countries. They controlled the high mountain passes. For two centuries, they'd been smugglers. It was in their blood. We didn't know what Riggs was up to; hopefully just making himself feel important, handing the cash out to the locals. That was fine. It would make our job easier.

"We didn't really care about him buying off tribes. We just needed a safe house near the border. We were barely ever there."

"Riggs said he was your commander."

"On paper. But mostly we were out working in denied areas on our own or taking commands that came from the Pope—the head of JSOC. I met Riggs face-to-face only a handful of times."

"You were on an infiltration mission?" I wanted to find out what he had been doing, what they had brought back with them, what was in that box.

"That's right."

"What were you after?"

He smiled. "You should have done intel, Byrne. Our job was simple. There was a very bad guy working in the region. We were operating autonomously in the wild for months on end. We had developed our own intelligence stream on him, and he was about to get his hands on a very dangerous item. We had to stop him."

"What was it?"

"Something you don't want falling into the hands of a lethal nonstate actor."

A terrorist.

"Al-Qaeda? Islamic State?"

"No. Our target was an altogether more frightening guy. Among Western intelligence agencies, he's known as Samael. The name comes from an archangel in Jewish lore, the seducer, accuser, and destroyer, the angel of death. Literally it means 'poison of God.' The Mossad were the first to speculate that this man existed.

"He has an intelligence background, but no one knows if he has a sponsor or if he's freelance. His fingerprints are on a variety of operations and militant groups: Lebanon, the Af-Pak border—"

"Afghanistan?"

"The campaign of strikes against our forward bases. He provided weaponry that could beat the anti-rocket defenses. Really did some damage. Camp Halo, FOB Storm King, Camp Dagger, Mustang. Rolled back the whole front."

"Dagger." The blood on my hands. The dead woman. Samael had been behind it.

"Yes. But there are no reliable photos of him. He can come and go as he pleases, could waltz through JFK if he wanted to. Some people think he's been made up to justify intelligence spending, keep the black budgets fat, a bogeyman to replace bin Laden."

"Do you?"

He shook his head.

"I've seen him twice. We learned he was trying to acquire a certain kind of weapon, was in the last stages of the deal, taking delivery from dissatisfied scientists employed by a hostile nation. Our plan was to enter that nation, do a long incursion in denied territory, and stop him. We'd chased him halfway around the world. If we were discovered behind enemy lines, it would have been considered an act of war, triggered a regional conflict or worse.

"So we go. It was a hard slog in a denied area with no support. We went through the mountains, high altitude. We had one sleeping bag, and when a guy went hypothermic we would load him in it until he could talk again. It was a tough route. The enemy figured no American would survive it, so they left it unguarded. We neutralize the package. Kill a few guys. Lose some skin but nothing too bad. The hard part is over, and we're on our way back through the high desert to the safe house, hot food, and a shower. I was finally going to get to go home and see my daughter.

"And then we were ambushed. The bad guys had good infantry maneuver. We close and kill the enemy. A group of them get away. From the dead and what they left behind, we find out they have brand-new American M4s. They have clean American hundred-dollar bills in shrink wrap. Worse, they had our routes and extraction points. We hadn't given anyone our extracts. I lost one of my sergeants. We're good, but, frankly, I can't believe we managed to fight them back. We get within a hundred meters, and I see their leader."

"Samael."

"Yes. And I finally understood how he had been able to live so long as a ghost. He has blue eyes and can easily pass for Western European."

"Where is he from?"

"We don't know anything about him for sure. There are rumors. That he joined the fighters when he was a child, not as a soldier but as a *haliq*."

In the borderlands, in the second generation of war, there are no women. The men live in the mountains and the most powerful among them take younger boys as lovers — *haliqs,* they call them, or "beardless boys." They treat them like spoiled little princesses. It's the strangest goddamn thing I've ever seen, these bitter old warlords, eyes and fingers missing, courting and cooing over these boys, who act like high-maintenance mistresses, wearing kohl eyeliner and dancing for the fighters' entertainment in the middle of a war zone.

"One of the more over-the-top rumors has him killing the warlord and taking his place. Whatever happened, he disappeared from the view of our intelligence agencies. It's so simple: we'd been searching for a foreigner, and we never found him because he looked like one of us."

"But how did he find you?"

"Someone from our side was helping Samael. At the end of the ambush, we came under heavy mortar fire. Visibility went to zero. A sandstorm came in hard, scoured the paint off our vehicles. He got away.

"Our injured were barely holding on, but we couldn't call for medevacs until we got back to the border. We were black. We couldn't be found in that country. When we finally reached the line, we called for help for our casualties. But there were no helos available. They were all tied up because Riggs was filming himself entering a compound the Rangers had cleared the week before, conquering-hero-type stuff. 'Psyops,' he called it. It was a highlight reel for his résumé, for the commanders in Tampa. One of our men died on the drive back."

"But who from our side would help Samael?"

"We had no clue, but it had to be the colonel. He styled himself as the 'hard choices' guy, working with these warlords. All the Cold War, pre–Church Committee, golden-age posturing. 'They may be sons of bitches, but they're our sons of bitches.' But they played him. Samael must have known he could hook this naive officer. The local forces Riggs was working with must have been funneling everything he gave them—arms, cash, and intel—up the chain to the real bad guys.

"But at the time, we were just trying to make sense of what was happening. Riggs had cut us off from all our other contacts; everything went through him. He probably started to guess at what went wrong. The only people who knew about his skimming and his work with the local clans were the interpreters he used, the bad guys, and us."

"Wait," I said. "Why are you telling me this now? Back at the restaurant, you couldn't say a word."

He gave me a look—*I think you know*—then changed lanes.

"Because I'm a dead man," I said.

"Sorry, Byrne. Riggs has figured out that you've gone off the rez. He won't let you go given what you know. You're the enemy now, same as I am. No one will ever believe a word you say again. They're hunting you too."

I looked out the window, watched the other cars creep ahead of us.

"So what did Riggs do when you found out what he was up to?"

"What does any good bureaucrat do? He covered his ass."

Kelly looked through the peephole. The cop had checked his jacket and then said his ID was in his car. He'd left to get it, but several minutes had gone by and there was no sign of him. Kelly didn't like it. She was going to get out of there. She went into the bathroom, still wearing the towel, and put her contacts in.

There were circles under her eyes. She hadn't slept. Eighteen dollars and some loose change was all that remained of the money. She didn't know where she would go next.

A breeze came under the bathroom door. Then the room went dark. She reached through the blackness for the wall, touched the door frame, found the light switch, and toggled it.

Nothing happened.

She felt along the sink for her makeup bag, pulled out a metal nail file, and held it like an ice pick.

"Hello," she said. "Hello!"

She opened the door and tried the light in the bedroom.

Nothing.

The blackout blinds had been pulled. She sidestepped through the room as her eyes adjusted, banged her shin on the radiator, and cursed. She limped to the blinds and threw them open, blinking as the morning light flooded the room.

It was empty.

She took a deep breath, then walked over and checked the closet. No one was there.

Her left hand trembled slightly. She shook it and sat on the bed for a moment until she calmed down, then walked to the bathroom.

The door slammed into her shoulder and knocked her back. A man slid forward as she stumbled and hooked his heel behind her right leg. She tried to stab him in the temple with the file, but he blocked her arm and shoved her to the ground in one smooth motion.

She rammed her elbow into the bridge of his nose as she fell back. The bone crunched. Her towel fell off. She came down hard on thin carpet over concrete and banged the back of her skull. She lay naked. The man threw the blinds closed and towered over her. He wiped the blood from his nose, leaving a long red streak on his forearm.

"Listen, bitch. Let me tell you how this goes."

"Cop," I said. "A quarter mile back."

Hayes eased off the gas until we were driving exactly the speed limit.

"We're almost there," he said.

"So Riggs killed them all just to cover his tracks?" That seemed like a stretch, but I did what I could to keep the doubt out of my voice.

"We're not sure. It seems monstrous, but I've seen worse in war. We got close to the base. I still couldn't find Riggs, but we heard gunfire in a valley where a lot of our interpreters and their families lived. It was a fog. We had no clue what was going on.

"We came to the village. These people had risked their lives to help us. It was a tribe that had been serially screwed over by every local and occupying power for the past two hundred years. They had been driven from their homes because of what they believed and were under constant threat of violence.

"Dust was still blowing everywhere. As we pulled into the valley, we saw the warlord's men standing outside a mud hut. They were executing the villagers. I had a long-barrel SCAR-heavy, and they were out at the end of the range. I lined up the shot, zeroed the SCAR for the cold barrel, and then I saw him in the crosshairs.

"It was the colonel, watching as they killed the villagers, one by one. I scanned left and saw that Samael was standing beside him. The dust rolled in, and I lost the shot.

"Whatever it was, it was criminal. We flooded the valley. We saw a child of one of the terps crawl out of the building through the dust. One man stood over him and shot him in the head.

"I tried to inform the colonel over the radio that he was committing a grave breach, that the real enemy was beside him. War is ugly. I've done things I'll never get over, killed the wrong people. I understand that there are gray areas. But that was black and white, and I didn't care if they were going to hang me afterward, I had to stop it.

"As soon as we identified ourselves, they retreated, taking potshots at us. We secured the valley floor. They'd rounded them up in the mud huts and slaughtered them. It was probably a hundred and ten degrees outside, a hundred and thirty or a hundred and forty inside. As we moved in, we heard moaning, a few weak thumps.

"There were fourteen bodies in the first house. Our terps and their kids, whole families, three generations taken out in a few minutes."

Hayes's voice went gravelly. He cleared his throat. "It was bad. They took the entire village. Most were dead, lying among the few possessions they had chosen to carry to safety—Korans, stuffed animals, family photos, deeds to houses their grandfathers had been driven from.

"There was one kid left, about eleven. He'd survived by pretending to be dead. We used to play soccer with him. He told us that Riggs had sent someone to the interpreters who'd told them that they were being relocated, sneaked over the border. They'd get them someplace safe and then secure asylum for them in America to thank them for what they'd done. Imagine the false hope giving way as you watch your whole family die, your bloodline wiped out in an afternoon. The parents stood in front of their children, trying to protect them, but there was nothing they could do to stop those rounds.

"I left Green to work on the wounded and we went after the colonel. He and Samael took the high ground. It was a firefight. We were better trained but there were dozens more of them. I don't know if it was me or one of my men, but someone shot the colonel. They hit the building with an RPG, killed the last of the victims and two of my men." He tapped his finger idly on a long scar, a patch of white that cut through his hair.

"They retreated, over the ridge. We didn't know why. There was a moment of peace. Then the Rangers came. It was a whole company. We thanked God for the backup, and then they started shooting. My team sergeant went down.

"Ward was our comms. She was able to listen in on the Rangers' tactical net. The order had gone out: The base was under attack. We were the hostiles; go green, weapons free."

I knew the order. It meant fire at will.

"After nine months in the wild, dressed to blend in with the local population, we looked like a bunch of muj. I can't blame the Rangers for following Riggs's orders, and we weren't going to kill those boys. I had trained a lot of them at Benning. Me and my team broke contact. Got in the trucks, went back into the mountains. We'd been operating independently for months from caches, self-supplying. It was part of our work to have safe houses, false papers, and contacts among the smugglers. Being on the run wasn't all that different from our day job."

"Was there anyone you could go to?"

"No. You know what a drop weapon is?"

I nodded. If the Marines found an AK or an enemy grenade, supposedly some of them would hang on to it, and if they accidentally killed an innocent local, they would lay it down next to him to justify the shooting. None of my guys had ever done that, and I liked to think it was a myth.

"Riggs killed dozens. There was no way he could cover it up, so instead of a drop weapon, he used us. The whole thing was lined up. They'd caught us up to our elbows in the blood of innocents. The scene confirmed everything the Rangers' commander, Riggs, fed into their ears and then told his friends in Tampa.

"We took everything we had left from the incursion and disappeared. We tried to get the truth out, but the colonel had it wired at every level. It was done. He was an insider, and we were ghosts, living borrowed lives. We'd been on our own for months with barely any contact with the command. Our unit was designed to be denied and disavowed. Who better to take the fall?"

I checked the speedometer and leaned forward in my seat.

"Easy, Byrne, we're almost there."

I had to get to Kelly, make sure she was safe. The old ghosts were everywhere; the dead woman in the backseat looked at me with those green eyes full of reproach. And that was the funny thing: I wasn't all that scared of Hayes, but he should have been scared of me. She could have told him the truth—that I'd killed her, that I'd killed those Marines at K-38, and that I would kill Kelly, kill him, kill them all if they didn't get away from me. But he couldn't hear her. No one could ever hear her but me.

I shut my eyes.

"Why would the colonel get in further with the people who attacked you?"

"There's a lot about it I don't know. Of course he wanted to cover his mistakes, but to double-down with the enemy? That seems too far. I don't know what Samael and the warlords told him, if he simply lost his compass or if he somehow, in whatever corrupted way, thought he was doing the right thing. It doesn't make sense a man could turn like that, even an ass like Riggs."

The motel was five blocks away.

"So you're the only one who has seen Samael?" There was so much about Hayes's story that didn't make sense, that seemed too convenient; he was the only American who could recognize Samael, and no one would believe him. "Could you identify him if you saw him again?"

"I saw him last night, with Riggs, in a black Mercedes as they closed in on us near the border. He's inside the U.S."

We pulled up to the curb.

"But what would be worth that risk?"

"That's what scares me—" Hayes broke off. I followed his gaze to the second floor of the motel as he took out his SIG Sauer pistol. "What was the room number?"

"Two twenty."

"The door's open."

We jumped out of the car and ran for the room. I sprinted while Hayes stayed a few feet behind, moving more deliberately, scanning the scene.

I heard a crash from the room, a groan of pain. As I neared the door, I could hear more grunts and blows. I saw legs on the floor, a figure standing above the body, blood on the carpet. Rage coursed through me so strongly, my whole being fixed on one purpose: kill anyone who hurt her.

Hayes followed, pistol out. "Byrne. Wait!"

I gathered this wasn't the tactically wisest entry, but I didn't give a shit. I couldn't let another one die. I shoved open the door and found myself staring down the barrel of a 9 mm.

CHAPTER 19

KELLY LOWERED THE gun, threw her arm around me, and pulled me inside. She wasn't wearing any clothes. Blood streaked her torso.

"Jesus, Tom," she said. "I nearly shot you."

"Are you okay?"

She ran her hand through her hair and gave the man on the floor a kick in the ribs.

She followed my eyes to the blood drying on her side.

"It's not mine," she said.

The man lay on the ground with a bruise growing around his eye and an obviously broken forearm, half wrapped in the towel.

"I threw the towel at him and twisted it around his arm," she said.

I checked his pulse.

"Alive?"

"Yes," I said as Kelly pulled on her clothes.

Hayes stepped through the door. She aimed the gun.

"He's with me," I said. "This is Hayes. He's…an old friend."

I heard sirens in the distance.

"Time to go," Hayes said.

"What the hell is going on?" Kelly asked.

"There's more where he came from. We should get moving." I grabbed her bags. "I'll explain on the way."

"Fine."

Hayes rolled the man over and stood above him with his pistol drawn, ready for an execution.

I wheeled away just as Hayes put his foot down on the man's good forearm, grabbed the wrist with his free hand, and jerked it up, cracking the ulna and radius like pieces of kindling. The man screamed and buried his face in the carpet. I remembered Hayes's words: *went in nonlethal*. This guy wouldn't be giving us any more trouble.

We trotted down the steps as the sounds of the police sirens grew louder to the south and east. Kelly took the backseat behind Hayes. I rode shotgun. He drove.

"You sure you're good?" I asked her. I could tell she was so hopped up on adrenaline she probably wouldn't have noticed if she were walking on a broken leg.

"I think so. You?"

"Yeah."

"Thank God," Kelly said. "Because I got a call from the police. They said you'd been taken, to call them if I saw you. And to be on the lookout…"

I turned. She had the pistol pressed against the back of Hayes's seat. "On the lookout for military types." I looked from her to Hayes. In action, there was a command presence that gave him away. Kelly might have thought this was all coercion.

"Don't," I said. "It's cool."

She didn't respond. I watched her finger inside the trigger guard, watched her weigh the choices as the sirens chased us.

She pulled the gun away, looked at me grimly, then put her lips to my ear.

"Thanks for coming to get me, Tom. Now please tell me you didn't join up with the men who stole that truck. Because you won't have to worry about the police or these soldiers or whoever the hell was following us yesterday. I'll kill you myself."

"'Join up' seems a little strong," I said.

She sat back. Hayes looked at her in the rearview. "Kelly, was it?"

"That's right. Kelly Britten."

"You have some training?"

"I'm a first lieutenant in the Guard. Army. Combat engineer."

"Sapper?"

"Yeah." That meant she'd made it through special training in small-unit tactics, explosives, and urban combat. I didn't know she'd earned the distinction.

"I like your style, Britten. Thanks for not shooting me."

CHAPTER 20

THIRTY MINUTES LATER, I was looking for orange peels.

Hayes had told me that was our danger signal. We were trying to reconnect with the rest of his team, but they had lost a radio in the raid back at the safe house, so we couldn't use that to communicate until we met in person and were able to set up new encryption keys. We fell back to a series of predetermined rally points.

"And if I see an orange?" I'd asked him.

"It means someone is about to kill us." The meeting site would be under surveillance, and we could be walking into an ambush.

He led us through a patch of dry grass and palms in the shadow of a freeway overpass.

"Here we are," he said.

I looked around. A plastic shopping bag blew by and snagged on the scrub.

"And how do we find your people?"

He lifted a rock next to a stanchion. There was a Chinese menu underneath it, a crumpled piece of garbage no one would have noticed. It was the second drop we'd checked.

"We go to China," he said.

It took me a minute to understand. Different ethnic menus were prearranged codes for different sites—they told team members where to meet or pick up a message.

"Old-school."

"Electronic communications are the government's strong suit these days. You can just sit at a computer and strong-arm Google. So we go back to mono. Everyone's weak on the classic stuff, in-person, hand-to-hand. The orange peel is an old KGB favorite. When my instructors from Peary were getting trained, it was hard to find a good spot for dead drops around DC that wasn't already marked with a few other intelligence services' chalk and pushpins."

"Who's on the other end?"

"Friends," he said. "Even I don't know everyone."

"Compartmented. Cells," Kelly said. "Like…"

She didn't say it.

"Know your enemy," Hayes said. We started walking.

"What about the car?"

"Forget it."

After I explained everything that had happened, Kelly didn't say much. She seemed to be considering her options. I was hoping it was simply deliberation and not shock. The police were on our heels. Our first priority was to get somewhere safe.

We worked our way downhill past Petco Park toward downtown. Hayes had run inside a Goodwill, and we had swapped our working gear for polos and button-downs. As the neighborhood changed, from skid row to business to upscale tourist district, Hayes's stride and manner adjusted accordingly. If anyone was tailing us, it would have been impossible for him to blend in among the changing demographics we passed through.

He moved quickly but never rushed, and by his example I forced myself to relax my manner, to disappear among the locals, to stop looking over my shoulder like a hunted man.

Hayes checked the windows of stores as he passed, using the reflections to look behind him. We came closer to the bay front, the embarcadero, and the tourist areas around the USS *Midway*.

"Why don't you go to...not the police or the press, but there must be someone," Kelly said to Hayes.

"It's not how we operate. If I got killed downrange, they would tell my wife it was a training accident. The other men and women, my closest friends, would lie to her. But if I got caught behind enemy lines, thrown in a labor camp—tough shit. The government never heard of me."

"But they accused you of all this, pinned it on you. At some point you have to say, 'Deal's off.' If they're lying, why can't you tell the truth?"

"One of the younger guys on our support crew tried that, tried to come out of the wilderness. He was from white Special Ops— unclassified teams. He was shot outside the wire before he had a chance to say a word. In any case, that's not how we do things."

"There must be exceptions."

"We knew what we were getting into, the mission we were working. If people found out where we went, where we had come from, which nations had helped us, it would be enough to start the dominoes tumbling—proxy attacks, a war in the region. So if me and my guys were the sacrifice for holding that off, then fine. It's the job."

"So what will you do?" I asked.

"We fix our own messes."

"Kill Riggs?"

"No," Hayes said. "I could have done that back on the peninsula. Would have been easier. We have something better in mind."

"Something to do with a hijacked truck?"

He didn't answer, just looked into the distance. I followed his gaze, caught a glint of light on a rooftop. He kept moving, scanning everyone in the crowd. Every face was a potential threat.

"Correct." He turned to me and used the cover of our conversation to check the harbor in both directions.

"Stay here," he said, and he walked toward a cluster of wood-shingled tourist-trap shops along the waterfront.

Parents helped their children onto the horses of an antique carousel in the center of the plaza. My attention kept going to the trash cans. Something orange eight feet out from one seized my attention like a signal beacon. I froze, but it was only a discarded tube of sunblock.

Hayes looked behind a hedge on a little-used walk between two of the stores. That must have been the China drop site. Traffic coursed behind me. I was just starting to relax when someone tossed a piece of litter out the window of a van. It hit the ground next to the trash can.

It was an orange peel.

I started moving and gestured for Kelly to follow. Hayes eye-checked me, and I glanced back at the trash. He saw it too and tilted his head toward North Harbor Drive.

A black Suburban pulled up at the light a block away. As I turned I saw more coming from the other direction. Hayes crossed the street at an intersection, moving as fast as he could without drawing attention.

We followed him, a hundred feet back, and jogged across the street just as the traffic light was about to change.

The Suburban blared its horn and pulled through the red light. We took off sprinting, up the hill toward Little Italy. The Suburbans tried to plow through traffic at a red light, and the holdup bought us some time. We ran up the steep grade. The warning lights flashed at the crossing for the coastal train line ahead. We picked up the pace and crossed the tracks just as the gates closed.

Sirens sounded to the east, and we ducked down another street. More police on foot at the intersection ahead. They were closing a cordon.

We hauled ass down an alley. There was an underground parking garage ahead, lots of exits and entrances. The police hadn't turned the corner yet. There might be time. We raced for the garage and fifty feet out heard an engine gunning up the cross street ahead.

A van shot out at the end of our alley and pulled up short, rocking on its springs. The door banged open. I stopped, but Hayes kept going and jumped in.

"Come on!" he shouted.

It was a twenty-year-old maroon Astrovan. I recognized it; the driver was the one who had thrown my orange peel. Kelly and I dived in too, and the van pulled away.

Hayes slammed the door shut as we hauled ourselves from the floor to a bench seat. I looked at the driver in the rearview. He was in his mid-sixties with a white beard and hooded eyes. He skidded the van around a corner, grinding the rear panel against the brick. A glance back in his mirror, then to Hayes.

"Not bad for a blind guy, huh?" he said, tapping on his glasses.

"Thanks, Foley," Hayes said and clapped him on the shoulder.

The chatter from a police scanner filled the car. The old man shifted routes on the fly, outflanking the choke points and avoiding the pursuing vehicles.

"All units, be on the lookout for two additional subjects sought in connection with an armed robbery and attempted murder," the voice on the scanner announced. "Suspect one identified as Thomas Byrne, age thirty-eight, white male, approximately five feet eleven inches, brown hair, medium build, clean-shaven. Suspect number two identified as Kelly Britten, age thirty, white female, approximately five feet seven inches, blond hair. Check mobile data terminals for photos and additional description. Possible links to terrorism. Both are considered armed and dangerous. Approach with extreme caution."

Kelly's face turned white. I saw her throat working against the nausea.

A helicopter growled in the distance, someone making announcements from a loudspeaker. I couldn't understand the words.

"Ditch the van," Hayes said. We pulled into an underground garage near the convention center and crossed on foot to the marina.

He and Foley moved down the D dock. The chugging of the helicopter blades came closer.

Ahead of us on the dock, a woman I recognized from the first safe house stood on the deck of a thirty-foot cabin cruiser with *Odessa* painted on the stern. Hayes and the old man made for it.

"Come on," the woman shouted to Hayes, "you've got to hear this!"

The helo approached from the east. Kelly ducked behind a dumpster. I watched Hayes vault over the transom of the boat and then I crouched beside her.

"Do you trust him?" Kelly asked. "If we join them, there's no turning back."

"He's saved our asses twice now."

Hayes waved for us to come.

"Go to the police," I said. "Tell them we took you. You had nothing to do with this. Give me up. I don't want you to get hurt."

She looked back. The sirens grew louder.

The boat's engines churned to life. They threw the stern lines off. Hayes watched us and beckoned. He'd stalled them but couldn't any longer.

I stayed low, ready to sprint, and looked to Kelly.

"Oh, for fuck's sake," she said, then she stood, ran down the dock, and jumped in. I came up behind her. We disappeared into the cabin as the boat pulled away and a helicopter cruised above the docks, beating the air overhead.

CHAPTER 21

As I STEPPED into the cabin, a cat leaped onto the counter next to me, bared its teeth, and growled like a little lion. I flinched, drawing laughter from the crew inside.

"That's Quinn," Foley said, and he scooped up the tabby. "Guard cat."

He climbed through the companionway. Hayes spoke with him on the deck outside, Foley's head bowed slightly as he listened carefully, like a student. Hayes joined us in the cabin a moment later.

"The helo kept going north," Hayes said. "They're looking for us on the roads. We're clear. This is Ward and Cook," he said, pointing to two of his teammates. To them he said, "Meet Byrne and Britten."

Ward nodded my way. I recognized her from the first safe house. She was pretty, solidly built, looked like she'd grown up on a ranch. Cook glanced up from the map he was reading and gave me a friendly look.

Ward sat down at the galley table and started working on a laptop. One man was lying down on top of a trunk with a cap over his eyes. "That's Speed," Hayes said.

"Is that ironic?"

Hayes looked at me. "No. When he's awake, he's really fast."

Speed lifted the cap with one finger, checked us out, murmured, "Hey," then let the cap fall back. I recognized him from the Valencia hotel and from his trigger-happy performance in the walk-in freezer at the safe house.

I could feel the boat rocking with the swells now that we were in open waters.

The cabin steps had been pushed to one side. The throb of the running engine filled the space. Hayes stood beside them and poured water into a brown pouch.

"When's the last time you ate?" he asked me.

"Yesterday."

The pouch he handed me burned my fingers. It had been a long time but you never really forgot those brown packets—meal ready to eat. This one was beef ravioli. At least it was beef. Those were the best.

"You hungry, Britten?"

"I'm good, thanks."

I dug a plastic spoon to the mush, a darker shade of brown, and swallowed some down.

"Who's our captain?"

"Old friend," Hayes said. "Facilitates what we need."

"You trust him?" I asked.

Hayes laughed. "More than anyone. And he's spread around enough goodwill." Hayes rubbed his fingers together: bribes. "So we'll be all right as far as getting into and out of port. We have a fixer helping us with supplies."

Cook sat talking to Ward as she worked on the computer, a headset over one ear. Their discussion grew louder.

"Seagal has no fight record!" Cook said. "It's all hearsay. You get him in a clean match, he's useless."

Ward looked up. "I'm telling you, Van Damme is just a ballet dancer with a pretty face."

A woman with long black curly hair tied back stepped out from the engine compartment and wiped her hands on a rag.

"How are you supposed to be the world's greatest fighter," Cook went on, "when—"

The woman stood over the table and twisted the cloth.

"One more word," she said. "One more fucking word on this issue and I will kill you both. Understood?"

They leaned back. Cook started to say something but thought better of it.

"Clear?"

"Clear," Cook said.

Hayes turned to me. "And that's Moret."

Ward lifted a headset to Hayes and said, "It's ready." He took the computer.

Cook and Ward looked at each other awkwardly in silence for a moment, and then Cook checked to make sure Moret was gone.

"All right," Ward said quietly. "Who wins in a fight, a silverback gorilla or a tiger?"

"Bengal tiger? Siberian?" Cook asked.

"Whatever."

"No contest," Cook said, and they dived into the debate.

Kelly and I climbed and stood at the entrance to the cabin, out of earshot of Hayes's crew.

"The people who tried to kill you after you escaped from Hayes—are you sure they were with the police?" she asked.

"Yes."

"Hayes helped us out, but I still don't know if I trust him. The old woman who told you the story about the interpreters, what was her name?"

"Nazar."

"She backed up what Riggs said about the massacre, right?"

"Yes. She even testified about it."

"If Hayes is telling the truth, if Riggs did kill her people, why would she lie and support Riggs's version of events?"

"I don't know," I said. "And I can't figure out why they took me when I was with Riggs. Hayes said he was protecting me from Riggs, but Riggs didn't try to kill me until *after* Hayes got me. The rescue almost confirmed for him that I was working with Hayes. If—"

The door that led to the forward cabin opened. Hayes stepped through and saw us talking. We went back inside the main cabin with him.

He leaned against the counter beside us. "I know this is a lot to deal with. You guys good? You have any questions?"

"I'm fine," I said.

Kelly nodded. No one said anything.

"Seriously?" Hayes asked. "No questions at all? You're just going with it?"

"Why'd you take me from Riggs?"

Hayes pressed his lips together.

"We wanted to get you away from him because he's bad news. You saw that when he came for us at the safe house. But we used you too, we put a tracker on you. You led us to him. Getting you out was a safeguard, in case he thought you were in on it."

"What did you do at that house? You were inside for a while before you came after us. And if you wanted Riggs, you could have gotten him there."

"We bugged all his comms. Ripped all his keys. If we'd wanted to kill him, he'd be dead. We took away his strength when we hijacked that truck, but there's a lot more going on. We have to find out what he's up to and why Samael is in the United States. I'm not going to stop until I have both him and Samael. We don't just kill people. We develop intel, infiltrate, stop plots."

"You're not trying to get away?"

"No. We're going straight at them, and I understand if you want to bail."

"What had Ward so excited? What did you need to hear?"

He took us over to the laptop. "You should hear it too," he said, and he pressed the trackpad.

Audio played from the computer's speakers. It was a commanding voice, a woman with a faint British accent, a poor-quality recording. It sounded like a cell phone. It took me a minute to recognize the speaker: it was Nazar, and the voice on the other end was Riggs.

"You said you would protect me," Nazar said.

"I will."

"Those men nearly killed us last night on the peninsula."

"I'll take care of them," Riggs replied.

"Forgive me if I doubt your abilities. I don't need promises."

"Are we going to have a problem?"

"You know that if something happens to me, the evidence will be released," Nazar said. "It's all arranged. Everyone will know what you did at the village. So don't try anything."

"Don't you dare threaten me."

"Or what? You'll kill me? Go ahead. It'll be the last thing you do before they haul you off to prison."

I turned to Hayes. "She's blackmailing him."

"So it seems. We'd never been able to figure out why she lied and corroborated Riggs's story of the massacre. We had our theories, mostly that he or Samael was threatening her."

"It was the other way around," I said.

I looked to Kelly. If this was true, her main reason not to trust Hayes—Nazar's account of the massacre—would be gone.

"She must have some evidence of his role in the killings," Hayes said, "and she blackmailed him with it in order to get asylum in the U.S."

"That's twisted. It was her own people," I said. "But—Christ. This is perfect. If she has this evidence, you can clear your names, right? Riggs will go down, and that will clear us all. She was the primary witness against you?"

"In every proceeding."

I couldn't understand why they weren't more excited. "Isn't this everything you've been hoping for?"

"Yes," he said. "Which is why it scares me. This is intelligence work, not combat. The weapons are hope and fear and trust. That evidence is what we've been dreaming of for two years, a way to clear our names, to get back to our families. They've used hope as a weapon before: they lured those villagers to their deaths with the promise of freedom, of safety, of home."

"What's the plan?" I asked.

"Same as before," Hayes said. "Regain the initiative. Take the fight to them. Go after Riggs. But now we have an advantage."

"We can turn Riggs and Nazar against each other."

"Exactly," Hayes said. "She sounded like she was ready to let the evidence go public. And he sounded like he was about to come after her. If we can escalate that, bit by bit, we might be able to push them past the breaking point. Riggs is scared. The truth cuts both ways; it's our biggest hope, and it's his greatest fear."

"Can you find out what the evidence is and where Nazar is keeping it?" I asked.

"Maybe. But we don't need to in order to put the fear into Riggs."

"Where would she take the truth?" Kelly asked. "Who conducted the investigation where Nazar was a witness?"

"Senate intel. Closed committee," Hayes said, and then he thought about it for a moment. "That's a strong idea, Lieutenant Britten. Before we hit the colonel, we can rattle him and see what shakes loose."

CHAPTER 22

LATE THAT MORNING, Caro and Riggs drove to a private residence on the western slopes of Mount San Jacinto. The meeting was the culmination of two years of planning and quiet politicking. The members of the small cadre in attendance held a variety of formal and informal roles in the defense establishment; the company included a former CIA director, a special assistant to the National Security Council, and an industrialist who financed political movements and small but influential journals. They were mandarins.

As the convoy carrying Riggs and Caro turned up the private drive, Riggs's phone rang. He glanced down. The incoming call was from 202-224-1700. The first six digits meant that it was a Senate office. The number looked familiar, but he couldn't place it.

He answered it.

"Hello, this is Carol Weigel. I'm a staff member on the Senate Select Committee on Intelligence. I'm calling because we were looking for an up-to-date phone number for your counsel."

"Counsel?" Riggs asked. "What's going on?"

"It's for the task force investigation. The Cyrine Nazar testimony."

"That was all resolved over a year ago."

"Is there a good contact number for your lawyer?"

"Why?"

"No one has talked to you recently? From the committee?"

"No. Explain to me what is going on." His stomach tightened. The investigation was closed. This couldn't be happening. Not now. Not at the worst possible moment.

"I'm sorry, sir." He heard papers shuffling. "My mistake. Let me check with the director and have him give you a call."

"Put him on the phone."

"He's not here. We're out of session, though he might be back this evening. I think there's just been some mix-up."

"What is Nazar's testimony? Is there new evidence?"

"I'm not sure, sir. I'm just updating all the information. I can see if there's anyone here who might know. Could you please hold?"

"What is your—hello? Hello?"

On the boat, Hayes ran his finger across his throat. Ward ended the call. "How was that?" she asked.

"Perfect. He must be scared out of his mind."

Riggs called back, but the office was closed. The committee had blundered and tipped its hand. Nazar was going to leak the evidence.

The cars in the convoy pulled through the compound gate and came to a stop.

Riggs turned to Caro. "That was the Senate Intelligence Committee. They're reopening the investigation. I think Nazar is about to tell everyone what really happened."

"No, she isn't," Caro said. "Leave her to me. She is simply afraid. As long as we go after Hayes with everything we have, she'll be fine."

Riggs put two fingers to his temple and looked out the window at the estate. The shipment was gone. The whole thing was crashing down on his head. He looked back to see Caro studying him. Riggs swallowed, dabbed the sweat from his brow, tried to hide his fear and anxiety.

"These are the most powerful men in America, and they're looking to you for guidance," Caro said. "This is our one chance. These are the moments that turn history. Show these men the way."

They didn't have time for doubt. They had to go inside and sell this plan. Everything was ready. They just needed the yes, and then they would pull the trigger.

Riggs straightened up and opened the door. He stepped onto the pavers, buttoned his jacket, and strode toward the house with a full colonel's bearing.

He walked through the front entrance and started shaking hands.

After five minutes of small talk in the parlor, the host, an immensity of a man wearing a navy-blue sack suit and a permanent scowl, raised his hand. The guests turned and gave him the floor.

"We're all busy, so indulge me in getting down to business." Normally the chitchat, cocktails, and introductions stretched out for an hour—one of the sacred rituals of politics. "I've brought you here to consider the proposal that Colonel Riggs has suggested.

"You all know the problem we are facing. From North Africa to Central Asia, America has been bruised and bloodied in our war against terror. Fearsome enemies remain, but no one in DC has the stomach to risk American lives to destroy them. Our friend here is closer to the action than anyone, and what he has told us is troubling."

Caro had caught rumblings of plots through his networks, and Riggs had passed them on to the host.

"There are foes determined to hit America, and we need a way to kill them without upsetting the politicians."

Riggs looked over the faces of the listeners, considered the power assembled in that room. He knew Washington. His father had once been the acting CIA director, had been a perpetual second in command for most of his career. Riggs had spent his childhood playing at the feet of influential men.

He stood at ease while the crowd examined him. The guests were hard to impress, but the three-car security detail for Riggs, unusual for anyone below cabinet level, did draw their attention. They knew there had just been an attempt on his life, that he was in the fight.

"Colonel," the host said, and held his hand out. Riggs stepped forward. He didn't have to say it. They all knew; since 9/11, they had won every battle and lost every war. A new strategy was needed.

"It's a simple proposal," he said. "Fight the enemy as they fight us. We need deniable direct action, provocations, proxies. All I ask is unofficial sanction and room to maneuver."

He didn't need to go into details. All of that had been discussed already, developed for years at gatherings like this through face-to-face conversations that were never recorded on any official schedule.

He outlined the plan. It would be a dirty war, with no fingerprints. Riggs would be the indispensable man for this new strategy, combining the best elements of contractors and Special Operations with none of the inefficiencies of the big army. He had the means and the expertise. The money and operations could be taken care of off the books through his private force and Caro's connections in the region. It was exactly the kind of unscrupulous tactics that the nation's enemies had used to outplay the U.S. for years, and now the U.S. could play the same game through its proxies. Caro was the fearsome son of a bitch they needed downrange to get it done.

Riggs finished. "Are there any questions?"

They returned only silence. These were shrewd men and women, and they knew that ignorance was often a smart move. In the past, a plan like this would have involved false-flag attacks. But certain questions are best left unanswered. Deniability was crucial. There were still men who specialized in such operations—who made bombs that couldn't be traced—but of course, America didn't engage in those types of tactics anymore. They didn't ask. The specifics would remain with the colonel, as would the risks. There were countless qualified O-5s waiting for promotion. Colonels were expendable, easily replaced.

This was simply a last face-to-face meeting, a gut check.

"How long will it take to arrange?" the host asked.

"We're ready now." All Riggs needed was the green light.

He looked around the room once more, waiting on a verdict.

A bell chimed in the anteroom.

"Lunch is served," the host said. As they walked out, he took Riggs aside.

"We'll have your answer after we all eat."

There was a four-course meal on the terrace, with the snow-covered peaks of San Jacinto towering over. Any questions came now, in whispered asides. They tested him, judged him more by his demeanor than by anything he said. You reached this level in politics only through instinct.

They asked about the attack on the safe house on the peninsula. "Sound and fury," Riggs said. "We'll roll up Hayes any moment." He dropped a few humble reminders of his actions after the massacre.

That day, when he'd faced off against Hayes alone, had made him a hero, had earned him his promotion to full bird. Today he was cashing in on that bullet.

Caro helped sell the plan, looking utterly relaxed, with no tie and his sunglasses hanging from the chest pocket of his suit. He was their dream made real, a blue-eyed campaigner, the guy who had seen flies crawling on dead men's eyes, their man in the Middle East. They gathered around him, eager for stories from the real war. Riggs noticed that there was a quiet confidence about him that conveyed a sense of history being in the room, like de Gaulle in London for the Free French. They were building a new resistance for a new age, on a far grander scale.

By the time coffee was served, Riggs was calm, felt his old self again, gruff and wry. These proud men and women were eating out of the palm of his hand.

"You'll excuse us, Colonel?" the host asked.

"Of course."

The host joined the rest of the assembly at the table, and an assistant led Riggs and Caro back to the entryway. It was time for a decision. It took only ten minutes. The host joined them and put his arm around Riggs's shoulders. He leaned in close enough that Riggs could smell his stale breath.

"You have the green light. Go ahead, Colonel, and Godspeed."

*   *   *

Caro and Riggs took their leave, made apologies for their haste, and walked back to their vehicles.

"The green light," Riggs said as if in disbelief. "But we don't have the shipment." The whole plan rested on the crate Hayes had stolen.

"We'll find it."

Cox, the lead investigator from the Department of Defense, was also on the hunt for Hayes and his team. He was keeping Riggs updated on his progress, and Riggs dutifully passed everything on to Caro, including the last location where the police had seen Hayes.

"But how?" Riggs asked.

"Leave that to me. It's time for more severe methods. I'll find Hayes, and I'll finish this."

Riggs nodded. Caro still had his knife; he understood what was about to happen. That was why their partnership worked so well. War was ugly, and the West had lost its nerve for ugliness. Caro filled that gap and gave Riggs cover.

"Whatever it takes," Riggs said.

"And the call?"

"Make it."

It was time to pull the trigger.

Caro took a separate car. Riggs was left alone and couldn't stop thinking about the call he had received as he'd arrived at the meeting, about Nazar and the possibility of the evidence going out. His mind raced through the awful consequences of the truth emerging, of the committee reopening the investigation.

But the success at the estate steeled him. Whenever he was

around Caro, he felt stronger, felt like the man he projected to the world. He would take care of Nazar himself, put the fear into her. If worst came to worst, he had options. There was a place he could take her and silence her once and for all.

He lifted his phone.

CHAPTER 23

CARO PARKED HIS Mercedes in the underground garage, killed the engine, then looked at himself in the rearview. It was faint, but he could see it: his pulse beating in the hollow of his throat. Fear; he knew it intimately as a tool but didn't often get to see it in a mirror. Decades of work rested on this moment.

He stepped out of the car, walked up a level, and found his second vehicle, a compact SUV, completely unremarkable.

He needed to be in two places at once, to take down Hayes and make the call that would start everything.

To be two people.

The security around Riggs made that much harder than it needed to be. It took Caro nearly an hour to finish his surveillance-detection routine, an hour of driving with his eyes fixed on the mirrors, surrounded by threats real and imagined.

Another hour's drive brought him to a public library near Riverside. There were no security cameras, and the staff had plenty to keep them occupied. The libraries in this country were the de facto homeless shelters during the day.

As Caro walked through the parking lot, he felt the recordable CD in his pocket. His secure computer was air-gapped; he had never connected it to the Internet, never exposed it to the NSA's channels. Files went in and out on CDs, which made it much harder for malware to sneak onto his machine or data to sneak off.

The wind piled the desert sand against the curb. The lot was empty.

He saw his courier, a plain young Indonesian woman with her hair up, as he walked in but gave no sign that he recognized her. He went to the Natural Sciences section, scanned the shelves, and found it. *On the Origin of Species.* Every library had a copy. No one ever read it. He pulled it out.

Behind it was a small black phone. He slipped it into his pocket, flipped a few pages in the book, and then put it back and walked away down the aisle. The smell of decaying paper made him nostalgic.

He stopped in Classics, found the copy of Aeschylus's plays, and slipped his CD in among the pages of *The Persians.* A group of children sat on the carpet along the far wall, listening to a volunteer read a story. He circled around them, passing his courier on the way.

Their eyes never met. The decades of tradecraft, the endless hours of training, were all to prepare for moments like this, deep inside an enemy nation where the slightest mistake meant death and, worse, the foiling of his one chance to bend the arc of history.

She now had the CD, his final orders to the bomb maker. Caro had lit the fuse.

*   *   *

He had been building up to this operation his entire life. The skin and blue eyes that let him slip unseen into the West, his blessing, had once been his curse, a target on his back marking him as a child of the infidel.

He had run off at twelve and found the first real home he knew, a mud-walled hut full of sixteen fighters. They would paint his face, and he would dance for them, and the grizzled old chieftain would take him to one side of the room after the lanterns went out and there would be the smell of olive oil, and the old man would be on top of him, grunting, gripping Caro's shoulders with his right hand, the one with the two fingers missing.

The other beardless boys always teased and wheedled their masters for chocolates or money or sweet-smelling scents—it was astonishing the power an object of sex could hold over a warlord whom whole regions feared—but Caro wanted only one thing.

He would whisper in the old man's ear as he eased back and wiped himself off: *Teach me to kill.*

The chieftain brought him a gift, one of the Kalashnikov rifles, the kind the fighters referred to simply as "the Russian," and while the boy worked the action, the man leaned down, looking into the kohl-rimmed eyes, and kissed his smiling bow of a mouth.

But that wasn't enough. Caro proved himself hunting mountain goats, riding straight across the cliffs behind the hounds, careless of death, driving the prey into snowbanks and killing them one after another with unerring shots. When the others tried to seize his prize, he shoved them back, picked up his knife, and began taking the skin off the animal in long, clean cuts.

They brought him to the next firefight. The old man was jealous of this rare treasure, a fair blue-eyed boy, but in the end Caro grew stronger, and he refused to stay back. So the chieftain taught him how to survive the war, how to kill.

He had never seen a student like Caro, so cool when death was in the air. Caro exerted a strange control over the old man, who would do anything to please his young lover.

But all Caro wanted to do was fight, to shed the blood of the foreigners that had dishonored his family, the blood that ran through him and marked him as an outsider. The chieftain knew about Caro's background, and when the first hairs began to appear on the boy's upper lip, he told him that he too had once been a *haliq*, and he brought him a gift.

He took him into a room in the mud-walled hut, and there was his present: a handsome foreigner with blue eyes, bound, on his knees, a man who could stand in for Caro's father, for the man who had cursed Caro as a pariah among his own people.

The chieftain handed Caro a knife and told him not to worry; it was just like skinning an animal at the end of the hunt. And Caro saw the fear in the captive's eyes and listened to the pathetic begging he couldn't understand. He felt the rush of power and stepped forward with the blade.

Caro's orders and the data from the CD did not go from the courier directly to their final destination. They would be sent first to an intermediary, transferred by hand to a new device, and resent through a network of couriers using a different location each time—a *mirror system,* in the trade.

His commands bounced from the U.S. to an agent in Algeria and then to Sudan before finally reaching his explosives man.

He was known by the nom de guerre the Mechanic. His phone buzzed on the crowded but obsessively neat workbench as he leaned over it and poured a white powder from a spatula into a beaker. It bloomed red in the water like diluted blood, and then the crimson smoke billowed past him as the reaction accelerated, on the brink of going out of control.

He wore terry wristbands on both forearms to absorb the sweat. He had been selected for his skill in improvised explosives. The job required a certain heedlessness of danger and a mastery of organic and inorganic chemistry in order to synthesize controlled chemicals that would have attracted the authorities' attention if purchased on the open market.

The green glove on his right hand fit strangely. Missing fingers and facial scars were the price of his profession.

He added his mixture to cool water, and the RDX crystals precipitated out. He filtered them, washed them down, then removed his respirator and checked his telephone.

When he was young and known by a different name, he had been at the top of his class and wanted to be a pharmacist, or even a drug researcher, but his father couldn't afford the bribes necessary for him to sit the exams, and besides, his family worshipped the wrong prophet.

He dissolved the plasticizer from glue rat traps and combined it with the RDX to form a stable plastic explosive.

The ingredients he had used—acetic acid from a camera shop, fertilizer, formaldehyde—were readily available. In the end, the cost came to about four dollars a pound, and the result was equal in power to the C-4 used by the U.S. military. Three pounds of it would destroy a truck. He rolled the casing of a 7.62 mm NATO bullet between his finger and thumb; packed with gunpowder, it would serve as a blasting cap.

He formed the RDX putty into bars and placed them in a weight vest from a sporting-goods store. Four caps went into the charges on the vest. Normally a second layer of ball bearings or other shrapnel would be used, but not in this case.

The glass of the school would serve that purpose, because the point was to maim, not kill. As always in such operations, the strategic goal wasn't the death of the victims but the reaction of those who witnessed the blast and its aftermath.

And that was Caro's genius. The Mechanic lifted the vest. Such a small thing. This tactic had been used thousands of times before. The body count would be minimal, a rounding error compared to the wars the West forgot. But the simplest thing at the right place and the right time—like a box cutter on an airplane—could alter the course of nations.

He paused. The muezzin called the faithful to prayer over the loudspeaker of a nearby mosque. He ignored it. He wasn't religious.

He went to his phone and downloaded all the data he had received to its main memory, then pulled the SIM card, dropped it in a jar, and watched it disintegrate and cloud the acid.

The orders had come from Caro.

It's time.

CHAPTER 24

WE SWAYED BACK and forth in the cabin of the *Odessa* as the boat crossed the coastal waters. Speed checked the batteries in his optics, then dangled a line of tobacco spit into an empty Rip It can. Muted heavy metal leaked from Cook's headphones. I recognized the song, though I couldn't remember the title; it had been popular when I was with the Marines. Cook loaded a thirty-round magazine from a stripper clip, then slapped the mag against his palm.

The precombat inspections went quietly, with none of the pumping up or slamming helmets together I saw in movies. There was some small talk—old video games, the foods they missed—but mostly they focused on making sure their gear was ready. The point was to stay loose. Once in action, the training would take care of the rest.

"What do you miss most, Moret?" Speed asked.

"Close air support," she said, then went back to jury-rigging a rifle sling with paracord.

Riggs was hunting us, but he wouldn't have to look hard. We were headed for the coast, for a safe port, and then we were going straight at him and Samael.

Moret handed me a Beretta M9 and an empty magazine. I cleared it and started running the function check: slide forward, mag in, slide back, drop mag. The motions came automatically, drilled into my muscles years ago. Safe, double-action, single; I cycled through each, working the slide, pulling and releasing the trigger, watching the hammer fall.

The gun was ready. I didn't know if I was.

Cook tossed a tourniquet to me.

"Thanks."

Kelly was still in the head, cleaning herself up from when she took down the man at the hotel.

"Fifteen minutes!" Foley shouted from the deck.

We were closing in on our target. I needed to talk to Hayes, to decide what I believed. I stepped into the forward cabin. Dust swirled through a shaft of light from the porthole.

Hayes was alone. He swallowed a pill dry, then slipped the packet back into his bag. He sat in front of a laptop and a map covered in pencil marks: choke points, police and military bases, terrain and demographics. A Bible lay near his elbow.

It was an AO—area of operations—map. I'd seen them only for the front lines in Afghanistan.

"Any word from Riggs?"

"He's inland, the deserts. We'll connect with the other cell, and then it's fix and finish."

"Kill him?"

"Not necessarily. He's the means to get to Samael. Samael is the main objective."

"And Nazar? What about getting the evidence?"

He put his pencil down and looked straight at me.

"It's her lifeline. You heard her. There are ways, but we don't have time. We could take her and interrogate her," he said. "An ugly option, and coercion often yields unreliable information. We don't know enough specifics to make it a priority."

"So you take Samael out and it's over?"

"We'll try to take him alive. You kill a man, you never know what plots he's left ticking."

"Even after everything he's done?"

"I can't let this be about revenge." He glanced down at the Bible. "'Recompense to no man evil for evil,'" Hayes said. "'Avenge not yourselves, but rather give place to wrath: for it is written, Vengeance is mine; I will repay, saith the Lord.'"

"You ever think of helping Him along?"

"The thought's crossed my mind."

"What about clearing your name?"

"This isn't fantasy," Hayes said. "I can't let my personal concerns cloud my judgment. Samael is the threat. If going after him marks me as a terrorist, so be it." He let a breath out, stared down at the table. "It's all I have left, Byrne. That duty, the promise I made. They took everything else."

"Your faith?"

He hesitated.

His pupils were dilated. I guessed he was taking dextroamphetamine, a go-pill that pilots and Special Operations Forces occasionally used so they could stay awake for days.

"I lost sight of God a long time ago."

The Hayes I knew was an all-business sergeant, never spoke a word of doubt or expressed anything but eagerness and determination that we would come out fine. You would be running with your unit, starving and wet, near delirious from hypothermia, and if you stumbled, he would jog alongside you, not a word of censure. *You've got this, Byrne. Come on.* Even on the worst days with the squad, he could turn morale around just through his example. It's why it killed me to see him like this.

"What about your wife?"

Hayes looked straight at me with a face so cold I thought he was going to kill me right there.

"I have nothing to go back to," he said, and he kept his eyes on me for a long moment. I looked away, to a hanging locker full of mildewed orange life jackets.

"Since we're asking questions—why'd you really quit the navy, Byrne?"

My eyes kept moving, over the sleeping berths, but all I could see was her lying there, the life going out of those green eyes, the blood on my hands. I looked down at my hands on the table.

"It was my time." I pointed to the Bible. Hayes slid it to me.

The book was open. I don't know what I expected to find. It was Revelation, and the ink was slightly smeared, as if someone had run a finger along the passage countless times:

His eyes were as a flame of fire, and on his head were many crowns; and he had a name written, that no man knew, but he himself. And he was clothed with a vesture dipped in blood: and his name is called The Word of God.

I flipped back to the rider on the pale horse, Death, with hell following after, to the sun black as sackcloth and the moon like blood.

I glanced up to see Hayes working his jaw slightly. Definitely amphetamines. I looked from berth to berth, wondering if the shipment he had stolen from the armored truck was here on the boat.

"How long have you been awake?" I asked.

"Thirty, forty hours. I'll crash when we're done. You worry about yourself. Just let me know if you want to come with us or run."

He must have seen me looking around.

"It's not here."

"What?" I asked.

"The box. It's safe. Don't sweat it. Worry about yourself. We're landing in a few minutes."

My eyes returned to the page: seven seals opened, seven trumpets sounded, hail and fire mingled with blood, a third of mankind dead by plague. *Don't sweat it.* Easier said than done.

"I—"

Ward stepped in.

"Hayes," she said. "You've got to see this. We have something on Nazar. The bluff worked."

Samael sat on a white cooler on a floating dock, leaned back on one arm, and watched a formation of Marine Super Cobra helicopters fly low over the Pacific.

The fixer that Hayes and his team had been using to aid their port calls was a bad liar. Once Samael set to work with the knife, it didn't take long for the man, who went by the name Ferrante, to give up what he knew about the *Odessa* and where it would be landing.

As the pain started, the man had tried to buy Samael off, confessed there was four thousand dollars in hundreds in a Ziploc at the bottom of the cooler. Samael took the money after the knife work was done and then was certain it had come from Hayes. They were hundred-dollar bills fresh from the currency strap.

The fixer's body was now in seven pieces inside the cooler. Fog crawled over the water toward the dock. Hayes's ship would be here any moment.

At the ambush on the way back from Hayes's infiltration mission, Hayes had managed to escape, and he had only impressed Samael more since then, surviving the American manhunt, finding the shipment, and taking the armored truck.

A fog bank approached from the south. Samael leaned forward and peered into the mist, excited to meet Hayes face-to-face at last and finish what had been started years before on that barren plain.

CHAPTER 25

HAYES HUDDLED OVER the laptop with Ward. As I left the forward cabin I saw Kelly near the entrance to the galley, finishing the check on a Glock pistol. I started toward her, but Moret stepped in front of me.

"Did you talk to Hayes about his family?"

"I mentioned it."

She shook her head. "Don't. He and his wife separated before his last deployment. Her idea, not his. It may have been before she knew she was pregnant. There's a daughter he's never seen. I don't need him in some screwed-up head space."

"Got it."

"Good," she said, and then she joined the others at the galley table, sitting around the laptop. I watched them for a moment. All of them had their own ghosts, the friends who had been killed, the families that had been taken from them during their exile.

Ward glared at me. "Can I help you?"

"I'm good." I leaned against the bulkhead as she played the audio recording. It was another phone call, Nazar's voice.

"What now?" Nazar said.

"What the fuck are you pulling?" It was Riggs, with an anger in his voice like I hadn't heard before.

"What are you talking about?"

"I know what you're doing. If you talk, you cease to be useful to me, and you know what that means."

"I haven't done anything. If you recall, our deal was that you would get me asylum here and protect me. I don't feel protected right now. So why don't you get those animals who came after us under control?"

"Don't tell me what to do. If you let that evidence go public, I'll kill you myself."

"You're a coward," Nazar said. "Now calm down. I haven't spoken with anyone. The phones are not safe."

"If you talk, you die. Do you understand?"

"Use the BlackBerry next time. It's encrypted. I don't want to hear your voice. Let me know when you have my money."

The line went dead.

"Who ended the call?" Hayes asked.

"Riggs."

Our plan to frighten him into overreacting had worked. "They're at each other's throats," said Hayes. "Riggs made the threat. This could work."

The swells died down. I looked out the window. We had left the open ocean and entered a channel between two jetties.

The rest of the team looked to Hayes.

"Change of plans. We go after Nazar first," he said. "Ward, you have the keys for Riggs's BlackBerry. Can you spoof Riggs's phone so it seems like the messages we send to Nazar are coming from him?"

"Yes."

"Set up a meeting with Nazar." He leaned over the map and read out an address. "It's good terrain. What were Riggs and his crew driving?"

"Suburbans."

"That's good. We can get a couple on short notice."

I heard the squeak of rubber on fiberglass as the boat came alongside the dock.

"Time to go," Foley barked. Without a word, the team moved onto the deck and started loading out the boat calmly but with startling speed.

"Wait," I said as Ward stepped through the companionway with the last trunk on her shoulder. "What's going on?"

She turned to me. "New objective. We're going to hit Nazar. Now she thinks Riggs may be trying to kill her. And you heard her. She has the evidence set up as insurance. The truth of what happened during the massacre will go public if she dies."

"So what are we doing?"

Speed threw me a black duffel and smiled. "Killing," he said. "Finally."

CHAPTER 26

THE *ODESSA* SLICED through the thick fog. Foley turned after the last channel marker, pulled up to a dock, backed the engines with a growl, and stopped perfectly parallel two inches from the bumpers. He jumped onto the wood decking and tied off the lines. "Ferrante," he called. "Ferrante!"

Foley had dropped Hayes and the team off at a port a few miles north and was supposed to meet the fixer here. He ducked his head into a small office to his right. It was empty except for a white marine cooler.

He walked up the gangway to the top of the seawall. "Ferrante?"

He stopped, then turned. Something was wrong. He scanned the dock ahead and behind him. A seagull with a gnarled foot landed on top of a piling. No one was here.

He stepped back on board, started the engines, and pulled away. The diesels churned and set a foot-high wake through the marina. Once he was past the mouth of the bay, he put the engine on idle and stepped down into the companionway.

"Quinn," he said, and clicked his tongue. "Quinn."

The cat never ventured far from his side. He'd found it half starved with no tags cowering under a VW Westfalia in Bellingham. With his thick beard and perpetual squint, Foley looked tough, but he'd always had a soft spot for strays.

He stepped into the cabin. It was darker there, and he had trouble seeing. Something moved at the end of the passageway, near the forward cabin.

"Quinn?" he said. Then he heard a hissing sound.

"There you are, buddy." He stepped forward.

The blow came from nowhere. The pain flared from his temple. His vision flashed white and he heard his glasses skitter along the fiberglass flooring.

He was blind without them.

The engine died. The boat drifted in open water, rising and falling, creaking with the swells. He got to his knees, one at a time, with a groan, and started crawling, feeling along the floor for his glasses.

A shadow crossed the white floor in front of him. "Quinn?" he said. He looked up and could barely make out the unfocused contours.

"Who the hell are you?"

He reached for his knife, but the sheath was empty. A kick. The world spun. He hit the ground hard. As he staggered to his knees, he felt the cold blade against his skin, and his arm was wrenched up behind his back.

Music often filled Samael's mind at moments like this, but this time it was an image, a fresco by Michelangelo called *The Last Judgment* that adorns the altar wall of the Sistine Chapel. Dozens of characters stand before God at the End of Days, rising to heaven or descending to hell. In the lower right-hand corner, you can see Saint Bartholomew, who was martyred, flayed alive. He is carrying his own skin, and a knife. And if you look closely at the loose skin he carries, you can see that its face is Michelangelo's, a hidden self-portrait.

Foley came to. His arms were bound with wire, looped to an overhead bar. A saline lock had been inserted in a vein in his arm.

"Welcome back," Samael said.

The knife moved closer to his face. It had a wide, curved blade. There were plenty of fillet knives on the boat, but this one was different; it was for gutting and skinning bucks.

There were other people in the cabin, but he couldn't make out their faces.

"I want you to know that although you might feel very weak right now, you are in command of this situation. Do you understand?"

"I don't understand what's happening. Who are you? Do you want money? The boat?"

Samael moved close to Foley, almost nose to nose, then reached up and, with an index finger, caressed the meat at the base of Foley's right thumb. There was a hard patch of skin and some scarring: a shooter's callus down to the bone. It takes firing thousands of rounds a day for weeks, years on end to build it. It was a product of the kill houses, the ineradicable mark of a former operator.

Samael smiled.

"You've been trained. You know that everyone breaks. Everyone. So save yourself the pain."

"I don't know what you're talking about."

Samael picked up the tube leading to the saline lock, screwed in a syringe, and pressed the plunger. Near their feet was a wooden board. It normally covered the bilge, the area under the cabin sole where water collects and can be pumped overboard, but it had been pushed aside.

Foley's pupils dilated. The lights burned huge and white in the cabin. Whatever was in that syringe, it was fast-acting.

"Who are you?" he asked. "Why are you doing this?"

"Don't," Samael said, then pressed the point of the knife into soft flesh just below Foley's ribs and jerked it down. The blade sliced through his belt, his pants, and his underwear. They sloughed onto the floor. A faint red line was the only sign on the skin that the razor's edge had passed so close.

Foley hung there, naked from the waist down, the tail of his flannel shirt draped over his buttocks. He looked around the cabin. The bulkheads were out of focus. They seemed to breathe. His mind raced, far too fast. Every sensation in his body felt amplified a thousand times: the cold against his bare skin, the wire cutting into his wrists. He could see the pain from whatever Samael had given him. It arced and danced across his vision like licks of fire.

"I want the safety signal." It was the sign that would indicate to Hayes that it was safe to meet.

"I don't know what you're talking about."

Samael lifted the blade so Foley's penis draped over the razor-sharp edge.

"Okay, okay. It's an orange peel next to a trash can."

"Good. Now I know the danger sign. What is the safe signal?"

Foley licked his lips. His mouth was parched. The drug had taken full effect. The interrogator hung an IV bag from the railing and attached it to tubing in his arm.

"You won't die. I can replace the fluids. I have days."

Samael stepped behind Foley and placed the blade at the small of his back, almost flat against the skin; the edge dug in at the smallest angle.

"Have you been to the Sistine Chapel?"

"What?"

"In the Vatican?"

"What?" Foley gasped. "No."

"That's a shame."

The knife pressed in, sliced through the skin.

The pain was beyond anything he'd ever felt, a wash of stinging fire, tearing him apart from bottom to top. He screamed and wrenched his body away. He felt the slightest give. The screws at the railing had pulled out of the old, waterlogged plywood. He stood as best he could, then seated them back in the hole.

Foley tried to catch his breath as he felt the blood drip down.

"You want the box?" he asked.

"I want everything," Samael said, and readied the knife for another stroke.

Foley had been trained, and he held on as best he could. It was true. Everyone breaks. The idea was to begin with the least valuable information you had and hope that by the time the interrogator got what really mattered from you, it would no longer be of any use.

But whenever Foley tried to lie, Samael sensed it and brought the knife back, and the world was on fire again. The drugs clouded his mind, made it impossible to be consistent with the lies and concealments, and soon Foley wasn't sure what truths he had given away during all the torments.

He screamed, long and loud, and the noise died in the wind as the boat drifted and rocked with the swells on the open ocean.

Foley turned and squinted at a photo tucked into the nav station: a young mother and child. He could barely make it out, but it still brought him comfort.

The pain retreated.

He was an old man. He had had a good life. He was glad he could die doing something worthwhile instead of rotting away in an assisted-living facility, sucking down everything he'd saved through a ventilator. Better he go now. It would be a good death.

Foley turned and saw Samael looking in the same direction. The cutting stopped. Samael plucked the photo off the station and walked to the other end of the cabin to examine it in better light.

It brought a smile to the monster's face. As much as he tried, Foley couldn't hide his hate.

That confirmed it.

"The wife and daughter," Samael said. "Where are they?"

Foley couldn't fool himself. The interrogator was an expert who now knew about Hayes's child. *You old ass. You lost the day with your sentimentality.* It would all come out eventually. That's one thing he knew. Everyone breaks.

Samael studied the picture, taking note of the background, of identifying marks.

Foley looked at the handrail along the companionway. It was metal, about three-eighths of an inch in diameter. The last six inches pointed up in the air. He usually hung his hat on it.

He jumped up, and with what strength remained, he pulled with his arms as he fell, wrenching the handrail free.

Samael turned back at the sound of screws tearing against the plywood. The act of resistance seemed almost amusing in its futility, a desperate move by an unarmed man short of blood. Foley threw himself at the handrail, eyes wide open. He felt peace and a certain satisfaction, as he was sure Samael realized what was happening. He couldn't hurt his interrogator, but he could hurt himself.

He thought of the wife and child as he fell, and he was happy. He was protecting them. He had done his best. He hadn't given them away. A good death. The old man was glad to be of use.

Samael lunged to stop him, but it was too late. The IV pulled out, dripped against the fiberglass. From the flutter of Foley's feet, Samael knew he was dead.

Foley hadn't brought his arms forward, had faced death square and unflinching. Samael couldn't help but admire the old soldier.

He had held up for a long time and given up far less than Samael had expected. But still, it should be enough.

A trail of blood ran along the sole and drained into the bilge. The pump whirred below them.

"Get the gas cans and head back to land."

CHAPTER 27

HAYES ACCELERATED ONTO the freeway. I was in the backseat, leaning forward so I could talk with him over the engine's hum.

"What are you going to use with Nazar?" I asked. "Sniper?"

"It's the least dangerous, but it's kind of Hollywood for an assassination," Hayes said. "No one's travel is that predictable. Scouting lines of sight takes weeks, and a kill with one round from a cold barrel is harder than you think. Poison's out. That leaves us guns or explosives. You always get the target in transport. It doesn't matter if it's an old woman or a prime minister—they're most vulnerable when they're on the move.

"The state of the art with this stuff is the Kidon. It's part of Mossad, the assassination squads. They like to use a small shaped charge on the door or a few grams of explosive in a cell phone or headrest. If they're using guns on the fly, they'll take motorcycles and a four-man team: a spotter, a man to guide the bike to the target, the bike driver, and the shooter on the back. You steal the motorcycles and use a container against the cartridge port to collect your brass. Totally untraceable."

"Hollywood is what we're going for here. We're not actually killing her."

"Sure," Hayes said. "Force of habit."

Our plan was to try to kill Nazar and fail. Riggs had just threatened Nazar, so we would pose as Riggs's men, make an attempt on her life, and miss. We had spoofed Riggs's BlackBerry and sent a message to Nazar to meet. She had just responded. She would be at the meeting site, a hilltop park, ten minutes from now. It was six miles away. We were speeding west in a Suburban.

The dome light had been pried open and disabled, to avoid any chance of our being detected at night, I gathered. A small module hung down from the diagnostic port under the dashboard. The truck was stolen. We used to scrounge for medical supplies downrange. In the military, the polite term to describe hot goods is *skillfully acquired*. In the navy they're referred to as *cumshaw*.

Hayes scanned the map again. "She's going to be meeting us here," he said, and pointed to an out-of-the-way section of the park. "I can put Moret here. Though if it's a sniper shot that misses, Nazar might not even notice."

"I have the high-explosive rounds," Moret said. "One in the car and one in the ground, and she's definitely going to pay attention. It'd be all the payoff of a bombing with none of the prep."

"I like it," Hayes said. "Byrne, we'll wait on you to ID her. You stay with Moret."

"Rog."

We drove along an access road up the foothills, then stopped on a knoll in a grove of pepper trees.

I stepped out. Hayes and Moret took wind and distance readings and set up cover for the SR-25.

Kelly and I were alone. "Are you sure about this?" she asked.

"There's a big difference between running away from a threat and being party to an execution."

"Hayes isn't going to kill her."

"So he says."

"You heard the intercepts of Riggs and Nazar. It confirms what Hayes said."

"I did. But those could be faked."

"Why bother to trick us into coming along? They can handle it themselves."

"You're the only one who has had a good look at Nazar. Just because Riggs turned out to be a bastard doesn't prove that Hayes is innocent. The enemy of your enemy means nothing."

"You believe what Riggs said about Hayes killing those people? They're saying we're terrorists too."

"I don't know. I don't know what he stole from that truck or what else he's hiding. And I sure don't know if I'm willing to bet an innocent woman's life on it."

I thought back to those dark passages from the Bible, to Hayes's dilated eyes. I remembered the Marines, that moment when Hayes pulled a hilt-deep knife from a man's eye.

And now he was cut loose. He had lost the only things binding him to this world, his wife and child.

I thought back to the photos from the massacre, and what Riggs had said about him: *You have to be careful with him, Byrne. He could turn you without your even knowing it. He draws people in, uses them as tools to kill others, then discards them. And we've never seen anyone better.*

I had dragged her into this, and we were one bullet away from clearing our names, from the truth going out, from Riggs going down. What was the alternative? To run for the rest of our lives?

There was a curse following me. This was my own damn fault, and I couldn't let it bring her down.

"I believe him," I said. "But you should—"

"I'm not leaving you behind." She reached for me, rested her hand on the side of my face. "I've always wanted to ask you, Tom. Why don't you sleep?"

"What?"

"You think I haven't noticed. I've had guys bail, but you, you stay, but you never sleep. What is it?"

The other woman; my hand plunged into her chest. Her face serene, her body a shambles.

"I can tell," Kelly said. "You're lost. You need something to believe in. Are you sure it's him?"

"You're right about me. But that's not why I believe him."

"Always running away. There's someone else, isn't there?" She said it matter-of-fact, without pain or recrimination.

Hayes shouted, "Byrne, she's coming! We need you on the scope to ID Nazar."

"No," I said to Kelly. "There is . . . there *was*. But it's not like that."

"Byrne!"

"Go," she said. "I trust you on this."

"Byrne! Go time!"

I stepped away. *I trust you.*

Don't, I wanted to say. *Please don't.* Because that's when I kill them. But there was no time. Nazar was coming, and Moret had zeroed her rifle and chambered a round.

Hayes handed me the spotting scope. I looked over the brown hills surrounding the lagoon, scanning to where the sun glinted off the Pacific just over the 5. From a hill on the far side of the valley came the roar of gas filling hot-air balloons for the sunset rides. A few drifted toward Black Mountain in the east.

I watched a silver Toyota Avalon wind up the road toward the park entrance where we had told Nazar to meet us.

"Is that her?" Hayes asked.

I pressed the scope to my eye, but the sunlight reflecting off the windshield was blinding.

"Byrne?" Moret said, her cheek pressed against the rifle stock.

The car turned slightly. Through the window I saw the gray hair and the scars near the eye. It was Nazar.

"That's her."

"You're sure?"

"One hundred percent."

"As soon as she's a hundred meters from the car, you light it up," Hayes said.

"Roger," Moret replied.

The car approached the entrance.

Moret watched the car through the crosshairs of her optic, leading the target to account for its speed. She could see the woman driving. People always looked so vulnerable sitting unaware in her scope.

Her own mother was about the same age. After the massacre, the FBI had come for her. She was Turkish, and her father French, though Moret hadn't seen him since she was six. She had been raised outside New Orleans as a casually observant Muslim. Her mother would have a glass of wine now and then, and she attended services every Friday but didn't bother with the daily prayers. Moret went to mosque once or twice a year and still fasted, but only on the days during Ramadan when she was going to attend an *iftar* with family, mostly because it seemed rude to go to a breaking of the fast with a full belly.

She liked the fast, found it cleansing, an invitation to reflect. The other soldiers would invariably give her shit when they found out her background, but it had been indispensable for intel work and deep recon. After the village massacre, FBI counterterrorism had come for her mother, jailed her for ten months on a trumped-up charge, and spent days grilling everyone from her mosque. Now her mother talked to no one, just sat alone in her apartment with the TV.

Nazar's car pulled into the parking lot, slowed, and then accelerated to thirty miles an hour, turning hard toward the exit.

"Where the hell is she going?" Hayes asked. "Moret, do you have a shot? Ahead of the car?"

"No. She's behind the rise."

"Is she calling?"

"Message from Nazar," Ward said, and read it out. "'Change of plans. Come on foot.' It's a new address." She had switched the location.

"Speed, I want you on the sniper rifle," Hayes said. "You tail her. Get over there and get yourself a shot.

"Moret. You're with us. I need you in case we have to do the shooting drive-by."

Delta consisted mostly of direct assault troops, and from those a small number of operators graduated to sniper/recon teams. Hayes, Speed, and Moret had all worked "recce." The unit was modeled on the British SAS and borrowed some of its lingo. Speed had plenty of experience on the SR-25 sniper rifle, and Moret was the better shot overall, so they kept her near Nazar in case there was a need for on-the-fly close-quarters work.

The team climbed into the Suburban and pulled out with Hayes at the wheel. Speed drove the pickup truck behind them. Three quarters of a mile from the park, Ward held out the laptop to Hayes with a map of the address Nazar had given.

"Jesus Christ," he said.

CHAPTER 28

THE MECHANIC DRAPED a black flag across the concrete-block walls. He knew that there was more to a bombing than ketanes and vapor points, and that is why he had prepared the room: soft lights, a table with a Kalashnikov and a long sword.

The space needed to be prayerful, reverent, sacred. The Mechanic had pieced it together from the martyrdom ceremonies he had seen on the Internet.

Bradac stepped into the room and lowered his head slightly in awe. For his entire life, he had known only the seedy and pathetic. His mother had been an addict, and the drugs were probably responsible for the fact that he had an IQ of around 80. He had bounced in and out of prisons since he was a teenager. They had found him before he came to the attention of any Western intelligence service.

Caro had confirmed it, using the colonel's resources. Bradac was a cleanskin, unknown to Western intelligence and able to slip past borders without a second glance.

As he neared the altar, his eyes grew wide behind the thick glasses he wore to help with his lazy eye.

"Can I touch it?" he asked.

"Go ahead," the Mechanic replied. "It's not armed."

He reached a hand out and traced the threads in the nylon vest, then began praying quietly.

The Mechanic wiped the fabric down with alcohol to remove the fingerprints. There would be no trace of the real author of this operation.

He opened the files he had received from Caro; included with the instructions for the bombing was a set of fingerprints belonging to John Hayes. Planting false clues would be an interesting challenge but well within his powers. The only evidence from the bomb would point to the wrong culprit.

A half dozen cell phones sat on the counter, all with their batteries removed. To communicate with Caro over the mirror network, he had had a phone specially built for privacy using a forked version of Android. They each had one. Messaging and, in an emergency, direct voice calls could be encrypted end to end.

The Mechanic put the gauze down and looked over the tracks in Bradac's arm. He had attempted suicide twice before. That was an excellent sign, and the intellectual disability would keep him from overthinking, from doubt. They had plied him with very weak intravenous heroin, enough to keep him responsive but too docile and clouded to second-guess what he was going to do.

The Mechanic had sent him on a trial run the month prior. Bradac had thought it was real and performed flawlessly, flicked the trigger without a moment's hesitation. The bombs were mock-ups. But he had moved simply, without hesitation, his mind numbed, like a wind-up toy marching ahead.

For months, they had fed him an endless stream of propaganda videos—footage of Western-led humiliations and massacres of the faithful—and told him of all the promises of heaven waiting for him after the bombing. He was taking a few lives to save thousands more, to unite the people under the One.

After the trial run, he was so distraught they had to double his dosage. He wept for days because he thought he had missed his chance at heaven. He begged and begged for another chance.

The central fact of Bradac's existence was that no one had ever paid attention to him before, and he had never seen anything but abuse and mockery, violence and penny-ante betrayal. To be treated as special, to have a role, to be important for one moment; it was an easy trade for the rest of his sad life.

Though it stood to change the fate of nations, it was a simple mission: walk up to a school that had essentially no security, no standoff distance.

The initial charge would be placed on the ground. It would simply burn, throwing sparks, to draw the children to the windows. It would look like fireworks, and children loved fireworks.

Then all he had to do was stand near the glass and press the trigger.

Caro ran his thumb over the black phone, then dropped it on the seat of the Mercedes as he sped through the desert night. Enough information had been extracted from Foley for him to find Hayes and recover the shipment, and now they would be able to control Hayes through his wife and child.

That type of leverage was a basic tool of Caro's profession. There are things worse than death, he knew all too well.

Caro hadn't spent a night at his own apartment in months. He didn't like to be at home. It was a comfortable place, far more modest than his role.

But in the back, he could always hear the boy. He would always think of him as the boy, even though he was older now, with hair on his chin and arms. Caro didn't consider him his son; he was just the timekeeper, a metronome ticking away empty seconds.

He hated the hospital sounds of that room.

It was the only time the West had ever come close to killing Caro, at least until the fierce fighting when he ambushed Hayes on the way back from his infiltration mission. An Israeli F-16 dropped a bomb on a Hezbollah compound that they had just fled. The concrete from an imploding apartment building blew through the window of their car and fractured Caro's son's skull. That was it. He was paused.

He could murmur a few responses, but it was like seeing a one-year-old in a man's body, and every year he grew older, and the gap between his handsome face and his drooling incomprehension grew more unsettling. Something had to be done.

He was alive only because of Caro's wife, who would come in and spoon food into his mouth.

"It would be a crime against God," she said whenever Caro brought up the subject. But Caro knew that this limbo between life and death was the real crime.

He stole into his room at night and watched the blank eyes. He placed his hand over his mouth and pinched his nose until the boy would start to fuss, slapping weakly at his wrists, his face turning redder and redder, those instincts so strong, to hold on to a life not worth keeping.

Caro watched him struggle and heard his wife's footsteps on the carpet.

He let his hand fall away.

He hated that boy, the empty shell of his son, but there was a lesson in it. It filled him with anger and a desire for revenge, of course, but Caro refused to be affected by distorting passions.

Such feelings were the tools of terror, and to master them he needed to master himself.

When Caro was a young man, he learned to hate with an intensity that nearly destroyed him, and then came the hard part: learning to control it, to make it useful.

Ever since the Twin Towers fell, so many of the young fighters clamored to go bigger: blasts, body counts, nuclear arms.

But the West barely noticed when a hotel went down. There had been so much killing over the past dozen years. Two hundred thousand die in Syria. Five million in the Congo. The world shrugs, hides away in comfort and numbness.

No. Terror was a tactic. What mattered wasn't the strike, but the reaction. You could kill millions and no one would flinch, but if you touch the right spot, if you find the right leverage, a soft target, a simple act could ignite the world.

It was an insight that would save lives. Instead of mass killings, there would be targeted violence. He felt bad for the children, but it was a sacrifice of a few young bodies to save thousands more, the same way the Americans had killed those in Hiroshima to save the world from a much bloodier war. That was Caro's strength, to see past the immediate violence to the larger game beyond.

The Americans would never stop meddling in his part of the world. Attacking them head-on was suicide, but martyrdom had plenty of devotees. When he watched the Shia march on Ashura, covered in blood and slamming knives into their foreheads, or the Palestinians striving to be the perfect victims, he could only shake his head. Why make a cult of losing?

The answer was to use the Americans' own strength against them. They could be tied down and bloodied, and their belligerence could even be made useful, redirected to destroy one's enemies.

Caro dealt with the men who paid for his true mission only through the most secret channels. Some were allies of the U.S., oil-rich states, cowards really, who used Caro to bite the hand that fed them. But nothing was ever black and white with him, and his patrons would often remark, with an uneasy laugh, that no one could be certain if he was working for them or if they were working for him.

Caro had looked at his son and thought of what stirred men's hearts, the pressure point that could turn a nation. One death is a tragedy; a million is a statistic. Stalin had said it. Caro's great innovation was to make the political personal.

Family. Instincts stronger than Semtex that even he could only just control. He would join the ambition of terrorism with the intimacy of murder. And through the children, he could control the men who control the world.

There are things worse than death, Caro knew, and that led him to this one opportunity and the idea that would deliver him: What if you had a bomb that didn't kill?

The message came back from the Mechanic.

Trial run went perfectly. Waiting for green light.

He was close. He would have the shipment back soon, and then he would pull the trigger.

His other phone rang. He answered it, held it to his ear. "We have her," said the voice on the other end.

Caro punched the throttle and raced through the empty land.

CHAPTER 29

WE PULLED UP a quarter mile from the address where Nazar had told Riggs to meet her. It was a new subdivision in the foothills. Hydroseed and muddy patches ran up the slopes, promising future developments under the high-power electric lines. Hayes scanned the higher ground—plenty of positions for Speed. We stopped across the street.

The address was a combined elementary and middle school. A few kids skateboarded in the parking lot. Others waited for their parents, but most had gone home. A quarter mile up the road, there was a police substation.

Innocent bystanders, cops.

"She's spooked," I said.

"Good," Hayes replied. "The coward is using kids as a shield. There's a reason she was the only survivor of the massacre."

"Where is she?" I asked. We walked to the corner, and I spotted Nazar's Toyota parked beside a wooden fence, just beside a playing field, opposite the police station. A whistle blew. I turned. A ten-year-old pitched a soccer ball over his head back into play. The kids sprinted after it, a seven-on-seven game.

I ran back. "She's on the bench near the clothes drop."

Hayes looked to the hills and raised his radio.

"Speed. Speed. Do you copy? Speed?"

"No radio?" Moret asked.

Hayes looked up. "It's the transmission lines. There are high-explosive rounds in the rifle?"

"Yes," Moret said.

"He's in the hills. His angle's too low. He can't see the fields. The bullet will go right through the car and the fence. He can't take that shot."

Speed centered the reticle on Nazar's head and measured her shoulders, her head, and height against the tick marks. He knew the average dimensions of the human body and adjusted for Nazar's stature. That give him his distance to target. The calculations were automatic. He factored in the tailwind, the altitude, the downhill angle, and the temperature, since propellant burns faster on a warm day, then figured the drop and dialed in the vertical minute of angle.

The road was still warm from the sunny afternoon that had passed. He saw the heat lines rising, magnified in his Nightforce scope. The lines rippled away at sixty degrees, which meant ten-mile-an-hour winds. He ran the numbers and dialed in his horizontal adjustment.

Speed lay in the bed of the pickup and felt his lungs fill, his diaphragm expand. The bullet would drop slightly less than two meters over the half a kilometer to the target. He focused on his breathing, cleared his mind, and waited for Nazar to open the door.

He would light up the Toyota as soon as she was a hundred meters away.

Nazar glanced up the street to the police substation, then craned her neck around to listen to the children playing. She would be as safe here as anywhere. Riggs could kill her—no one would miss a lonely old teacher—but he couldn't kill kids, not American kids, at least. It would bring too much attention.

She didn't like using them in this way, but she was a survivor, and she would do what she must. She hadn't always been like this. A long time ago, she had been young and naive. She had told the story of what had happened to that girl to Riggs once. It was the story that led him to make Nazar his lead interpreter and fixer, his guide among the local tribes.

Growing up, she spent her time reading the few books about America and Europe she could find, books by Henry James and Proust and Tolstoy. She read them as much for the luxuries as the stories. She had to hide them from the rest of the villagers. She made it through the hard and hungry days by dreaming of escaping to those lands.

And when a foreign army came through the village for the first time, she was drawn to the blue-eyed invaders and sought out their friendship. She found a man. And he was her first, rough and sure, and he brought her more books than she had ever seen, and fine clothes, and food like she had never tasted. And he told her he would take her away to a better place.

And one morning he was gone, without a word. The whole army had left.

She was alone, and after the summer passed there was no way to hide the pregnancy. Everyone she had grown up with called her a whore and a collaborator, and after the birth, they threatened the child, a son.

She took what she could carry in two woven bags and ran because they were going to kill her, or worse. The elders had strange punishments, doled out by the young men in the central square, where only the shame eclipsed the pain.

And on the cold nights as she fled, she remembered those books, and the weave of the cloth on the covers, and the smell of the pages. The villagers had burned them all.

She was just another refugee in a land of refugees and shifting borders. That strange-looking child marked her as a traitor to her people, and she could never rest, never hide from the rumors. Her son heard them when he was still a boy, and her son, even as she tried to protect him, hated her for what she had done. He called her a whore and was even worse than the others in order to protect himself, in order to belong. And he left her. She was alone for a long time, lost.

Then another army came. The Americans took her in. She found work interpreting.

She told Riggs her story, and he understood how much she had suffered and sacrificed because of her love for the West. He brought her books and took her into his confidence.

When the news went through the village that the Americans would be taking them away to safety, that they would finally have a home, she knew it couldn't be true. She had been burned before.

She watched. She had been betrayed once already by a man with promises from the West. And she looked on, hidden, as they rounded up the others, friends and family, and the killing started. She watched it through the shaky viewfinder as she made a record of it all, and then rushed off to leave the photos somewhere safe.

A new life at last, a home; the promise *would* be made good, but only for her. She went to Riggs. She told him she wanted to come to America. She knew he would need someone to back up his story after the massacre. He was a smart man. The mere mention of the evidence was all it took for him to understand that she would expose him if he didn't agree to her request. They made their uneasy pact.

And why did she do nothing but watch as her people died? Because she wanted to record the truth? To expose what happened? No. Because she wanted out, and that film was her only chance.

She would corroborate Riggs's version of the massacre. From her work she knew that that was the secret of translation: the story changes with every telling.

She found a way to live with herself. She wouldn't be betrayed again. All she wanted was her books and her electric kettle and a quiet place to do her work.

Nazar was sorry for those who had died, but she had done what she must for her freedom, and she would do what she must to keep it. She opened the door and stepped out of the car.

Speed watched her walk away. She would be clear in a few seconds. He focused on his breathing, the way it moved the reticle up and down, up and down, within a half minute of angle. With that long a shot, even the heartbeat in his chest and the pulse in his finger affected the scope, faster rhythms than his breathing, like wind chop on top of ocean swells.

She would be clear in three, two . . .

He took a breath, held it, and pressed the ball of his finger against the trigger.

One.

"She's clear of the car," I said. "He's going to shoot."

"I can't get him on the radio," Ward said. "There are fucking children there."

"Hayes," I said.

But he was already gone, running in a crouch toward the sniper's line, his arms crossed at the wrist in an X.

"Did she see him?" Ward asked.

I looked through the scope. "No, she's turning around."

Hayes ducked behind the car as Nazar scanned the street, then took out her cell phone and tapped the screen.

As she turned, Hayes worked his way back, keeping out of sight, then rounded the corner toward us.

Nazar glanced at her phone again, and Hayes joined us.

"Now what?"

"We wait. At least we know she's getting rattled."

"And then?"

"We do the drive-by. There's nothing but empty hills on three sides of this place. We'll have a chance. Just brandishing a gun might be enough to scare her into releasing the evidence."

Nazar dropped her phone into her purse, took a last look around, then stepped back into her car.

"She's moving," Hayes said and pulled a black balaclava from inside the van. "Let's finish this."

The pickup stopped at the end of the block. It was Speed. Hayes met him halfway. I couldn't hear exactly what they were saying, but it was getting loud. They were in each other's face. I took a step toward them.

Moret put a hand on my arm. "Let it be."

I moved closer. I heard Hayes say something about killing her.

"That is an order," he went on. "We're going to finish this my way. Do you understand?"

Speed laughed. "We're not soldiers anymore."

Hayes stormed back.

"You good?" I asked.

"More or less," he said. "None of us have had a good night's sleep in two years. Two years, they've been calling us terrorists, murderers. And after a while, no matter how much you fight it, you start to feel like one. It eats away at you, turns you into the lie."

"She's on the move," Ward said. "And I'm getting a cross signal."

"On the BlackBerry?"

"No. Her regular phone."

Speed walked our way. Hayes jumped into the Suburban. He opened a Pelican case, took out a silenced submachine gun, loaded a magazine, and pulled back the charging handle to cock it. He held the map out to me.

"Byrne, you and Britten take the pickup and meet us here." He pointed to a spot two miles away. "We'll need to burn these vehicles as soon as we're done. We probably won't even have to shoot, but I don't want you nearby once we go kinetic. There might be a lot of fire, and you're not up on the tactics. I don't need any blue-on-blue."

"But—"

"It's an order. I don't want you getting killed and we need a ride."

"Understood."

He handed me a radio. Speed tossed me the keys.

They climbed into the Suburban and took off. We rolled out a minute behind them in the pickup.

Hayes's voice came over the radio. "Wait till Nazar is out of the residential areas."

We crossed an overpass above the freeway and entered a section of low-rise commercial and industrial buildings—warehouses, wholesalers, machine shops—laid out on a grid of four-lane roads.

"Traffic ahead. She's slowing down. Looks good. Byrne, are you all clear?"

"Yes."

"We'll see you at the rally. Get out of here. Speed, we'll flank her at the next intersection and then execute."

"I don't like this," Kelly said. "Why did they get rid of us?"

I turned twice and headed south on a street parallel to the direction Nazar and Hayes were moving. I didn't want to get too far ahead in case they needed us.

Our radio was still live. Ward came on. "I've got an intercept. Nazar's talking on her phone."

"What's she saying?" It was Hayes or Speed.

"Hold on," Ward said. "She called someone. Identified herself. She said, 'I think they're coming after me. Do you still have the package that I gave you?' The other speaker confirmed that it was safe and ready to send. He asked for confirmation on whether to send it or not. Nazar told him to wait."

Hayes's voice cut in. "Perfect. That's the evidence. Hit her at the traffic light."

I heard pops up ahead and, an instant later, over the radio. It sounded like automatic fire.

"Shots fired," Ward said. "Nazar gave the order to send it. The other party confirmed. Holy shit. That's it. The evidence is going out."

I pulled over to the curb beside a corrugated-aluminum warehouse, some kind of remodeling company.

"Is that it?" Kelly asked.

"If she sends it out, the whole story goes public."

"Riggs goes down, and we'll be able to clear our names. Are you serious? It's over?"

"You heard what she said."

She leaned in and wrapped her arms around me. "We're going to make it out of this."

"Thank God," I said.

I held her close, felt the dread leave my body for the first time since the police had knocked on my door. She took my face in both her hands and kissed me.

I would tell her everything: the ghosts, the way everyone around me ended up dead. We might be all right. Maybe I wasn't a death sentence for everyone who trusted me, for everyone who came close. Maybe one day I would make peace with the shades, with the green-eyed woman from the past, and remember her as she was, beautiful and warm, not as the distortion of my guilt. One day I might close my eyes, lie beside Kelly, and sleep.

"Kelly, what I said before, about there being someone else. It's not like that. Years ago, when I was deployed—"

Gunfire ripped through the night, and I heard the screech of tires, then the crunch and shatter.

A woman screamed.

CHAPTER 30

We looked at each other for a moment, then took what guns we had, the 9 mm Glock and 9 mm Beretta, stepped out of the car, and started walking toward the gunfire. I took point around the corner of the building and looked to the right.

A block to the north, Nazar's Toyota had swerved across an intersection and crashed into the base of a liquor-store sign on the far corner. A seam of bullet holes ran up the side of the car. The engine compartment was on fire. Black smoke billowed out.

Kelly came up behind me.

"They fucking shot her," I said.

I could see Nazar dragging herself along the asphalt away from the intersection.

The Suburban parked halfway up on the median. A cardboard sign scrawled in marker lay on the asphalt, abandoned by a panhandler.

Shooters in balaclavas knelt at the southeast and southwest corners, the two closest to us. It looked like they were covering sectors. Another grabbed the shoulder of Nazar's shirt and hauled her away. They disappeared behind a parked truck.

I walked up the block, the gun at my thigh, aimed down, finger outside the trigger guard.

"Hayes!" I shouted. One of the kneeling men turned toward me as I yelled. I was on the east side of the street and he was on the west, at the far end of the block.

"What happened? Is Nazar all right? Need medical?"

He waved me closer. I stepped between the parked cars and walked ten more feet. Then I saw the barrel of his MP7 come square, aimed at my head. I dived to the ground between two cars as a three-round burst hissed past me. I landed hard, taking the skin off my elbows, and low-crawled behind a truck for cover.

It was Hayes. There was no way he could have mistaken me for someone else. And he had tried to kill me. They were getting closer now, one on the opposite side of the street and one on the other side of the row of parked cars I had taken cover behind. They moved quickly, one running, the other using a minimum of fire to keep me down every time I looked out.

Kelly had dived behind a transformer about fifty feet away. The gunman shot a burst in her direction. She grunted in pain.

"You okay?"

"Yes," she said.

I crawled out to make sure. We'd be overrun in a few seconds. I signaled for her to run from the shooters, down the street around the corner, back the way we had come. She shook her head, crawled to a better position, prone beside the transformer. There were bushes around it. It was good cover, no silhouette, not where they expected us.

I signaled again: *I cover, you run.*

She shook her head again.

Bullets punched through the panels of the car I was crouched behind. The adrenaline poured through me in a hot wash from my head to my feet. I felt strong, like I could flip the car over, but soon a tremble worked its way into my gun hand.

Every instinct told me to freeze, take cover, but the way to survive was to keep moving, keep the pressure on, keep the initiative.

I edged around the truck and slipped into its bed, out of sight. It was a hauler, with panels around the bed. They wouldn't be expecting me over the top, and it would give me a line on the gunman on our side of the road.

I signaled back to Kelly to suppress the man on the other side of the street. *Three, two, one.* She put rounds into the car he had taken cover behind. I came over the top of the truck. My shooter was surprised and aimed a burst in my direction, but coming from cover, his fire wasn't accurate. I was dropping back down when I heard the click of steel on concrete; he was changing mags. I vaulted over the panel, came around, and lit him up.

The bullet leaned him back a few inches. He didn't react for a second, then he seized up with pain and grunted, fumbled the magazine, and glared at me with a strange, indignant look.

Kelly kept going, keeping the other shooter out of play. Six rounds, seven, eight. She had fifteen in the Glock. I had to move. I ran toward my injured man as he managed to get the magazine in and cock the gun. He lifted it and took aim.

I shot him in the stomach, and he flinched, but it wasn't enough.

He got up on one knee, tried to raise his gun again.

Two, three, four shots. Two of them hit.

He staggered toward me, still trying to lift the gun. Goddamn 9 mm. He wouldn't drop.

Six. Seven. Another hit. He fell back, unconscious. The crack of gunfire came from my right, but they were God-willing shots, way wide.

I ran up, grabbed the injured man's MP7, and put three rounds into the minivan the shooter across the street had taken cover behind. I ducked behind the hood of a car on my side of the street and peered out from under the bumper.

He was gone. I ran forward.

The pulse of the man I had shot was thready. Bright red blood flowed from his arm.

"Kelly!" I shouted. "Clear."

No answer.

I looked back. She lay on the ground next to the transformer.

I ran to her and checked her pulse—weak. Her face, turned to the side, was beautiful and untroubled. But then blood dripped from the hairline and began to flow down her forehead.

I was reaching for something to wipe it away when bullets ripped through the steel of the transformer. Oil poured out and covered the green sheet metal.

The blood ran into her eyes and down the side of her face.

I mopped the blood off with my sleeve, being careful not to move her neck. I could stop the bleeding. But that didn't matter. There was no time. I had to kill the other man first. It was a choice I'd never wanted to have to make again. The gunman was moving closer and closer, and soon he would be straight across the street from us with a clear shot, and then we were done.

The bushes might give me cover to circle the building and flank him, but that would take too long. I looked ahead. There was a storm drain. It must run under the street. The third dimension. People always forget it, but it's crucial in urban operations. I could get behind him.

He moved even closer. I took her pistol and loaded a new magazine. My heart pounded in my chest and my vision sharpened. The blue of the sky and red of her blood looked impossibly bright, hyperreal. The fear and the noise and the chaos faded out, leaving a simple imperative: destroy this man.

Another burst of fire chewed apart the steel of the transformer. A shower of sparks burst out.

The bullets sawed the air next to my head, and then I felt a wall of heat.

I turned away and lifted the gun. No sound but the ringing in my ears. The transformer blew.

As I went down, I knew the truth: Hayes had lured me in. I helped them kill Nazar. Everything false was now true; I had aided terrorists, abetted whatever horrors they were going to unleash with the stolen shipment.

In my blindness, all I could see was Kelly's face: no pain, only repose, her lower lip tucked under just slightly, like when she slept, and then the blood pouring down.

The world exploded around me. Pressure bloomed in the back of my head. Everything went black.

CHAPTER 31

THE ORDER CAME from Hayes. "Is the box ready?" he asked.

"Yes."

"Move out."

Hayes's associates dropped the crate in front of the consulate general of Egypt, on Wilshire in Los Angeles's Miracle Mile, then disappeared into the endless traffic of rush hour.

The black, white, and red flag of Egypt hung slack from the pole. A dog walker who approached forty minutes later was the first person to see the crate. She noticed the strange Arabic markings, jerked the leash, and quickly moved away from the consulate, an imposing tower of brown stone and black glass.

A guard came by next and called down the embassy's chief of security. After a brief back-and-forth with the head of mission, they contacted the Secret Service, which is responsible for diplomatic security.

There was a private elementary school across Wilshire, and a public middle school on the same street.

The box sat partially obscured by the walls of the parking lot. The Secret Service closed off the street. LAPD cruisers blocked off Wilshire and the side streets for half a mile in either direction. They emptied the four-story terraced apartment buildings next door. Most of the office buildings were empty, but the cleaning crews were evacuated as well. Crowds gathered at the roadblocks. People filmed on their cell phones and craned their necks to see as the mine-resistant ambush-protected truck trundled past the police cars.

If the box was full of ammonium nitrate and fuel oil, like the explosive in the Oklahoma City blast, the lethal radius would be a hundred and fifty yards. That attack killed a hundred and sixty-eight people and injured six hundred and eighty. If it was full of C-4, it would leave a crater fifty feet wide, spray lethal shrapnel for a quarter mile, and send a mushroom cloud four hundred feet in the air. The effect would be about 50 percent more devastating than Oklahoma City.

The explosive-ordnance disposal team stepped out of the MRAP wearing short-sleeved black uniforms. They moved purposefully but kept going back and forth to check with their commander and the LAPD, who were maintaining security at the scene. A few phones remained in the air snapping photos, but once the spectators saw the two techs help the third into the bomb suit, they began filing away from the barriers as quickly as they could.

The EOD team sent a robot to do an X-ray inspection. The results were inconclusive. Two hours had passed. The Miracle Mile, a traffic nightmare even on a typical day, had been reduced to a snarl of horns and cursing drivers all the way back to Beverly Hills.

The techs double-checked the specialist's helmet, and he began to lumber down the center of the empty six-lane boulevard.

They called it the long walk.

The radiological and bioassays found nothing. He took a pry bar and forced it under the lid of the crate. The nails creaked as he wrenched it open.

Inside, there was a trunk the size of a dresser. He didn't recognize its origin. It was made of brass and bone, which he mistook for ivory, inlaid in an intricate design.

He checked again for any signs of radioactivity or a bioweapon. Nothing.

A drop of sweat fell from his nose and beaded on the inside of his face mask.

"Opening the package," he said into his helmet mic.

He reached for the clasp. It was unlocked. He took a deep breath and lifted the lid.

CHAPTER 32

Vehicles from half a dozen law-enforcement agencies filled the marina parking lot. A towboat had pulled the burned wreck of the *Odessa* into the harbor. Cox had caught the stench of burning oil and scorched fiberglass from a half mile away.

He crouched next to the body. Half of the corpse had been burned beyond recognition, with the flesh charred and tightened, giving it a mummified look, but the upper torso and head were intact. Shallow cuts and missing skin. Death from head trauma, not exsanguination. Given the extent of the flaying, that meant an expert interrogator with a steady hand and a strong stomach.

Cox looked at the face. It was definitely Foley. He had found a photo of him and Hayes together and got some background on their relationship from one of Hayes's former commanding officers. Foley was not Hayes's father, but he might as well have been. He had been a Special Forces vet, a track coach who saw something in Hayes when he was a foster child and took him under his wing.

The more Cox learned about Hayes, the less this made sense. He was the child of refugees, abandoned to foster homes. He didn't know his own race, his own people. He could be anyone. The Joint Special Operations Command seized on that chameleon nature and his deep psychological desire to join, to blend in, to belong. He was born to go behind enemy lines.

Hayes had been the best in Force Recon, and then the Marine Special Operations Command. They pulled him into the JSOC classified units because he wanted to be more than a trigger puller. He liked working with Special Forces, studying languages, going deep on cultural background.

That's why the massacre of the villagers didn't add up. Hayes was a refugee himself, always searching, always looking for a home. Maybe that need to be a part of something was too great. He had stayed too long behind enemy lines. He'd lost his wife and kid. His own country had placed him into a deniable unit, ready to disavow any knowledge of him if anything went wrong. In the end he'd decided he belonged there, on the other side.

Foley had been the key person Cox wanted to find and interview. Now he was dead. Cox's only other good lead had turned up in seven pieces in a white marine cooler.

He shook his head. He had been just a few hours away from finding these two men, but he was too late.

Hayes was a step ahead of him, covering his trail through violence, killing as needed. How could Cox, operating within the law, possibly outstrip that sort of evil?

The medical examiner arrived and gave Cox an unwelcoming look. "Can I help you?"

"Probably not," Cox said. He had what he needed. He climbed out of the cabin and stepped onto the dock.

Once he was clear of the local law enforcement, he lifted his cell and dialed Riggs's number. The colonel should know: Hayes was coming, and he was out for blood.

Riggs picked up. There was an echo, as if he were in a tiled room.

"Hayes just killed our two best leads."

"Foley?"

"That's right. Looks like Hayes tortured him. I want you to think about coming onto a base, where it's safe."

"I'm safe," Riggs said. "I'll take care of my security."

Was that a dig? Cox wondered. If so, he deserved it. Hayes was winning.

"So Hayes is killing anyone who might lead us to him?"

"Seems like," Cox said.

"It's inhuman," Riggs said.

"Yes." But Cox wasn't sure. He thought of the body again. Tortured. But you don't torture if you're covering your tracks, eliminating anyone who has information about you. You torture to get information. You torture if you're *following* tracks. Which could mean that someone else was hunting these men down, just as Cox was, only better, more ruthlessly, without a thought for human life or suffering.

"What's up?"

"It's..." Cox hesitated. "Nothing. I'll keep you posted."

Riggs hung up the phone and stepped through the metal passageway toward Caro.

They were on a ship called the *Shiloh* that Riggs controlled through his military-contracting firm. It was often used by the Special Operations command for off-book jobs. They were on the third deck, below the waterline, surrounded by the sounds of running engines and waves washing along the hull.

"They found Foley," Riggs said.

"And?"

"They think Hayes tortured him to death. What did you do to the old man?"

"Nothing," Caro said, waving the question away.

"How did you make it back here so fast?"

He ducked that too. "So we're good as far as the official investigation?"

"Yes," Riggs said. "Did Foley give up anything?"

"Not as much as we hoped. But we have a few of their rally points and codes. We can go through them by process of elimination and tighten the noose around his network. They're using country names as codes for the rally. We're heading to a site referred to as Italy. We don't know if it's a safe house or a waypoint."

"We?"

"I have some men in-country," Caro said.

Riggs nodded, doing a decent job concealing his surprise and what looked to Caro like a hint of suspicion. "What are the grids? I can have my men help."

They both knew what was at stake. Whoever took Hayes would also control the shipment.

Caro knew he had to get there first, had to have control over the box. He put his hand on Riggs's shoulder.

"Excellent," he said, and he opened the door to his right. It had once been the cryptography vault on the *Shiloh*. A dial-combination lock, the type used on safes, secured the door.

Hall, Riggs's deputy, stood guard just inside. Caro stepped through and looked at the captive. Her wrists were bound to the railing above her head, and she was slumped against the bulkhead with a blood-soaked bandage on her neck. It was Nazar.

He noted the shock of recognition in her eyes, less fear than sadness, a look of love lost, maybe even misguided hope.

Caro didn't react, just turned back to Riggs. "What exactly did she say when she made the call about the evidence?"

"She said to get it ready to release. And then she panicked and told him to do it. We think she gave the photos to her lawyer for safekeeping."

Hall stepped toward Nazar, racked a .22-caliber pistol, crouched slightly, and pointed it at her temple.

"Not yet," Caro said, ignoring her as she whimpered around her gag.

"Wait until we hit the lawyer and get the evidence. We have to destroy every copy. We may still need her."

The Mechanic slipped the bomb vest over Bradac's head and then stood behind a camera. There would be no recording, of course, no evidence.

Faking the fingerprints hadn't been too difficult. He'd printed them out on a transparency, using as much ink as possible, and took an impression from the toner with liquid latex. The only clues from the bomb would point in the wrong direction: to Hayes, and to false enemies.

The Mechanic stoked the visions in Bradac: the entry into a new life; the forgiveness of sins at the moment the martyr's blood is shed; the immediate admission to heaven, no suffering in the tomb, the privilege of standing in the highest gardens of heaven, next to God, among the prophets, saints, and righteous believers, and the marriage to the houri, the heavenly maidens.

"Can you see it?"

"I can see it."

"Can you see it?" It was almost a chant.

"It's beautiful." Bradac stared into the middle distance of the dingy warehouse, ran his thumb along the handheld detonator, and began to weep as he smiled. "I can see it, I can see it."

In his unsteady gaze, the maidens danced in the garden.

CHAPTER 33

THE PAIN WAS everything when I came to, a ringing in my ears, electric-blue lines arcing across the inside of my eyelids. I was on my back on what felt like a tile floor. My head rested on rolled fabric, a used T-shirt, from the smell of it. I opened my eyes. White light flooded in. I closed them again. The injuries were plenty, but they seemed so small next to the guilt I felt, filling my body like some black poison.

Kelly; where was she? My mind raced quickly to the worst: she was dead. And that was just my small, private pain. I had helped Hayes kill the main witness against him, led him to whatever Nazar was hiding, moved him one step closer to his goal of using whatever tool of destruction he had stolen from Riggs.

I had wanted to believe that Hayes had done no wrong. That he could be redeemed. That anyone could. Because I needed redemption.

Riggs had warned me. Kelly had warned me. I'd refused to listen. And Kelly would pay.

Kelly. Goddamn it, why hadn't they just done me a favor and killed me during the firefight?

I opened my eyes again, just a millimeter or two. The light diffracted through my lashes. I was in a modest home that looked brand-new. It was unfurnished. The solvent smells of paint and processed wood lingered. To my right there was a medical kit and some bloody gauze. Men moved in and out of the room. I closed my eyes, waited for the men to leave.

My hand stole to the side.

I waited for the shouts, the kicks in my ribs. None came.

"Over here." It sounded like Hayes. Footsteps drew closer.

"Speedy, have you seen the shears?"

He moved away. Then stopped. I felt the plastic handles under my palm, the metal point against my wrists. They would kill me five seconds after I went for it, I knew, but they would be doing me a favor.

I gripped the shears tightly and steeled myself to attack.

This wasn't the first time I'd lain on a cold floor waiting for death.

The first was after I killed the woman, Emily. She was an anesthesiologist I worked with in Afghanistan, part of a forward surgical team at Camp Dagger.

Dagger; that's what made me angrier than anything else. Hayes had said Samael was behind the Camp Dagger attack, had used it as a way to draw me in. He had exploited the death of a woman I loved, profaned her. And I had fallen for it, given in to revenge.

The camp was little more than a collection of plywood huts and tents, but it was our best chance to save the casualties near the line. It sat in a valley not far from Gardez. We were hemmed in by ice-covered mountains and rock-filled defiles on all sides, but the valley itself was beautiful in summer; sheep and goats grazed, and green fields surrounded an oxbow in the river.

Emily was a few years younger than I was and came from the sticks outside Louisville. I didn't have time for much of anything outside of medicine, hadn't had for years. I liked being busy. It kept me from thinking about the dead boys at K-38, about what I had done. It had been so many years since then. I was a doctor now, a lieutenant commander.

Between the helicopters shuttling urgent surgical cases in and all the cutting, there wasn't time for sleep, let alone relationships. She was a good doctor, one of the best I'd ever worked with, and that was the end of it. I couldn't let myself be distracted by the thought of those green eyes looking at me from over the mask.

I remember the day it started. A kid came in, a nineteen-year-old Marine with an unexploded rocket-propelled grenade in his abdomen. The EOD techs called us out to a second operating room, surrounded by blast barriers. We wore flak jackets and helmets over our scrubs.

One of the corpsmen started to say that if anything happened to him, someone should tell his wife and kid that—and Emily cut him off, sent him out of the room. No nonessential personnel. "I don't need a fucking jinx *and* a bomb in here."

The anesthesiologist runs the OR. Emily knew exactly what to do. She shut off everything electric. Took the patient's pulse using the second hand of her watch, dosed the anesthesia by counting drip by drip.

I cut out the RPG and put the kid back together as best I could with the tissue that remained. He'd be using a colostomy bag for the rest of his life, but that was better than the alternative.

Afterward, Emily and I ducked outside and watched the EODs blow the grenade a mile off.

She offered me a cigarette. Most of the doctors smoked. I would take one now and then, but I passed that night.

"How'd you know what to do in there?" I asked.

"An article I read."

"That's it?"

She nodded, dropped her head in her hands, and sighed. "Jesus Christ."

She had been pure confidence the entire operation, had steeled our whole team, and now she could finally let the fear out.

"Sometimes I picture myself in a nice gastroenterology practice in Buckhead," she said. "Six hundred K a year. In at eight, out at four, just sitting in an ergonomic chair at the head of the table and watching the GI guys look up people's asses all day."

"Sorry, Miller," I said, and I thought of everything I knew about her. "I think you'd get bored with asses."

"A girl can dream."

It's hard explaining what it's like downrange. The rest of the world is an abstraction. Death is everywhere, so life draws you in. We weren't looking for it, but it found us.

Personnel weren't supposed to sleep together, but that only added to the tension as we passed each other in the halls every day, sat side by side in the DFAC—the dining facility. Even before we got together, others could see it coming off us like a cloud of guilt as we talked like old accomplices or sneaked off after a sixteen-hour shift to drink some of the moonshine her father made in his own still and shipped to her in perfume bottles.

She liked Afghanistan, liked that people still rode horses there. It reminded her of where she had grown up.

We were good. We kept it secret, never flouted the rules. The only chance to be open about it was on R&R. It probably shows how fucked up things were that we went to Kashmir for R&R. We rented a houseboat on a lake in the mountains in Srinagar, looking out over the Mughal gardens and floating lotus.

We were together for fourteen months and due to return to the States soon. There would be time for everything.

Two nights after we got back to the base, we were walking back from the operating theater to our B huts when she turned to me with a look on her face like she was about to do a cliff dive.

"I'm late."

I was too surprised to say anything. When she was thirty-one, doctors had told her she most likely wouldn't be able to have kids.

"How late?" I asked.

"I'm eight weeks pregnant."

"But…"

"Never count out a Miller. My mom was forty and on the pill when she got pregnant with me."

We were standing at the edge of a dusty airstrip. The Spin Ghar Mountains and the Khyber Pass were silhouetted against the stars.

"Marry me," I said.

"What are you doing, Byrne? No, no, no."

"Say yes," I said. I dropped to one knee.

"What? Come on. Get up."

There had been so much death, so much blood, and now life.

"I'll get up if you say yes."

"You're serious."

"Don't I look serious?"

"You look ridiculous."

"Say yes."

"Yes… we can talk about it."

I stood up, lifted her in the air, and kissed her.

"All I heard was yes."

* * *

She died within the month—a rocket attack. Shit luck, was all. We took fire all the time, would hole up in the bunker for hours. She had sneaked into my quarters. The blast woke me up. Everything was chaos and noise. She was beside me, and her body was torn apart.

We had just been lying there, but her body protected me. The rockets kept coming. She was awake for a minute before shock set in.

"It's deep, Tom," she said. "See what you can do."

They called us into the bunkers, but I ignored it.

They blew up the main OR. I carried her to the secondary operating theater. There was penetrating trauma to her chest and abdomen.

She tried to say something else, but I couldn't make it out. I've spent two years wondering what she said. She went unresponsive, not breathing, pulseless, but with some electrical activity in the heart.

I had two corpsmen with me. The procedure is called an emergency thoracotomy, or sometimes a clamshell. I cut her chest from sternum to flank and spread her ribs.

The only good thing was that the injury was to the right side of her heart. That gave her a chance. The shrapnel had torn the right ventricle. Blood poured out with every pump. The heart muscle around the wound was shredded, but I gathered enough tissue to sew it up. Fifty-six stitches and a double square knot. She was hemorrhaging in the lower abdomen, but the lungs were fine, and I had sealed up her heart.

The heart stopped. I took it in my hands and began to help it beat. The sutures held. No blood came from the ventricle. The gunfire crackled outside. I kept going, a hundred beats per minute, far slower than my own heart rate. And it started to move in my hands.

I thought I saw her fingers extend to reach for me, but I knew that she was too far gone for the movement to be intentional. Her heart continued to beat. I closed up the thoracic cavity and set to work on her abdominal wound. The pulse was strong, and then nothing.

She was gone.

The autopsy found that the ventricle had ruptured near the repair. They had had to pull me away from her body.

I worked through the night on the rest of the casualties. Operated for fifty hours before they forced me to bed. I didn't want to stop, couldn't stand to be alone with my thoughts. I had been caught by a secondary blast, a chunk of stone blown out from a Hesco barrier. I didn't tell anyone about the broken ribs, about the pain. I couldn't stop moving.

I don't know if it was the ribs or what happened to Emily, but I couldn't sleep. I would work until I couldn't stand any longer, and when I had to catch a few hours' rest, I would dose myself against the pain. It was a way to shut my mind down, to keep the thoughts at bay as I lay there trying to pretend it hadn't happened, that I hadn't failed her, killed her.

I had been going too hard, for too long.

I was in the pharmacy tent. I slid the needle into my arm, and within a few seconds, my legs crumpled. I'd grabbed the wrong vial. I knew it must have been a paralytic because I hit the floor like a sack of dirt. The muscles in my arms drew tight in spasm, then let go: fasciculation. That meant it was succinylcholine. We called it sux around the OR.

It paralyzes the patient. My diaphragm slowed, a last shallow breath from my still lips. My lungs emptied but didn't refill.

You would never use it without a ventilator. The patient would asphyxiate. And you never use sux alone, without general anesthesia, or the patient would be fully conscious but unable to move or breathe on his own, a living death. You could end up operating on someone who feels every stroke of the blade but can give no sign or reaction as you cut.

I could see the syringe at the edge of my field of view but couldn't control the muscles to turn my eyes toward it. The plunger was a third of the way down. Thirty-three milligrams of the typical one-hundred-milligram dose. I weighed a hundred and eighty-five pounds. The paralysis would last two to ten minutes. Brain cells typically start to die after one minute; real damage kicks in at three, and by ten, no one recovers.

A horse race.

I was buried alive inside my body. The air started to run out. I willed myself to breathe but couldn't. Sixty seconds without oxygen. My mind played with the numbers. I tried to distract myself, hide in the calculations, but in the end it was a coin toss whether that first gasp would come before my life ended.

My vision began to waver, an early sign of hypoxia.

I didn't care.

I couldn't stop thinking that maybe I made the wrong call on the thoracotomy. Maybe I missed something. Maybe I'd killed her when I cut her open and grabbed her heart. The ventricle had given out. The surgeon's stitch is like the runner's stride; it's personal, distinctive, the foundation of everything else. And mine had failed. I didn't care what they'd said about underlying tissue damage. It was my fault, my table, my stitches. I'd killed her.

I waited for death.

Ninety seconds...one hundred.

I blacked out, but my body kept fighting, and somewhere in the dark came that last saving gasp.

The paralytic wore off. I was breathing again. I would live, like it or not.

But I was done.

I left the navy. They cleared me of any blame, commended me, but I knew the truth. I skipped the ceremonies. The medals came in the mail. I signed up with a locum tenens shop, worked trauma at a string of hospitals. I tried to make up for the lives I had taken with the lives I saved but I always came up short.

It gave me an excuse to keep moving. When you stay in one place, you find people, you get close. They trust you. And everyone who had ever trusted me was dead.

Over time, I started to believe what the others told me. That this was crazy. That I had to stop. That I couldn't be alone forever. But it had been greed on my part.

I'd wanted what I didn't deserve. And then I brought Kelly in and made her trust me.

And now I'd killed her too.

"They were right over here," Hayes said. His voice was close. I could smell him. His fingers touched my neck, probed for the pulse of my carotid artery, held there. I lay still, focusing on the breath coming and going from my belly, trying not to betray that I was awake.

He put his hand on my cheek. It felt like 220-grit sandpaper. His thumb touched my eye, pulled the lid up. I looked at him, fought the impulse to squeeze those shears tight. I couldn't afford to show any sign of consciousness. He shone a light in my eye, watched the pupil contract, let the lid shut.

I heard the brush of his boots as he stepped away, then I leaped for him.

He had his hand on his pistol by the time I hit his back. I pressed the shears under his jawline, felt the skin stretch and tent, looked around the room, and found myself at the intersection of three gun barrels—Hayes's team, arrayed to one side. I kept my head behind Hayes's as much as possible. These guys had drilled hostage rescues in the dark, on bucking ships and planes, practiced shooting until their hands bled. Killing me would be as tough as opening a jar.

"Don't fire," Hayes said. "Byrne, you have to listen."

"Where's Kelly?"

"This isn't what you think."

"Where the hell is she? Is she okay?"

I saw it in their eyes before I felt it. Someone was behind me. A hand clamped on my shoulder.

I turned, kept the shears on Hayes's neck, and hit the person behind me with my forearm.

"Tom!"

Kelly stumbled back.

CHAPTER 34

Caro and Riggs waited in the wardroom, a cramped dining area with vinyl-upholstered chairs; luxurious by shipboard standards. Riggs ran his thumb over the handle of an empty coffee cup and glanced at the clock.

"Where are they?"

Caro had traced Nazar's call releasing the evidence. It had gone to an estate lawyer named Shah in Laguna Niguel. Caro sent his men to Shah's office to intercept him before he could deliver the evidence.

That had been forty minutes ago.

Caro checked his phone. "I don't know. I can send—"

The mobile buzzed in his hand. He answered it, and the other man's voice came through the line. "You're sure?" he asked.

The other party spoke.

"Do not move. I'll deal with you later."

He ended the call.

"What happened?" Riggs asked.

"They found Shah. He must have seen them. He fled. A hundred and twenty miles an hour on the Five in his Jaguar. He couldn't handle it, lost control, and went headfirst into a divider. He's dead."

"The evidence?"

"He exited his office with a strongbox. They were able to take it before the police and EMTs arrived, pulled it from the car. But it was empty."

"What?"

"They think he was going to retrieve the evidence."

"From where?"

"We don't know."

Riggs threw the mug against the bulkhead. The ceramic shattered.

"Now what the fuck do we do?"

"Nazar is still alive?" Caro asked.

"Yes. No one touched her."

"Good. Because she's the only one who can lead us to it."

"She'll never give it up."

"There are ways. What about this mess up in LA at the Egyptian embassy?"

"I don't know. There's no word."

"And Hayes?"

"We have narrowed it down to his rally site, Italy. We'll have a team there in five minutes."

"It's not his style to wait. We have to assume he's coming for us." Caro took a photo from his pocket and slid it across the table. It was a woman holding a child.

"Who is that?"

"Hayes's wife and daughter," Caro said. "Cox found their address. It's near Raleigh." Lauren Hayes had gone back to her maiden name, Parker, and moved three times since the scandal. She had cut off all contact with the command and the other unit wives in an attempt to distance herself from her husband's crimes.

"We should have gotten to them first. We need the leverage."

"There are still ways to use her to control Hayes, even after the authorities get involved," Caro said. "Tell them that she is dangerous and involved in the plot, harboring, collaborating. We can still get to her. Hayes will have to choose between coming after us and saving his wife."

"I'll get started."

"Leave Nazar to me," Caro said.

He climbed down the ladders to the third deck. Hall stood outside the compartment. Caro approached, dialed in the combination to the door, and opened it.

Riggs remained in the passageway as Hall followed Caro inside. Caro flicked open the knife and moved toward the old woman chained to the bulkhead. She looked up, stared straight into his blue eyes.

"You couldn't kill me before, and you can't kill me now, Aziz."

Of course it was his mother. Always the whore for whatever army passed through.

He wasn't going to kill her. That was true. Not yet.

"Leave us," he said to Hall.

The door slammed shut behind him. He balanced the knife in his hand and took a step closer.

CHAPTER 35

"Kelly!" I said and reached for her as she stumbled back. She caught my hand and kept herself from falling. "Are you okay?"

She straightened up, touched her face. "Drop the shears, Tom," she said. "These guys saved us, both of us. They weren't the ones shooting at us. It was Riggs and his men."

She had a gun holstered on her hip. If she was being coerced, there's no way she'd be armed. I saw it in her manner as well: she was telling the truth.

My hand fell to my side. Hayes hovered to my left, close enough to take me down.

The shears dropped from my fingers to the floor, and I wrapped my arms around Kelly, feeling her warmth and the heart beating in her chest.

"Thank God you're okay," I said.

"You too."

A faint red mark showed on her cheek where my arm had hit.

"Sorry about that," I said.

"Don't worry. I thought you knew how to throw a punch."

That got me smiling, Hayes too.

A neat row of stitches ran just above her hairline. "That's nice work," I said.

"Hayes did it," she replied. "He and Cook had to fight their way to us."

That made sense. I hadn't been able to understand how I'd managed to buy time with my 9 mm against two guys with MP7s.

A crumpled menu lay on the counter—Volare Pizza Restaurant. "Let me guess. We're in Italy."

"Yes. Should be safe for now."

I looked into the living room and saw a man lying on the floor, bandages covering his shoulder and neck. Standing over him was a man I barely recognized. The last time I had seen him was back at the safe house near the Mexican border. It was Hayes's medic.

His left hand was bandaged, the broken fingers still splinted. The neck wound was covered but clearly wasn't causing any problems since he was in good enough shape to be checking on the casualty.

"Green, was it?"

"Yeah."

"How are you doing?"

"All right. Takes some getting used to." He lifted his hand. "Thanks for fixing me up."

"Don't mention it. What happened to him?"

I knelt over the casualty. It was Cook, the youngest of the crew. His right cheek and most of the ear was gone.

"Multiple gunshot wounds, shrapnel. Blunt-force trauma to his chest."

"Was that for us?" I asked Hayes.

"He was doing the job, that's all. Don't worry about it."

"Had him stable, but something's off. Heart rate is rising, BP is dropping."

Cook looked up at us with terror in his eyes. He tried to talk but could only pant.

I looked at his trachea, shifted almost imperceptibly to his left. His chest seemed hyperexpanded.

"This is going to suck for a second, okay?"

Cook nodded. He was barely breathing now. If this kept going, circulatory collapse was a few minutes away.

I put my ear to his chest, tapped it on the left and then the right. The right sounded like a drum, and there was no trace of air moving.

I looked to Green.

"Tension pneumothorax?" he said.

Trauma to the chest, often a broken rib, can tear a lung. With each breath the patient takes, air enters the lung and then escapes into the chest cavity. Sometimes the tear works like a one-way valve, allowing air to leave the lung and enter the chest but not letting the air back out. Pressure in the chest cavity builds, causing the lung to collapse and, as with Cook here, compressing the vena cava and other major blood vessels, obstructing the blood flow to the heart.

"You have a chest tube?" I asked.

"No. Just the needle kit." He handed me a package containing a 15-gauge needle catheter attached to a syringe, a length of tubing, and a valve, and we both put on gloves.

"You want to do it?" I asked as I tore open the plastic, doing my best to keep everything sterile. Green had been shattered, but he could rebuild.

He looked from me to the kit and back. Cook moaned and blacked out.

"Sure."

Green took the needle catheter in his right hand as I swabbed the right side of the chest wall with Betadine. He inserted it into the skin about two inches below the middle of the collarbone. His hand didn't shake.

He advanced the needle into the chest, pulling back on the plunger, and suddenly air rushed into the syringe. Green smiled as he threaded the catheter farther into the space and then removed the needle and syringe. The trapped air that had been compressing the heart and lungs now had a way out. He'd just saved this man's life.

I grabbed a stethoscope and listened; the lung had partially re-inflated, and there were breath sounds bilaterally. "Good," I said as I secured the catheter.

Green reached for a Heimlich valve, a one-way valve that would let air out when Cook exhaled but seal off when he inhaled, preventing another tension pneumo.

"It's broken," Green said.

I found a sterile surgical glove, snipped off one of the fingers, cut the tip off that, then taped it to the end of the catheter. It looked like a small windsock hanging from a plastic tube.

As Cook exhaled, air passed through the latex sleeve. When he breathed in, it sealed off, wrinkling up against itself, maintaining the vacuum in the space around the lung.

"That's how we used to do it before the kits, with a glove or a condom."

"Hayes told me you were a corpsman. You're a full doctor now?"

"Yeah."

"How long did that take?"

"A decade, not counting pre-reqs and military obligations."

"Jesus. I'll be lucky if I can stick a vein."

I pointed to his injured hand. "Let me take a look at that."

He held it out. I unwrapped the bandage and inspected the damage. There was minimal swelling, and he had full strength and normal sensation in the splinted fingers. It wasn't as bad as I'd thought.

"A good orthopedist and you'll be a hundred percent."

"I'll be lucky if I live to see tomorrow."

"We'll make it," I said, and I handed him a pair of shears. Medics and corpsmen wore them on their chests, clipped to the webbing of their body armor, almost like badges. "And then find an ortho guy. You'll be all right. From everything Hayes told me, you'd make a fine doctor."

"Thanks." He put the scissors in his chest pocket, then checked Cook's blood pressure, moving confidently.

"Hey," Cook said, eyes closed and slurring the words as he came to. "Green. You're alive. That's fucking awesome." He opened his eyes and focused on the tube coming out of his chest. The finger of the surgical glove filled and collapsed like a flag in a light breeze.

"What the hell is that?"

"A flutter valve. It's keeping you alive."

"Okay. Cool. My face hurts, man. How's my face?"

"It's not too bad. You're going to be fine."

"You're lying through your teeth, Green, but thanks. How'd I do?"

"You did great. Just take it easy."

"It feels so good to breathe. Oh." He closed his eyes again, took long deep breaths for a while. "Green...come here. I need to tell you something."

"You should rest."

"Green." He waved him closer. Green knelt beside him like a priest administering last rites.

"What is it, Cook? Are you okay?"

"How many South Americans"—he paused, winced against the pain—"does it take to screw in a lightbulb?"

"I don't know, Cook."

"A Brazilian."

Green snorted, then started laughing.

I left them and walked back to Hayes. "So Riggs went after Nazar at the same time we did."

"Yes."

"Jesus. I thought...I thought you were coming for us."

Hayes and his crew had done everything they could to pose as Riggs's men in order to mislead and provoke Nazar when they ambushed her. So when Riggs actually showed up, guns out, I assumed his shooters were Hayes and the team. "How'd they find us?"

"Ward picked up a second signal coming from Nazar's cell. They must have been tracking her, eavesdropping on her conversations. We tried to turn them against each other. We did our job too well."

I took one of the water bottles, poured some out into my hand, and wiped my face off.

"I'm sorry," I said to Hayes.

"You had no way of knowing who was taking shots at you. You trust me now?"

I drank some of the water. Swallowing made the pain in my skull flare up.

"I have to see that shipment you stole from the armored truck," I said. "I need to know what I'm part of."

Hayes crossed his arms. "For a guy who just tried to kill me, you're asking for a lot of trust." He considered it for a moment. "You've earned it, but you can't see it. The trunk is gone, Byrne."

"What is it?" I couldn't shake the images from Revelation, the seven seals, the seven trumpets. "Riggs had me thinking it was some kind of weapon, nuke or bio."

"It's the ultimate weapon, really."

"What did you do?"

"We dropped the trunk outside the Egyptian consulate. They should be opening it any second now, depending on their security posture."

"And then what?"

"Nothing. It's empty. The trunk was a false front, Byrne, to smuggle the shipment in. The Egyptians will have it in a museum soon unless some cultural attaché turns it around on the black market. We just needed to get rid of it. What matters is what was inside."

He walked over to a black trunk, one of eight stacked against the wall. I stepped closer, and he opened the lid.

CHAPTER 36

HAYES'S WIFE, WHO now went by the name Lauren Parker, turned a page in the textbook. She rested her elbow on the table and her head in her hand as she copied notes down onto an index card. The house was a modest ranch, neat, though showing its age, with deep-pile brown carpet and linoleum in the kitchen.

She was still wearing the scrubs she'd had on for fourteen hours. A year of coursework remained for her to become a nurse-practitioner. It had taken her a little longer than the others in her class because she was raising Maggie by herself and working full-time as a registered nurse. Plus things had been hard ever since Hayes...she tried not to think about Hayes and focused on the page:

The Cockcroft-Gault Equation for Creatinine Clearance

She worked through the problem set. Her daughter stood on a chair next to her. She had started asking questions about everything recently, which was normal for her age. But more and more, she asked about her father, and those questions Lauren didn't know how to answer.

Maggie mimicked her, placing her head in her hand and, armed with a crayon and a Babar book, pretending to work her own calculations.

Lauren couldn't help but crack up. She checked the clock on the stove: eight p.m. She should have put Maggie to bed fifteen minutes ago, but this was the only time they had together. The child thrived on the schedule, and it was selfish to let her stay up. But it was nice not to be alone, especially at night, out here in the middle of nowhere, with good reason to believe every creak of the house or engine in the distance represented a coming threat.

Ten more minutes, she told herself, and she returned to Cockcroft and Gault. She couldn't focus. After everything that happened, she was used to having eyes on her. For two years, every car, every passing stranger had seemed to be following her. And she'd learned to deal with the paranoia, but today had been different. She couldn't convince herself that it was all in her head, that no one was hunting her.

Were the police going to take her again for endless hours of questioning? Would the rumors start again? Would she have to move for the fourth time, change her name and cut ties once again? Part of her believed it would be Hayes, and she was never sure whether to be hopeful in those moments or afraid. And then it would cycle: hating the men who did it to him, hating him, and sometimes hating herself for hating him.

Maggie put her finger on a graph of drug concentrations and did her fake-reading bit: "Blah-blah-blah."

Lauren looked at the page.

"Exactly what I was thinking, kiddo." She scooped her up in her arms. "Time for bed."

Maggie rested her head on her mother's shoulder. She pointed out the kitchen window. "What's that?"

Lauren turned. She could see the dome lights in the vans and trucks. There were at least four. She went to the bathroom, kept the light off, and looked out the window. Two squads of four men were approaching the house.

There was a pistol in a safe above the fridge. A long gun locked in the hall closet. Instinct told her to grab one or both and defend her child. She was a better shot than 90 percent of the guys at the range. But that would only give them what they wanted, confirm their fears, grant them a reason to kill her.

"Bailey!" She snapped her fingers and pointed to her daughter's door, closest to the living room. The chocolate Lab slipped inside, and she closed the door behind him.

They would come from the front. Lauren took Maggie into the kitchen. She knelt down and looked at her.

"Sweetheart, we're going to play a game. We're going to lie on the floor and keep our hands out to the sides no matter what happens. It may be scary, but we're going to be brave and just stay where we are and not get up and not run. It's all a game. Do you understand?"

"No."

Lauren's hands were trembling so badly she could see them shaking her daughter's arms.

Maggie's lower lip stuck out. "I'm scared."

"It's going to be fine. Will you play? For Mommy?"

"Okay."

"Here we go, baby." She kissed her on the forehead and laid her down.

"Police!" The door splintered in, and something metal tinked against the wall. A half a second later, the explosion shook the house. Pure white light burned Lauren's eyes.

Maggie was silent for a moment, then opened her mouth wide and held it, held it before the sobs broke through.

"Stay there, sweetie! It's just a game!"

This was a night raid. It was what her husband did for a living, in Afghanistan and Iraq and Pakistan and the Horn of Africa and God knew where else.

She heard the rattling of the load carriers. It was bad enough that they were here but worse that she had seen them coming. This was not her husband. These were small-town police, tweaked on adrenaline.

One glint, one move, one shout. An ashtray, a wallet, a silver necklace. Anything could set them off. She had to be brave at the wrong end of the gun, give them nothing to react to. If she let the fear take her and grabbed Maggie and ran like every nerve in her body was screaming for her to do, they'd kill her.

The sliding door to the patio blew out and sent a shower of glass into the living room, skittering along the floor toward her daughter. She looked back, saw the men throw the forty-pound battering ram down and rush in: four, eight, twelve. She stood up and tried to count as they blinded her with flashlights.

"Where is he!"

"Who?"

"Your husband!"

"He's not my husband. I haven't seen him in years. My daughter is here. Please. It's just the two of us. Please. We're cooperating. Please don't shoot."

She knelt down. He pushed her to the ground, spread her arms out to the sides.

"Put your hands out. What are you carrying? Who else is here? Do you have any weapons?"

"It's just my daughter and me. There's a pistol in the kitchen. Rifle in the closet. They're locked and I have a permit. There's a dog in that first bedroom. He's friendly. Please don't hurt—"

Another man stormed over. "Where is your husband! You got any guns?"

Maggie screamed for her mother, boosted herself onto her knees. The lights crossed to her in the dark.

"Just stay there, sweetie," Lauren said. "Please...please don't hurt my daughter. Please don't take her away. Her aunt lives fifteen minutes from here. If you're going to arrest me, please let me call her to take my—"

"You're lying. We know he's—"

Wood splintered in the hallway. The dog's barks echoed down the hall. They kicked down the bedroom door.

"He's friendly! Please don't hurt—"

Three cracks of rifle fire. The dog whimpered.

"Did you have to shoot my dog!" she screamed.

Other men heard the gunfire.

"Shooter? Shooter?"

The voices drowned each other out. More shots. The cries of the dog, hurt badly. Maggie screaming, and someone else groaning in pain.

"I'm hit! Shooter! Shooter!"

More shots. The room stank of smoke. Lauren gagged.

Some cops yelled for order, but the panic was contagious.

"Bailey!" Maggie screamed. Lauren saw her stand. She was going to run.

"Stay still, baby. Please." Lauren reached for her. "My daughter. Don't hurt her!"

"Don't you move!" A light mounted on the barrel of a rifle shone in Lauren's eyes. "Are you trying to warn him? Where is he!"

Lauren saw the gun lights converge, the lines pass through her and her daughter, reflect off windows, illuminate the sweaty faces of the men, veins plump in their necks, eyes wide with fear and panic, their fingers too tense on their triggers.

"Lie down, baby! Please—"

Her daughter took a wobbling step toward the dog, arms outreached.

"Freeze!"

Lauren saw the officer near the kitchen, wearing black goggles and a black helmet, take aim.

"No!"

Her daughter fell to the floor.

CHAPTER 37

HAYES STOOD TO my right. I put my hand on the lid of the trunk and looked inside.

At first it seemed like reams of printer paper wrapped in thick blue and clear plastic. Through a transparent section, I could see it was made of many smaller plastic-wrapped bricks. Then I saw Benjamin Franklin, with his scraggly hair and sad eyes, staring back at me.

"How much is it?"

"Sixty-eight million," Hayes said. "All four of those are full."

"Jesus, you could buy an F-16 with that."

"Two, actually. Or a Pakistani nuke. It cost only half a million to pull 9/11 off, and those guys didn't have the kind of connections and state support Samael has."

Hayes lifted one of the bundles, considered it, then let it fall back. He shut the case. "The root of all evil, prior to every bomb, every bullet. Sell your cloak and buy a sword."

"It's the black money Riggs stole. You stole it back."

"That was our first step. Take the money, his strength. He doesn't have all those people working for him because they believe in him."

"What was he doing with it?"

"He plays it off as some service project, giving jobs to warriors after they leave the military, but he's hiring guns. We didn't know exactly why. Then we saw him with Samael. He doubled-down with him. He had the funds and the means and he's working with one of America's most dangerous enemies.

"I don't know what his exact motivation is, but he was a 'the worse, the better' kind of guy, believed the U.S. should let things fall apart, let the bad guys wipe each other out, and then step in to start rebuilding the region from scratch."

"Is stealing this enough to stop him?"

"No. We took his legs out, made it hard for him, but there are other ways. All we know is that he is planning something big, he has unofficial sanction, and he could pull the trigger any minute."

"Who did Nazar call? Didn't she order the evidence to be released?"

"A lawyer, an Iranian exile up in Orange County. He's dead. Car crash. Tried to outrun Riggs's men."

"And the evidence?"

"It's still out there. We were able to pick that up from their comms. They hit him too early. He tried to run, lost control of his Jaguar. They forced the lockbox he was carrying. And it was empty. He must have been going to get it."

"So Nazar is the only one left."

"Yes."

"Can we get to her, maybe turn her against Riggs?"

"If we can rescue Nazar, after what Riggs has done, she would almost certainly turn, but Riggs already has her. He took her in the firefight. That's the last audio pickup we got: 'Keep her alive enough to talk.'"

"They're going to torture her."

"Yes."

"Where is she?"

"They're all together, on a ship that Riggs controls docked about an hour from here."

"How much time do we have?"

"They're skilled at this sort of thing. Hours, if that."

"It's all right," I said. "We'll get to her in time."

A look of doubt crossed Hayes's face.

"They killed Foley," Kelly said.

"God. I'm sorry."

Hayes took a deep breath, refocused. "Foley was tough, but they may have broken him. They're going to come for us with everything now."

"Then let's get to them first."

Things were uneasy between Riggs's and Caro's men. The colonel's soldiers dressed like typical contractors—ball caps, jeans, beards—while Caro's wore two-thousand-dollar suits and carried themselves like City of London bankers. Caro's lieutenant, a man named Kasem, had insisted on driving separately and now kept a side conversation going with his men in a language the others couldn't understand.

This was rally point Italy: a dry creek bed along the side of the highway, surrounded by new subdivisions.

"Are you sure you have the grids right?" asked Kasem.

He looked over the map and checked the GPS. "They must be using SARDOTs."

Kasem cursed in a foreign tongue. SARDOT—an acronym for

search-and-rescue dot—is a sort of geographic code word that's changed daily or even more often. When locations are communicated on open radio nets, they aren't given exactly but with respect to a predetermined point known only to friendly forces, an offset that obscures the real location to anyone listening in. These men were a mile from the home where Hayes and Byrne were hiding, but they had no way of knowing that.

"They must be close."

"Most likely. But we won't be able to find them unless they screw up, break radio silence, or move out."

Kasem lifted his binoculars and scanned the hills, passing without notice over Hayes's safe house where it stood among the thousand other newly built homes.

CHAPTER 38

HAYES STEPPED OUT of the truck and lifted his spotting scope. Sheer cloth covered the lens to stop any reflections. We were on a hill looking down over a commercial marina with three concrete docks. Across the bay came the sound of sailboat halyards clanging against masts like church bells.

"That's it," Hayes said, pointing to the docks.

Our chances of rescuing Nazar were dwindling by the second. It's called progression of captivity. When you're taken by hostile forces, no matter what your situation is, it's only going to get worse: more secure, deeper in enemy territory, harder to overwhelm or escape.

Ward, Cook, and Green remained at Italy with the money. Ward had tracked Riggs's communications to this port where Moret, Speed, Kelly, and I had just arrived.

I followed Hayes's extended finger. On the closest pier, I saw a ship's silhouette against the ripples of moonlight on the water.

"The *Shiloh*," Hayes said.

"You know it?"

Hayes nodded. "Every bulkhead. Operated out of it for months. It's a prototype, built under contract. It sucked up billions, but never went into production. It wasn't technically navy, so they used it for classified missions and then turned it into a floating brig to hold prisoners they wanted to keep off the books. A floating black site."

"Riggs controls it."

"Yes. Our only chance is to snatch Nazar back while they're moving her."

I could hear the ship's engines droning. To reach the *Shiloh*, first we needed to get past a chain-link fence that surrounded the whole complex, then past another fence inside, which ran between two industrial buildings and was topped by razor wire. Finally, at the base of the dock, there was a tall metal barrier.

"There's probably conventional security at the perimeter, shared for the commercial marina. Riggs looks like he has his own people closer in on the *Shiloh*'s dock."

"How many?" Speed asked.

"Can't say. Safe side, given his habits, eight to twelve, another dozen or more on the ship."

"We should take her now," Speed said.

"If we can take them by surprise. We only have the numbers for a stealth approach."

Moret set up a prone sniper position behind a tangle of sage bushes and cut away the low growth. It would hide her muzzle flash and let her overlook the entire port.

We sneaked down to the base of the first fence. Hayes pulled out a twelve-inch pair of wire cutters and clipped the fencing right next to the post, then pulled it open wide enough for us to pass through. He took a length of gray paracord and laced it through where he had cut the fence.

If you didn't look close, it was impossible to tell it had ever been breached.

"You two stay here and cover us," he said to me and Kelly. "We'll see if we can get through the next fence. Wait for my signal."

"Check," I said. Kelly and I put twelve feet between us and watched Hayes disappear down the hill toward the razor-wire fence.

Hayes and Speed moved silently toward the *Shiloh*'s dock, avoiding the sight lines of the cameras. Speed raked open the American padlock on the razor-wire fence in a few seconds. There was a main gate through the high metal wall that guarded the dock, but Speed assumed the guards would be watching that entrance. Instead, he and Hayes were headed for a small secondary door.

They moved toward it, passing behind two corrugated-aluminum trailers and a parked truck, then a large steel job box. A crane on six-foot tires covered the last twelve feet to the gate.

Hayes halted. He could hear footsteps on the other side of the crane. He listened as the guard moved closer and then stopped. The flint of a lighter rasped, and they could smell smoke. Hayes unsheathed his knife.

The guard started moving again, the footfalls growing quieter. Hayes edged around and saw him disappear behind a trailer.

He raised his finger to Speed: *One minute.*

They ran for the door through the high metal barrier, their last obstacle before the *Shiloh*'s dock.

It was solid steel, with an Assa Abloy lock, certified to stand up to a skilled lock picker for thirty minutes at least. Speed unzipped a pouch on his chest and pulled out a tool that looked like a small power screwdriver. It was a Falle decoder, a skeleton key available only to select military, intelligence, and law-enforcement agencies. Hayes and Speed had met with Falle. He was a former British commando who worked out of a little-known factory on the island of Jersey.

The business end was shaped like a key. Most keys have notches—called bits—at different heights. The correct combination opens the lock. But this decoder had bits that were adjustable.

Speed started with them all level at the full height of the key blade. He slid the decoder in and applied a light twisting tension. A thin metal rod ran through the handle of the device and allowed Speed to jiggle each bit and each corresponding pin inside the lock. If the pin was at the correct height to open the lock, he would feel the slightest wiggle. If wrong, there would be no give at all.

He moved the rod and felt each pin. Number five was correct. He took the decoder out, and using another tool, he lowered each bit slightly, except for number five.

He put it back in and felt the pins.

Nothing. The rest were still bound.

He lowered them again.

One and three were now at the correct height.

The Falle tool allowed intelligence operatives to decode a lock over multiple visits. All they would need was ten seconds unattended. They would do one height at a time in the embassy, under the noses of their targets. And the decoder, unlike other nondestructive entry techniques, left no forensic evidence.

"He's coming back," Hayes said.

Speed worked his way down the bit heights. Then he felt the slightest give. The door was unlocked. It had taken sixty seconds. He pulled the decoder and hid behind the crane.

The guard continued on his rounds. Hayes radioed for Byrne

and Britten to join them through the gate they had left unlocked in the razor-wire fence. As the two crept up to meet them, Speed put the decoder back in, with the correct combination still set, and opened the door a crack.

Hayes checked in with Moret for an overview, then peered through the door. He could see the *Shiloh*.

Little Bill walked across his path, then turned back. Hayes saw only that one man covering one sector. Moret had a better view and had given him the position of several other sentries. Together, that was enough for Hayes to understand Riggs's entire security posture around the ship.

They were waiting for an attack. He craned his neck, and the assault plan came to him: *Put Byrne and Britten on the carbines for cover. Remain in the shadows beside the gate, take Bill from behind with a knife, and make a cut to the carotid on each side of his neck; he'll bleed out in a half a minute. Go over the port side, skip the pilothouse, stack on the door with Speed; breach, bang, and go below shooting.*

The steps came naturally, without conscious thought, like moving his legs on a ship to keep his balance.

"Let's go," Speed said.

Hayes had been at the christening of Bill's boy, but that wasn't what gave him pause. Another guard was making rounds in the distance. They didn't have enough guns for an assault against a well-prepared enemy. If they were at sea, in the chaos of noise and darkness and wind, they could take them by surprise, but not here, not with security on land and on the ship. Their chance was to take Nazar in transit, but now she was buttoned up. He knew the hold where they would put her, an old crypto vault they used as a cell. He needed a half a dozen shooters at least, and Moret's rifle would do him no good once they went below.

He ran it every way, longer on stealth, faster now, coming over the bowlines, shooting first, pure kinetic violence.

The end result was always the same: they would be dead before they reached the second deck.

There was a better way. They had the gear cached.

"No," Hayes said. "We can't take them head-on."

"You're worried about killing?"

"No," Hayes said. "Just killing for no reason. We're not murderers."

"You're the only one who believes that."

"It's the truth."

"How many did we kill?"

"That was war. It was different."

"Why? Because a bastard like Riggs told us so? Killing is killing, and a few more traitors doesn't matter. You want to screw us all by playing prince? You're a warrior. Act like one."

Hayes watched Bill lift his radio. "They're waiting for us."

"Fuck this," Speed said, and he fixed his sights on the sentry.

The deckhands on the *Shiloh* threw off the stern lines. "They're leaving," Speed said. "We need to take them now."

"Speed. We've lost surprise. We've lost the initiative. We have the gear to take that ship, but this is not the way. We need to fall back. If we go direct assault, we'll have to kill every one of them, and we'll die before we finish."

Hayes had seen it before, many times, anger short-circuiting reason. The only way to sate it was by killing. It was as dangerous as enemy fire. And he could see it infecting Byrne as well, the adrenaline rising, the fear giving way to a taste for blood.

"You're afraid," Speed said. "You've lost the will. There's no time. I need suppressive fire. I'm going."

"Speed," Hayes said. "Listen to me. They want us to come. It's a trap, a shooting gallery. There's a better way. The water. I'm ordering you—"

"You can't. We're not soldiers anymore. We're nothing. Now, give me a base of fire." He brought his rifle across his chest.

"Don't." Hayes grabbed for his arm, but he took off in a crouch along the dock.

He was ten feet out when the first shots came, every fifth a tracer, burning red through the night. Hayes took a knee and aimed at the shooter. The fire stopped, but more picked up from the ship.

Speed got twenty more feet. Hayes moved into the open door, taking out the enemy guns one by one.

More fire. Speed took two stumbling steps, then fell forward into the shadows.

Byrne lifted the radio. "Speed. Speed."

Hayes ducked back and grabbed his arm.

"Stay off the comms."

Floodlights fixed on the body. The volley had taken Speed's head off from the jaw up. Rounds filled the corpse. The tracers burned in the flesh.

"Fall back," Hayes barked to Byrne and Britten.

"What about you?"

"I'll take those shooters. I need to get to the body. They can't take our radios.

"Go," Hayes said, and he moved toward the gunfire as it closed in on them, thundered against the steel.

Byrne and Britten ran fifteen feet before they were hemmed in by fire and took cover behind the job box. Kelly reached forward and squeezed his arm. A tracer round punched through the metal, burning red, and slit the air between them.

CHAPTER 39

WARD LIFTED THE Italian menu. On the back, with a ballpoint pen, she had sketched Sandstone Falls on the New River Gorge. Green glanced over without letting her see his interest. She didn't like to show her work, but he could never get over it. One minute she would be arguing about *Bloodsport,* and then she would go quiet and start drawing with startling realism.

The water seemed to rush down the page. She began sketching a figure; a child's form slowly appeared on the cheap paper. Green knew his anatomy and could see every contour drawn true to life. She stopped at the neck and jaw.

She never drew faces. Everything was exploitable.

She stood up, held the paper to the blue flame of the range, and watched it burn near the sink. Her radio crackled, but no voice came.

"What's that?" Green said. "No one should be on the net."

"Help." It was a man's voice, strained, racked by pain.

"Help."

"Go ahead."

"It's Speed. I need help. I'm hurt. Where are you?"

"Speed, are you in some kind of trouble?"

"Yes. I need help. What's your location?"

"I say again, *Are you in some kind of trouble?*"

"I need help."

She turned off the radio. *Are you in some kind of trouble.* They used the phrase as part of their coded communications. If a team member seemed to be under duress, he or she would be asked exactly those words, which would sound innocent enough to any captors. If the team member had been taken hostage, the response was *I'm doing all right* or *I'm not doing all right.* If free and clear, the response was *I'm doing good* or *I'm not doing good.* In this way, they could communicate with one another without tipping off the enemy.

The voice on the radio had said, *I need help;* whoever was on the other end of the line wasn't up on the codes. Ward had suspected it, but now it was confirmed. The man talking wasn't Speed, but he had his radio. She knew enough about Speed to realize that he wouldn't give it up alive.

He was gone.

"It's a trap! They must have been tracing us. We need to go, now!"

She lifted three bales of money, about a hundred pounds, and started for the truck.

"What about Cook?" Green asked.

"We'll get him last. The less time he spends moving, the more likely it is that he'll make it."

They ferried the cash out to the box truck, stacked it, and strapped it against the walls. Green carried his under his good arm.

Ward checked her watch—eight minutes since the call. She thought of trace times, SWAT response, as she hustled back inside.

She grabbed an IV bag and put it at the foot of Cook's litter. "Can you get that end?" she asked Green.

"Yeah," he said. He taped down the catheter with the improvised valve, then put the IV bag in his teeth and hoisted the litter with his good hand. Ward carried the other end.

They loaded Cook into the back of the truck. Ward followed him in.

"Get the engine going," she said, and she threw Green the keys. He snatched them out of the air and walked toward the cab. She cut a length of paracord and lashed the IV to the tie-down bars. As the truck shuddered to life, Cook opened his eyes.

"We going for a ride?" he slurred.

She put her hand to his cheek.

"Yeah. Sit tight."

"How'd I do back there? In the firefight?"

"You made us all proud, Cook. You did great."

"Did I tell you…"

"Tell me what, Cook?"

"About the corduroy…the corduroy pillows."

"What? Cook, are you okay?"

"Wait, it's, ah…"

"Why don't you tell me later, Cook," she said as she pivoted out of the back of the truck. "We've got to roll."

"Okay," he said, and he shut his eyes. "It's a good one. I think I got it this time."

She slammed the back door shut and was about to turn when she felt something press against her temple. It was cold and round, about the size of a quarter: the muzzle of a gun. The man holding the pistol came around and pressed the barrel against her forehead. He was wearing a suit.

"Hands," he said.

She raised her hands in the air, close to her temples, and to the gun. He took her sidearm.

Pfft.

A suppressed gunshot. She heard a cry and then a muted thump as a body hit the ground on the other side of the truck. Green. She held back the emotion and used the moment, the distraction, to swipe her right hand a few inches through the air as she stepped in the other direction.

The gun near her face fired. The blast from the pistol burned the skin of her cheek and ear and deafened her. The bullet gouged the side of her scalp. She grabbed the wrist of the man's gun hand, jerked it down and toward her. As he stepped forward to gain his balance, she threw her shin against the side of his knee and dropped all of her weight into it. The pop from a ligament, probably the ACL, sounded like a snap of the fingers. As he crumpled, she took his gun. He reached for hers, tucked inside his belt, but she kicked his hand, and her pistol went flying.

She hauled him off the ground, threw her arm around his neck, and held him in front of her body, the pistol to his head. He covered most of her. The key was to keep moving now, to not give them time to line up the shot at her head where it stood out from behind his.

She moved to the side of the truck. The man in the suit stumbled along with her, crying out from the pressure on his blown-out leg.

A truck pulled up. The headlights blinded her. She shot out the right light and put four bullets through the window where the driver's head should be. Two more vehicles pulled up, with floodlights on the roofs. She took her time, emptied the pistol into where she thought the windshields were but couldn't see because of the glare. Glass shattered. She dropped the empty magazine. Three figures stepped into the light.

M4 carbines. These weren't cops. They looked like Special Operations guys or contractors. She was pinned down, outnumbered. She needed to play for time, get a better weapon.

She dropped the gun and pulled her knife in one motion, then flicked open the blade and pressed it to the man's throat.

"Let him go," shouted a voice behind the lights.

Another man with thick black hair, wearing a suit and an open-collared shirt, came toward her.

"We will shoot the injured man in the truck, and then we will kill you. Drop the knife and we will not harm you."

Her captive squirmed. Blood dripped down the blade.

"I'll let him go," she shouted, "if you get care for the guy in the truck."

"Of course," he said as he sidled toward her. "Understood?" he shouted to the other men.

"Roger," the voices came back.

She eased the pressure off the knife, lifted it, stepped back from her hostage. Once she was a foot away, there was a crack behind the lights. Her upper right arm exploded in a spray of blood. The pain drilled through her. She fought back with her good hand as they rushed her, gouging eyes, breaking someone's ribs in the scrum with a dropkick, but there were too many. They took her down, pressed her face into the grit on the asphalt, wrenched her arm up behind her back.

Others vaulted inside the truck. "We had a deal!" Ward yelled.

They lifted Cook by his arms and dragged him away. The catheter in his chest tore out.

"The tube!" Ward shouted. "He'll die!"

"It's the money! It's here!"

The man in the suit walked over. Ward heard someone call him Kasem. She watched him silently counting the cash. She couldn't see Cook anymore, could only hear him, trying to breathe.

"Is it all here?" asked Kasem.

"Looks like almost all of it," said one of the soldiers. "Hayes probably used some to pay for operations."

There were a few others like Kasem. They seemed like civilians, Mediterranean or Middle Eastern. They conferred quietly for a moment.

Flashlights moved on the other side of the truck. Ward could see Green, bleeding from his head onto the pavement. She watched as they hauled off the boxes, one by one, everything that she and Hayes had worked for. The money was gone.

"Great work," Kasem said as he slapped the soldier on the back. The man walked away, and one of Kasem's colleagues pulled a silenced pistol from a holster inside his suit jacket and aimed it at the soldier's head.

Ward watched from the ground, and as the shooter tightened his grip, Kasem put his hand on the gun.

Not yet, he mouthed.

CHAPTER 40

CARO STOOD IN the cell with Nazar. He held the knife at his side and lifted his encrypted phone to his ear.

Kasem gave him an update on his progress. "We have the shipment back. We'll need to pick the right moment to finish the rest."

To eliminate Riggs's men. Caro had no doubt of his abilities. "As soon as you can."

He ended the call. The money was his alone. It was time. He turned away from Nazar.

It never failed to amaze him about Americans, the unreason of their isolated country. The insane notion that they had sold to themselves, that there could be a life without pain. That they could bomb the children of the world but not one setback or want would ever burden theirs. That love was their weakness, and his opportunity.

He remembered the school, pictured the glass windows, the children's hands pressed against them, the excitement in their wide-open eyes that were inches from the glass.

This was the end. The new beginning.

He lifted the phone and typed the word that the Mechanic had been waiting for.

Vesper.

The Mechanic read it once more, then pulled the battery from the phone. It was well before dawn. He double-checked his detonators as Bradac bathed himself to prepare for heaven.

The martyr prayed, butchering the Arabic pronunciations. While in prison, Bradac had heard that Muslims got better food and he'd converted, though the Islam of his understanding was barely recognizable to the bomb maker.

The Mechanic helped him into a North Face jacket. It was winter, and brown slush melted on the curbs. The parka that concealed the explosives would not be out of place.

He handed Bradac the distraction charge, a small U.S. Postal Service box, and then gave him a last once-over.

"Are you ready?"

"Yes."

"Let's go."

He kissed him on both cheeks and pressed the switch on the wall. The metal door rolled open, clanging and echoing in the cavernous space.

The journey to the target would take some time. They drove off in the Mechanic's sedan and made their way through the hills of Prince George's County. The capital lay below them, and the red lights at the top of the Washington Monument watched them like two unblinking eyes.

CHAPTER 41

Two MORE BULLETS ripped through the steel. I glanced over, and through the doorway I could see Speed's body, the buried tracers still burning. Shots hissed by. We clambered on our knees along the concrete. And then the shots stopped. Hayes must have drawn the fire, or Moret had silenced the guns with her sniper rifle.

This was battle as I remembered it. Thirty seconds after our last order, and we were in chaos and darkness, separated from our commander, with zero situational awareness, my nerves running like I had just mainlined epinephrine.

The gunshots picked up again from where we had left, and I heard voices coming for us. I could see men prowling along the route we had taken to enter the complex. They spread out along the razor-wire fence. The only way out was through one of the industrial buildings. Gunfire flew over our heads. Guards ran at us from the docks.

"Kelly, this way, come on!"

I turned, and she was ten feet away, messing with a jerrican. They would take her any second.

"Kelly, what the—"

A wall of fire leaped up between her and them, and she came sprinting toward me.

"What'd you say?" she asked.

"Never mind. Great work." I pointed to the building.

We ran for it. Every few seconds I could hear the snap of a .308 round and groans from behind us. Moret was up there with her rifle, silent and unseen, holding them off.

We rounded the side of the building. I threw the door open. It was some sort of power station. Heavy equipment churned in long rows, and a low throb shook the concrete floor.

I started working my way toward the far side. If we found an exit there, it would put us past the razor wire and leave only a short run to the outermost chain-link fence.

We crept along the edges, wary of guards. A door to my right creaked open. I counted five flashlights, five men, as I took cover behind a boiler.

Kelly ducked down, six feet away. I raised my hand: *Five of them.* She nodded.

Flashlights crossed the echoing space. It was a systematic search. I peered around the edge, watched them come. I waited for the right moment, then waved Kelly over. She crouched next to me. The footsteps came closer. I could hear the men breathing, the rattle of their gear. I readied my carbine, Kelly her MP7, and waited. They stopped just on the other side and began to spread out. They would come around our corners any second.

"What's that?" one asked. "Say again." It was his radio. I couldn't make out the transmission.

One man stepped into view. I aimed my carbine center mass,

brought my finger against the trigger. The fight was two against five, and they were better armed and in better practice. But we had to try.

He started to turn.

"Move out of here," one said.

"What's up?"

"They've got a damn sniper and one of their guys is loose near the docks. They can't kill him."

Hayes.

"They need help. Back to the *Shiloh*."

My man moved toward them.

We waited. My heart pounded; I opened my mouth wide to keep my fast breaths from making any noise. I heard them step away, then heard the creak of the door opening.

Kelly and I looked to each other. I squeezed her thigh.

"You stay here," one said.

"Sure."

The door closed. A flashlight beam swept over our heads.

The man's footsteps were relaxed, but he was moving along the perimeter. He would find us any second.

I reached down against the corrugated-aluminum wall and found a stripped screw and a hex bolt. It would have to do. I would distract him, take him from the side.

I signaled it to Kelly.

Something was wrong. She was blinking too much, looking around as if she were trying to force her eyes to focus.

Are you okay? I mouthed.

She gave me the A-OK.

You sure? I mouthed.

She nodded.

I eased around our boiler and pitched the bolt. The clang of metal on metal echoed through the dark. The man's feet scuffled, giving away his position, and I could discern his outline. He turned and started walking toward where it had landed, oblivious to me as I crept along.

I moved fast, catching glimpses between the equipment. At the end of the next row, I had a clear shot. His rifle was down.

I took aim. I had him.

Then I heard a thump to my right, where Kelly was.

Shouldering his rifle, he shouted, "Who's there?" and took off toward Kelly's cover.

I moved alongside, praying the grating electric buzz from the machines would mask my steps.

I turned to Kelly and saw only a flash: her on the ground, bleeding from her ear. After a head injury, bleeding from the ear could mean a fractured skull.

The man came around her cover, but before he could see her, I aimed and shouted: "Drop it and lay on the ground!"

He froze for an instant, then began to turn my way with the rifle. I shot four times, the last as he began to fall. I sprinted over, kicked his rifle away. He was down, shot twice in the chest, once in the upper thigh, and once where his trapezius met his neck. The thigh shot had happened as he was falling back.

He was gasping for air. The chest rounds had hit his plate body armor, knocked the wind out of him. I pulled the flex cuffs from his belt and cinched his hands. He would be out long enough for me to check Kelly.

She lay beside the transformer, up on one elbow, looking confused but breathing.

"Thank God," I said. "Are you okay?"

She nodded and eased back. "Get him."

The man tried to push himself along the ground with his one good leg.

I stood over him. Blood slicked the fabric of his pants and his fatigues. I was reacting more than thinking. The only things driving me were the vision of Kelly hurt, the knowledge that he had done it, and the heft of the carbine in my hand.

"Please," he gasped. "Please."

I remembered this feeling, the animal need to kill.

He backed against the wall until he could go no farther, grunted at the pain. I raised the gun. He shut his eyes as tight as he could.

A gunshot would draw the attention of the other guards. I brought the Heckler & Koch around hard, driving the stock into his temple, and he slumped over.

As he turned his face up, I drew my knife.

"No, God. Please," he said, holding his hands up in front of him.

I grabbed his shoulder, brought the knife up, and sliced off the collar of his shirt. I stuffed it in his mouth.

Kelly had pulled herself up and was leaning on the transformer. She was still alert. I checked her ear. The earlobe was lacerated, probably from her fall.

"What happened?" I asked.

"I don't know. I just...my vision kind of narrowed. And then I guess I fell."

"You blacked out. Postconcussive syncope. It's common after a head injury. Can you walk?"

She took a step. "Yeah, yeah. I feel fine."

Her pupils were reactive, and I rattled off the cognitive tests: What day is it? Where are we? Who's the president?

She passed the tests and I decided she was all right for now. I turned back to the guard. The trap shot was through the muscle, clean. I slit open his pants near the thigh injury and probed the wound. A lot of muscular damage and blood oozing, but the femoral vessels were okay. I opened my trauma kit, pulled the QuikClot, cut two pieces, and stuffed one deep into each wound.

He screamed through the fabric between his teeth. "You're welcome," I said, and taped his mouth shut. He could have avoided the pain if he had dropped the gun when I'd told him to.

I walked back to Kelly.

"Okay," I said. "Let's go."

We crossed the building and found the rear door. It opened to two hundred meters of scrub and a steep climb between us and the chain-link fence.

"How do you feel?"

"Fine."

"You think you can run?"

"Definitely."

We started out and were clear halfway across when the ground exploded to our right. I could barely hear the gunshot. It was a marksman, far off, putting down accurate fire. Kelly moved ahead of me. The dirt puffed up at my heels.

A running target in the dark was a hard shot for anyone. I scanned the fence ahead. If we stopped or tried to climb, we would be easy marks. I ran faster, felt my lungs burning for air. Another bullet whistled close. I cut right.

The fence loomed twenty feet away, ten. I pulled my knife and sprinted for the corner. The sniper closed in. I barely stopped, just slashed in one long stroke through the paracord and threw my body into the fence.

It gaped open.

I stepped back. Kelly hurled herself through.

I followed.

Bullets sparked off the fence behind us as we ran along the access road. Headlights blazed ahead, coming for us, fast. I raised my gun. Then I heard the radio.

"Byrne, it's Moret. Do not shoot. Hop on."

She pulled alongside; we jumped in rolling, and the truck took off into the night.

"Hayes?" I asked.

"He went into the water. We're going to get him."

"Speed?"

"He's dead."

I saw the *Shiloh* moving across the black water of the bay. Our only salvation, Nazar, was locked in the hold of that ship. And we had lost her.

Hayes dived pencil-straight into the water. He swam with a combat sidestroke, barely bringing his mouth and nose above the surface. From the shore, he was almost invisible.

The lights passed over him. Bullets splashed to his right. He dived and swam fifty meters below the surface, and then something began to shake his guts like heavy bass.

A boat was coming.

He came up and took three long breaths before the light found him, then dived again, straight into the path of the oncoming boat, drove himself lower until he hit the muck of the bay bottom. The churn of the propellers was deafening and getting louder. The currents pulled him toward the blades.

He fought them and came up in the furrowed wake on the far side.

It was a tug.

He reached for one of the thick lines hanging from the bumpers. It ran through his hand, scorching his palm as he slammed into the barnacles along the hull. He got his hands into one of the tires and hung on as the ship chugged toward open water.

Blood trickled into his eye. He caught his breath, watched the port recede, and saw the point ahead. He let go and stroked toward the black rocks and crashing surf.

"The point, I'm on the point."

Moret put the radio down and we sped along the breakwater. Hayes ran out and jumped in the truck. I listened to the scanner and helped her skirt the roadblocks. They had called out everyone: state and local police, some National Guard, Customs and Border Protection.

They didn't have a description of the truck, but we needed to change our look, ditch the cap and swap plates. We pulled under an overpass alongside a dry concrete culvert. Tarps and shopping carts were scattered along the gravel banks.

I set to work in the bed of the truck, under the cap, stitching up Hayes's eyebrow. The police scanner chattered in the background.

"The *Shiloh*?" he asked.

"Gone," Moret said.

"Riggs's men got Speed's body. We need to switch radio keys," he said. "Find another way to get back to Ward and Green. As long as we have the money—"

"It's gone," Moret said.

"What?"

"I intercepted a radio call. His men found the safe house. Took the money. Ward, Cook, and Green were overwhelmed."

"Christ," Hayes said.

"You all right?" Moret asked.

"Hang on." He leaned over and turned up the scanner.

"National terrorism advisory system has issued an imminent

threat alert. Heavy weapons units deployed around US Bank Tower. Vehicle restrictions in place for LAX and Port of Long Beach—"

"It's starting," Hayes said. "Samael's attack. He was waiting until he got the money back. They're all on the ship?"

"Yes. That's the last thing Ward confirmed."

"Why is Riggs going along with Samael?"

"I don't know," Hayes said.

"Is there a way to take them down?" I asked.

"We have the gear. The RHIB we picked you up in, the Drägers. It's all cached. Foley. Foley saved us."

I looked out the rear window. A few of the homeless men and women were gathering, taking an interest in our presence.

"There's a way onto that ship?" I asked.

Hayes nodded.

"And off?"

Hayes looked at me. "Unlikely. This is our last chance. We'll leave everything out there. I can't ask you to give that up. We've got a few caches left: money, IDs. Take it, Byrne, and run."

I took a deep breath, looked to Kelly, sitting in the passenger seat. I counted the stitches threaded through her skin.

I was done running.

"I don't want you to have any illusions," Hayes said. "This isn't about clearing our names. If we fail, we'll go down as terrorists, traitors, maybe even take the fall for whatever they're planning. Even if we live, they may hunt us for the rest of our lives."

I hadn't been living these past two years, just dying on the installment plan, trying to make things right. If we didn't stop Riggs and Samael, a lot of people were going to get hurt. I could do some good here. If I was going to throw my life away, I might as well make it count.

I watched Kelly rest. I would miss her. But I didn't want to think about it too hard. I was exhausted beyond reckoning. In the end, it was selfish. I was going to find the man who had hurt the people I loved and take him down.

"I'm in," I said.

He put his hand on my shoulder and was about to speak when Moret turned with a Toughbook laptop in her hand. She held it out to Hayes. "You need to hear this," she said. "They have your wife and daughter."

CHAPTER 42

WE READIED OUR gear on the concrete floor of an abandoned boat works. We were just south of a lagoon, on land cut off by train tracks, about twenty miles from where we had picked up Hayes. The building smelled like low tide and decaying fish, but it had a fenced-off yard and a boat ramp that was cracking up but still serviceable.

Hayes stacked ammo boxes and checked inside. It was green-and-white-tip .50-caliber ammunition—high-explosive incendiary armor-piercing rounds, each a half an inch thick and as long as my hand.

I could tell something was off with him, had been ever since he heard about his family.

"You all right?" I asked.

"No," he said. "Not until I know they're okay."

Going after his home was a tactic to destroy him, turn duty against family, distract him from his real target. It was working.

"God forgive me," he said. "This is where I need to be."

We would be wearing and carrying twenty thousand dollars' worth of diving equipment—rebreathers, fins, dry bags—and had packed enough small arms for a squad: HK416 carbines, an SR-25 sniper rifle, MP7 submachine guns, and navy-spec SIG Sauer P226s that would have no problem shooting after being submerged.

You could do a lot with sixty-eight million.

"Foley." Hayes looked over the gear and then shut his eyes. "He never let me down."

Moret zipped her sniper rifle shut in the waterproof bag, and then pivoted the .50 cal M2 heavy machine gun to the side so she could double-check its mount at the bow of the RHIB. She wore sunglasses to preserve her night vision. She wasn't trained on the combat-diving rigs we were using, and as the best shot of us by far, we needed her watching over us on the .50 and the SR-25.

Hayes and I finished loading the gear and climbed onto the RHIB, a thirty-three-foot-long fast boat with a turbo diesel. Kelly finished the radio checks and gave me a handheld unit.

"I'm going with you," she said.

I climbed onto the seawall and stood beside her.

"I wish you were. You've saved my ass twice. But you've got a grade-two concussion. And we're diving with closed-circuit rebreathers. You wouldn't make it."

"Are *you* going to make it?"

I ducked the question. "Before, you asked if there was another woman. There was someone. Someone I loved. She got hurt and I couldn't save her. A lot of people close to me have died, died with my hands on them. It messed me up pretty bad. It's why I kept running, kept people out."

"Their deaths are not your fault."

"But—"

She put her hand on my shoulder and looked at me squarely. "You can't live like that." I could see the concern in her eyes.

"I know that now."

"You can't think it's your fault."

"I know it in my head, but still—"

She nodded. "Don't believe it, Tom. You're a good guy."

"I haven't felt this way about anyone in a long time. I didn't think I could. Until you. I need you to live, Kelly." I handed her a case.

She opened it. Inside there were two hundred thousand dollars and three passports. "Those won't get you into the U.S. or Europe, but they will work everywhere else."

"You pushing me away?"

"No. I need you to live. Someone needs to live. To get the truth out."

"But Tom, this is crazy—"

"Please," I said. "I need to do this. I made it out when so many others didn't. Maybe this is why. They need me here."

She started to speak, then stopped, swallowed. I could see that she understood.

"I want to fight. I'll come with you."

"You'll have your chance. Every badge in the U.S. is looking for you."

"You're not a killer, Tom."

"Prove me wrong, then. Live through this."

I put my hand to her cheek and kissed her.

"Go ahead," she said, and put her hand over mine. "You're not going to kill me, Tom. You can say it."

"I love you."

"Likewise." She kissed me, then stepped back and slung her carbine over her shoulder. "I'll see you soon."

I stepped into the RHIB.

"We ready?" Moret asked.

"Ready," I said.

She gunned the engines, and we took off toward the *Shiloh*. The reflected light from town glimmered and ran like mercury on the surface of the water. I watched Kelly recede in the distance, saw her climb into the truck, but soon the waves came, and it was all I could do to hold on as we launched off the back of a shoulder-high breaker.

There are three ways to take a hostile ship: fast-rope down from a helicopter, throw caving ladders over the side and come over the gunwales, or blow a hole in the hull and enter through the breach.

The first two were out. There was no helicopter. We didn't have the numbers to shoot our way through the whole ship. Also, the men on board were simply hired guns who had no reason to doubt Riggs's version of events. They thought they were doing the right thing, and Hayes preferred not to kill them.

Even if we could somehow make it to the cell where Nazar was being held, Hayes would have to open it, and that would take time. He had walked me through the basics of the tool he would use to open the door. He needed two minutes, at least; an eternity in an operation like this.

We had to find some way to hold Riggs's men off without killing them or getting killed ourselves.

Hayes had figured it out.

"The water," he said. "We'll breach below the waterline and flood a compartment. The water will keep them out and give us time to work."

"Has that ever been done before?"

"No. Since World War Two, there's been only one mission with combat divers against a ship, during the invasion of Panama. This is definitely not SOP."

"Will it work?"

"We're going to find out."

We rode on in silence, Moret at the wheel of the RHIB.

She called out three minutes, and Hayes turned to me. "If we get Nazar out, and I'm stuck behind, I want you to take her and head for shore."

"We're not going to leave you behind."

"It's not your decision. I need to finish this."

"We're going to get her, and you're coming home with us."

"You get Nazar, you go."

I watched him for a moment. Nazar could testify to what really happened at the massacre. Hayes still believed that the truth mattered. That people would do the right thing. That Riggs and corruption couldn't win.

"You have faith," I said. "After everything."

"I don't know anymore. But if I'm going to die, I'd like to die believing in everything I fought for."

As we rose and plunged over the swells, Hayes did a final check on my diving rig.

It had been over a decade since I had used the Dräger rebreather. Dräger diving was one of those activities, like riding a motorcycle, where you wish you had a little less medical knowledge.

The rebreather isn't like regular scuba tanks, which contain a breathable mix of air. The Dräger recycles your own breath, filtering out carbon dioxide and replacing it with pure oxygen. It releases no bubbles, allowing for complete stealth, and is an eighth the size of scuba tanks.

The largest tank on my back contained dry chemicals with the consistency of cat litter, primarily lime—a base that can be as caustic as acid but on the other end of the pH scale. That would absorb the carbon dioxide, and a small computer would add just enough oxygen to keep me alive.

Hayes had given me a refresher on the apparatus, pointing to the different elements, while all I could think about were the scratches and dents and signs of age on it. The equipment looked like it had fallen off a truck.

"That's the diluent. Don't touch it or you'll die. And this is pure oxygen. Ditto. And this is the bailout. Lose that…you get the idea. And remember, you're breathing your own exhaust." He gave me a half smile. "So relax."

Or else I'd die, exhale too much for the Dräger to keep up. And if my regulator got knocked out of my mouth before I could seal it, water would rush through my loop, dissolve the lime, and pour into my mouth a slurry—known as a caustic cocktail—that was corrosive enough to eat through metal.

Relax.

And the Dräger was keeping me alive; forget about the real threats ahead.

"One minute!" Moret shouted.

We pulled our fins on and strapped our dive bags and submachine guns across our chests. They were over-the-beach modified MP7s and could fire even when full of water.

Moret brought the boat to idle and loaded a strap of high-explosive rounds into the .50 cal. Hayes and I sat on the gunwale. He spat in his mask and wiped the inside.

"You know why I gave you such a tough time, right?"

"I just figured you were a hard-ass."

"Because you were the best corpsman—not just that, the best guy I had. And I wanted to push you. Byrne, you saved the rest of the squad at K Thirty-Eight. I would have bled out without you. You were our best shot then, and you're our best shot now."

He slapped me on the shoulder.

"Thank you, Doc," he said. "Let's roll."

He pulled his mask down and slipped backward into the water.

CHAPTER 43

THE MECHANIC WATCHED Bradac disappear among the morning commuters streaming toward Dupont Circle, then turned away and walked south on Connecticut.

He stopped in front of a hotel lounge and stared through the plate-glass windows at the TV screen mounted over the bar.

CNN showed standoff barricades going up around the White House, the Pentagon, the Capitol Building, and the New York Stock Exchange. Armored Humvees rolled into the downtowns of America's cities, and soldiers with automatic rifles and German shepherds patrolled the airports and key transport hubs.

The terror alert had gone out.

He needed to keep moving. The Mechanic broke protocol and messaged Caro. *They know,* he wrote. *How can they know?*

He was walking down P Street away from the crowds, through a quiet section of turn-of-the-century town houses, when the message came back.

Because I told them. All is well. Proceed as planned.

*   *   *

Caro put down his encrypted cell and leaned against the ship's railing. Waves crashed into the side of the *Shiloh*'s hull.

His deputies had painted the online networks with chatter warning of an attack. Why tip off the authorities? He wished he could explain it all to the Mechanic, but there was no time. There was the simple purpose of distraction, like the British had used against the Ottomans in the Sinai campaign. While the Americans ringed their landmarks with steel barriers and overmuscled police, they'd left their soft belly exposed, blinded themselves to their real weaknesses: sentimentality, overreaction.

But Caro's game was more complex. He had been planting the seeds for this moment for years. Every scrap of intel, every bread crumb he fed to Riggs—it all pointed to the wrong enemies. And after the bombs blew, and the Americans' anger raged, it would overcome all reason, and they would launch themselves into attacks, into wars like those that had bled America in Vietnam, the Soviets in Afghanistan. It was the only way to tear down an empire.

All the while it would be his voice whispering in their ears.

For months he had warned Riggs and his circle of such an attack, had railed against U.S. complacency. When the bomb hit, it would only cement his rumors as truth, and he would lure them toward quagmire and bloodshed.

Caro looked to the *Shiloh*'s bridge, where Riggs was standing behind glass, thirty feet overhead. He might be able to decipher Caro's role in the bombing. He was the only one who knew all the details of their collaboration.

Kasem had already executed Riggs's men and taken the money. Caro stepped inside and began to climb toward his target. Within the hour he would kill Riggs himself.

CHAPTER 44

AFTER THE LONG ride to the *Shiloh,* action came as a relief. Riggs had anchored in the wind shadow of the Catalina Islands. To conserve our oxygen tanks, we approached the ship by turtlebacking: swimming on the surface, on our backs, with our gear and guns rigged to our bellies.

We moved through the darkness by dead reckoning. I had forgotten the terror of the open ocean at night, with swells and currents dragging us back and nothing but cold black water for miles. Hayes carried the attack board, a mounted compass and watch used to navigate on combat swimming missions. Its tritium hands gave off the faintest green glow.

We stopped one mile off the starboard side of the *Shiloh,* far enough out that the crew wouldn't be able to see us. We switched to our regulators and let the air out of our buoyancy vests. Once we had dived to eighteen feet, we continued underwater.

I could hear and feel the ship well before I saw it. Its turbines churned and pulsed the water. As we moved closer, I could see a shadow, a deeper black, and then I recognized the outline of the hull.

"Expect it when you least expect it" was a combat diver motto. They would wait for the killing hours before dawn, for bad weather, for their targets to take cover and grow bored, and then they would strike.

Our plan was to disable the ship first. Then we would breach the hull below the waterline, flood a compartment, and enter. We had four charges to lay down. Two on the driveshafts just forward of the propellers would immobilize the *Shiloh*. Two more shaped charges would cut two holes through the hull in the compartment that contained Nazar's cell, fill it with water, and give us a way in.

We started with the explosives on the props, which were the easiest to place, satchel bombs full of C-4 on a remote RF detonator. We came around the stern twenty feet underwater, then rose to six feet. The diffraction of moonlight allowed us to read the vessel's name, reflected upside down on the surface of the water. I followed as Hayes dived into the black. We had no lights, so he went by feel, counting the riveted panels on his way down.

He returned one minute later, materializing out of the lower depths, and gave me the A-OK. We cruised in shallow water up the port side of the ship, then Hayes signaled for me to stop. He had one shaped charge lashed to his gear bag. I had the other.

We found the seams in the hull we would use as guides, about twenty feet apart, then dived down. I counted the steel plates by feel in the blackness as we descended. My respiratory rate was elevated, but acceptable. The silence, the dark; it was strangely peaceful, but that wouldn't last.

My explosives for breaching the hull were on a two-foot-square metal frame. Each side was a linear-shaped charge, and the corners were hinged so that I could carry it collapsed flat as we swam.

I opened it. The corners clicked tight. When the long strips of explosive blew, they would shoot copper against the steel of the hull, slicing a neat hole. In theory, at least.

I laid the frame against the hull, easing the magnets down to avoid any noise. As soon as I placed the charge, I started to float up. My buoyancy was off from dropping the weight. The light filtered through the water as I neared the surface.

I reached around to my vest and vented. The bubbles rose. If the guards on the ship saw them, they would know we were here.

With my buoyancy neutral again, I dived down, lost in the blackness. Running a hand along the body of the ship to orient myself, I found what felt like my seam and swam back to my charge.

A hand closed on my shoulder. I threw my arm out, but the hand squeezed—two short, two long—and I realized it was Hayes. That was one of our signals. I don't know how he found me in that obscurity. He checked my explosives rig and double-primed it.

We swam under the hull, running the double-stranded detonation cord out behind us. As we sank into the depths, I could feel the pressure building against my chest. We crossed under and began to rise on the starboard side.

The blast from an explosion is three times more powerful underwater. Hayes had told me we needed to use the hull for cover. That's why we had come to the opposite side. We would detonate the charges, and then Moret would speed in on the port side and use the .50 cal to take out the *Shiloh*'s helicopter, its fast boat, and its close-in-weapon system: a 20 mm Gatling gun mounted near the bow of the ship that could shoot seventy-five rounds per second.

We had radios fixed to the side of our face masks, but we would use them as little as possible, for stealth. Hayes checked with me. I gave him the okay.

He tapped the radio. "Jericho, Jericho, Jericho."

It was the code to begin the assault. Hayes started counting down the twenty seconds Moret would need to race into effective range on the port side. He lifted the detonator, pushed aside the safety cover.

Fifteen.

Ten.

It was strange to wait in silence, knowing what was about to happen. A long swell rocked us and the ship up and down.

Five. They would be able to see her in seconds. It was time.

My heart beat louder, a pulsing roar in my ears, amplified by the water pressing against them; it was one of the most unnerving parts of diving. I cupped my hand over my ass to protect my organs and opened my mouth so I wouldn't shatter my teeth.

Hayes triggered the driveshaft charges. The explosion surprised me: a low thud instead of a crack. The pressure didn't hit me in the ears and mouth. It traveled through me, carrying me back with the water. I couldn't hear, and the shock wave tore at my stomach and lungs, seemed to wrench them loose as I was thrown back, straining the muscles in my arm.

The M2 Moret was firing was a fearsome gun, sixty-five inches long, capable of shooting down aircraft and killing from a mile and a half away. Even underwater we could hear it popping. Our first two explosions rocked the ship, and the distraction should have given her enough time to destroy the *Shiloh*'s other defenses and disable the helicopter on the flight deck.

We waited as she rained gunfire down above the waterline. The timing of the bombs was critical. Hayes knew the tactics and procedures aboard the *Shiloh*. He checked his watch. They needed time to raise the general alarm, time for all hands to get to their stations. As part of the standard protocol, they would leave the prisoner. The ship compartment that contained her cell would be unguarded.

The chug of Moret's .50 cal died out. Between her fire and the prop bombs, we had stranded the *Shiloh*. Hayes gave the crew ten more seconds, and then swam to the surface. All attention would be fixed on the other side of the ship, where Moret had attacked. He placed a suction cup with a ring handle against the hull, gave my vest a tug to signal going up, then hauled himself out of the water.

I surfaced next to him and reached for the ring as well. We were about to blow the breaching charges, and at that range, the pressure would kill us if we remained underwater.

I hoisted myself up. Above the water, the sounds of battle leaped out at full volume: the rattle of gunfire hunting down Moret, the shriek of the sirens on the *Shiloh*, the cries of the men on deck.

Hayes focused on his watch and the detonator. He pressed his thumb down, as calm as a man changing a channel on a TV, and triggered the last two charges.

The ship shuddered and cavitated through the water. I could hear the steel tremble and strain, like teeth grinding inside my own head amplified one thousand times.

The *Shiloh* was divided into a series of watertight compartments. It was designed so that even if two of those compartments flooded completely, it would still float, though barely. We had just taken one. The ship heeled slightly as seawater surged through the holes we had punched in the hull and filled the interior.

The plan was to wait until the violent rush of water abated and then swim under and enter through the breaches.

A light scoured the water a hundred meters back. "They're coming," Hayes said.

We had hoped the gunfire would keep their attention fixed on the port side of the ship, but they had kept their heads and were now looking for attackers from every direction. I dropped back to the surface. Hayes unfixed the ring and slipped below the water. I followed.

Once we were ten feet down, we didn't even have to kick toward the breaches. The water pulled in a slipstream along the hull, dragging us along the barnacles toward the razor-sharp edges of the holes we had blown. We were in the black now, blind and barely able to steer ourselves with our fins.

I could hear the driveshaft turning, the wrenched metal grinding in its housing. Running the propellers was a standard antipersonnel measure. The ship went nowhere.

I felt myself rising, moving faster. We were close. I kicked hard, oriented myself with the flow, and waited.

Something slammed hard into my lower back as I was pulled through the breach, but it was less violent than I had feared. The compartment we had flooded was nearly full, the pressure almost equalized.

Red and white lights shot by in a flash. I was upside down. Hayes was ahead of me, shining his spot around the compartment. Now that we were inside, light security didn't matter. We had entered through the larger breach, about three by four feet, with the hull plating curved in, torn into jagged edges. I half expected to see maimed bodies, viscera, and blood snaking through the water, but it was clear.

The large breach led into a machinery room lit by the glare of a single emergency light, with an open door to the passageway that ran up and down this side of the ship. I followed Hayes through.

It was empty except for pipes and junction boxes along the bulk-heads. To our left, toward the stern, the passageway ended in a heavy watertight door.

Riggs might have known that divers had played a part in the assault, or maybe he believed that it all somehow came from another boat. But there was almost no chance he would imagine that we were already inside, with a hundred and fifty thousand pounds of water pressing against the door between his crew and us. It would give us time to rescue Nazar—if we didn't drown her first.

We turned and headed right, toward the bow of the ship. There were three rooms along the passageway, all on the same side, just inside the hull. We had come through a breach in the first. Next to it was the vault room, and finally there was a third room, with the door blown open, where we had breached the second, smaller hole.

We swam toward the door to the vault. Then I heard a *tink* behind us, like the highest key on a piano.

I turned.

Tink. Tink-tink-tink.

Hayes shone his light back down the passageway. The partitions and doors within the compartments weren't nearly as strong as the massive walls that separated the watertight compartments from one another. If there was an area within this compartment that hadn't flooded, the weight of the water would build up on one side of the partition with nothing but air on the other until the partition blew in an implosion.

There was another *tink,* then a loud crack as a bolt sheared.

Hayes said something, but there was so much noise inside the ship, my radio was useless. I grabbed for a railing along the bulk-head. At the end of the passageway behind us, metal screamed, and the partition began to crumple away from us.

It gave out with a blast as the unflooded area swallowed enough water to fill it completely in seconds. The rush of water grabbed me, hauled me back down the passageway, nearly pulled my regulator from my mouth.

I bit down, held on as I smashed into rivets and pipes and prayed that I wouldn't tear my loop or puncture either one of the counterlungs that were keeping me alive. I rag-dolled through the compartment and slammed hard upside down into a pipe as the water dragged me, folded me around it, tore at my equipment.

Finally, pressure bounced back the other way and threw me off the pipe. I was upside down, breathing far too fast for my Dräger.

After a half a second of peace, a jet of froth and bubbles filled the passageway and roiled the water. I couldn't see. I patted myself, checking for lacerations. I tried to calm down, slow my breathing, waited for the drunken feeling of too much carbon dioxide in the loop or the nausea and tunnel vision of too much oxygen.

I could hear water in my rebreather, a faint gurgle with every breath. Some water I could survive—there were traps in the loop to catch it—but a leak would be fatal. And the danger of the Dräger is that once that careful balance of breathable air is gone, you're likely to die before you even figure out something is wrong.

Debris filled the water: upended chairs, fire extinguishers, papers, and a whiteboard. I reached for my chem light—my flashlight was gone—and scanned for Hayes.

He was ahead of me in the passage. I swam toward him as he lifted our bailout, the backup tank we had been carrying. Divers on rebreathers always carry a small tank of breathable air, like those used in traditional scuba, for emergencies. He ran his finger across his throat. Our bailout was gone. The next mistake would kill us.

* * *

The strong room was the first door on our right, protected by a steel door in a steel frame. It was originally a vault built into the ship for holding cryptographic equipment, but Riggs had found a new use for it. There was a small glass panel, about two inches high and eight inches wide, set in the door at eye level. I peered through it.

In the blue glow of my chem light, I could see Nazar leaning forward, shackled to the bulkhead, as water poured in all around her, flooding the vault. I could barely make out her condition.

She was still alert enough to cry for help. The door had held. It was more than enough to keep the water back, but the cell was filling fast, the cold black Pacific up to her knees and rising. It flowed from the vents and the pipe fittings near the overhead—what the ceiling is called on a ship.

The vault was filling faster than we had anticipated. And something was off. The water wasn't clear. The surface was a rainbow. I couldn't smell anything, but I knew that fuel was leaking somewhere nearby.

Hayes sank down a few feet and faced the door lock. It was a combination dial, group-three navy standard, that could be used on vault doors and safes.

I floated above and to Hayes's left, near the window, with a grease pencil and a small slate. He tried an old combination, with no success. He was going to have to decode the lock, and for that he needed a partner to keep track of the numbers.

The traditional way to crack a safe is by drilling at certain points, positions that are carefully guarded and specific to each model, that would allow the bolt to be drawn. We didn't have time for that and couldn't run a high-speed drill.

But every vault already has one hole drilled through it, for the dial, and that was the weakness Hayes would exploit. It was how he had managed to break in and steal his own classified records.

He pulled out a case marked *Falle Safe,* then jammed his knife behind the lock dial and pried it off.

That left the spindle exposed, poking out of the front of the lock. The spindle turns with the dial and lets the user manipulate the four wheels stacked inside the lock. Each wheel has a notch in it. The correct combination would leave those notches perfectly aligned, allowing a bar to fall down into them and the bolt to be drawn.

The spindle is a long threaded rod with a groove down its entire length. Hayes needed to remove it, but first he had to reach a wire all the way down that groove to the very back of the lock. There, a small piece of metal, called a key, had been hammered into the groove and bound the spindle to the wheels. If he knocked it out, he could unscrew the spindle.

He started feeding the wire in, then stopped.

This, he had told me, would be the critical moment. Attacking the spindle is one of the oldest, least sophisticated ways to crack a safe. Amateurs would simply hammer the spindle back into the vault. It destroys the wheels or pushes them off entirely, allowing the bolt to withdraw.

Any real safe has a countermeasure known as a relocker. These are inch-thick bolts held in by heavy springs that rest against the back of the lock and the wheel pack.

"Destroy the wheel pack?" Hayes had said. "The pins fire. Punch the spindle? You knock off the back of the lock, and the pins fire. Those pins can't retract. They permanently lock the vault. Not even the combination will open it. It takes hours of drilling at secret points known only to the manufacturer to disable those pins."

If Hayes moved a few millimeters too far and set off the relocker, Nazar was dead, and our fate was sealed as surely as that vault.

It sounded like surgery.

He shook his hand out and tapped on the wire, pushing out the tiny piece of metal that held the spindle in place. It moved in, millimeter by millimeter.

He looked to me, put his hand flat, then raised it from his belly to his chest, asking how high the water was in the cell. I looked in, saw Nazar's desperate eyes, turned back to Hayes, and held my hand up to my neck.

He tapped the tool with the butt of his knife. Again; harder. Harder. It gave.

I held my breath, sure that he had gone too far and triggered the relocker. I listened for the clunk of the pins firing and heard nothing, but that didn't mean much. The noise could have been covered by the chaos in the water and the alarms sounding above our heads.

He unscrewed the spindle until it was free and put it aside. Nazar began to scream, which at least meant she was still breathing.

Hayes screwed a special replacement spindle into the lock. It had a hollow center that would allow him to feed a decoder— a thin rod—deep inside the lock mechanism. At the end of the rod was a metal clip that would reach around and let him feel the edges of the wheels and find those notches.

Nazar stopped screaming. I looked through the glass. Her eyes came above the surface one last time, then disappeared. We had two or three minutes until brain death started.

Hayes fed the rod in and turned it slowly. I waited with the slate. He found the first notch, and signaled: *68*. I wrote it down.

The second wheel took another thirty seconds: *10*. I could hear the chains rattling as Nazar struggled under the water. She was only wasting her oxygen.

The third wheel: *52*.

One more.

The clanking inside the cell stopped. She was unconscious. She was dying.

Hayes pointed to the loop of my rebreather. I grabbed the tube to my counterlung and pulled it forward. Bubbles trickled out, slow and steady: a leak. I felt okay and double-checked the read-out on my Dräger's display: no alarms.

He gestured for me to surface, but I didn't move.

He started on the fourth wheel: *27*.

That gave us the combination, but it was relative. He needed one last measurement, of the wheel that would draw the bolt, to tell us the offset between our readings and the true zero of the lock. That was where I came in.

There was a chalky taste in my mouth, bitter and sharp. I thought at first it was just the coppery bite of fear, but I soon knew it was something far worse. I held on, held my breath. We needed those numbers.

Hayes gave me the offset, and I added it to our four numbers. As I wrote out the last figure, the pen in my hand seemed to recede to a small circle at the end of a long tunnel. I held the slate out to him.

Hayes entered the combination, tried the handle. It didn't work.

My chest spasmed, desperately sucking for air. I couldn't stop it. The caustic liquid rushed into my mouth. I vomited instantly into my mouthpiece, then spat it out and watched as the yellow plume melted the rubber of my loop and floated past me in a cloud.

I stroked for the surface with my last strength and bumped against the steel overhead. A small air pocket was trapped between two supports. I put my face in it and tried to breathe. Water ran into my mouth with each gasp, some into my lungs, and I coughed violently, swallowing more with each fit. My vision wavered. Hayes lifted me, kept my face in the pocket.

My eyes were an inch from the steel. I could taste diesel. The water rose, up my cheek, to the corner of my mouth.

"Take my regulator," Hayes said. It would take me minutes to make up for the carbon dioxide poisoning, minutes Nazar didn't have, and there was no way Hayes could work the dial with me buddy-breathing on his back.

"No. Open that door."

"The relockers must have fired. It's over. She's dead."

The water splashed against the overhead. I craned my neck, sipped the last air.

"They didn't," I croaked. "You can open it."

"There's no point killing yourself—"

Nazar was in worse shape than I was. "I can't let another one die. Open that door."

The water came over my nose and mouth. There was no air left.

He pulled out his regulator and handed it to me.

I kept my mouth shut, shook my head no. Hayes exhaled in anger and frustration, then brought his regulator back to his mouth. As my vision narrowed further, he turned down, grabbed the dial, and spun it hard.

Then the darkness took me.

CHAPTER 45

THE PAIN BLOOMED in my cheek, again and again. Someone was smacking me. I opened my eyes and threw up water that tasted like salt and gasoline. I looked over and saw Nazar, barely conscious, and Hayes, swimming between us.

We were inside the vault, in an air pocket near the overhead. The door was open.

"The key I pushed out must have fallen into one of the notches. I spun it out. You were right."

My mouth and throat burned from the chemicals. In the red wavering light, I filled my chest, over and over, ignoring the choking diesel fumes to take in everything I could before the air pocket disappeared.

"Is she okay?" I asked. "Injuries?"

"Nothing immediately life-threatening."

"Torture?"

"No sign."

I felt along her neck, found the pulse; strong. The rainbow surface of the water rose closer to the overhead.

"No. No," Nazar muttered and began to weep.

"We're going back underwater," Hayes said.

"No!" she screamed.

"We're getting you out of here." He backed against her. "Hold on to my shoulders and breathe through this."

Hayes brought her arms over his shoulders and turned the mouthpiece on his Dräger around.

"Byrne, can you make it out of here in one?"

The air felt like fire against the swollen, burned skin of my mouth.

"Yes."

He held Nazar's arms tight against his chest with one hand, held his regulator in the other.

"If you spit this out, we're all gonna die. Understand?"

She nodded. Hayes pushed the regulator into her mouth and opened the valve. He watched her suck the air in.

"Slower," he said.

Nazar was still in shock, taking short, shallow breaths as the water rose over her chin and lapped against the overhead.

"We've got to go," Hayes said. He dived through the door and entered the passageway. I took a long last breath. It was twenty-five meters to the breach. We had done fifty on one breath during training at Camp Pendleton. I had this, I told myself, ignoring the years since and the fresh trauma to my body.

I slipped under the water. We turned back the way we had come, toward the room where we had blasted the larger hole.

Hayes stopped, grabbed my shoulder, and pointed up. There was a small pocket of air trapped in a hatch. I came up inside it.

Metal clanged ahead of us.

"What is that?"

"They're opening the door. They carry scuba on every deck. They're coming for us."

"What?" If they opened the doors, a second watertight compartment would flood, and the *Shiloh* would barely be able to float. "But anything goes wrong and the ship will go down."

"That's how bad Riggs wants us." He grabbed Nazar and held her above the water, dunking his own head for a moment.

A red light strobed below us. The door was opening.

"I'll hold them off," Hayes said. "Bring her to the other breach." He started to remove the Dräger.

"You'll need it more," I said. "We can make it. I'll get her out and come back for you."

"No. Stay with her. She's more important."

Hayes pulled his knife from the sheath on his chest rig. "I'll be behind you with the loop if you run into trouble."

The siren sounded and the door shuddered in its track. I wrapped my arm around Nazar's chest like a lifeguard, dived, swam in the other direction, past the vault and toward the second breach. I hauled her through the door and saw the hole through the hull. It was smaller, and jagged around the edges, but Nazar and I would be able to get out one at a time. The alarms seemed to grow louder, and I could hear and feel the grinding of a motor through the water. Nazar started to panic. I grabbed a pipe next to the breach, took off my small inflatable vest, and looped it over her neck. I pointed through the hole. The veins bulged at her throat; her chest spasmed. Her limbs started to shake.

Divers called it the sambas. She was working too hard. I pushed her toward it. She groped for me, knocked my mask to the side.

Gunshots behind us, low *poof*s underwater. The door was

open. If we didn't get through that hole right now, we were done.

I shoved her through and put my chest and shoulder out halfway at the same time. The metal tore through my wet suit, cut my ribs. Cold water flushed down my side.

A current streamed through the breach into the ship, growing stronger by the second. They had opened the door behind us, and as it flooded it was pulling water down the passageway and in through the holes.

Three more gunshots cracked behind me, where Hayes had gone.

I fought against the current and yanked the red tab on the vest. It inflated instantly, and Nazar began to rise outside the ship. I grabbed for her ankle but the torrent of water picked up and pulled me back through the breach. I held it off for a moment, but now it was like a waterfall. I grabbed hold of a pipe and tried to fight against the weight of all that rushing water.

The current grabbed her, slammed her into the side of the ship, but as she bounced off the steel, the buoyancy took hold, and she began to rise toward the surface outside the ship.

My arm trembled, and gave out. I shot toward the passageway. I reached for the bulkheads, for anything, cut up my fingertips against a bolt, then finally caught a handle as the water rushed past me. The desperation built. My chest bucked for oxygen.

I looked back down the compartment. There was no sign of Hayes. The ship began to heel to one side. Nazar was floating up there on the surface, easy pickings for Riggs and his men. I had to get out to get her. I had to get out to breathe. I dived down, fought the easing current, grabbed the rough edges of the main breach, and hauled myself through.

I stroked for the surface as my body shook harder, my burned mouth screaming in pain, my vision narrowing to a pinpoint. The surface seemed to move farther away with every stroke.

I broke through, gasping the second my face hit the air, sucking in diesel fumes and the water I churned up.

Through the fog, there was no sign of Nazar, only the rolling swells crashing me into the side of the ship. I looked up. The starboard gunwale was moving closer, the hull leaning farther and farther. Ships can shift ballast to offset flooding, up to a point, which the *Shiloh* had long since reached.

The twenty-foot-high side of the ship slowly tilted down over my head. I swam hard as it moved faster. The rush of displaced water picked me up and washed me out as the steel loomed. The tilting slowed as the ship found its new equilibrium, the main deck just a few feet off the water.

Gunfire snapped overhead. I swam away as fast as I could. The fog gave me some cover. A hundred meters out, I turned on my back, taking in great breaths as the pain finally cut through the adrenaline. My body was wrecked, the skin over my ribs shredded and bruised.

I checked my watch; fourteen minutes since Hayes had called out *Jericho*. It had felt like an eternity.

I scanned the water. Nothing but spilling whitecaps. "Hayes," I said into my radio. "Nazar," I said, then again, louder.

The only answer was the splashing of water as the rifles closed in on my voice.

Moret came on the channel. "Byrne. Are you okay? What's your location?"

"Midship, starboard. A hundred meters out. They're shooting. I can get farther away."

"I'm coming, lights on."

I reached for a small infrared beacon on my shoulder and

flipped the switch on the side. I couldn't see it shine, but she would. I tried to raise Hayes, but heard nothing. Then a roar grew on my two o'clock: a diesel engine.

"Is that you?"

"Yes. Be there in a few seconds," Moret said.

I detached my submachine gun and brought it up just in case. The diesel coated my skin. The fumes were overpowering. I started to retch, and every gag scorched the burns inside my mouth.

The RHIB materialized out of the fog. I lifted the beacon. Gunfire burst behind us, threw curtains of water. The men on the *Shiloh* must have gotten their own .50 cals going.

As she angled toward me, I braced for the impact. She passed close and I grabbed for the rope, wrenching my left shoulder out of the socket. The boat dragged me along, planing on the surface of the water. My right hand closed on a plank seat and I hauled myself over the gunwale as the gunshots walked closer and closer. Moret threw the boat into a 180-degree turn.

"You okay?" she asked.

My teeth ground together from pain. I shoved myself across the deck to the center console of the RHIB. After two deep breaths, I gripped my left arm with my good hand, raised it up and behind my head, and pulled hard. The joint wouldn't reduce. I steeled myself and pressed my elbow against the console until the humerus popped back into place with an audible snap.

A string of obscenities poured out of my mouth and my vision started to darken; I was on the edge of passing out.

"I've had better days," I joked to Moret, but the words were unintelligible. I sounded like Frankenstein's monster.

"What?" She turned and got a good look at me for the first time. "Jesus, you—"

A bullet tore through her right shoulder. She grunted and went down, grabbing the wheel. The boat lurched hard to port and buried the gunwale in the water. I slammed into the pedestal, planted my feet, fought my way against the spin toward the throttle, and pulled it back.

She was on the deck, eyes shut, blood streaming from her shoulder.

"Stay with me, Moret." I stood and gunned the engines on the RHIB to get us out of range.

"I'm all right," she said, and tried to sit up.

"No, you're not."

Once we were clear, I checked the wound: in and out under her right armpit. That's high-value real estate, brachial plexus and the brachial artery. She could be dead in a minute.

I pulled the shredded fabric back and checked the wound channel. No frothing, no pulsing, no arterial blood.

"Can you move your hand?" She touched her thumb to her index finger. "Good," I said. "I'm going to put something in it to stop the bleeding. It's going to hurt."

She nodded.

I pulled out the QuikClot and stuffed it into the hole. She gritted her teeth and groaned as I leaned her forward and plugged the exit wound. I could fit four fingers in it.

She took long, deliberate breaths. I could see she was counting them out.

"That's good. You're going to be fine."

"Where's Hayes? Did you get the woman?"

"Nazar got out. Hayes, I don't know."

"Find them. I'll hold up."

I took the wheel and lifted her NVGs. The whole field of vision blazed white. I took them down, figuring they were broken, and then saw red light flare through the fog, and smelled the acrid petroleum smoke.

The water was on fire.

The flames illuminated the sea near the ship, under the bank of cloud. I scanned the surface again; no sign of either one. Near the bow of the ship, I caught a white flash, the reflector built into my buoyancy vest. My breath caught. It was Nazar. The rush of water must have carried her there. A massive slick of diesel covered the water between us and her, covered the entire starboard side of the *Shiloh*. The fires near the ship hadn't ignited all of the fuel yet but would any second.

I reached for the throttle.

"Mako One, Mako One," a voice came over the radio. It was Hayes. He was alive.

"This is Mako One. Where are you?"

"Twenty meters out from the stern, starboard side."

"I'm on my way."

"Where's the woman?"

"In the water. Starboard bow. I'll—"

"Get her first," he said.

I turned the wheel to port to take us to Hayes.

"I'll get her after—"

"This is all about to burn. You don't have time for both of us. Get her first."

"You have your rebreather. Dive. I'll find you."

"Don't worry about that. Get the witness. Take her home."

The flames jumped from puddle to puddle across the water. The whole slick was ready to blow. I knew the choice he was making: he was trading his life to clear his name, to finish this.

Another one who trusted me. Another one dead. I couldn't.

"I'm coming for you."

"This is what I want, Byrne. Now go."

I growled in anger and kicked the pedestal so hard I shattered the fiberglass, then I gunned the throttle and turned the wheel hard the other way, heading for the bow. The flames raced us to Nazar. They moved closer, rose behind us as we threw a giant tail of water, making straight for her. I switched hands, held the wheel in my right, and leaned toward the gunwale.

I could smell the nylon and rubber burning behind me. Nazar splashed in the water, then looked back to see the wall of fire speeding at her. It was so loud.

My hand skimmed over the surface of the water. I braced, grabbed her life vest with my left hand, and hauled her through the water, away from the flames. I lifted with both my legs, threw her onto the deck, and spun the boat around. The shoulder didn't dislocate again, but the pain tore through the whole left side of my body. My vision tunneled for a moment, and my legs went weak, but I held on.

I flew at the edge of the flames toward the stern, toward Hayes. The heat choked me, left me coughing.

"You're going to lose the boat, Byrne," Moret said. "It's too hot."

There was no oxygen. I couldn't see through the fire. I reached the water near the stern, at the border of the fire, ran out, turned back for another pass. Bullets ripped by. Two more passes. A gunshot blew out the Plexiglas on the pedestal. Fire raged where I had last seen Hayes. I turned away, scanned the water, yelled for him on the radio.

"He's gone, Byrne."

"He can't be."

"Mission first," she said. "It was his choice. Getting us killed won't save him."

The enemy .50s threw a torrent of bullets our way, sent a wall of water at the RHIB. I pulled away, choking from the smoke.

"We have to go, Byrne," she said. "We can finish this."

I circled the flames as they spread farther and farther, well beyond the distance Hayes could have swum.

"I couldn't save him," I said quietly. I pictured him floating dead in the dark water and knew that the image would never leave me.

"You got her. You got the truth. You saved all of us. Now turn to shore."

CHAPTER 46

I POINTED THE boat to the east, away from the wreckage. Our shadows flickered in the orange light, growing longer. After we'd gone one hundred meters, Nazar cried out, "My son."

It was a relief to hear her talking.

"My son!"

I thought it was shock at first. I brought the boat to neutral and knelt over her. The veins in her neck stood out like thick, dark cables. They were massive, distended.

No.

I tore open her shirt and searched the skin with my light. It was a small red dot just beside her sternum that looked like a speck of paint. A puncture wound to the chest. The bruises around it were growing quickly, indicating major trauma. I took her pulse, rapid and weak, then listened to her heart. It sounded muffled, distant, like it was beating under the sea.

She put her hand to my face, stared at me, and screamed, "Son! No. Please!"

Altered mental status. With the other signs, that confirmed it. She had a cardiac tamponade. Her heart was drowning in its own blood. When the heart bled, it filled the sac surrounding it, and the pressure built, constricting the heart, killing her with every milliliter.

She had vital signs. But that wouldn't last.

I reached for the trauma kit, pulled out a 16-gauge needle, and attached it to a 20 cc syringe. My only hope was to buy her time.

"Do you need help?" Moret asked. "Is she okay?"

"It's all right. You rest." A piece of metal must have stabbed Nazar in the chest, probably in the chaos as I helped her through the breach. I had missed it, and now she was dying.

The pressure was increasing on her heart as it pumped less with every beat. She blacked out. Two more breaths, then nothing.

The RHIB rocked on the swells. The burning *Shiloh* cast a faint red glow through the fog.

I sterilized the skin just below her sternum. You enter there, at the base of the sternum, aim the needle at the left shoulder, and drive it in at a 45-degree angle toward the heart. In hospitals, they use ultrasounds to help guide the needle, but I didn't have that option. I had to stab her in chest, break through the pericardium — the sac around the heart that was now filled with blood — and stop before I hit the ventricle and killed her. It was a margin of millimeters.

The RHIB slid down the back of a swell.

Hayes had traded his life for hers, and I had squandered it. Another woman dying in my hands. Another shade.

I lifted the thick needle and pressed it to the left of the bottom of her sternum. The skin tented, and then the needle broke through. I slid it forward as I pulled back on the plunger, my body moving with the rolling ocean, my eyes fixed on the syringe, waiting to puncture the membrane around her heart, waiting for the blood to pour out.

Suddenly I was back at Dagger, covered in blood to the elbows, Emily's heart in my hands.

Gunfire tore through the night. I pushed the needle in deeper. A wave crashed into the gunwale.

Blood spurted into the syringe.

CHAPTER 47

Riggs stood on the tilting fantail of the ship and reached for the rail. The men squinted as the diesel smoke blew into their eyes and the flames roared off the side of the *Shiloh*. This was supposed to be a straightforward coastal run—with a skeleton crew and the close-in weapon system off—and now they were crippled, under full attack.

"What's happening below?"

"They breached the crypto vault."

"Nazar?"

"She's gone. We saw a RHIB take off."

Riggs placed his hand over his mouth, then brought it down. It was impossible to believe. The attackers were still out there. They might lose the ship.

"Hayes is close. He wouldn't come this far and not finish it. He'll come back for us. You get the fuck out there, all of you, and search that water until you find him. Understand?"

"Yes, sir."

"Go!" Riggs shouted, and then crossed the deck. He went in and kept to the high part of the passageway. The metal was warm to the touch, but at least he wasn't on the main deck, where swells and fire washed over the side.

He could hear the water splashing below him. Two compartments had flooded. The ship was barely above the waterline.

He keyed his radio. "All available men out?"

"That's right," Hall replied.

"And we're seaworthy?"

"For now."

"What about support?"

"The Marines are sending Super Cobras from Pendleton."

Attack helicopters. Riggs killed the radio, laid his arm over the top of a coiled fire hose, and rested his forehead against it.

One of Riggs's guards, a former Ranger, climbed down a ladder to the mess, a large dining area. The flooding rose halfway up the bulkheads, deeper on the port side due to the ship's tilting. He waded in up to his chest and began to cross.

Behind him, a shadow emerged from the black water. It was a man, rising to his chin and breathing deeply but silently, his eyes taking in the whole space.

Hayes rested like that for thirty seconds, until the panic and oxygen starvation abated. He listened to the guard's radio chatter, memorized every call sign. The guard began to turn, and Hayes slipped back under the water.

They would be looking for him out on the surface, so Hayes had come back in through the breach.

He wanted Riggs alone, or Caro. He waited until the soldier climbed back out, then rose and caught his breath. He dived and slipped through the water in silence toward the bow.

He surfaced at the end of the passageway and climbed up a level. He was near the center of the ship. Ahead of him were the staterooms for the senior officers. He moved down the corridor and was halfway through it when he saw one of the dogs on a watertight door turning. He pressed against the bulkhead next to the door, his pistol ready at chest level.

Through the glass porthole in the door, he saw Bill. He lowered the gun, and as Bill stepped through the door, he swung his left fist as though driving an ice pick into his temple. Bill stumbled. Hayes brought his left arm around his neck so Bill fell forward into the V of Hayes's elbow.

Hayes brought this right arm up, clasped his own biceps, and vised down on the man's arteries, applying enough pressure on the airway to keep his cries quiet but not enough to crush his trachea. Bill clawed at Hayes's forearm and head and blacked out after eight seconds. Hayes lowered him to the deck and flex-cuffed him. He pulled one of the straps off Bill's ammo vest and stuffed it into the man's mouth.

He stood and caught a reflection in the porthole just as he felt the pressure against the back of his skull.

Hall, Riggs's deputy, stood behind him with a gun to his head.

"So stupid," Hall said, looking down at Bill. "You should have killed him." He pressed the pistol in harder.

Hayes snapped his neck back, driving the muzzle up, at the same time he lifted his knees to his chest fast enough that his feet came up off the deck. His whole body free-fell for a split second in a deep squat.

His right hand snatched Hall's wrist and brought the arm forward, past Hayes's ear and down. Once Hayes had the wrist and the gun hand, he slammed his feet down, stood up to his full height, and drove his right shoulder into Hall's elbow. He felt a soft pop and a crack as the ligaments and then the bones gave in to the hyperextension. The pistol dropped from Hall's hand.

Never put a gun that close, thought Hayes.

He caught it by the barrel in his left hand and gave it a half turn as he pulled Hall forward by the broken arm as if he were going to throw him over his shoulder. That brought Hall's body against Hayes's back and slightly to the right as Hayes reached with the gun around his own torso, pressed it against Hall's chest, and fired twice.

The body, as he had hoped, muffled the pressure, which could have blown his ears in that confined space. Hall fell to the deck, bellowing. Hayes shot him in the eye. As Hayes wiped the blood from his face, he could hear footsteps clanging down the passageways.

"Eagle? Eagle?" A voice came from the radio handset clipped near Hall's shoulder.

They'd heard the shots. They were coming.

Hayes picked up the handset, stretched it toward himself, and put on labored breathing.

"This is Eagle. Riggs. Riggs. Where are you? I'm hurt, he got away. He is heading toward the stern, the port-side passageway."

That was the opposite side of the ship.

"Who is this?"

"This is Eagle," Hayes said. "Riggs. Where's Riggs?"

"Heading for the CO's stateroom."

That was closer to the bow of the ship. He heard guards closing in on the doors at both ends of the passageway. The water was rising. Hayes would have to go down to move forward. He opened a hatch and pulled the radio from Hall's corpse. After three deep breaths, he disappeared under the surface.

*   *   *

Hayes navigated by feel, using the pipes along the overhead, and swam forward far enough to come under the passageway near the CO's office. He climbed through a hatch, and as he rose from the water, he tilted his gun forward to drain the barrel.

He slipped down a passageway filled with the sound of seething water and the general alarm, then came to a corner and peered around. Riggs stood twelve feet away. It was sweltering. The fire was close. The bulkheads seemed to waver with heat.

Hayes closed in before Riggs could turn. He pulled his knife and in one movement chicken-winged Riggs's right arm behind his back and pressed the blade against his throat. With his grip on Riggs's wrist, he torqued the arm all the way up to the shoulder. The only way to relieve the tearing pressure on the joint was to lean forward, into the blade.

There was justice, order, duty. They gave Hayes's life meaning. But they had been torn apart. The moment they came for his wife and child was the moment they moved past all limits on barbarity, on the animal instincts that had been sharpened in him over decades. He had seen the darkness poison Speed, but there was a time when killing was just.

He could feel the fire getting closer. Sweat dripped and stung his eyes. He gripped the knife tighter, twisted Riggs's arm harder, and turned his face away to avoid the wash of blood.

"No one hurt them," Riggs pleaded. "They're okay. Your wife and child."

Hayes said nothing, made no sound save for measured breathing from his nose.

"We can work this out," Riggs said.

Hayes relaxed the joint lock.

"Where are they?"

"Police custody."

"And Caro?"

Riggs didn't respond.

"Caro," Hayes said. "Where is he?"

"He's secure. That's all I'll say. You're going to kill me either way. I'm not going to help with your revenge."

Riggs deserved to die, for the killing he had stood by and condoned and for what he had taken from Hayes. But this wasn't about revenge. Hayes had a mission to defend and protect his people, and that meant stopping Caro. It was a mission he had taken on two years ago for a country that now called him a traitor. But that didn't matter. The duty remained. And he wasn't going to stop until he finished the job.

He needed answers, not blood.

"Nazar is gone. The truth is going to come out. You're going down for the massacre, but you can still do the right thing. Caro is the real enemy. Tell me where he is."

"You talk about the right thing?" Riggs laughed. "I did what needed to be done in that village. You, though, you're a traitor. Your job was to get burned. It's what you signed up for when you went black. You disobeyed orders. Everything you've done from that day to this is a disgrace."

"I'm happy to suffer for my country's sins, but not yours. Where is Caro? What are you planning?"

He wrenched Riggs's arm until the tendon almost tore.

"False flags and proxy battles. We're going to win this. You don't have the stomach for the war we need to fight," Riggs said.

"You still don't understand. Caro is Samael. He's the terrorist we hit on the incursion. When they ambushed us, they had brand-new Colt M4s. They had fresh hundred-straps, CIA money.

You helped him. You made a mistake. That's understandable. It's chess. It happens, but for Christ's sake, don't double-down with a terrorist."

"What are you talking about?"

"You have to know. Jesus. Why would you get in bed with him? You saw him kill those people in the village," Hayes said.

"Those people gave your location to the enemy," Riggs snarled. "The interpreters betrayed you, set you up for that ambush. We had to get rid of them. It was ugly, sure, but they stabbed us in the back. Then someone had to take the fall. That's your job."

Hayes understood at last.

Caro had fed Riggs a bullshit story to cover up his own role in the ambush. He had blamed the interpreters, painted them as the true enemy. Riggs had thought killing them was a necessary evil, frontier justice. It was a grave crime, but now at least Hayes could understand what had happened. For Riggs, embracing the lie about the interpreters was easier than admitting he had been wrong, that he had aided the enemy. It was tragic in a way.

But even Riggs couldn't have been that willfully stupid, that blind.

"You saw him doing the killing," Hayes said. "And then you believed him when he turned around and gave you that story. Why? Jesus, just think for a second—"

"Believed him? No. I didn't believe *him.* I wouldn't have taken his word alone. He wasn't the one who first told me about the villagers stabbing us in the back. I believed—"

The booming pressure swallowed the words, and then fire roared through the compartment. It knocked Hayes forward. The flames felt cool at first, a strange numbness along his back as he stumbled and Riggs threw himself to the side.

The explosion swallowed the oxygen in the passageway. Hayes

gasped for breath but no air came. The initial shock of the blast resolved into pain now, tearing across his back. He rose to one knee. Something had exploded. Molten rubber and plastic coated his back, burning down through the skin.

He couldn't see Riggs through the choking fumes. He rolled twice but had no way to tell if he had extinguished the flames. Then the first bullet came through the smoke, sparked blue against the bulkhead. Shrapnel rained down on the passageway.

He rose to his feet and sprinted around the corner. Footsteps clanged on the metal. Voices came on the radio: "Forward, move... move. Protect the bridge."

He tried to think through the fog of pain. He could understand their tactics from their comms. It was typical for teams that hadn't spent enough combat time together; slow, cautious, deliberate. They couldn't flow, couldn't anticipate, couldn't work with the speed, silence, and violence necessary. They knew they had contact. They were closing on the bridge.

The *Shiloh* had a wide tower—known as a superstructure—roughly at its midpoint that rose thirty feet above the main deck of the ship. Hayes and Riggs were inside the base of the tower, where the commanding and executive officers had their offices and staterooms. Above them was the bridge, the windowed room at the top of the tower with a panoramic view of the sea where the commanding officer could control the ship.

That would be the standard place to evacuate the principals, where the watch would circle and protect them. That's where Riggs had been headed and that's where Hayes knew he would find Caro; *he's secure,* Riggs had said.

The only way to get in was by climbing the ladders inside the tower or by climbing up the rungs on the back of the tower in the open air. With those few access points, it was a kill funnel for anyone attempting an assault, and it's where Hayes needed to go.

But there was another way.

Hayes lifted the MP7 and shot along the bulkhead. The hollow-point rounds were the best choice for close-quarters work on ships because they fragmented and spalled. Hayes used the narrow angles to bounce the shards of bullet around the corner, covering the passageway behind him.

It felt like the skin was sloughing off his back, but Hayes kept calm, checking the route ahead while firing behind him, intending more to suppress than kill his pursuers.

He was in a room at the very front of the tower. Ahead of him a door opened to the outside and the forecastle, the main open-air deck at the bow of the ship, shaped like a triangle.

He grabbed an emergency escape breathing device off the bulkhead, a small tank of air with a plastic hood attached for use in case of fire or gas leak. Inside the pack was a green cylinder of pure oxygen.

They shouted after him. He opened the door to the forecastle and laid the green bottle across the frame.

"Grenade," he shouted. Fair warning. He didn't want to kill them all. He wanted Caro.

He stepped outside. Swells threw burning water over the deck. He slammed the door shut with every ounce of strength, and the closing steel sheared off the tank's valve.

He'd seen oxygen tanks go before. They didn't even need a flame. The gas was under a few thousand PSI and the friction as it expanded was enough for ignition. Hayes's unit had lost an apprentice armorer who thought he was swapping out the valve on an empty oxygen tank. All they found afterward was the case from his Omega and his left foot. The tank was a quarter mile away, embedded two feet deep in a concrete wall.

The blast lit up the passageways at the base of the tower. The overpressure alone would knock out anyone approaching through the confined spaces, and likely wreck the doors. Glass blew out over his head.

He stepped onto the forecastle. The wrecked turret of the ship's 20 mm Gatling gun stood near the bow. He turned and looked back at the tower looming over his head and the bridge windows thirty feet up.

The front of the tower was a vertical plane of painted steel, a hard climb even without the smoke and the flames. He traced a route: the footholds in the dogs of the door, the railing above, and then the wires of the standing rigging that led to the antennas sticking out from the top of the bridge.

It was the only way.

He lifted his radio and made the call.

The smoke closed in. He jogged at the steel bulkhead, jumped, planted his foot, and grabbed the railing. Ignoring the agony from his back, he hauled himself up.

Riggs came to in the passageway at the base of the tower. Caro was the first to reach him and found him looking like a broken man, gasping on the deck. He draped the colonel's arm over his shoulders and helped him walk away from the smoke after the oxygen explosion.

"Was it Hayes?"

"What?"

"Hayes!" Caro shouted.

Riggs opened and closed his eyes twice.

"Was it—"

"It was him."

"Where is he now?"

"I don't know."

"Did you talk to him? What did he say?"

"What?"

"What did Hayes say? I heard you talking."

Riggs grabbed the handrail of the ladder leading up the tower to the bridge.

"What did he say?" Caro asked. He had kept the truth hidden for so long, and now it could destroy him.

Riggs looked at him for a moment, as if deep in thought.

"Nothing," Riggs said. "Nothing."

"Let's get to the bridge. Leave your men down here on watch," Caro said.

"Wait here," Riggs said. He radioed for his guards and didn't move until they arrived. "I'll check out the bridge," the colonel said.

"I'll come with you," Caro offered.

"No," Riggs said, and turned to his men. "Guard these ladders. That's the only way up."

He closed his good hand on the railing and started climbing.

Caro watched him go. He had seen doubt like that on Riggs's face before, on the day of the massacre.

After Hayes had been ambushed on his way back from the infiltration, Riggs couldn't understand what had happened. He knew that Hayes had been hit and that arms and information from Riggs's command had possibly made it into the enemy's hands.

Caro had calmed him down. "He was ambushed in the badlands near the border. We know who leaked his location—it was the interpreters."

They were the traitors in their midst. "Where are they? They may try another attack to kill the rest of your men."

Riggs was silent, and finally he'd turned to Caro.

"Can you help me take care of them?"

Riggs was desperate. *Take care of them.* What did Riggs think Caro would do? Give the villagers plane tickets? Resettle them somewhere? No.

And Caro was sure that Riggs hadn't thought about it too hard, because his primary goal was saving his own career. However it had happened, the ambush reflected terribly on Riggs. The leaks had happened on his watch.

Caro sent his men to round up the villagers. Riggs arrived just after the killing started, and his mouth fell open with horror. He pulled Caro aside. It was a moment when Riggs had to decide what kind of man he was.

He had lived only in the United States, had never seen combat up close before, had never seen how things were done in the hard corners of the world. That day Caro showed him what it took to win wars in a land where mercy was interpreted as weakness and weakness was death.

Caro offered Riggs a way forward, an escape from his own mistakes. They would sacrifice the villagers' lives—people whom the world had forgotten anyway—in order to protect their own, to go on and save countless more. Caro broke him out of the CNN mentality that flinches from violence and ties America's hands in battle. "This is what you do with traitors."

And there, looking at the huddled villagers, Riggs had to make his choice. He stood at the entrance to the house with his sidearm out, unsure.

He turned back to Caro and said, "Whatever it takes."

He had to believe the villagers were guilty. What was his alternative? To admit that it was all his fault? To sacrifice his career? No. The truth would have destroyed him, so Riggs doubled-down on a lie. Who wouldn't?

From then on, Caro held the secret of Riggs's role in both the ambush and the massacre, and that secret proved to be a powerful weapon. Caro owned him, whether Riggs cared to admit it to himself or not.

When Hayes and his team arrived at the massacre, it could have ruined everything, but there was grace in the bullet Hayes fired. It shattered Riggs's hand as he pointed into the valley and then tore through his upper chest. Hayes's men were down in the village, trying to save the dead, painting their hands with blood.

Hayes made it easy for Riggs to pin the blame on him. He had tried to relieve Riggs of command, had shot his superior officer. It was mutiny, and the punishment for mutiny in a time of war was death.

As Riggs lay unable to move and bleeding into the dirt on that hill, Caro put the idea in his ear: "The crimes. Let them fall on Hayes."

They called in the Rangers.

Through the agonizing recovery, Riggs nursed his grievance against Hayes, the man who had rebelled against him, the traitor. Caro wondered sometimes if Riggs had finally come to believe his own lie, that Hayes had cut those interpreters down.

It hardly mattered. That was the fire that drove Riggs, half crippled by Hayes's hand, half blind with revenge, and he and Caro had labored together ever since, building their plans.

But now the work was complete and Riggs no longer useful. Caro stepped outside. There were two guards watching the ladder that led up the rear of the tower to the bridge. He thumbed the safety down on his pistol and waited for them to turn their backs.

*   *   *

Hayes reached for the next and highest railing, just below the wide windows at the top of the tower. He pulled himself up and eyed the wires running to the antennas. Adrenaline was the only thing keeping him going through the pain. He could haul himself onto the top of the bridge and then drop down to the wings, open platforms on either side, like terraces.

He grabbed the wire with his right hand, leaned out, and gripped it with his left as well. He planted his feet against the sheer face of the tower and began to walk his way up the gray steel. He stopped, waited.

Black smoke billowed past, offering concealment. He pulled himself up the wire, hand over hand, and was nearly to the top of the bridge when sparks blew beside him. He turned and saw guards on the forecastle below him. They had finally forced their way through the door he had wrecked when he blew up the oxygen tank. He posted his legs out, held the wire with his left hand, and fired the MP7 in three-round bursts at the men below.

Blue sparks burst from the side of his gun. He felt the fire jump across his hand, his neck, his face. His gun dropped to the end of its sling. A bullet had hit his MP7, maybe his hand. He couldn't feel anything below the wrist, just the white-hot nothing of a fresh injury, the shock before the pain set in.

He had no time to think about it. He hauled himself up on the wire, pushed hard with his legs, and landed on his right side on the starboard bridge wing. His head pounded against the steel deck but he carried the momentum forward into a roll and came up in a crouch as a cloud of black smoke passed over.

The blood was seeping into the collar of his shirt. He took a quick look at his hand. The skin was shredded. He felt the cuts on his neck and cheek. The bullet must have fragmented off the gun. He felt the pressure. It was flowing slowly, nothing arterial. The shot had wrecked the chamber of the MP7. The pistol was gone. He reached across his body with his left hand, pulled his knife, got down low, and started toward the door of the bridge.

As the smoke cleared, he saw that the door was open. Riggs was just inside the pilothouse with a rifle aimed and ready in his good hand. Hayes stood, held the knife out front. And then he heard footfalls on the steel.

He turned. Behind him, on the bridge wing, Caro raised a pistol. He hadn't come through the bridge. He must have climbed up on the outside ladder on the back of the tower.

Hayes watched the surface of the ocean ripple in the firelight—a gust of wind. The billowing smoke neared the railing. It would hide him. He might have a chance in the blackness to kill them both. He had to try.

He readied himself for the lunge to get Riggs's rifle, prayed for the smoke to come, but it was too late.

Blue flames sprang from the muzzle in the shape of a star. Riggs fired an automatic burst.

CHAPTER 48

THE FOG OF diesel fumes closed in and Hayes saw nothing but the suffocating smoke. Then he heard it behind him, something slamming against the deck.

Caro's body.

Hayes pivoted, leaped toward him, and felt along the man's side through the slick of blood until he found the pistol. He dropped the knife and took the gun with his uninjured left hand.

Another gust, and the smoke cleared. Hayes and Riggs stood facing each other.

"He was coming for me," Riggs said in a monotone. "I ordered my men to secure the bridge."

Hayes looked down. "There are two bodies on the main deck. Not my work."

"I heard it on the radio. Caro must have executed them. He was going to kill me, kill us all, and then blame you." He lowered his gun. "Again.

"You've earned it," Riggs went on. "Take the shot."

"That's not how this works, Colonel."

"Do it."

"You made the wrong choice in the village. Make the right one here. Call off the rest of your men. And work with me. What was Caro doing? What were you two planning? We have to stop it."

"No," Riggs said. "Just end it."

Hayes stepped closer.

"After everything I did to you." Riggs shook his head. "Your wife, your daughter. The people you had guarding the money are dead. Do the honorable thing and take the fucking shot."

The colonel deserved to die, but Caro had risked coming to the U.S. for a reason, and Hayes needed Riggs alive to find out what it was.

"Call off your men," Hayes said. "We need to stop what Caro set in motion."

"It's too late. No one will believe you. This is the only justice you'll get. So don't waste it. Take the goddamn shot."

Riggs raised his gun, and Hayes his. Hayes weighed the choice with his finger on the trigger. A nonlethal shot on the deck of a shifting ship was almost impossible. It was suicide by cop, and if he murdered Riggs, he didn't know if he could ever convince the authorities that he was innocent.

The barrel aimed straight at Hayes's face and then kept moving up as Riggs brought the gun around. Hayes dived at the colonel as Riggs buried the muzzle under his own jaw.

He struck the gun arm. The shot boomed through the bridge. The muzzle flare blinded Hayes for a moment, and as his vision returned, he saw Riggs on the deck, with blood on his face. Hayes stepped on the wrist of his gun hand, took the carbine, and slipped its sling over his shoulder.

He cleared the blood away. The cheek was torn apart and

scorched from the muzzle flare. Blood trickled from Riggs's right ear, but he wasn't dead. Not yet. Hayes tore off his sleeve and tamped it on the injury. Ears ringing, he dragged Riggs toward the bridge wing.

He could barely hear as the door inside the pilothouse opened. He turned. Four guards stepped out.

Hayes threw his injured arm around Riggs's chest and lifted him up as a shield. It was Bill and three others. Hayes brought the gun forward with his left hand, pulling the sling taut to steady his aim.

"Drop the weapon and we can get this sorted out. We don't want to kill you," Bill said.

Hayes stepped back, over Caro's dead body, crushing a pair of sunglasses that had fallen from his pocket. Caro's head had been torn off by the gunshots.

He backed toward the edge of the wing. It was a forty-foot drop to the water, and he needed to make it far enough horizontally to clear the gunwale and not break his neck. Flames surrounded the ship, a slick forty feet wide.

A hard swell lifted the *Shiloh*. Helicopter blades chugged toward them. Hayes tried to keep Riggs close, but he knew that as their bodies drew apart, one of these men would get the shot. He had trained two of them in hostage rescue himself. Hayes stared down the muzzles of four carbines.

Marine Super Cobra helicopters closed in. Riggs couldn't talk. He was still in shock. The truth wouldn't save Hayes now.

He saw the barrel line up perfectly, and just before Bill's muzzle flared, Hayes pulled Riggs tight to his body, compressed his legs, and threw himself over the edge.

The fall seemed to last minutes as they dropped toward the flames on the water. They passed through a chaos of heat and fire. The surface hit them like a car crash and then all was cold silence and darkness. The water soothed Hayes's burns. He clamped Riggs to his side and stroked underwater with his good hand, sliding through the dark, the red glow dancing above their heads.

Forty feet. Thirty. Twenty.

He could see full dark ahead, and pulled hard, drove himself with his legs.

Ten.

He kept on, then angled to the surface, broke through into the night air, and filled his lungs.

Hayes hit the IR beacon on his shoulder, floated on his back with the swells. He watched the clouds drift overhead.

A helicopter came in low, searching with its light like a circle of midday sun on the water. He dived and waited, dragging Riggs's limp body down with him.

When he came up, he saw the floodlight moving away and heard another engine over the chug of the helos.

It was the RHIB. Fifty feet out he could see the man standing at the pilothouse: Byrne. Hayes had called him on the radio before he assaulted the bridge. The boat pulled alongside. Hayes hauled himself in, and he and Byrne dragged Riggs over the gunwale. Byrne brought the boat through a fast 180-degree turn and gunned the engines for the shore.

Hayes flex-cuffed Riggs, then took the helm with his good hand while Byrne tended to the colonel.

"He's in shock, but he should live," Byrne said. He stepped to the pilothouse and started dressing Hayes's neck and hand.

"Nazar has major trauma to the chest. She's going to die if we don't get her to a cardiothoracic surgeon."

"Oceanside," Hayes said, and scanned the skies behind him: no aircraft. He could hear them in the distance, but they weren't in close pursuit. "There's a cache. It's our best chance."

"We can't go in over the beach with these casualties."

"The harbor," Moret said. "But they'll catch us."

Hayes looked to Moret, to Nazar. A syringe attached to a catheter in the old woman's chest was half full of blood.

"I'm not letting anyone die," Byrne said. "The harbor."

Hayes turned the wheel.

"You dive when we're close to shore," Byrne said to Hayes. "Run for it. I'll take the casualties in."

"I'm not running. We stopped Samael. We brought them Nazar, brought them the truth. I did what I needed to do. We have to warn them."

"They'll try you."

"I knew what I was doing. If I broke the law, I'll pay the price. I wouldn't want it any other way."

"Don't," Byrne said. "They might execute you."

"I can't kill them all. I can't make them believe at the point of a gun. This is too big for Riggs to control anymore. I have to trust my country."

Nazar moaned, and Byrne crouched next to the old woman. The swells picked up.

"How are we doing, Byrne?" Hayes shouted.

"Blood pressure's dropping. Give it everything."

Hayes pushed the throttle. The boat skipped over the surface of the ocean. The chug of helo blades never quit the horizon as they saw the mountains rise behind Camp Pendleton and the glow of Carlsbad and Oceanside resolve into lights, and then houses.

"We're losing her," Byrne said. They rounded the mouth of the harbor. He cleared the blood from the syringe.

Hayes headed for the end of a dock. The attack helicopters

came in fast from the west and south. They had held off, and now they were tightening the noose. There was no way out of the harbor.

The dock came closer as the helicopter lit them up with a flood. Police and navy aircraft touched down in the parking lot beside the water. The Super Cobra hovered just ahead, its 20 mm turreted cannon aimed straight at the RHIB.

In the lights from the circling aircraft, Hayes could see the SWAT teams closing in on land. There were a dozen SUVs, more patrol cars, and two armored personnel carriers. The tactical teams fanned across the parking lot and surrounded the dock. The police took aim from behind the doors of their black Suburbans. The whole waterfront was a circus of blinking lights.

"Drop your weapons! Drop your weapons!"

Hayes brought the boat to the dock, stepped onto the concrete, and raised his hands.

"Don't give them an excuse to kill you," he said to the others.

The SWATs circled him. He watched them move in slowly and cautiously, checking off each step, like they had just watched a long PowerPoint presentation on squad tactics.

He kept his hands in the air. "I have Colonel Riggs and Cyrine Nazar on this boat. They are innocent and require medical attention. Do not hurt them."

A squad leader moved in.

"The woman has trauma to her heart and needs an airlift to a surgeon. She can tell you the truth about who we are and what we have done."

An officer shoved Hayes forward and tried to trip him to his knees. He didn't go down.

A man in a suit parted the crowd. He looked like he hadn't slept in days.

"I need to talk to your CO," Hayes said. "Do what you want with me, but listen. There is an imminent threat. Listen to Riggs. People are going to die."

"What did he say!" someone barked.

"On your knees!" A rifle butt slammed into Hayes's back. He took a knee but didn't fall.

Cox tried to move through the crowd. "Don't shoot! Don't shoot!" But his voice was lost in the chaos.

"A plot is under way. People are going to die. You can stop it. Let me talk to your CO."

"Is that a threat? Is there a bomb?"

The SWATs crowded in.

Hayes could see the fear in their eyes, their hands tight on the grips of their rifles, the fingers on the triggers, the discipline ebbing. Caro was dead. Hayes had completed the mission. He could die content.

"Listen to Riggs. To the woman."

They slammed him facedown onto the concrete.

"What did he say! He could trigger it!"

"What's he doing? Do I fire? *Do I fire?*"

A deputy, the youngest and most inexperienced of the forward squad, leveled his rifle and aimed at the back of Hayes's head from five feet away. He would later swear he had heard the order.

"Take the shot. Now!"

His finger pulled on the trigger.

CHAPTER 49

BRADAC BOARDED HIS second bus of the morning and fed his dollars into the fare box. His ride toward Sidwell took him away from downtown, and the bus was uncrowded. The Mechanic knew the checklists that American law-enforcement officers used to spot suicide bombers—freshly shaved face, the scent of flower water to prepare for heaven, mumbled prayers—and had coached Bradac to avoid them.

Many of the warning signs were unconscious—sweating, nervous tics, unnaturally fast or slow breathing—but as Bradac sat on the 30N, he gave no indications of his intent. He had been through this before. The only thing that could upset him would be the denial of his chance at heaven. The twenty minutes passed as in a dream, and he was beaming the entire ride.

He caught the eye of an older Salvadoran woman holding the hand of a grandchild. Most of the riders stared into space, at their phones, or at the floor, but Bradac's bliss was infectious. The woman smiled back at him, and the little girl turned her brown eyes his way and followed suit.

The bus climbed the long hill toward Sidwell Friends School.

He waved to her, and she laughed and hid her face in her grandmother's side.

As they approached Tenleytown, a massive office building made to look like a colonial mansion rose to their left. "Upton Street," chimed the prerecorded female voice.

Bradac pulled on the yellow cord to signal for a stop, then exited through the rear doors of the bus. School had been in session for thirty-five minutes at Sidwell, and students had settled in for their first lessons.

The vice president's daughter, age twelve, raised her hand to ask a question in pre-algebra on the second floor. The national security adviser's grandson, age seven, sat at a cluster of desks listening to a reading lesson on silent *e*'s. The House Whip's daughter, a speech therapist, was working in the resource room by the south stairwell with a small group of children, including the niece, age six, of the deputy secretary of defense for Special Operations.

A fence ringed the entire campus except for the entrance to the middle school. Bradac walked along Upton, turned south on Thirty-Seventh Street, and saw his target. There, the windows on both floors of the school were only twenty feet away from the sidewalk. He didn't have to enter the campus or deal with the security guards at an institution that had educated the First Families of the United States since Theodore Roosevelt sent his son Archibald through its doors.

He stopped across the street, placed his USPS package on the ground, and tore away a tab—a friction fuse.

Nothing happened. He waited, and watched. A dark spot appeared on the box, turned into black ash, and then sparks flew crackling from the top. They poured into the air, sixteen feet high, red and black and brilliant electric white.

The morning was still. The smoke rose straight toward a clear blue winter sky.

Bradac crossed the street, hands plunged in the jacket of his coat, thumb pressed against the trigger. He watched the colors flare. It was beautiful. Children crowded around the windows, awestruck, their eyes open wide, inches from the glass.

Their souls were pure, and they would enter heaven too, without ever having to suffer the tomb, and his mother, whom he'd found when he was their age dead with her skirt up and a needle stuck in her groin because her arms were too scarred to shoot, would be there, and she was alive again and as beautiful as he remembered and they were all there in heaven because on this one winter morning he had been so brave.

"There is no god but God."

He gripped the detonator, shut his eyes, and pressed his thumb down on the toggle switch.

CHAPTER 50

THE NAVY C-20 jet cruised at four hundred and sixty knots at forty thousand feet. From the sounds, Hayes could tell they were in flight aboard a small jet but knew nothing else. He had been blindfolded and shackled wrist and ankle since his capture. At some point they cut his clothes off without loosening the restraints and left him naked in a cold cell. They stitched up his face and hands, then placed him in coveralls and readied him for a long flight.

He knew the drill. They were taking him to a black site, or maybe the Fort Leavenworth supermax prison, to be warehoused, disappeared in a cell where the light shone twenty-four hours a day until the mind destroyed itself.

But his own fate wasn't his concern right now. They hadn't believed him. Caro was gone, but whatever plot he had started could still be ticking. How many would die?

He heard footsteps, the breath of a man, figured him for a hundred and eighty-five pounds.

"There is an imminent threat," Hayes said. "Please listen. I understand that you don't believe me, but people are going to die and you can stop it."

He felt the blacked-out goggles tugged away from his face, pulling at the deep cuts along his cheek and ear. The light blinded him.

As his eyes adjusted, he looked at the man standing over him. They had met before, at Bragg. His name was Cox. And Hayes recognized him as the man who had broken through the crowd at the last minute and stopped the SWAT team from killing him on the spot.

Cox said nothing and reached into his pocket. He placed a key in Hayes's shackles and released his feet, then his hands. He put the restraints on the seat across the aisle.

Hayes's mind worked quickly as he surveyed the jet's interior. This must be a trap. Maybe an attempt to build rapport, which meant he had a trained interrogator with him rather than a sadist. He preferred sadists. They caused more pain but were less effective.

"I've been hunting you for a long time," Cox said.

Hayes narrowed his eyes, trying to puzzle out this man's game.

"And now I need your help, Captain Hayes. Riggs told us what happened."

Hayes refused to believe it. It would be snatched away. He held on in silence while the prospect of freedom, of making this all right, stood before him like a false vision before death.

"There is a terrorist attack under way," Cox said. "The suspects are inside the country. We don't know where they will strike."

Hayes had faith in his country, in the truth. He'd figured that for a martyr's cause. But it had worked.

"It must be Samael," Hayes said. "He was using the name Caro and had somehow managed to gain Riggs's trust. They were developing an operation. I don't know what the goal was. We had a source on Samael before…before everything fell apart. We were tracking him on that deep infiltration. What did Riggs say?"

"He doesn't know how much he can believe of what Caro told him. He thinks that he was planning a provocation, a way to start a war by striking at political elites."

"Samael has been building up to this for years. Our source talked about him going after leaders where they were most vulnerable, deriving the greatest effect from the smallest cause: targeting the families."

"Riggs believed it would happen abroad, against America's enemies."

"No," Hayes said. "It's the same strategy, but he's doing it in the U.S. That's why he tried to kill Riggs, who knew the logic of his plans. The provocation is the first domino. He's trying to draw us into a conflict. The U.S. will walk right into his trap. It could bring decades of bloodshed."

He looked down. "I know where he's going. Washington. We need to get to Andrews."

"We have an imminent-threat alert out. Metro SWAT teams. The National Guard. We have security up around every target."

Hayes shook his head.

"No, you don't."

The patrol car stopped at the corner of Thirty-Seventh and Upton. Officer Paul Santoya scanned the street, then glanced down at the box on the passenger seat. It was a vapor-ion detector. For work at range, the bomb-sniffing dogs were ineffective.

There was a red bar on the screen: *Nitramine detected.*

The call had gone out from the tactical operations center downtown: a full alert. They wanted added security at the schools.

Everyone was carrying a long gun. He figured it was just the politicians looking out for themselves as usual, and today would be an easy job, babysitting VIPs' kids. He had been assigned to Sidwell.

White smoke rose down the hill. He called it in and was trotting toward the school down Thirty-Seventh Street when he saw sparks pouring into the air. He had been army National Guard infantry, with two deployments. He had seen plenty of IEDs go, but this looked like fireworks.

As he came around the corner, he saw the man standing in front of the school: bulky coat, hands in pockets. The vapor detector went to five bars. Could have just been the fireworks. New Year's wasn't that far away.

He dropped to one knee to steady his rifle, took aim, and keyed his radio.

"This is Santoya. I have a man on Thirty-Seventh, Sidwell Friends, outside the middle school. Bulky coat, hands in pockets. There's some kind of fireworks going off. Should I approach?"

He aimed his rifle at the man's center mass, as he had been trained, felt the cold wind against his cheek, and moved the target a few mils to the left in his scope to compensate.

Santoya remembered the day insurgents had blown the checkpoint outside his forward operating base. Even the high-powered rifle round to the insurgent's chest hadn't killed him fast enough to stop him from pulling the trigger.

But this guy didn't look like a bomber. He was smiling.

"Stand by, Santoya."

The man in the coat watched the fireworks blaze, then looked up at the children, their faces against the windows.

"I say again, do I approach?"

He kept his finger outside the trigger guard. Santoya had a good thing going with a younger girl he'd met online, no drama, a steady job, enough for the alimony. He was not going to throw it all away by acting like he was still downrange and killing some poor guy who was just out for a morning walk.

A head shot. That was SOP. He aimed two mils higher. He had qualified on this carbine, a law-enforcement version of the M4, and remembered that his cold shots always flew a little low, one minute of angle or so. Propellant burns more slowly in a cold barrel.

"I say again, do I approach?"

The man's hand reached deeper into his jacket pocket.

A thirty-foot bank of video screens filled the front wall of the tactical operations center—the TOC. Cox's face appeared on one of the dozens of displays. They relayed the message to him from Officer Santoya at Sidwell. The TOC commander didn't want to take the shot.

On-screen, there was a man to the side of Cox who looked like he had just been dragged back from hell, his cheek bandaged and face scratched up.

The whole staff wondered who they were, these people who had authority straight from the White House and had ordered roadblocks around half the schools in Washington.

The fireworks. A distraction before the main blast. To draw them to the glass. To cut them when it shattered. Hayes had seen it before.

"Take the shot," he said to Cox. "The head. Take the shot. Now."

The command went from Cox to the TOC to the officer's radio. Santoya laid his finger on the trigger and pulled it smoothly.

The head of the man in the jacket disappeared in a cloud of red. His body fell back as it crumpled, out of view from the school behind a low concrete wall. Only a few children witnessed anything.

Most of them knew nothing of what happened that morning until years later. Their eyes were fixed on the colors pouring from the small package as the sparks slowed, then stopped, and left only a cloud of white smoke drifting into a clear sky as their teachers called them back to their desks.

CHAPTER 51

"Hey."

A hand closed on my shoulder.

"Byrne."

A figure rose over me. I sat up, startled, and grabbed the wrist.

It was Kelly, holding a cup of coffee in her other hand. She stepped back.

"It's okay," she said. "We're at the hotel. Everything's cool."

I looked around the room: generic landscape paintings, a minifridge, light angling in between the drapes.

"Right."

She was smiling at me like I was the last one to get the joke.

"What time is it?" I asked. There was something strange about the light.

"Nine thirty."

"Wait. Was I…"

"Yup," she said. "Like a log. I didn't know you snored."

"Neither did I."

I lifted myself up on one elbow, put my hand to the side of her face, and kissed her.

"I haven't been able to do that in a long time."

"You look like a little boy when you're asleep."

"All right. Don't get cute."

It was Kelly who had first told Cox the truth of what happened. It took two dozen officers to catch her, in the sloughs near the Mexican border. Without her giving Cox the story, preparing him for the truth, we never would have been able to stop the bomber in time.

It takes a while to get off the no-fly list and undo the damage of being branded an enemy of the state. Forced R&R with Kelly was fine by me.

"Here." She handed me an orange pill bottle and then took a bottle of her own and dropped a tablet into her palm. We were like a couple of old fogies, but the injuries were healing, and I was starting to be able to use my shoulder again.

"Cheers." I swallowed my pills down with a glass of water from the nightstand. I had had them put us up at La Valencia. She stepped onto the terrace. I followed and put my arm around her waist.

Swells filled in the cove, a ten-foot set, peeling beautifully as the late-season Santa Ana blew offshore.

"That's gorgeous."

"The ocean?"

She nodded.

"I'm off oceans for a while."

She had her phone in her hand and was fiddling with it. Something was on her mind.

"Any news?"

"My CO called."

"And?"

"Cox straightened everything out. And my unit-transfer request went through."

"Great. Where are you headed?"

"Bragg."

Fort Bragg, in North Carolina, home to Airborne and Special Forces.

"It's the cultural support teams."

"Congratulations." That's the closest women could get to front-line combat, at least officially, accompanying Rangers and SF on raids. And she would be first in line for Special Operations if the policy changed.

"Cox pulled some strings. I still have to make it through assessment."

"You will. I am damn sure of that. I feel sorry for the bad guys. When do you leave? Fall?"

She pursed her lips. "A week."

I did a decent job hiding my disappointment. I was happy for her and didn't want to bring her down.

"They're trying to stand it up by summer. If it works out, I'll be gone eighteen months."

I didn't say anything for a while. We both stood there, pinned by the awkward question in the air.

"I'm sorry, Tom. I've got to do it. This was supposed to be—"

"Of course you're going to do it. We were always on the same page. Don't worry about that for a second."

"I meant everything I said."

"Me too."

Sure, I had slept through the night beside her, but I still had a lot to deal with, and I wasn't going to rush into anything. It wasn't fair to me, or her.

"Thank you for trusting me, and for…"

"Not dying?" she said.

I almost laughed. "Well, yeah." She'd proved me wrong. I wasn't a curse.

"You're easy to please."

"I didn't think I could have this again. That I would deserve it."

"You do, Tom."

I kissed her and brought her to my chest.

"You're a good guy. Don't be too hard on yourself, okay?"

People had been telling me that for more than a decade. I'd always known in some way that I hadn't caused those deaths, but that didn't matter to the guilt. I knew it, but I could never fully believe it. Now I could start, and maybe I could stop running.

"I won't."

I held her close. And for once, a morning felt like a beginning instead of an end that would never come.

I looked out over the cove, then back into the room, waiting for the punishment for my pride, my happiness, my gall. Nothing came. Where were the shades that had haunted me? Gone for now and, I prayed, for good.

Those visions weren't Emily. They were my own twisted guilt, my head looking for ways to hurt me.

And I remembered her as she was, beside a mountain lake, young and strong and beautiful. I remembered the first time she handed me a glass of her father's moonshine. She'd warned me it was strong. *Come on,* I said, took it down, then broke out in a fit of coughing, water welling from my eyes. She started laughing, under the summer sky so clear.

That was Emily. That was the truth. That's what I would remember now.

* * *

We watched the ocean for a long time.

"One week," I said.

"Yes."

"You want to stick around?"

"More than anything. And then..."

"You're going to Bragg. Don't worry about me."

"I'm not. And life is long, Byrne." She pulled me in close and kissed me. "I'll be seeing you around."

CHAPTER 52

THEY BURIED COOK on a Wednesday. It was a cold, brilliant morning at the Main Post Cemetery at Fort Bragg. Hayes and Moret joined Cook's father and brothers to carry the casket. Moret used her left hand. Her right arm was still in a sling.

When Caro's deputies had turned on Riggs's men, Ward took advantage of the chaos and managed to escape, carrying Cook with his arms over her shoulders. She broke into a construction trailer and did everything she remembered from tactical combat care for the tension pneumothorax. She'd stayed there in the cold with her friend for hours, talking to him about old action movies like they used to. But he had never regained consciousness.

Ward's two sons, three and five, sat in the fifth row beside her ex. She had tried to draw them so many times, but she couldn't get their faces right, couldn't picture them anymore. Every time the guilt had devastated her, and finally she just stopped trying.

Now they were here, trying their best to sit still, though the three-year-old couldn't help but swing his dangling legs.

They watched her stand at attention beside the rifle party at the full-honors funeral and lead the three-volley salute.

After the burial, Hayes and Moret and Ward went to a dive bar in Southern Pines well known for its clientele: built guys with beards and Wiley X tans who kept to themselves and, if pressed, claimed to have the most boring-sounding civilian jobs imaginable: systems engineer, compliance analyst.

Byrne and Britten wanted to leave them alone, to talk, to grieve, but Hayes had insisted that they come.

They took the back room with the pool table and the dartboard. Moret passed Hayes a medal, the Distinguished Service Cross, the second-highest award in the U.S. military. Hayes had skipped the ceremony at the Pentagon. If they wanted a hero, they'd have to find someone else. Even after he had been cleared, Hayes didn't like mingling among the generals who had spent two years trying to kill him. The award was classified. It was really about the brass honoring themselves for their magnanimity.

It felt odd when he'd pulled on his class A uniform after so long on the run and operating undercover before that. He barely recognized himself in the mirror.

The investigations had been an endless slog, but the glad handing from the command afterward was worse, the way they treated him as if nothing had ever happened.

Hayes's teammates were glad to be together here, on their own, away from the base. Mainly they checked up on one another, made sure everyone was getting on in the transition, families were okay, that they all had everything they needed.

They'd been in the crosshairs so long that there was something unsettling about peace and calm and empty days. They hunted for jobs, went through bills, shopped for basics, and were never able to stop looking over their shoulders for a kill team, even while dragging the trash cans out to the curb.

But every day was a miracle. They talked about what they had missed, the small things: using their own names, eating a decent burger, taking the kids to the lake, mowing the lawn and smelling freshly cut grass.

Byrne brought back another round. It had grown late.

"Ask Hayes," Moret said.

Ward turned to him. "When Cook came to at the last safe house, he was trying to tell me something. I think it was a joke. Corduroy something."

Hayes shook his head. "You haven't heard that one?"

"No."

"Come on." He sighed. "Everybody knows that joke."

"How does it go?"

Hayes relented. "Did you hear about the corduroy pillows?" he asked, and looked around the circle. "They're making head lines."

Britten laughed first. Moret joined in. Ward groaned. Even Hayes seemed to enjoy it.

"He finally told a decent joke."

It grew quiet again, and there was some crying. They had held it back for so long. Hayes shut the door and they comforted one another, brothers and sisters, let it overflow at last, the warring feelings of sadness and joy for what was lost, and for what remained.

They drank to the dead, and to one another, and to the lives they had saved. And they drank to Hayes, who had brought them home.

As they lowered Cook into the ground, Samael woke from a deep sleep in the business-class cabin of an Emirates 777 and pressed the button to raise the lie-flat bed. The attendant approached and asked when would be a good time to serve dinner.

The menu featured grilled lamb cutlets, roast chicken with a pistachio crust, and Thai-style fish curry.

"As soon as possible," Samael replied. "The curry." It was a long flight, and there was a lot of business to take care of in the east.

It was a shame about the Sidwell attack, but they could start again. They still held the most important weapon: the millions in black money taken from Riggs.

Caro was dead. It was a great loss, but the networks were intact. The logic of the plan was good. It would succeed eventually. The first time they attacked the Twin Towers, with a truck bomb in 1993, they failed, and the world seemed to forget until the planes hit. It would take time to rebuild, but they would be back. There was much work to be done. The first priority was sleep.

The attendant offered a glass of Moët et Chandon. Samael declined and couldn't help but smile at the extravagance. Not bad for a dead man.

CHAPTER 53

THROUGH THE WINDOW of the Suburban, Hayes watched the split-rail fence roll by. The last time he had come here, he had been in disguise, moving undercover toward his family's home as if it were enemy territory.

He saw the curtain pull back for a moment, and the outside lights came on. His truck crunched down the gravel driveway. He stepped out and saw the fresh paint and new windows where the bullets had torn through.

He climbed the stoop. He'd taken hundreds of doors in his time, but he'd never felt fear like this. He had spent his whole life looking for a place to belong and spent years trying to get here, to get home. He always knew he might arrive to find that there was nothing left for him. He would be a refugee with no homeland, wandering endlessly, like those who had died in the massacre.

He let out a long breath, lifted his hand, and knocked.

No answer. He waited ten seconds and knocked again.

The door cracked. A hazel eye peered out. Lauren opened it and stared at him, and her face fell. She began to cry.

"I'm sorry," Hayes said.

He had flowers and the oatmeal raisin cookies from the bakery in Southern Pines that Lauren loved. He looked down at the gifts and cursed himself. *Idiot. Like a first date. She's still traumatized and you come in a black truck and pound on the door.*

"No," she said.

"I shouldn't have come."

She smiled. "No, not like that." She grabbed his free hand, pulled him through the door, and threw her arms around him. "It was just too much for a second." She laughed and wiped her eyes. "I don't know. Welcome back."

He held her and felt peace for the first time in years. But it was clouded by the guilt that he hadn't been there to protect her, that he had put her in danger. And the knowledge that this peace wouldn't last.

He and Lauren had separated before his last deployment, before she found out she was pregnant. He knew her well, knew she made up her own mind. He needed to come here so he could tell her the truth and so he could apologize for the pain he'd put her through. He owed it to her.

"Thank you. I know what you said, before I left. I needed to tell you in person. I'm sorry, Lauren, for—"

She put her hand on his cheek.

"Don't worry about any of that right now." She took the flowers and cookies. "Come on in. It's still a bit—"

"Who's that?" Maggie stood in the arched entry to the family room, holding a toy hammer. Hayes took a step toward her.

"Hi, there," he said. All he wanted was to be part of his daughter's life, but he wouldn't be the one to tell her who he was. It wasn't his call. He had missed so much already, left his wife to shoulder the weight alone. He looked from her to Lauren, waiting on the verdict.

She crouched next to Maggie and pushed a strand of the child's hair back behind her ear. "That's your daddy. Do you remember what I told you about Daddy?"

"She knows?" Hayes asked.

"Of course. It's been hard, but I always believed in you, John."

He ducked down next to his daughter. "Can I give you a hug?"

Maggie shrugged. Hayes picked her up, held her to his chest.

"I remember him," she said.

Lauren tilted her head. That was impossible.

"He was outside," Maggie said.

Lauren looked to Hayes.

"I came by the house before I went after the men who did this to me. I had to see her. I didn't know if it would be my last chance."

He looked at the fresh patches in the drywall.

"Are you okay?"

"We're fine."

"I'm sorry."

"Don't be. You did nothing wrong."

"And Maggie?"

"I think sometimes I was relying on her more than she was relying on me."

Hayes held her, and they stayed like that for a long time, in silence.

Maggie started to fuss. Hayes let her down. She took his hand.

"You want to help me put her to bed?" Lauren asked.

"Of course," Hayes said.

A chocolate Lab limped out from the kitchen. Hayes leaned

over and rubbed his head. Lauren led him toward the hallway bathroom. He reached down and picked up a red vest where Maggie had left it.

Hayes sat in a rocking chair and watched his daughter sleep.

"Where are you staying?" Lauren asked him.

"Foley's cabin. Taking care of his affairs."

"You can stay here as long as you want."

"Thank you," he said.

Maggie rolled over, and after fifteen minutes, Lauren said good night.

Hayes watched over the child. The night was long. He didn't sleep, didn't want to lose a minute with her. He'd never felt anything as strong as that love.

And he'd never had so much to lose. Other thoughts crowded in. The CIA black money had never been recovered. There was more chatter about terrorist operations, signs pointing to Samael. Cox had told him that perhaps it was a successor, a deputy attempting to resume Samael's work.

But Hayes knew more about Samael than anyone, and he had devoured every piece of intelligence there was about Caro.

He knew something was wrong. The evil was still out there. Mother and child. The overwhelming power of those instincts, of family. In that room, he began to understand, and he made his decision.

She wouldn't be safe until he finished it. No one would.

Lauren came by the door just before dawn.

"Did you sleep?" she asked.

"Caught a couple hours," he said, and stretched his arms over his head.

"I can't believe you lie for a living."

"You're the only one who could ever tell."

"Something's wrong," she said.

"This isn't over."

"You have to go?"

"Yes."

That was what had pulled them apart before, the endless cycle of deployments. That was the trade. He couldn't be here for them, because he was out there for them, for everyone.

Hayes called Cox and drew a hard line. For weeks, the Pentagon set had been trying to slap him on the back, give him the Ira Hayes treatment.

"If I help you on this, you're not parading me around like a hero," Hayes said. "I'm going to be a ghost."

"That's what I was hoping you would say. Full black. No one will know what you're doing."

"No brass. No bullshit."

"We'll have national command authority. From you directly to me and the NSC and the White House. That's it."

"I need everything you have on Caro. And I need to talk to Riggs."

"He's buried."

"Where?"

"Leavenworth. It's a heavy lift. Everyone just wants him to disappear."

"Make it happen."

The arrangements with Cox took a while. Hayes stayed at the house, got to know his daughter. On the day he was set to depart, Lauren and Maggie walked him to his truck.

"This is the last time."

"That's what you said last time."

Hayes looked down at Maggie. It was too much. He couldn't leave them.

"Go, John," Lauren said, and put her hand on his cheek. "I understand. We need you out there."

He said good-bye to Maggie. Lauren stood next to the open door of the truck. They knew each other well enough. The question was clear: *And you and me?*

She embraced him, brought her cheek against his, and whispered in his ear.

CHAPTER 54

SAMAEL LOOKED OVER the Mediterranean from the terrace of the villa. It was owned by a sympathetic financier of the mission and stood empty for most of the year. Samael disliked luxury as a rule, but the only buildings secure enough for the work were these mansions. It would do. It would give them time. Theirs was the long game.

The Americans were like children near a flame. They would blunder into this part of the world, get burned, retreat, forget their mistakes, return. How could they possibly police the whole planet? It's as if they believed in all those superhero stories. Against them, Samael brought focus, simplicity, determination. It would take years, decades, but they would succeed.

Twelve miles away, there was an aging stone warehouse that still smelled of the tobacco it once housed. At 6:50 p.m. local time, six ten-pound charges of C-4 detonated simultaneously against its vaulted walls. The high explosives incinerated everything inside, though some witnesses would later claim that they saw, falling through the air, burning U.S. hundred-dollar bills.

The black money that Samael had stolen was gone.

Samael counted out the recordable CD-ROMs on the desk. They contained instructions to the cell leaders and would be sent by trusted courier. E-mail and even thumb drives were too vulnerable to American methods of interception.

The departure was set for five minutes. The plans lay on the desk. It was everything they needed to start again.

Samael lifted the radio and called the guards at the front door.

"Is the driver here yet?"

There was no answer. Samael keyed the radio again, and checked the battery LED.

"Hello?"

Hayes slipped through the front door and took cover in an inside corner of the villa's foyer. Outside, a small fire burned in a trash bin. He had unscrewed the fuse from a flash-bang and dropped it in the garbage. The fire grew quickly and drew out the guards at the front door.

Now they both lay dead on the walk.

Samael was on the move. Hayes had come alone on a last-minute patrol, intending only recon, but once here, he had to act. He had seen too many high-value targets slip away while he waited for approval from above. Other members of his unit had gone to blow the warehouse where the black money was being stored. He had called in for a helo team but didn't have time to wait.

It was dusk. He preferred three and four a.m., the time of night raids, the killing hours. But there was an advantage to going alone: the silence. He had used a suppressed .22-caliber pistol with half-loads on the guards at the front door, but inside, even that would be too loud. Often a raid against an enemy like Samael would be a kill order, but Hayes wanted to take the target alive, in silence, so there would be as little time as possible to torch intel.

He crept into the grand entrance hall, a large central area with spiral staircases on either side. They led to open landings on the higher floors where anyone could stand, look over a railing, and take in the entire space. He needed to make it upstairs unobserved. He heard footsteps coming from a hallway to his left.

He jammed the button on a radio, turned the volume all the way up, and slid it along the marble floor. It came to rest in the corner, and he took cover in an alcove fifteen feet away.

A few seconds passed, and then the sound of someone laboring to breathe, perhaps due to an injury, perhaps out of fear, came from the radio.

He waited.

"Hassan?" one of the guards asked. The men moved through the entrance hall, searching out the source of the noise. They raised their submachine guns and approached the corner.

"Hassan?"

Hayes came from behind. He had been whispering the noises that came out of the radio in order to draw them into a trap. He took one man with the knife, a straight vertical stab behind the clavicle into the aorta. The guard died instantly.

The other turned, but Hayes was already on him. There was a brief scuffle as Hayes twisted his arm until the shoulder joint broke, forcing him to the ground. He killed him with a stroke of the blade, then dragged him out of sight.

Hayes had spent years in the gray area, hiding from his own country. All that time he had tempered his thirst for revenge with the knowledge that the American soldiers hunting him were good men doing their duty.

But now it was black and white. He gave in to vengeance, the simple moral duty to kill these men before they could kill the ones he loved. Two years of suppressed rage flowed out of him like clear water.

He pulled the guard's radio and inserted the earpiece.

"Hello? Is the car here?"

It was Samael's voice.

It had taken six weeks of rehab for Hayes to be able to handle a weapon again. He tore the scar tissue apart between his barely flexing fingers. It was another six weeks of fifteen-hour days to get back into form. He tracked down everything he could about Samael and Caro. And as he regained his strength, he knew that Samael was out there, rebuilding at the same time, determined to strike again.

That unsettled feeling had started at his home, in the room with his wife and daughter. As he and Cox worked the investigations, the clues lined up. Caro couldn't possibly have been the one who tortured Foley to death on board the *Odessa*. He had been a hundred miles away, driving through the desert. Caro and Samael were two different people.

Hayes always thought back to what he had seen and heard aboard the *Shiloh* as it burned. There was one line from Riggs that had replayed ceaselessly in Hayes's mind. *Believed him? No. I didn't believe him*, Riggs had said. *I believed—*

He never had a chance to finish. And Hayes had never found the answer to the question that troubled him the most. Why would Riggs double-down with Caro, a man he had just seen slaughter an entire village? Why would he trust him enough to continue working with him? It never made sense.

It took two months and orders from the national security adviser herself for Hayes to be cleared to visit Riggs in his windowless cell. Riggs had confessed everything to the authorities. He had 30 percent hearing in one ear, none in the other. Hayes had to shout to be heard, but slowly, Riggs unspooled the story of the massacre.

"Who did you believe? Who told you that the villagers betrayed you?" Hayes asked.

Riggs told him. And though the crime was inexcusable, Hayes could at least understand why Riggs had let them be killed.

A person Riggs trusted had told him that it was the villagers, not Caro, who stabbed the U.S. in the back. The information came from an unimpeachable source who had sacrificed everything for the West. It was tragic, in a way, because as Riggs joined in the massacre, he really had believed, by some twisted logic, that he was doing the right thing.

And despite all the death, Hayes knew the true enemy was still alive, once again plotting safely while Hayes buried his brothers and sisters.

Hayes climbed the staircase of the villa, then crossed the landing to the top-floor suite. The door was half open.

"Hassan," he whispered. "Hassan."

He ducked back behind the door frame as the barrel of a rifle appeared, and then a man. Hayes grabbed the barrel and found himself facing a six-foot-four bodyguard in a competent stance. With Hayes in too close for the long gun to be effective, the man pulled a knife with his free hand and came in lunging. Hayes released the barrel and let the blade come, moved six inches to the side at the last minute, and grabbed the back of the man's neck. He pulled him forward and down as he dropped and fell backward.

The momentum brought the aggressor tumbling toward the iron railing. Hayes planted his feet at the man's waist as he rolled onto his own back, pushed hard with both legs, and lofted the bodyguard up and over the edge.

As the man fell, Hayes jerked his head back and broke his neck over the railing. The guard rag-dolled down and was dead by the time he hit the marble floor.

Hayes moved across the top floor, clearing it systematically, then came to the office, the only closed door. The time for silence was over. He mule-kicked the knob and threw in a bang.

White light and a deafening blast blew out. Hayes ran in, clearing the corners in that strange slowed-down time that always came after he took a door.

On the desk lay a neat row of CD-ROMs and stacks of files. He was in the sitting room of an office suite. He quickly scanned the library, the other exits, then crossed the vaulted passage.

Samael started for the desk and a pistol lying behind the files but couldn't make it in time. Hayes took aim with the carbine. The concussion grenade's effects on Samael were clear: unsteady steps, a hand held to the ear.

Hayes had known whom he would find, but the sight still threw him: Samael was an older woman, her black hair touched with gray and piled in a loose bun. She had the look of an academic.

"You've come to kill me," Nazar said.

"That would have been a lot easier."

He was going to take her alive, extract everything she knew, and destroy everyone she worked with. She would be responsible for the ruin of all she had built. No martyr's death, just humiliation, cowardice, and compromise.

She lifted her left hand and extended the fingers. The spoon from a Soviet F-1 grenade flew off and tinked against the window.

*   *   *

Her body, when Hayes saw it on the *Shiloh,* had been a crucial clue. She hadn't been tortured. Caro hadn't touched her. As Hayes dug in and began collecting intelligence, he was able to trace Nazar's and Caro's roots back to the borderland where the massacre had taken place. They had been working together, mother and son, against Riggs from the beginning. She played the part of the refugee and fulfilled the American dream of a kindred voice in a hostile land, a local yearning for freedom. As a sympathetic interpreter and guide, she was able to infiltrate the invading armies, steal their secrets, whisper in their ears, and steer them wrong.

She had done the same thing decades before with the previous army that occupied her lands. She played her role as a collaborator with that foreign army so well that her own people turned on her, rejected her and her bastard son. It would have broken most women, but she used it to burnish her legend as an ally of the West, to prove to the Americans that she could be trusted. She had suffered for decades and sacrificed her son to sell the lie.

After Hayes's team was ambushed on their way back from the infiltration, she knew it would be clear that there had been leaks from Riggs's command. Someone had to take the fall. She blamed her own people in order to cover up her role.

She rounded up the villagers and lured them to their deaths. She told Riggs that they were guilty of the treacheries she and Caro had committed, and she watched as they were slaughtered. The massacre eliminated the only souls who could help piece together the origins and true nature of her and Caro's relationship.

Riggs's role in the massacre provided them with valuable leverage. Caro couldn't use the evidence of the massacre to blackmail Riggs himself. The colonel would never trust someone who was coercing him, so she took over. She kept Riggs in check with the evidence while Caro promised to protect him. She made Riggs a hero by backing up his story and helping him frame Hayes as the man who had committed the massacre. That got Hayes—the only one who knew the truth about Caro—out of the way. Hayes would be hunted down and killed by his own military.

They had Riggs cornered and developed the best source ever recruited in the West. She would never actually release that evidence. The threat alone was enough to control Riggs, to force him to do everything he could to destroy Hayes, to keep Riggs scared and dependent on Caro.

There had been only one mistake: they had sold their story too well. Riggs believed Nazar's bluffs. He overreacted and came after her, shot up her car, and dragged her away. But Caro had been able to step in and stall long enough for his men to get the black money back and kill Riggs—the only one who knew enough about Caro's plan to link him to the Sidwell bombing.

The F-1 grenade had a four-second fuse, and Hayes started the count:

Three.

He ran toward her as she held the pineapple-shaped bomb out like a talisman.

He ignored it, and seized her biceps.

Two.

As the fingers of his right hand depressed her brachial nerve, her hand relaxed, and the grenade fell into Hayes's open left palm.

One.

He threw it hard left-handed through the open door and heard it hit the marble in the hall. It was a stone house, Beaux-Arts French, probably at least a hundred years old. The walls were plenty thick. He dragged her down behind the desk. The grenade blew. Shrapnel rained through the suite and dug into the beautifully carved oak panel they had used for cover.

He turned her arm, put her facedown on the floor, then took her other arm and bound her wrists.

Nazar prayed that death would come but knew that it would most likely be a worse fate, with her last years hidden from the sun in a long betrayal of everything she had built, everything she had sacrificed. How many of the militants who spat on her, thinking that she was a traitor, would never know the truth: that she was the best soldier and commander they ever had.

That was her lot, and her choice, and she wasted no time regretting it. Only the work mattered. There would be helicopters and planes, and the Americans would bring her hooded and shackled to a cool place that smelled like a cellar where time stretched endlessly and daylight never reached.

They would break her. Everyone breaks, just as she had broken Foley. Even as she held out, she knew in the end she would give them the intelligence they wanted. And after so many years she'd spent pretending to be the West's lackey, the lie would become the truth.

She was old and seemed harmless. Treating her as the threat she was would only embarrass her interrogators. They were always men. In time, they would grow complacent. There were ways out. A prisoner swap, perhaps, or one of the American Congress's periodic retreats into isolationism and penny-pinching. She was a patient woman, and Americans were a forgetful people. They didn't like to think about the darkness in the world.

Through it all, one thought gave her strength. Among all the lies, there was one truth that mattered. She had found her son.

Caro had grown into a great fighter. And she had been able to tell him the truth of where he came from, and who she was, and why she had done it all. And they were able to use his curse—the blue eyes of the infidel—as a weapon. In the end he understood everything, and that was enough. The Americans could never take that from her.

Hayes heard the growl of engines in the streets, and through the window he saw the militiamen arrive. Two Toyota Hilux trucks sped toward the villa, .50 cals mounted on their beds.

He lifted his radio and called the quick reaction team. "How we doing?"

He checked his watch, took a C-4 charge, and went to the landing. He primed it for six seconds, then threw it toward the front door. He ran back into the office and began pulling hard drives and files and dumping all the intelligence he could grab into trash bags.

The charge blew. The wreckage at the front door would hold off the militants for a few more minutes at least.

He threw Nazar over his shoulder and stepped through the French doors leading to the terrace. It looked out on a courtyard and, beyond that, the Mediterranean. Gunfire popped in the streets below. The Little Bird helicopter started as a speck in the sky, chugging toward him, its rotors growing louder. There was nowhere to land, so the pilot nosed down until one skid rested on the terrace railing. Hayes threw the garbage bags through the door.

Inside were six operators, kitted out for a raid.

"Sorry, guys," he shouted above the rotor wash. "It's over. I just need a lift out."

He looked inside the bird. Typical. It was full up. Everyone wanted in on the action. There was nowhere for him to sit. They took Nazar, and Hayes planted his ass on the narrow pod above the skid as the helicopter rose, spun, and took off for the last red glow of sunset streaking over the desert.

A hand reached out and tapped him on the shoulder. The medic handed down a four-by-four square of gauze and pointed to Hayes's neck.

Hayes touched it, felt the blood. The big guard must have gotten a touch in with the knife. He'd barely noticed with all the adrenaline. He pressed the gauze down, let his rifle fall to the end of its sling, and watched the bombed-out city flash by underneath his boots.

He remembered what Lauren had whispered just before he left.

Finish this. Then come back to me, John. This is where you belong.

He was going home.

ACKNOWLEDGMENTS

My wife, Heather, joined me on countless brainstorming walks as this novel developed and always steered me right. My family patiently acted as a sounding board as I untangled the plot. Shawn Coyne, my agent, provided invaluable help editorially and professionally as I struck out in a new direction. He is a story guru, business sage, and great guy.

Hachette Book Group and Little, Brown and Company are publishers of exceptional talent and principle, and I have the good fortune to remain part of their family as I join the ace team at Mulholland Books.

My editor, Wes Miller, brings an extraordinary level of care and insight to his craft and vastly improved the manuscript. Hachette Book Group is full of great people, and I am indebted to all of them, but I would particularly like to thank Reagan Arthur, Michael Pietsch, Pamela Brown, Joshua Kendall, Lauren Harms, Nicole Dewey, Heather Fain, and Sabrina Callahan.

Dr. Drew Wilkis and Dr. Steven Davis helped me with the trauma scenes and procedures. Tracy Roe is a superb copyeditor *and* a physician. She saved the day with her artful edits and medical expertise.

I couldn't have written a book about war without getting to know the subject through the work of correspondents I have long looked up to: Mark Bowden, William Langewiesche, Jeffrey Goldberg, James Bennet, Sean Naylor, Jon Lee Anderson, George Packer, Dexter Filkins, Robert Young Pelton, Spencer Ackerman, Mark Kukis, and Graeme Wood. I am especially grateful to the last three for their help with this novel and their friendship over the years.

Dozens of books and other resources were consulted in my research, but a few were particularly indispensable: *Delta Force,* by Charlie A. Beckwith; *The Mission, the Men, and Me,* by Pete Blaber; *Black Hawk Down,* by Mark Bowden; *The Command,* by Marc Ambinder and D. B. Grady; *Locks, Safes and Security,* by Marc Weber Tobias; and *Not a Good Day to Die,* by Sean Naylor.

I sought to be as realistic as possible for a thriller. The Special Operations folks I talked to reminded me that my first task was to tell a good story, so I have taken liberties to that end.

Thanks to Kevin Reeve and everyone at OnPoint Tactical, a company that provides survival, evasion, resistance, and escape training to elite military units and civilians alike, for kidnapping me and chasing me through Los Angeles. Deviant Ollam, Chris Gates, and Matt Fiddler advised on technical security matters. David Swinson, a former special investigations and major crimes detective with the Metropolitan Police Department of Washington, DC (as well as a terrific author with Mulholland Books), helped with law-enforcement questions. Abraham Sutherland, who spent three years with the State Department in Kunar Province, Afghanistan, brought that dangerous world to life for me.

Roger Pardo-Maurer, former deputy assistant secretary of defense and Special Forces veteran of Iraq and Afghanistan, was a continual source of inspiration, good sense, and laughs. Lieutenant Colonel James R. Hannibal, a former stealth bomber and predator UAV pilot (and a first-rate military-thriller writer), kindly guided me on drone details. Don Shipley, a retired Navy SEAL senior chief, very generously answered my questions about combat diving missions, and army captain Cornell Riley took the time to review the manuscript and saved me from many errors. And to the others who will go unnamed here: thank you.

It has been an honor to hear the stories of all those who serve and all those who put themselves in harm's way. I am in awe of and profoundly grateful for the work they do and the sacrifices they make.

ABOUT THE AUTHOR

Matthew Quirk studied history and literature at Harvard College. He spent five years at *The Atlantic*, reporting on a variety of subjects, including crime, private military contractors, terrorism prosecutions, and international gangs. His bestselling first novel, *The 500*, was a finalist for the Edgar Award and won the Strand Critics and International Thriller Writers awards for best first novel. He lives in San Diego.

...AND *DEAD MAN SWITCH*

Captain John Hayes and his teammates are racing against the clock to save their own lives, and thousands more. As with *Cold Barrel Zero*, Matthew Quirk has written a breathless high-stakes thriller where the gravest dangers are embedded deep within a tangled nest of politics, double crosses, and government conspiracies.

Following is an excerpt from the novel's opening pages.

John Hayes stepped from the rear door of the two-and-half-ton truck. Four gunmen covered him, their Kalashnikov rifles braced against their shoulders.

He ignored them and looked to the sky. It was a good night for an execution, summer in the high alpine. The snow was soft, and the crevasses in the ice spread wide enough to make a man's body disappear.

He'd spent nine hours crammed in the back of the truck, and his legs were rubber. They had switchbacked up the valleys all night on a gravel path so narrow and pitted by old shell craters that the rear of the vehicle hung over empty space through each hairpin turn.

The highest pass had been well above fourteen thousand feet. They were slightly lower on the southern slopes now, and Hayes felt the blood that had frozen while trickling from his nose starting to melt again. He wiped it off, a long smear on the back of his hand.

"Let's go," the driver barked in Dari, and the slanted muzzle brake of the rifle jabbed into Hayes's ribs just beside his spine. The cold burned his face as they marched him through a rolling door set in the hillside. They entered through a thick concrete portal into an underground garage. He climbed the steps, feeling the blood flush in his legs, the muscles regain their strength, the relatively rich air revive him.

A steel door opened at the far end of the garage, and they walked into an open courtyard. He had expected a mud-walled hut, or even a cave complex, but not this: an interior courtyard paved in marble with Moorish arches.

A man strode toward him, his hair gleaming. At first Hayes assumed the shine was due to the pomades popular among the officers in this country—he was wearing his regimental dress—but then Hayes realized that it was simply wet.

"I hope I didn't keep you," the man said as he stretched his right shoulder. "I was finishing a game."

Squash. It was a fetish among Pakistani military commanders. Imran Kashani was formerly ISI, the Pakistani intelligence service, an uneasy ally of the United States that still kept close ties with the Taliban and militant groups. But Kashani had gone to work for himself and become a power broker—a warlord, essentially—in the ungoverned lands along the Afghanistan-Pakistan border. He commanded a militia the size of a small army.

"Come in," he said.

This man had killed dozens of Americans. Hayes was here to make a deal with him.

They stepped through a long parlor into an office lined with books. Huge mirrors dominated one wall, windows with closed red drapes the other.

"English is okay?" Kashani said.

"That's fine."

"Excellent. I spent a year in college in the States. Arizona State University."

He sat back down at a desk at the front of the room, and Hayes stood between two guards on the carpet before him.

"Are you hungry? Tea?"

"No," Hayes said. He wasn't going to waste time on ceremony in this guano-reeking mansion. Kashani shrugged, and a moment later a third guard placed a glass cup of tea on the desk next to him. Kashani took a sip and examined Hayes.

"All business. Very American. I'll get to the point. What do you know about Cold Harvest?"

Hayes knew it well. It was a small group, culled from the U.S. military's classified Special Operations units and the CIA's paramilitary forces. They were kill teams, in essence, run as independent contractors with no official relationship to their home government. They pursued the gravest threats to national security in countries, most of them American allies, where the U.S. would never be allowed to perform lethal missions. They were a last resort.

Hayes had once been a leader, a legend in those elite tiers of American special operations, but he had spent years in exile, hunted by his old teammates.

"What do you want to know?" he asked Kashani.

"I want to know their names. I want to know where they live."

"Their outposts? Safe houses? Covers?"

"No. I want their addresses inside the United States. Their homes. We have some, but not enough."

Hayes considered it, ran the back of his hand along his chin, felt the stubble scratch.

"I can get you that information."

"For how many?"

"All of them, give or take a few of the most recent additions."

Kashani let out a short, startled laugh, like he'd just won something. The two men had no idea that from a hilltop a kilometer and a half away, they were being watched.

At the top of a glacial cirque overlooking Kashani's compound, Connor Burke slammed his gloved hand against his thigh, trying to warm up his fingers. After a minute he could feel pain buried somewhere in all the cold numb flesh. He huddled against his partner, Bryan Sanders. They were both former SEALs, senior chiefs in Team Six, but now they worked as contractors for the CIA. That allowed them to operate in the borderlands of a country like Pakistan, a nation with which the U.S. wasn't technically at war.

Sanders held the laser microphone steady and aimed it at the window of the formal office so he could pick up the conversations in the compound while Burke kept watch. They each had an earbud in and could hear everything Hayes and the other man said.

"I can get you that information."

"For how many?"

"All of them."

Sanders looked to Burke, eyes wide. Burke recognized the voice. He brushed the accumulating snow from his earpiece and raised the volume. Like most seasoned operators, they were half deaf from the tens of thousands of rounds they expended every year. But it was unmistakable. It was John Hayes. Burke had fought with him in Fallujah. It was Burke's second deployment, and Hayes had led the team through a baptism by fire in urban operations. Burke had since heard the rumors: Hayes had gone over to the enemy.

But Burke couldn't believe what he was hearing now. The flurries built into a steady fall, cutting through the laser's path and interfering with the microphone's operation. The audio broke up into static.

"Is Hayes going to sell them the names of our operators?" Sanders asked.

"More than that. The homes. The families. Jesus Christ. It's a kill list."

"It can't be. He was a good man."

"Was," Burke said.

Sanders looked over the compound, well defended and built into the side of the slope.

"I don't like it. Do we have the authority to kill an American if it comes to that?"

The batteries in the radios were dead. The cold drained them at twice the normal speed. They had been in the field for three days. There was no way to get authorization from above.

"You do the math. One life for how many? We've got to stop him."

Sanders nodded.

Burke slammed his hands together and flexed open his fingers. He lifted his rifle and started down the ridge.

In the office, Hayes waited for Kashani to absorb the full measure of what he was offering: a trove of intelligence that would allow him to destroy, root and branch, America's most effective defense against asymmetric threats.

Kashani's cool pose disappeared. He started blinking quickly and leaned forward.

"All of them? That information wouldn't be trusted to one man, or even put on one list."

"It's my business to know. They have been trying to kill me for a long time."

"Where is it?"

Hayes gestured to his temple.

"Memorized? All the names? Addresses?"

"Yes."

Kashani laughed again, regaining some confidence. "I guess you think that means I can't kill you?"

He said something in a dialect Hayes didn't understand, then waved a finger to the guard to Hayes's right, who approached Hayes from the side. Hayes's hand shot out, seized his wrist, and twisted it, wrenching the shoulder. A piece of black-and-tan-patterned fabric fell from the man's hand and landed on the floor. It was a *shemagh,* an Afghan scarf often worn by fighters over the head and neck.

The other two raised their rifles, but Kashani called them off.

"What is this?" Hayes demanded.

"Have you read Kipling?"

"It's been a while."

"It seems appropriate, given the circumstances. A test of your memory, to see if you can offer what you claim. Kim's Game," Kashani said. "Our instructors at the Farm used to use it."

Kashani had been trained in intelligence work by the CIA at its facility in Virginia, thirty years ago in this never-ending war. He had shaken hands with the vice president of the United States.

Hayes reached for the scarf. Kim's Game was a standard training exercise for spies and special operators. They would be flashed images of objects and told to recall them, or they'd simply be blindfolded for a quiz at random moments. They practiced until their senses were hyperaware and they could retain photographic memories of their surroundings at any time, recording every threat and exploitable piece of intelligence. It came from an old spy novel by Kipling called *Kim*, set not too far from these mountain passes.

If Hayes failed, they would most likely kill him. He folded the fabric into a long strip and tied it over his eyes.

"Arches in the courtyard?" Kashani asked.

"Thirty."

"Weapons on the guard to your right."

"AK-74M rifle. Beretta pistol on his hip. SOG dagger on his chest."

"Fruit on the table?"

"Four apples."

"Which direction are you facing?"

"Southwest."

"The red book on the shelf behind me. Is it to my left or my right?"

"There is no red book."

"Very good. And where are you?"

Nine hours driving in the dark, and Hayes had spent the entire time fixed on navigation: land speed, altitude, and the twisting azimuths of the stars that served as an endless unerring compass over his head.

When he stepped out of the truck he saw the Spin Ghar Mountains silhouetted against the sky: Sikaram, Barkirdar Sar, Tarakai. They might as well have been street signs as he lined them up and fixed his location.

He knew where he was down to a few kilometers. Enough for an air strike. And he suspected Kashani knew he knew it too. The test was not only to evaluate his memory but to see how observant he was, to determine if he could identify this compound. If this deal fell through, there was no way he was going to make it out of here alive.

"You understand, I want the names of everyone in Cold Harvest."

"I'm not going to give them to you."

Kashani's jaw tightened.

"I'm only going to deal with whoever you're working for."

"There is no one above me."

"You're a go-between. This is too big for you to handle on your own."

Kashani rolled his cup between his hands. "John Hayes," he said, shaking his head. "I have to say, you live up to the stories. Follow me."

The guards led Hayes back through the hallway, underground, and down a long concrete corridor. Then they left him in a room with a simple table and chair lit by a dim desk lamp.

He sat there for forty-five minutes, wondering what the odds were that this gamble would work, that he might be about to meet the real power behind Kashani.

Finally, the door opened, and the bright light from the corridor blinded him for a moment. Kashani stepped in. "This way," he told Hayes. "There's someone you should see."

Hayes followed Kashani and two guards toward the underground garage. He wondered if they were moving him again or if the leader was there, in a safe room. A guard pushed open a heavy steel door.

Hayes peered inside. There was no chief here, only two soldiers sitting against the wall bound hand and foot. They wore *pakols*—round-topped wool caps—and loose-fitting robes in the local style, but their gear was clearly American Special Operations'.

Under the glaring fluorescent light overhead, Hayes could see blood trailing from the ear of one of the men, and judging from the cuts on his cheek, Hayes guessed he'd been injured by a grenade frag at just outside of the lethal range.

"Who are they?" Hayes asked.

"Some of your American killers. We found them closing in on the house. Good tactics. We wouldn't have seen them coming, but they triggered a slide of snow below the peak."

"They came to kill you?"

"We think they came to kill *you*."

Kashani took a handgun from a guard and entered the room. He kicked one man, knocking him over, then stepped on his neck, driving his face into the floor, and aimed the pistol at the back of his head.

Hayes followed him in, and the guards posted up in the corners.

"If you are what you say you are, surely you won't mind," Kashani said.

Hayes said nothing. He had expected a test of faith.

He recognized the American that Kashani was threatening with the gun, a man with a reddish-brown beard and a few minor cuts on his face. His name was Burke. Hayes had fought with him in Fallujah, back when Burke was a SEAL, a kid on his second deployment; he had trained him in house-to-house fighting, and Burke had gone on to Green—the Special Operations shorthand for the unit commonly known as SEAL Team Six.

"Hayes?" Burke said. "Jesus. It's true. You son of a bitch." Hayes knew that if he tried to stop Kashani, the Pakistani would kill them all.

Kashani put his finger on the trigger.

"Wait," Hayes said. He stepped toward Kashani, who was smiling like a man who had called someone's bluff. The guards lifted their rifles.

Hayes gestured for the pistol. "How does the saying go? It's better that I kill my brother than a rival take him." It was a *tapa*, a two-line Pashtun poem often sung by soldiers or grieving wives.

"I've heard it," Kashani said. "Keep it in the family, you would say."

Hayes nodded. "Let me take care of this."

Kashani smiled and stepped back, then took the barrel in his other hand, and offered the pistol to Hayes. The guards kept their rifles at low ready, and Hayes traced the tendons standing tense along the backs of their hands.

Hayes stood over his former student. Burke arched back to look him in the eye as Hayes lined up the shot.

"I never believed what they said about you. Until now. Go ahead. You'll burn for this."

Once, things had been simple for Hayes. There were commanders and rules of engagement, opposing forces and friendlies. But now he was on his own, and he understood the terrible weight of choice, of his own calculations of the greater evil, of trading lives like coins.

"You don't know me. What they put me through." He cracked Burke in the mouth with the slide of the pistol and put his foot on his back.

He wrapped his finger around the trigger and brought the gun before him, facing away from Kashani.

He raised it, and pulled the trigger.

The light blew out with a pop and a rain of glass. The room went black. But in his mind, Hayes could still see where each man stood. Kim's Game. He ducked to the left and aimed the pistol at the first guard.

Burke felt the hot glass scratch his neck as the lightbulb exploded, and he rolled onto his feet. The images came like strobes in the orange flash of Hayes's firing pistol: one guard flinching back, struck by gunfire, then the other. Hayes sidestepped left to right, and six shots flared in the dark. Kashani spun with a pistol and shot. The muzzle flame reached out toward empty space and lit up Hayes behind him, his knife out.

The dark returned. A body hit the ground. A flashlight cut through the room, then came the cinching and popping of the cords as someone cut Burke's hands free, drawing the knife a half inch from the skin on his wrist.

Hayes pulled the injured soldier's arm over his shoulder and helped him up. He was dazed.

"Burke," Hayes said. "Sorry about the jaw. I had to sell it. Are you good to walk?"

Burke fought back against the shock. "I think so," he said. "You got Sanders? And what's going on?"

"I'm here undercover. I was trying to find out who he was working for, who wants those names."

Hayes aimed a flashlight that he'd pulled from one of the guards at the ceiling. "We've got to roll before they get backup."